FOR THE LOVE OF LLAMAS... HELP!

Needed: Temporary ranch hand to pitch in at our llama rescue/tourist outfit/fiber farm forty miles east of Taos, New Mexico. Our regular fella's off getting hitched and we need someone while he's finally making an honest woman of Rosie. She's been plenty patient.

The job: Help care for our herd of sixteen rescue llamas, thirty prize-winning alpacas, plus eight chickens, six goats, and two dogs (the cat looks after herself). Oh, and the bunny.

If that ain't exciting enough, my pal Jane says to tell you we've got spectacular views of the Taos Mountains, and our ranch offers thirty acres of wide-open wilderness to explore (but not exploit!). Nearby hot springs help you soak your bones after a long day of honest work.

Enthusiasm, spirit of adventure more important than experience. You bring a love of furry creatures and a willingness to learn, and we'll tell you what needs doing.

No smokers, please. I just quit.

BY HILARY FIELDS

Bliss
Last Chance Llama Ranch

Last Chance Llama Ranch

HILARY FIELDS

REDHOOK

www.redhookbooks.com

Copyright © 2015 by Hilary Fields
Excerpt from *Bliss* copyright © 2013 by Hilary Fields
Excerpts from Euripides's *Medea*, translated into English rhyming verse by Gilbert Murray, M.A., LL.D, copyright © 1906 by Oxford University Press

Redhook Books/Orbit
Hachette Book Group
1290 Avenue of the Americas
New York, NY 10104
www.HachetteBookGroup.com

Printed in the United States of America

RRD-C

First edition: August 2015

10 9 8 7 6 5 4 3 2 1

Redhook is an imprint of Orbit, a division of Hachette Book Group.
The Redhook name and logo are trademarks of Hachette Book Group, Inc.

The Hachette Speakers Bureau provides a wide range of authors for speaking events. To find out more, go to www.hachettespeakersbureau.com or call (866) 376-6591.

The publisher is not responsible for websites (or their content) that are not owned by the publisher.

Library of Congress Cataloging-in-Publication Data
Fields, Hilary.
Last chance llama ranch / Hilary Fields.
    pages cm
  ISBN 978-0-316-27742-6 (paperback)—ISBN 978-0-316-27741-9 (ebook)
1. Career changes—Fiction. 2. Travel writers—Fiction. 3. Llamas—Fiction. 4. Ranch life—Fiction. 5. Self-realization in women—Fiction. I. Title.
  PS3606.I357L37 2015
  813'.6--dc23
                                            2015013182

*I*t was a dark and stormy night...

Outside the cave, anyway.

Inside the cave it was actually darker and stormier. Because it was inhabited by one very grumpy troll.

"Goddamn it! Of all the rookie mistakes, this has to take the biscuit."

Mm, biscuits... One of Dolly's famously fattening, gravy-smothered, pillow-sized breakfast biscuits would definitely not go amiss right now.

"Your phone have any juice left?"

"Seriously? You guys barely even get service in the middle of town, let alone halfway up a mount—"

"I don't need service," the troll cut in savagely. "I just need enough light to find my ass with both hands and a map."

"Ah."

She depressed the "Start" button on her smartphone, and it gave a wan, nearly-out-of-battery glow.

The troll snatched it from her freezing-cold fingers. "Scrape up some of that dry moss and those dead leaves for tinder while I see about making sure we're still alive come morning," he snarled.

She didn't tell him where to stick the smartphone. Because the troll would, she hoped, be so kind as to save her life tonight.

It just happened that, in addition to being outstandingly bossy, he was also quite handy at building shelters and starting fires out of practically anything.

And Merry Manning was a huge fan of shelter and fire at the moment. She had never been so cold in her life.

That's what happens when you give a baby alpaca your only sweater, she thought, shivering and chattering fit to crack her teeth. But she kind of thought it was worth it.

She hadn't felt so alive in years.

Though how I explain this one to my readers, I cannot remotely imagine...

Istanbul (Not Constantinople)
Two months earlier

Fatimah was not having a good day.

This much became obvious as my ponderous host led me deeper into the steamy bowels of her domain. Her discontent was a miasma that seethed about her, oozing ominously from every pore.

Perhaps it was the worn and unlovely daisy-patterned swimsuit that wrapped less than graciously about Fatimah's sturdy figure, or the nubbly sea anemone bathing cap that strained to contain her bushy black hair. I really couldn't say. But whatever the source of her existential dyspepsia, it was causing her to stomp like a brontosaurus down the mildew-spotted hallway in her squish-squashing Crocs, muttering dire nothings beneath her breath.

I began to suspect my first spa treatment might also be my last.

The Topkapi Hamam caters primarily to tourists. And since that's what I am these days, it seemed like a reasonable place to try out this most traditional of Turkish experiences. But Fatimah, as cultural ambassador, was clearly less than thrilled with her day's task: take my ungainly carcass and give it the full "Sultana Treatment."

My guide pushed open a door marked "Tepidarium." My high school Latin told me to expect tepidness, and I was not disappointed. It was tepid. Pitch black, empty, and tepid. I peered in with trepidation.

"Five minute!" bellowed Fatimah, shoving me inside.

She slammed the door behind me, and it clanged shut with a boom like the gates of hell. When my shoulders finally felt safe to abandon their perch above my ears, I looked around. I was alone in utter darkness... with no idea where the door was. Five minutes of panting, slightly chilly terror later, I had yet to find the egress on my own when the portal was flung open and my glowering, pear-shaped Virgil was once again silhouetted in the doorway.

"You hot!" she snarled.

"Well, ah...that's nice of you to say," I began, but Fatimah had me by the scruff now—no easy feat considering I topped her by at least ten inches—and was marching me down the dim, grungy hall.

"Caldarium," read the sign above the next chamber.

And Fatimah tossed me in the oven.

"Five minute!"

Five minutes later I had a lot of sympathy for baked potatoes. My face flaming, my sweat-drenched hair plastered to my skull, I gasped and pitched forward woozily when my tormentor finally freed me, but Fatimah had no patience for fainting foreigners.

"Now wash!" And she goose-stepped me to the far side of the seemingly endless hall.

We entered the grand chamber. And indeed, it had once been grand—maybe two or three centuries earlier. A vaulted dome soared above us, little hexagonal skylights letting light slant in like something out of a Pre-Raphaelite painting. Everything was marble, from the walls with their burbling fountains splashing into foot basins to the cool, blue-veined floor and, in the chamber's center, a circular, raised marble platform roughly the size of a handball court. Intricate mosaic work patterned the walls and floors. Steam curled in tendrils about the room, coiling around pillars and masking my fellow bathers from close inspection.

It did a less thorough job of hiding the disrepair of the place.

Cracks in the floor were black with mold. Whole chunks of mosaic were missing in spots, leaving the fanciful figures on the walls without eyes, arms, or legs. The air was redolent with eau de BO and attar of foot fungus.

Fatimah shoved me toward the altar of sacrifice and ripped the towel from my body with one violent, magician-whipping-a-tablecloth-off-a-laden-table move. "Yiiiiiiikes!" I (quite naturally) howled. Before I could so much as figure out which of my bits to cover first, Fatimah was on me.

"Down!" she barked.

I ducked, then grinned sheepishly when I realized she wanted me to lay upon the central platform. Other female tourists were arrayed on the rim of the stone circle in a loose ring, similarly guarded by smoldering bath attendants in fifties-style swimwear. The head of one to the foot of another, the tourists made a daisy chain of naked flesh . . . and now I was to complete the chain.

Except, of course, I'm the tallest freaking daisy in the world. While I eyeballed the gap in the ring of soon-to-be-washed women, wondering if I would be able to wedge myself in without getting or giving a snootful of foot to the face, Fatimah disappeared into the mist. Thank goodness, I thought, hoping she might have gone on lunch break or Australian walk-about. But no. All too soon Fatimah was back . . . with a bucket.

An instant later, I stood agape as sudsy (thankfully warm) water sluiced down my body from where Fatimah had hurled it with some gusto (and a hint of a sadistic smile) all over my shocked form. As soon as I was suitably lubricated, my human loofah muscled me down onto the marble platform, muttering something I'm guessing meant "I oughta get paid double for this behemoth."

And friends, Fatimah proceeded to scrub me.

You might imagine this involved washcloths, and shampoo, and the occasional sliver of soap. You wouldn't be wrong. However, the remark-

able part of this supersonic scrub-down was how vividly it reminded one of a WWF wrestling match. As Fatimah attacked me with scrub brush and soap, my ungainly form skidded and slid on the slick marble with a distinct lack of dignity, forcing my attendant to grab for whatever portion of my anatomy was handiest—an ankle, a shoulder, my hair, and once, breathtakingly, a boob—to haul me back to my assigned slot. Around me, other tourists shrieked, slipped, and cursed as they were spun about like the famous dervishes I told you about in my last dispatch.

Ten minutes this went on, friends. Ten. Freaking. Minutes.

When at last the slapping, slopping, and sliding wound down, I was dizzy, half-drowned, and pretty sure I could pen a treatise on waterboarding.

And was I clean? In a word: not so much.

To sum up: My impression of the Topkapi Hamam was less one of luxury than a subtle form of vengeance. I was lovelessly hustled through a series of less-than-relaxing "traditional" treatments, performed by bath attendants with all the delicacy of a herd of wildebeests. The murky water, the musty environs, and the general aura of despair cloak the visitor in an ineffable coat of... well, there's no better way to put it than "bleh." But my true issue with the Topkapi wasn't the rough, Silkwood-style shower or the fear of flesh-eating bacteria. Honestly, the entire time I was undergoing my "hamam experience," all I could think was that the only thing worse than getting the Sultana Treatment must be giving it. What sins had these women committed to consign them to a purgatory of scrubbing overprivileged, culturally clueless foreigners seven hours a day? To sitting in soggy swimsuits and sweaty bathing caps in this steaming fungus-farm, soaping up women who undoubtedly earned astronomically more than their hourly wage, and were surely capable of taking care of their own basic hygiene? A little sullenness was to be expected, if not enjoyed.

Moral of the story, kids: When in Istanbul (not Constantinople), if you're gonna try the baths, bring sufficient Purell for a full-body dip. And don't forget to tip Fatimah and her friends.

'Til next time, I'll be...

—On My Merry Way

&

Merry scanned the screen, nibbling on a hangnail as she reread her article. She debated giving it another run-through, but after four rounds of rewrites she knew it was as good as it was likely to get. "Save...and...send!" she murmured, clicking the appropriate keys. She glanced at her Gmail and saw her boss was on chat. It didn't surprise her—Joel was *never* offline. As far as she knew, he showered with his iPhone and used his iPad for a pillow. She clicked on his name and started typing.

Just posted the last of my Turkey series. You ought to get a kick out of this one. I practically got waterboarded.

The answer was instantaneous.

Another clusterfuck? Can't wait.

Merry smiled wryly, even as she sent Joel a scowly emoji. Her editor seemed to have a particular fondness for anything that involved Merry's near drowning. (The waterfall incident during the Milford Sound cruise last month had given him quite the chuckle.) As usual, she'd filed her story with time to spare, not that *Pulse* seemed to believe in anything as pedantic as journalistic deadlines. With constant competition from *Slate*, the *HuffPo*, and *BuzzFeed*, all the online mag Merry worked for demanded was a steady diet of snark, slapdash, and sizzle.

Well, mission accomplished, she hoped. Her job for the past year had been to act as part tourist, part cautionary tale, and her column "On My Merry Way" explored some of the best and worst of high-end travel worldwide. It was, she reflected, a hell of a one-eighty from what she'd been doing before, and the learning curve had been steep, to say the least.

So glad you're looking out for me, she typed to her boss. She paused, her fingers hovering over the keyboard. Um, Joel?

"…" typed Joel.

Merry knew her boss well enough to know she was quickly losing his attention, but she still hesitated. At last she put her fingers to the keys, half afraid they might bite. Joel, do you think I'm finally getting the hang of this gig?

There was a pause that went on longer than Merry liked. Then…

You're doing fine, kid. Just remember, you're not penning the great American novel. The words appeared on her screen in a flurry despite the many time zones between his office in downtown Chicago and her hotel room in Istanbul. I know you're the product of seventeen Swiss boarding schools, but you don't hafta write like you're gunning for an MFA in comparative literature. Like I told you: This is a light, breezy magazine column. Who are we writing for?

Merry rolled her eyes. Five-Second Sally.

And what does Sally want? Joel prompted.

To be entertained. I remember, boss.

Entertained but not *challenged,* kid. You try to compete with her Facebook feed or her Pumpkin Spice Latte, and you're gonna lose.

Joel's criticism stung a bit, but honestly Merry couldn't blame the mythical Sally, quintessence of *Pulse* readership. She liked a good seasonally spiced latte herself. *Maybe I should tone it down,* she thought, but she hoped she wouldn't have to—she was finding she had quite the taste for linguistic acrobatics. But she *also* had a taste for gainful employment. Understood, she typed.

What's our watchword?

Merry's lips quirked. "Fluff."

Damn skippy, he wrote. Now get your ass on the next flight home. We ain't paying you to loaf around.

You got it, boss.

Merry clicked out of the chat and sighed, shaking her head in wonderment.

I write "fluff" for a living.

She was even starting to have fun with it—when she wasn't being pummeled by ballistic babushkas in bathing caps. Who *wouldn't* want to span the globe, tasting amazing food, meeting unusual people, and having exotic adventures? Most people would have looked at the gig as a dream come true.

But most people hadn't been Merry Manning, world champion downhill skier, five-time world-record breaker, and, until two years ago, the odds-on favorite to bring home Olympic gold for the good old US of A.

Yeah, Mer, her inner voice reminded her. *And most people didn't wrap all six feet, three inches of themselves around an eighty-foot spruce at Olympic trials.*

Merry slapped her laptop shut and sighed, leaning back on her hotel pillow. Thoughts like this weren't getting her anywhere. She had a good job—hell, a *great* job—and, even if it paid peanuts and was nothing to compare with the rush of competing against the best athletes on the planet, things could have been a lot worse.

Like, *dead* worse.

Probably the hamam from hell had just rattled her. Standing naked in that cavernous steam room, scars exposed in front of dozens of strangers, had left Merry incredibly off balance. She'd seen no reason to share as much with her readers, however. She rarely let her fans see her vulnerable side—a holdover from her days as a professional athlete.

Rub some dirt on it.

Walk it off.

Tough it out.

If she hadn't been the sort of woman who could slap some tape over a sprain, shrug off a concussion, and still crush her competition's best times, she wouldn't have deserved all those endorsements, the little girls with stars in their eyes holding out tiny ski boots for her to autograph...

But you didn't shrug off ten days in a medically induced coma. You didn't "walk off" a broken pelvis or torn ACL. You didn't "rub some dirt" on a shattered femur, collarbone, and elbow, or "tough out" a fractured jaw and eye socket.

No. You slunk off the stage and tried to figure out what the hell you were going to do with your life now that you were never again going to do the only thing you were ever truly good at.

And your body looked like Frankenstein's monster, to boot.

Merry's throat tightened, and her fingers curled into fists above the keyboard. *Don't smash*, she ordered the fists. *You need this laptop. You need the job at the other end of it.*

Because while Merry might no longer be a sought-after athlete, she was still a very popular gal with a certain segment of the population—*debt collectors*. Every time her phone rang, a shiver ran down her spine, for as likely as not it would be some dead-voiced hard case demanding to know if she was the "M. Manning" who owed eighty grand on her VISA, the M. Manning whose car lease was six months in arrears and whose credit rating currently hovered somewhere just above zero. *Amazing how that happens when your coke-addled agent forgets to pay the premiums on your health insurance plan, and no insurer will touch you because your "pre-existing condition" involves twenty-seven broken bones,* Merry thought.

Obamacare hadn't come soon enough to salvage Merry's credit rating or her savings. And if she were being honest, having grown up the way she had, she'd never paid much attention to her finances before the accident had wiped her out. That negligence had left her scrambling now for whatever work she could find to stanch the hemorrhage in her wallet. Travel writing wasn't much, but then again, her résumé wasn't exactly bursting with highly marketable skills now that skiing was off the table. And she'd be damned if she'd take the only *other* way she knew out of her breathtaking debt pit.

I'd rather sell what's left of my spleen than go that *route,* she thought, powering down the laptop and stuffing it in her satchel next to her passport and ticket home.

It had been Marcus who'd suggested the gig at *Pulse*—he might be a scoundrel, and more vain than even his supermodel status gave him any right to be, but her big brother knew her better than she knew herself sometimes. He knew she loved to travel (hell, they'd spent their childhoods roaming the halls of Four Seasons hotels in five continents), and he also knew she'd always had a secret passion for writing and literature, encouraging her even when their parents told her it was a waste of time, that her true value lay in her athletic prowess.

Writing is for asthmatic navel-gazers and university professors, Meredith, she could still hear her mother saying. *Not winners like us.*

Except Merry had lost. Spectacularly.

Pulse had given her a second chance, and Merry had grabbed it, best she could. She'd spent the past year striving to live up to the magazine's expectations with the same drive and dedication she'd once devoted to her kamikaze training regimen. *Though with a whole lot less sweat and, until today, fewer bruises*, she thought ruefully, rubbing one of Fatimah's little love taps.

Her mandate for the "Merry Way" dispatches was simple, as Joel had reminded her repeatedly. "Kid, you're there to have their dream vacations for them, tell them what's fun and what to avoid. Have a ball, make 'em wish they were hanging out with you, and move on when the story's played out. Don't get all deep or try to be the next Hemingway."

Shallow was just fine with Merry, because she wasn't keen on blasting the hot mess that was her private life all over the Internet. Her readers expected to see the woman they'd come to know on the slopes—funny and fearless, and yes, a trifle self-deprecating. They liked to laugh with her—and yes, sometimes to laugh *at* her if their comments on her columns were anything to go by—but they weren't there to learn what made her tick. They enjoyed her misadventures; her *misgivings* were her own.

Speaking of which…*Maybe I should take another shower*, she thought. But the three she'd already taken since returning from today's sog-tastic adventure would surely suffice. Well, that and some prophylactic Tinactin. Anyway, she had a flight to catch. And a stud-muffin to snog, if she was lucky.

∝

She was lucky.

Ish.

CHAPTER TWO

Contrary to every R-rated movie ever filmed, an airplane lavatory is not, in fact, a fantastic place to get laid. Particularly not for a woman of Merry Manning's altitude.

"Ow!"

"Shh!"

"Sorry, sorry... just, could you move your elbow a little... yeah, like that... oooh, yeah... oh... wait, I'm stuck on the..."

Freezing water doused Merry's keister. "Yikes!" she yelped, and her lover slanted his mouth across hers—as much to shush her as seduce her, she suspected. But a little discretion was called for, given the dozen or so sleeping first-class passengers and the peripatetic flight attendants who might so easily overhear their tryst. Merry's heart was racing. Just now she couldn't care less about the suboptimal accommodations. Well, okay, she *cared*, but she wasn't going to let that stop her from reveling in this moment. Because at this moment, she had an Olympic-caliber lover smiling conspiratorially down at her, his long, lean frame pressed hard against her yearning body.

And against the lav's accordion door.

And the ceiling, with the smoke detector one really shouldn't disable.

And the sink, with its bolted-on foaming soap dispenser.

And perilously close to the flight attendant call button, which *really* would have been a bad idea.

There were, Merry reflected, certain places tall people simply shouldn't fuck.

And Johnny Black was *tall*.

Like, *really* tall.

That might not mean much to most women, but it was a helluva selling point for Merry. When you topped six feet three in your stocking feet (except who wore stockings anymore?) with shoulders like a linebacker, finding a guy who could make you feel even moderately dainty was a...well, a tall order. Johnny, at six seven, never seemed daunted by her stature, which all too often made men dismiss her out of hand. Even other athletes gave her a wide berth, examining her as if she were a mountain they were ill prepared to climb, but Johnny wasn't intimidated by mountains. Or much of anything—except persnickety sponsors.

"I could get kicked off the team for this," he muttered, leaning in to suckle her earlobe. "Morals committee would *freak* if I got caught."

So would your corporate backers, Merry thought, desire cooling a degree. Johnny's squeaky-clean image as the snowboarder next door would be trashed if he were caught indulging in such tawdry shenanigans off the pipe. Especially when he was known to be dating America's favorite ice dancer, the sylphlike Melissa Christianson. Never mind that Merry happened to know Melissa was actually quite contentedly partnered with the reigning Norwegian record holder for women's speed skating. Reality wasn't what counted in the world of professional sports. Reputation was everything.

Is he worried about getting caught, or getting caught with a has-been like me?

The fact that he'd take this risk to be here with her—damaged, loser Merry—was both gratifying and a little bit galling. She and Johnny had had a flirtation going on for years before her accident, though it had never progressed beyond the occasional encounter at competitions and exposition games. They both knew they didn't have much in common beyond a love of defying gravity, of feeling the wind and the cold and the rush of pure speed—the triumph of knowing no one could catch you. Johnny loved the spotlight, the sponsorships, and the glory attached to being a world-class athlete. Merry just liked to *win*. While he sought attention, Merry had sought to outrace her own demons as much as anything else.

They were never going to sit around the fire discussing the latest Jonathan Franzen novel, or debating whether or not immigration reform was a good thing. But the sex was awesome, and wasn't that enough? It wasn't often she crossed paths with Johnny these days, and it was pure luck he'd been filming that spot for Turkish TV while she'd been in Istanbul. He'd be off to make his connecting flight to Aspen soon after they landed in Chicago. Which was fine with Merry. They'd never made a big deal of their hookups, staying under the radar so the media wouldn't make hay with something that didn't fit into a neat, all-American narrative.

And "under the radar" was cool with Merry. But since when had she become the girl you hid in the lav?

"You fucking the committee, or me?" she challenged, tossing her hair and nearly clocking herself on the paper towel dispenser in the process. Thankfully, Johnny didn't notice. He was too busy pressing her up against the sink with his lithe, ropy body.

"I love how you're always game for anything," he groaned, licking her throat. "So fucking fearless..."

So my cunning plan is working, Merry thought, letting his tongue do its mind-bendingly good thing against her neck. Maintaining the myth of "Merry Manning, all-around badass and intrepid adventurer" was a full-time job these days. Until the accident, it hadn't been a myth at all. Badass had been second nature—hell, the *only* nature Merry had. But now? She didn't know what—or who—she was, but it certainly wasn't *fearless*.

Johnny didn't need to know that.

She wrapped her fingers around his rock-hard ass and urged him on. "That's right, my boy. And don't you forget it."

"Put your foot up on the seat, baby," he panted. "Now, brace yourself..."

"Ohhhhhhhhh!"

Five minutes later, Merry's mile-high membership had been thoroughly renewed.

Seven minutes later, she was back at her seat toward the rear of the darkened airplane, fishing in the overhead bin for an Advil.

Johnny had given her a quizzical look when she'd slipped past him and out of the first-class cabin. She'd sent him off with a smile and a sneaky caress on that trained-to-the-hilt tush, not bothering to explain why she wouldn't be joining him for in-flight cocktails and warm nuts. "See ya at the gate, lov-ahhh," she'd said with an exaggerated wink over her shoulder as she'd headed back to her seat in coach. She wasn't about to tell Johnny how broke she was. She'd been just like him not long ago, taking first-class accommodations for granted. The team would pay. The sponsors. Whoever handled logistics while you were busy racking up medals and glory.

What Merry had been racking up lately were medical bills.

So not sexy.

And speaking of unsexy... *Yikes, what a cramp*, she thought, rubbing her leg as she folded the physique of an Amazon into a space better suited to a Keebler elf. The ride home wasn't going to be a whole lot of fun. Merry massaged her left thigh harder as the pain set in. The muscle would be wound tight in knots, if history was any indicator. *Ugly* knots. She was just glad their impromptu acrobatics in the loo hadn't required any actual nudity— *that* might have turned even her hot-blooded snowboarder cold.

Eighteen months since her last surgery, and the scars still looked gnarly—red, deep, and jagged, like riverbeds carved along the course of her left leg. Switzerland's finest orthopedic and plastic surgeons had done their best—and their best had been good enough to patch together what was basically roadkill—but Merry would always bear the imprint of the accident that had stolen her Olympic dreams. Along with the shattered leg, torn ligaments, and the pins that had knit her pelvis, there'd been the broken collarbone and elbow too.

And then there'd been the facial injuries.

Though not as physically devastating as the rest, the fractured orbital socket, broken nose and teeth had been psychologically damaging in their own right. Waking up from the coma the doctors had induced, eight days after the accident, she'd demanded a mirror despite her doctors' efforts to dissuade her...and when they finally handed one over, Merry hadn't even recognized the swollen, black-and-green monster she saw in it as her reflection.

From then on there'd been the "Before Merry" and the "After Merry." And "After Merry" was a stranger, a bizarro-world version of herself she could hardly bear to acknowledge. Months of painful rehab and several surgeries later, even Merry's mother, ever vigilant for flaws, swore you could barely tell anything had happened—to her face, at least—but Merry could still see the signs of the impact.

She still saw them now, on those occasions she cared to glance in a mirror. Even before the accident, she'd never been what one would call beautiful. While the rest of her family were striking, smooth-complected patricians who turned heads each time they entered a room, Merry had somehow come out like... well, like a cross between a Norman Rockwell painting and Pippi Long-stocking. Freckled, with a wide, expressive mouth and wide-set eyes that were a guileless denim blue. Thick red hair that had lightened to a sun-streaked copper after years spent mostly out-doors. As a competitor, she'd never been the Lindsey Vonn type, flashing white teeth and lush lips in a Chapstick commercial, posing for photo shoots in teeny bikinis. No, her niche as a pro-fessional athlete had been the Valkyrie in twin strawberry blonde braids—a Valkyrie who saved herself from Brunhilde compar-isons by cracking jokes at her own expense even as she shattered records on the slopes.

Now, she'd have given a great deal just to get back to her Brunhilde days, because after the accident... everything was just subtly *off*. There was that slight crookedness in what had once been a pert, ski-jump nose; the fine line that bisected her left brow, giving it a piratical lift; the front teeth that were impos-sibly perfect... and completely fake. You could feel the surgi-cal screws that had pieced her cheekbone back together if you pressed your fingers closely to her skin. But Merry was as leery of letting anyone touch her face these days as she was of getting naked anywhere other than alone.

So yeah. A face from a fun-house mirror and a body that no longer effortlessly obeyed her commands. That was her reality now.

Merry rubbed her eyes, catching herself in a yawn despite her discomfort and less-than-cheery musings. The day—and its unaccustomed activities both carnal and career-related—had taken its toll. She pulled her jacket over her shoulder and snuggled as best she could into the scrap of fabric-covered foam and sadism that passed for a seat in coach. Her days of riding high were over, and she'd best resign herself to it. *Pulse* might send her to far-flung locations for her column, but they sure as hell weren't paying for first-class plane tickets to get her there.

Suck it up, Merry. You don't rate special treatment anymore.

She sucked it up and, for good measure, sucked *down* a nip of Absolut she'd snicked from the first-class galley.

When she woke a few hours later, pain shooting through every nerve ending (and twice through a few), she wondered if Johnny had waited for her like he'd promised. Emerging from the Jetway, stiffness making her slight limp more pronounced, Merry looked around for her lover. Coffee and perhaps a few farewell kisses would not go amiss, she thought with a smile. But her smile died as a trio of buxom coeds standing around the waiting area squealed, "OMG, that's *him*!" and launched themselves at Johnny like charging rhinos in clingy tank tops. Their shrieks of "Johnny! Johnny!" were loud enough to be heard halfway back to Istanbul, and they already had pens out as they begged him to sign their boobs, pose for selfies, let them stroke the snowboard he'd been given special permission to carry on the plane. Their jumping and shouting attracted attention from all quarters, and soon Johnny was mobbed.

No one noticed Merry.

Her throat tightened. Once *she'd* garnered attention like that. Not the panting girls so much, but excited, eager fans who wanted nothing more than a moment with the girl who was going to bring home the gold. Back then, it had made her uncomfortable, self-conscious. But now...

Johnny's eyes met Merry's across the departure lounge. *Gotta go*, he mouthed, shrugging apologetically as he was carried away by the crowd. *Catch ya later.*

Much later, if at all, Merry guessed. His star was rising, and hers had quite clearly set. She turned her back. *Get over yourself, woman*, she thought, closing her throat against any possibility of tears. *It's over, you're done, and that's the end of it.* She forced herself to move toward the taxi stands outside the terminal, briskly and without a backward glance.

CHAPTER THREE

*G*wendolyn Manning wants to Skype with you," Merry's tablet informed her.

Merry groaned. Her mother had spectacular timing, as usual.

She'd barely collected her pet turtle, Cleese, from Andy down the hall, and was still debating whether to chuck or wade through the stack of mail that had accumulated in the box the super kept downstairs for her when she was out of town. Judging by the machine-addressed see-through windows and the "Past Due!" notices printed in angry red ink on most of the envelopes, she wasn't going to like the contents of that correspondence. Then again, correspondence with the fam was likely to be equally unpleasant.

"Do you wish to accept?" asked her device.

No, I really, really don't.

It wouldn't just be Gwendolyn (never "Gwen") either. Pierce would be beside her, stiff and uncomfortable in front of the webcam, doing his usual impression of Dignified Dad. Marcus, her evil, adorable older brother, would surely be there too, hovering over their shoulders with a glint in his eye that said he wasn't going to be any help at all. His Twitter feed—always a reliable means of keeping track of the twit—had announced "a visit to the ancestral pastures" a couple of days back.

The holy trinity of familial perfection.

And on the other side of the Skype session, Merry. The fallen one. The great disappointment. Merry—the girl whose sole saving grace had been her athletic ability. Without which...

Well. There wasn't much to say, was there?

Merry couldn't help remembering the morning of her first big competition. How her mother, swaddled in Arctic fox from neck to knee, had stood dwarfed by the unlikely daughter in team-sponsored spandex and space-age ski boots.

"I expect you'll win quite handily today, darling," said Gwendolyn, turning her collar up against the wind at the summit of the Aspen ski area.

Merry felt herself flush with the unexpected praise...until her mother finished her sentence. "Of course, with your height and build, we must be grateful you inherited my family's athletic abilities."

Merry had heard this refrain countless times since she'd started towering over her peers while still in grammar school. She clenched her fists around her ski poles, resisting the urge to flip down her visor and shut her mother out.

"Your uncle was quite the cricketer," Gwendolyn reminisced while Merry fidgeted, eager to join her teammates, "and your grandfather was captain of the royal dressage team for years before he got himself thrown by that blasted mare. I myself gave up a promising future as a figure skater to marry your father—but of course, all the men were after me in those days; I had my pick. It wasn't as though I *had* to excel at sports."

Merry's eyes stung, but she told herself it was just the sharp wind whipping off the slopes. *Focus on the course*, she told herself. *Crush the competition. And get as far away from Mother as possible, as fast as these fucking fiberglass slats can take me.*

"It's unfortunate you got more of the sportsman than the

sophisticate from my side of the family, Meredith. But you've found your niche now, and I know you'll make us proud." Gwendolyn removed a glove, one finger at a time, and reached up on tiptoe to fuss with Merry's wayward locks. Pursing her lips with motherly concern, she tucked hanks of hair under Merry's helmet—and then, as Merry flinched, wet her thumb with spit and ran it over her daughter's unsatisfactorily tamed brows. (Gwendolyn had a thing about unkempt "accessory hair," as she so delicately dubbed it.) "We must always put our best face forward, darling," she said. Unspoken was, *even if that face is homely, at best.* "One never knows who may be watching. And please, dear, dash on a little lipstick before the cameras catch you. Otherwise people might think you're one of *those* girls."

A fate worse than death, Merry thought now, tossing her mail on the bedside table and shaking her head to clear out the memory.

"*Do you wish to accept the call?*" the tablet asked again—a little impatiently, Merry thought.

Do I have *to?* she silently asked it.

But she knew the answer. She'd been ducking the Manning clan longer than was wise. Their emails, texts, and tweets (in Marcus's case) had been dogging her since well before she'd headed to Turkey. If she didn't talk to them now, they'd only become more insistent until she finally caved, and by then they wouldn't be best pleased.

Not that they were ever very pleased where Merry was concerned.

Flopping down on her bed with a sigh, she put Cleese on her tummy (he liked the warmth), gave him a bit of lettuce from the sandwich she'd grabbed at the corner deli, and settled the scratched and duct-taped tablet atop her bent knees. She tapped "Accept" and cringed.

"Happy birthday, darling!" trilled Gwendolyn, arriving on the screen poreless, lineless, and timelessly glamorous beside her equally attractive husband. A second later, up popped Marcus, thrusting his handsome face into frame and waving spastically.

"Hey, Sis, happy birthday!"

"It's not my birthday for another week," Merry muttered, trying to minimize the part of the chat screen where she had to see her own face. Compared to their movie-star sheen, she was a walking war wound—with jet lag, no less. She resisted the urge to smooth her eyebrows.

"We know it's not really your birthday, sweetheart," Pierce intoned. "We thought we'd try to catch up with you a bit early this year."

Oh, joy.

"Yes, darling. We were rather hoping to schedule our annual family détente to coincide with your big day," said Gwendolyn, pinching off the small smile that was all her Botox would permit.

Merry smothered a smile of her own, and across several time zones, she saw her brother do the same. *Détente* was more accurate than Gwendolyn, not known for her interest in wordplay, probably intended.

"Your father's just wrapped up that treaty in Ukraine," she went on, "and I've got some time off from the foundation, so we thought now would be a good time..."

"I'm free too," Marcus interjected. "I always make time for my little sis. Let the runways of Milan pine for my presence; I'm damn well going to give Sasquatch a squeeze for her big day!"

Merry winced. He'd probably still be calling her Sasquatch when he was a white-haired, white-toothed model for Cialis,

and she was a tooth*less*, towering old crone. She grabbed her
cell phone and, holding it out of sight of the webcam, quickly
thumbed a text message. Sasquatch, eh? Thought we'd decided to give that one a rest.

Her phone, which she had on mute, buzzed almost immediately.

Seriously, Sis, have you looked at your hair today?

Merry typed a tongue-stickie-outtie emoji, and on Skype,
Marcus responded by giving her a real, if silent, raspberry from
over their parents' heads.

"Yes, darling boy, we know how much you adore your sister,"
Gwendolyn said, oblivious to her children's covert bickering. As
if it could not help itself, one birdlike hand rose to smooth the
cowlick that ruffled the otherwise perfect coif of her son's silky
locks. "We're all eager to find out how you've been getting on,
Meredith."

Marcus shrugged away from her fussing, and Merry saw him
thumbing the screen of his phone. By which she means, "What
shameful circumstances you've gotten yourself into," Marcus
texted, as effortless with his smartphone as he was strutting his
stuff down the catwalk during fashion week. *Meredith.*

Gwendolyn always called her Meredith. Never mind that it
wasn't her name. Merry's mother refused to acknowledge her mistake in allowing the then-eight-year-old Marcus to name their
infant daughter after his favorite fictional character—Tolkien's
Meriadoc Brandybuck. "We were in a phase, darling," Gwendolyn had said once Merry was old enough to ask why she'd been
burdened with such an unusual appellation. "And I was never one
for fiction—I assumed if our Marcus chose it, it must be a re-
spectable name. Anyway, all the parenting books were saying it
was a great way to help siblings bond."

Perhaps it was true. Despite her near-constant aggravation with her brother, Merry loved Marcus fiercely. He was a scamp, a scoundrel, and a scalawag, but he was loyal to a fault—and smart too, though he did a pretty good impression of a dumbass when he wanted to. And after all, he was the only other person who knew what it was like to grow up with Pierce and Gwendolyn Manning for parents.

"I'm sure Merry is getting on just fine," Pierce said, patting his wife on one slender shoulder before peering into the camera to wink at his daughter. "Working hard at the new job, eh? Making us proud, I'm sure." His expression said he *wasn't* so sure, but at least he was sticking up for her, Merry thought. Her stomach suddenly felt heavier than the lunch-plate-sized turtle on it could account for. Because it was clear her mother wasn't on the same page with Pierce.

Gwendolyn faced her husband, turning her cameo-perfect profile to the camera. "Is that so?" Her voice, though still measured, could have etched glass. "Then why was she cavorting naked in Turkey only yesterday? And drunk in Denmark the week before that?" She faced the webcam again, glaring just left of dead-on into Merry's flinching eyes. *Now we get to the real reason Mother called*, Merry thought, letting her weight sink deeper into her nest of pillows. *Let the guilt trip commence in five...four...three...*

"You might have taken that job with ESPN, Meredith," said Gwendolyn. "They would have been happy to have you. There's no shame in being a sports commentator. Many athletes join the networks after they retire..."

I didn't retire. I did a Wile E. Coyote into a conifer, Merry thought.

"Of all the opportunities afforded to you, Meredith, I'll never understand why you chose to sign up with that website. If not the networks, you should have taken up your rightful place at the foundation as your grandmother wished," she continued. "Instead, you spend your days capering around like a monkey. It's undignified, and unbefitting an athlete of your stature. After all the years we worked to craft your image . . ." She stopped, pursing her lips with displeasure.

"I needed a change, Mother," Merry said wearily. There wasn't much point going over this ground again. How could she explain to Gwendolyn how exquisitely painful it would have been to spend her life attending sporting events, watching former colleagues doing what she herself could no longer do? Fawning over them in interviews, watching them beat her best times . . . Gwendolyn could never understand. *She* had *chosen* to give up figure skating (and an Austrian grand duke) to marry Merry's father. Merry, on the other hand, had gone down in flames. To see that knowledge reflected in the eyes of her peers as she gushed over their accomplishments for the cameras? *It would have killed me.* Never mind how welcome those TV bucks would have been—the cost to her pride was just too high.

And the cost if I slink back into the family fold and take my place at Mother's foundation, spending my days sponsoring society luncheons and arranging benefit balls? Merry shuddered. *Forget my pride . . . my very* soul *is at stake.*

Though her better judgment was jumping up and down, making "shut up and tell her what she wants to hear!" gestures, Merry couldn't help herself. "And the thing in Denmark wasn't some drunken debauch, Mother. It was an artisanal beer tasting that got a little out of hand. My readers thought it was funny—"

"Well, *we* did not, Meredith. People are talking."

"That's the *idea*," Merry said. "Creating buzz is what the magazine pays me for."

"*Buzz*," scoffed Gwendolyn. "This can't be what you want for yourself, Meredith." She shook her head, dripping disappointment. "To be some stand-up comedian on a...what do you call it? Blarg?"

"Blog," Marcus put in, helpful as always. "It's called a *blog*, Mother."

"Yes. That *blah* of yours. You were a *world-class competitor*, Meredith," she said. "And now you spend your time writing fluff that will be forgotten the next time some teenaged pop singer decides to tweak—"

"Twerk," Marcus interjected.

"—all over the Internet. You're undoing all our hard work, Meredith, making yourself a laughingstock instead of the legend you were meant to be. And for what? A travelogue on some garish little website no one's ever heard of?"

That "garish little website" gets millions of hits every month, Merry thought, stung. *Besides, it's not a blog, it's a magazine column. Totally more dignified.* Merry opened her mouth—to scream with frustration, to defend herself, or apologize—she wasn't quite sure. "Mother..." she began.

Pierce, ever the diplomat, stepped in. "Let it go, Gwendolyn dear. Merry's old enough to make her own decisions. After what she's been through, she may just need a bit more time to explore her options. If she makes a few wrong turns here and there, we need to respect that. Give her some space."

Yes, please, Merry thought.

"Really, Pierce," Gwendolyn said. "I'd hardly be doing my duty as a mother if I blithely gave my blessing while my only daughter turns her back on all our dreams."

"*Our* dreams?" he asked. "Or hers?"

Gwendolyn's mouth snapped shut.

Merry felt a stab of vindication. *Exactly.*

Thanks, Dad, she mouthed, and she saw her father blow her a kiss as he gathered the aggrieved Gwendolyn in his arms. Her expression turned tender as she looked up at her handsome husband, as unable to resist his charms as she'd been when they'd met nearly forty years earlier. Pierce was the only one who could soothe her ruffled feathers, and he seemed to quite enjoy it. Experience told Merry they'd be under each other's spell for a while.

OMG, Merry texted Marcus. Help me out here. Pull a fire alarm. Fake a seizure. *Anything.* She saw Marcus smirk as he read her message. Honestly, Poopyface, she continued, typing rapid-fire. I don't know how you stand being in the room with them when they get like this. And why are you even visiting? Calvin Klein run out of banana hammocks for you to model?

All part of my cunning plan, he typed. Every time *you* dodge the 'rents, *I* look more like the golden child.

What else was new. Merry rolled her eyes at him. Are you *trying* to make me look bad?

It's not hard...;-P

Merry scratched her nose, very deliberately, with her middle finger.

Marcus snickered silently, waggling his ears in a way his legions of sighing fans surely never got to see.

Merry stuck her fingers in her mouth, pulling a grotesque face.

"Meredith, you know it's not good for you to tempt fate that way," Gwendolyn said, emerging from her preoccupation with her husband with her usual uncanny timing. "After all we've gone through to put you back together, I would think..." She shook her head, her silver-blond bob unmoving. "Well, it's your face, I suppose. You've jolly well never listened to me before, so why should I expect you to start now?"

Merry knew there was little point arguing that mugging for her brother was unlikely to undo tens of thousands of dollars' worth of plastic surgery. "Yes, Mother. Thank you for the reminder." Stretching sideways toward her nightstand, she rummaged around for the container of Tums she kept in the drawer, grabbing a fistful. Cleese stuck his head forward, his turtly tongue darting out to lick one greenish tablet. "Stop it, you," she scolded under her breath.

Pierce heard. "I hope that wasn't meant for your mother, young lady."

"No, no, Dad," Merry assured him. "Just talking to my pet." She crunched three antacid tablets. A headache was starting behind her right eye, but there was no cure for that—barring hanging up on her parents. "No disrespect intended." She scrubbed a hand down her face.

"Yes, well." Gwendolyn seemed only slightly appeased. "I can see we haven't called at a very good time. You look like you haven't slept in days, darling, so we shan't keep you. Just promise me you'll make time for our get-together. I don't think it's too much to ask to see our only daughter once a year."

"I don't know when I'll have time for a visit," Merry hedged. "Now's not really a good time. I've got a very heavy schedule for the magazine, and I'm leaving on assignment almost immediately."

This was not true.

Merry had yet to accept her next adventure. She'd been hoping to have a few days off to just be a regular person for a little while. Renew friendships long neglected. Visit a museum just because she wanted to, not because she was writing about it. Maybe even hit a few thrift stores. (The "care packages" her mother sent—full of designer clothes that rarely, if ever, fit as intended—were doing Merry's social life no favors.)

"Merry," her father said ponderously, "I think it would behoove you to *make* time for a visit. Of course we want to see you— we do worry about this new bohemian lifestyle of yours—but we also have important family business to discuss. Your grandmother's bequest has to be addressed—in person—if you want to receive your inheritance."

Bzzzz.

There's the carrot… Marcus texted.

Merry let out a long breath. She knew as well as Marcus did what was coming. I'm not biting, she texted back. You may be a suck-up, but *I'm* above such shameful tactics.

Hey, don't knock it. Sucking up is a fine art! Marcus made fish-faces at the camera over their parents' heads.

Merry had to smile. Enjoy your filthy lucre, she typed. Cleese and I would rather starve in our garret. She looked away from her dueling screens long enough to feed her turtle another piece of lettuce. It might be the last bit of green either of them saw for a while. "I understand, Dad," she said aloud to the webcam. "And I do take this seriously. I'm just not prepared yet to…"

Her phone bleated like an electronic raspberry, interrupting her thoughts. You may not suckle at the family teat yet, Marcus's message said, but you know when it comes to that big, sweaty wad o' Granny-cash, you ain't gonna say no.

Merry did not type "fuck you," but it took most of her dwindling store of restraint. The truth was, her brother might be right. Their grandmother Renee had finally gone to her dubious reward and, with typical spite, had loaded her will with codicils guaranteed to confound her descendants. Chiefly, by granting Merry's mother complete authority to bestow—or withhold—the nearly ludicrous fortune her family had amassed over centuries of sticking it to the peasants. As her mother's executrix, Gwendolyn Hollingsworth Manning was now sole arbiter of what constituted the type of behavior of which Lady Renee Hollingsworth, scion of a long line of singularly unpleasant Hollingsworths, would have approved.

Which meant that if Merry wanted to claim her inheritance, she'd have to return to the familial fold—in whatever way suited her mother's sensibilities.

"I know this is a great privilege and responsibility, Mother," she told Gwendolyn. "And I'm not ungrateful. I just..." *Need time to figure out how to politely tell you to shove it*, she thought. *If I can afford to.*

Marcus read the consternation in her expression far better than her mother did. What's the problem, Sasquatch? he texted. You allergic to money?

Merry's fingers flew as she replied. No. I'm allergic to the strings that come attached to it.

Well, consider me strung up, her brother replied, and she saw him shrug philosophically. If it requires a little ass-kissery, I'll pucker with the best of them.

Merry rolled her eyes. Marcus often found himself a tad light in the wallet. It was tough work supporting an endless series of dubiously legal parties with swimming pools full of supermodels and celebs, controlled substances, backroom poker tables, and officials of various principalities who required hefty bribes to look the other way. "The life of a male model," as Marcus put it, "is fraught with back-end expenses."

I bet you don't even have to practice, she typed back, considering your whole job is to make Zoolander faces anyway.

Marcus staggered back, clutching his chest and pretending to be struck to the heart.

"Children, are you up to something?" Gwendolyn peered into the camera. "Meredith, are you tormenting your brother?"

Merry's tummy tickled, and it wasn't solely from Cleese's tiny claws as he trekked the distance from her belly to her breastbone. *Sure, assume it's me,* she thought. *Precious Marcus never instigates.*

"Good lord, Meredith," Gwendolyn gasped, *"what is that thing?* You haven't got some sort of pest problem in that ghetto of yours, I hope."

Merry glanced at the screen, then had to laugh as she realized her pet turtle must appear the size of a stegosaurus on the webcam as he trundled into frame. It grounded her a bit, reminding her that her family's dysfunction—as well as their ever-so-tempting money—was on the other side of a very wide ocean. At the summer cottage on the shores of Lake Como this time of year, if she remembered rightly. A far cry from downtown Chicago, perhaps, but the little apartment she'd leased with the last of her endorsement cash—partly because it was a great jumping-off point for travel, and partly because it was about a million miles from the nearest mountain—was hardly a ghetto.

"It's just Cleese," she said, stroking his little head gently with the tip of one finger before moving him out of camera range. "He hasn't seen me for a while so he's being extra lovey-dovey."

"Well, Meredith, *we* haven't seen you in quite a while either," Gwendolyn said. "And considering the substantial inheritance that's at stake, I should think you'd be a bit more accommodating with us than your...reptile."

Bzzzz, went her phone.

...And there's the stick.

Merry saw Marcus shrug sympathetically from across seven time zones.

"I'll try, Mother," she said. "I really just can't break away right now." She sighed, avoiding her father's eye, which wasn't hard over Skype. "And, Dad, I appreciate that I have to make a decision about Grandmother's bequest—"

"The paperwork has to be signed and witnessed within six months, or you forfeit everything, Merry," he reminded pointedly.

"I understand. And I *will* take care of it. I promise. I'll come to you, or maybe we can meet in DC this fall if you're in conference with the State Department. Certainly by Thanksgiving at the latest. I'll have made my decision by then."

"What is there to decide?" Gwendolyn asked sharply. "Of course you'll accept. And of course you'll come home. What else is there for you now?"

Penury.

Freedom.

Merry looked at the stack of bills at her bedside, the corners of which Cleese was currently attempting to ingest. If only it were that easy to make her debts disappear. *I really can't afford to say no this time, can I?*

C'mon, come hang with us, her brother texted. I'll introduce you to some Abercrombie & Fitch models. Marcus made the Zoolander face again. With all that Granny-money, you can stuff twenties in their low-slung jeans all day long.

And what would I do when that got old? Merry wondered with a tinge of bitterness. *Spend my days attending charity luncheons and getting my hair done with Mother? Host state dinners for my father's diplomatic colleagues? Watch Marcus strut his stuff down the runways of Paris while I pretend I'm not his loser, half-crippled baby sister?*

I'd die.

Some other time, she typed, mustering a wan smile. Now, help me get G&P off my back, 'k, Uglymug? I gotta go walk my turtle.

Sure, Squatchy. Love ya, furball! A pause. And really, seriously...happy birthday. Marcus turned to Pierce and Gwendolyn. "Why don't we let Merry-Contrary do her thing for a little while longer?" He threw an arm around each parent and smooched them loudly on the cheeks. "You don't want to see her until autumn anyhow. You know how frizzy she gets in the summer."

"Well..." Gwendolyn melted under her son's winning smile. She was clearly not pleased, but the prospect of Merry with frizzled hair seemed to give her pause. "I suppose we can put off our rendezvous until Thanksgiving, but *no* later. Understood, Meredith?"

Merry nodded. "Yes, Mother."

"And Meredith..." Her mother paused delicately. "Those brows. Really, dear. They have tools for that."

Merry hit "Escape."

And started thinking about *her* next escape.

CHAPTER FOUR

*W*e're renaming your column," Joel announced. He kicked feet shod in painfully fresh-out-of-the-box Converse up on his desk and beamed at Merry as though delivering the best news imaginable.

"Uh...we are?" Merry slung her bag off her shoulder and slinked over to the visitor's chair in her editor's office. A sign reading "Entering Upper Slobovia" was taped to the open door, and it wasn't kidding. Joel's den of iniquity/place of business was a graveyard of dead computer equipment, obsolete file folders, and crusted-over coffee cups into which Merry preferred not to look too deeply. With two fingers, she picked a gym sock off the chair's seat, searched in vain for a place to put it, then gave up and set it on the floor at her feet, nudging the dingy cloth aside discreetly with her toe.

Her editor didn't take offense. "Yup." Joel's smile grew, if that were possible. "From now on, we're calling it, 'Don't Do What I Did'!" He spread his stubby arms in a "ta-da!" gesture and looked at her expectantly.

Merry got a bad feeling in her tummy. It was not an "I shouldn't have eaten that sausage-egg-and-cheese dollar breakfast special from the roach-coach downstairs" feeling. No. This was more of an "Oh, fuck, am I out of a job?" bellyache.

"And, uh...why are we doing that?"

"Well, Merry," Joel said, putting on his Serious Editor face, which didn't quite jibe with his cherubic, triple-chinned features. "We're in a recession, you know."

There seemed no safe response to this, so Merry just waited.

"And in a recession, do you know how many people are spending money on high-end travel?"

This time, Merry suspected she was supposed to answer. "Well, I, ah, don't have solid statistics, per se, but—"

"Fuck statistics. The answer is *less*. Fewer. Whatever." He scowled, which suited his face better than the jollity of a moment ago.

"But, Joel," Merry began, dredging up her most unflappable voice—the one she'd learned early on to employ whenever her mother went into rant mode over Merry's unacceptable hair/clothes/shoes/general lack of social grace. "I've been getting *great* responses from my readers lately. I can hardly keep up with the comments on my page, and my Twitter feed totally blows up every time I publish a new piece. I know I'm still finding my sea legs, but I thought 'On My Merry Way' was starting to go pretty well."

Her editor was unmoved. "Have you seen the numbers from your most recent series?"

Merry's stomach was definitely in "I'm getting shit-canned" territory now. She dug into her bag for her trusty Tums and crunched down. "I actually hadn't had a chance to run the analytics..." she admitted. *Damn it, I should've done that first thing*, she thought. *Gotta stop making stupid mistakes like that.*

"Uniques were down a full *fifteen percent*," Joel said. "And click-throughs are thirty percent lower than this time last year. Sponsors are threatening to pull out, Merry."

Where had she heard that one before?

"We're sorry, Ms. Manning. Mountain Sports is all about freedom, excitement, healthy competition. Not..." The advertising rep, visiting Merry in the second of her long-term sports rehab centers, had paused delicately, then waved at the cast that had encased Merry's leg all the way up to the hip. He'd avoided looking at her swollen, stitched-up face.

Not losers.

They'd been the first of her sponsors to pull out after the accident, but they hadn't been the last. Endorsement deals had dried up faster than well drinks at a frat house happy hour. The loss of income had hurt—badly—but the shame of failure had hurt even worse. Merry swallowed hard. "Does this mean you're dumping me?"

Joel looked at her a bit more kindly. "Not dumping you. Just...*retooling* you a little bit. You've come a long way this past year. You still sound like you're trying to write the great American novel instead of a quickie service piece sometimes," he hastened to add, "but you've been coming along great. You're polling well personally, and the comments are as positive as ever. People still love to *read* about your travels. They're just not following in your footsteps the way they did when times were better—which means they're not buying what our ads are selling. Frankly, four-star resort and spa advertisers were never really our demographic to begin with, and sales is having more and more trouble landing them lately." He sighed. "What I'm trying to say, Merry, is that corporate ripped the ed board a new one over the latest quarterly figures, and if we don't keep Five-Second Sally happy, *Pulse* will go the way of the AOL home page." He looked down at his pristine Chuck Taylors, sparing a longing glance for the well-worn loafers that lolled exhaustedly under his desk. "We've all got to think younger. More hip. Less moneyed."

"Ah ha." *And that means?*

Joel seemed to read Merry's thoughts. "That means twenty-somethings who can't afford pedicures at the Parker Meridien, or a private cruise on the Caspian Sea. Millenials who fancy themselves adventurers, but still probably siphon cash off Mom and Dad to finance their backpacking expeditions. You know… *hipsters.*" He shook his head. "I fought for you, Merry. The board was all for replacing you with someone…more *relatable*, if you know what I mean, but I told them you had what it took. That you were a team player. And you'd play ball."

Team player? Is he kidding? I was captain *of the women's US downhill ski team.*

Operative word: *was.*

Sure, she'd been put up in some pretty swank hotels when she was being wined and dined by advertisers eager to score her for a commercial or a sports drink endorsement. And yes, she'd grown up traveling in style as her father's diplomatic duties took the family all over the world. But did that make her *unrelatable*? The thought stung. *I work hard, damn it. I've always worked hard. I'm not some entitled, whiny rich girl.*

Yeah? Well, hard workers don't bitch when their bosses give them bad news. Suck it up, Merry.

"Okay…" she said warily. "I appreciate that, Joel. I know you've always had my back." When it was convenient. Joel was supremely self-interested, a fact which hadn't bothered Merry previously because he was *also* a brilliant editor and a shrewd manager. He had to be, to have reached his fifties and remained relevant in the cutthroat world of digital media. "But what does that have to do with renaming my column 'Don't Do What I Did'?"

Joel's grin returned. He lumbered to his feet and rummaged

around in one of the precariously balanced piles cluttering the storage closet behind his desk. With a triumphant grunt, he pulled out a long, narrow object and held it up for Merry to see. It looked to be...

A canoe paddle?

Somehow, Merry wasn't surprised—she'd seen him pull weirder items out of those depths. She looked at him with an expression halfway between a raised brow and a full-on cringe.

"Here you go, kid. You're gonna need this." He handed her the paddle.

Merry stared down at the splintered wood in her hand, holding it as if it might bite. "Dare I ask why?" she asked faintly.

Joel paused as if he were waiting for an invisible bandleader to give him a rim shot. "Becaaaaaause," he drawled, "next stop is Shit's Creek."

CHAPTER FIVE

As you'll have seen, my faithful readers, your favorite travel series is sporting a new look as of today. Note the bold header, the change of title—my dashing new photo.

"Why the change?" you may be asking.

Well, the answer is, it's time to spice things up. After a year of leading you through once-in-a-lifetime river cruises, toting your lovely selves in my metaphorical back pocket to some of the finest restaurants, coziest inns, and palatial...well, palaces...this world has to offer, I thought it was time to take a look at the other side of travel.

The down and dirty side.

No more spas, no more beachside resorts. Instead, I'll be returning to my badass roots, charging headlong into new experiences just like I used to speed down the slopes.

What does that mean? Well, for starters, instead of dabbling my toes like a dilettante into the waters of the places I stay, I'll be getting into the nitty-gritty, taking on outlandish jobs from all around the world to pay my own way. Maybe I'll be a short-order cook in Bhutan for a week. Or a gator tagger in rural Louisiana. It'll be rough, tough, and potentially dangerous.

Hence "Don't Do What I Did."

Pretty cool, huh?

As before, I'll be selecting my missions with the greatest care, forethought, and research. Only now, I'll be scouring the globe in search of the shit you simply wouldn't do, the shit you wish you had the guts to do, and the completely ridiculous shit that just needs somebody to do it, so I might as well be the one.

Crazy? Possibly. Unhygienic? Probably. Fun? You bet your bippy.

I'll try to choose wisely... yet in the end, gentle readers, it is you who will decide my fate.

That's right. You get to choose between two one-of-a-kind adventures, and I, ever your servant, shall undertake the winning entry with "full devout corage" as old Chaucer would say.

So what'll it be for our maiden voyage, mates? The Pit and the Pendulum? The Lady or the Tiger? (Or in this case, the llama?) Here are this month's choices, culled from real rough-and-tumble opportunities our staff has researched.

This?

Bat Tagging in Belize!

Volunteers needed to help scientific expedition count and tag endangered sac-winged bats in the jungles of Belize. These unique creatures almost single-handedly keep in check the population of insects that are harmful to humans and livestock. However, white-nose syndrome is decimating bat populations worldwide. Our vital research may be the key step toward eradicating this pernicious fungus and preventing outbreaks of mosquito-borne illness.

Applicants must have spelunking experience, undergo a full course of antimalarial drugs, and be prepared to collect daily guano samples. College students welcome!

Or this:

For the Love of Llamas...Help!

Needed: Temporary ranch hand to pitch in at our llama rescue/tourist outfit/fiber farm forty miles east of Taos, New Mexico. Our regular fella's off getting hitched and we need someone while he's finally making an honest woman of Rosie. She's been plenty patient.

The job: Help care for our herd of sixteen rescue llamas, thirty prize-winning alpacas, plus eight chickens, six goats, and two dogs (the cat looks after herself). Oh, and the bunny.

If that ain't exciting enough, my pal Jane says to tell you we've got spectacular views of the Taos Mountains, and our ranch offers thirty acres of wide-open wilderness to explore (but not exploit!). Nearby hot springs help you soak your bones after a long day of honest work.

Enthusiasm, spirit of adventure more important than experience. You bring a love of furry creatures and a willingness to learn, and we'll tell you what needs doing.

No smokers, please. I just quit.

Okay, readers! Record your vote below:

- *Bat shit*
- *Llama shit*

>>Vote now!

Merry took her fingers off the keys and sighed. Forget the exotic animals. *She* was the one full of shit. Her chipper, gung ho attitude? Lie. Her balls-out dedication to her new mandate? Phony as a three-dollar bill. *"Care and forethought" my ass*, she thought, finishing off the entry and hitting "Publish" only with the greatest reluctance. *But there's no going back now*. Her new job was officially a reality.

And perhaps, for someone with her physical limitations, an impossibility.

She'd never dream of letting her editor—or her readers— know how daunting she found the idea of charging into these so-called adventures Joel had cooked up, but...*yikes*. Joel thought tossing her into the pit with the lions for the amusement of *Pulse*'s snarky audience would create buzz, and he was probably right. He had no idea how ill equipped she was to actually *fight* those lions. He knew she'd been injured—the whole world had witnessed her near-fatal wipeout—but she'd kept the long-term repercussions of those injuries to herself. Partly, it was self-preservation—a competitor since early childhood, her instinct was always to hide her vulnerabilities. And in the Manning family, weakness had not exactly been welcomed with an understanding hug. But the rest was pure pride.

Because if there was one thing Merry Manning hated, it was being bad at shit.

It wasn't a side of herself she showed many people—in her skiing days, she'd shrugged off her rare losses with a laugh and a wink—but inside, it rankled to be anything but the best. If she couldn't do something well...she didn't do it.

Lately, Merry didn't do a lot of things.

"Don't Do What I Did"? she thought. *How about "Don't Make Me a Laughingstock"?*

It had been uncomfortable enough learning to write for the magazine this past year. She'd taken great pains to teach herself about finding hidden gems and exclusive, one-of-a-kind events, but honestly, given her upbringing, that hadn't really been so hard. When her editor had told her of this new cockamamie scheme, however, she'd had no idea how she was supposed to find the kind of missions he had in mind. Nothing about her up-bringing or experience had taught her how to navigate, as Joel so charmingly put it, "Shit's Creek."

Her editor had been the soul of helpfulness—as well as brevity.

He'd pointed to the Wheel o' Craigslist.

This jury-rigged cardboard contraption was the *Pulse* staff's idea of a great way to procrastinate when they didn't feel like facing their deadlines. An intern with a couple of paperclips, a bicycle gear, and too much time on his hands had MacGyver'd the Wheel o' Craigslist, which consisted of an outer ring of city names drawn in Sharpie marker, taken from the many the anything-goes site served, and an inner ring of categories from jobs to housing, casual encounters to garage sales and more. A pointer made from a well-chewed pencil stub determined the result, and whoever was spinning the wheel had to respond to whichever ad was currently at the top of that category.

The point of this—if there was any point at all—was pure fun-pokery. The variety of human experience exposed by Craigslist was eye-opening, to say the least. Some of the ads they'd found had been laugh-out-loud hilarious. Others had been dubious, even pathetic, and some flat-out sketchy. Don, *Pulse*'s resident cartoonist (and donor of the masticated pencil) bragged he'd found a half-decent, bedbug-free sofa after one enthusiastic spin. Glenn, the copyeditor, had gotten a date with a woman named Beauregard, about which he had said little.

But Merry was pretty sure the Wheel o' Craigslist had never been used to send a reporter into certain career suicide before.

There's a first time for everything, I guess. And if Merry didn't want to be out of a job, she'd be having a lot of first times from now on.

I'll be fine, she told herself firmly. *Hey, I survived childhood in the Manning household, right? And I've turned disaster into triumph—or at least a reasonably satisfying substitute career—once before. Screw the bad leg. I can do rugged. I can do adventure. I'm the* Millennium Falcon.

Her mind flashed back two years. The mountaintop in St. Moritz. The time trials. "Don't worry," she'd told her coach as he taped her knee that fateful day. "She'll hold together." It was an old joke between them.

"Please, baby," Jim had said, putting his mouth close to the joint in question and doing his best Han Solo, "hold together!"

It hadn't. But Merry would. She *had* to. She'd rub some damn dirt on this situation and make the best of it, faking fun for her fans, grinning and bearing whatever came her way. Because unless she wanted to go crawling home to Gwendolyn and Pierce, she had no other choice.

And speaking of choices...which would be worse? she wondered. Spelunking into the pestilent, guano-caked caves of the steamy Central American jungle, or hauling hay and shoveling manure at the back-of-beyond farm laborer gig? Squeaky, rabid flying rodents, or playing zookeeper to a flock of fuzzies? Fuzzies to whom, not incidentally, she was sure to be allergic. Merry and wool were a toxic combination.

Well, it was out of her hands. Within an hour of her posting, she had more than enough comments to seal her fate.

Tony Bored-anus: 'Bout time you took it to the peeps, Miss Merry! Love the new format. Get down 'n' dirty! I vote llama-love.

Travelbiatch: Make with the fluffies, Merry!

Troll-lolz: No batz, plz. I read a post-apocalyptic vampire novel that started that way.

Snark442: That's why she should do it.

SniffyKazoo: Totally. Zombie vampire brain-eating Merry would be a trip.

GrlyGrl: Oh, please, please, please pick the 'packies!

HomerSimpleton: Farmer Merry FTW!

It went on like that for several scrolls of her mouse.

Alrighty then, Merry thought, popping three maximum-strength Tums. *Wild and woolly times, here I come.*

&

"Yel-lo," said a voice that sounded as if it had been dredged from the back of Harvey Fierstein's closet. "Last Chance Llama Ranch, can I help you?"

"Oh, um, hello, sir," said Merry with all her customary grace. She glanced at the ad for the contact information she'd deliberately left off her blog. "I was looking for Dorothy Cassidy. Is this her husband?"

"I knew I shoulda given up smoking sooner," said the voice, resigned. "No, honey, this is Dorothy her own damn self. Who's calling?"

Shit. *Way to win friends and influence people. Now, just ask her how many months along she is and when the baby's due, and you'll have this one in the bag.*

"Well, ah, my name is Merry Manning. I'm calling about your Craigslist ad?"

"Are you asking me or telling me?" The gravelly voice was amused.

"Telling you," Merry said with a laugh of her own. "Sorry about that. I'm just never sure what to expect when responding to a Craigslist posting."

"Uh-huh. You do this a lot?" Dorothy's voice grew a bit less friendly. "I've already had about six calls from Nigerian banking magnates this morning, and I'm neck-deep in marriage proposals too. Some for me, some for my animals. Not sure if I need a shotgun or a secretary at this point, but I sure's shit am second-guessing this Craigslist crap Jane got me into. So don't be a scam artist or a goat-fucker, okay?"

Merry snarfed her Diet Coke. "Ow," she muttered, rooting around for a napkin in her bag. Her shirt sported cola-colored spots and her nostrils stung. "No, no goat-fucking here!" she assured Dorothy. "I'm a travel writer."

Silence.

"I assure you, it's a step up."

"And you wanna be a ranch hand?" The skepticism was strong in Dorothy's voice.

"Well, for a little while, anyway," Merry acknowledged. "From your ad it sounded like you're just looking for someone to fill in."

"Right. My regular hand Luke's getting married and his gal Rosie wants him to spend a few weeks with her family down south. But the fluffies won't feed themselves, and I ain't as nimble as I used to was, if you know what I'm saying."

"Ah...sure," Merry said. "What exactly do you need done?"

"Mucking, fence mending, hay and regular rounds. Welfare checks, scan for bear or mountain lion scat in the far pastures. The usual." She sounded surprised Merry should have to ask. "Plus, help my nephew Sammy with his side of the business—that's the llama tours." Dorothy sounded proud, and Merry had a vision of a younger, cowboy-hatted Harvey Fierstein riding the range with a string of llamas in tow. Maybe the beasts would be doing a chorus number, she thought—high kicks and all.

"You strong enough to haul a forty-pound bale of hay?" Dorothy asked, bringing Merry out of her surreal suppositions. "Muck out a barn?"

It was a good question.

Am *I strong enough*? Frankly, Merry wasn't at all sure her leg was up to a lot of heavy farm work. For the past year, her adventures had been more "interested observer" than "derring-doer." She'd happily skydive—if she was strapped to someone who could take the brunt of the landing. She'd drink in Hemingway's dives in Pamplona, but she sure as hell wasn't running with any bulls, before *or* after boozing it up. She didn't like to think of herself as a wuss, but she knew her physical limits.

Now, if she wanted to keep her job, she'd have to challenge them.

"I'm sure I can manage," Merry said heartily. *My readers will relish my attempt, anyway*. Or so said Joel. As far as her editor was concerned, the more shit she stumbled into, the better. *They'll eat it up, kid*, he'd assured her. *This is the Internet. There's nothing these people love better than watching other people land on their fannies—even their heroes. Hell*, especially *their heroes. So be a good sport*. And he'd handed her a kit bag containing bug spray, sunblock, and half a tuna sandwich she suspected he'd forgotten from his lunch.

She'd accepted it without comment, too proud to share her misgivings. Because Merry Manning was a good sport.

"Mrs. Cassidy, what I'd like to propose is a kind of a work exchange," Merry continued. "You let me experience ranch life firsthand, and I get to write about it for my online magazine."

"You mean you don't even want to be paid?" Dorothy's voice rose to a practically feminine pitch in surprise.

Merry would, indeed, like to be paid. But despite what she'd said to her readers, she couldn't very well ask the rancher to provide wages when she'd undoubtedly be far less qualified than the other applicants for the job. The per-piece fee she earned for her columns would have to carry her through to the next assignment. Somehow. "Well, your ad did mention something about room and board," she said. "Would that be okay, Mrs. Cassidy?"

"Call me Dolly. And I just have one question, honey."

"What's that?" Merry found herself smiling despite herself. *Dolly the Llama Lady?* Her readers would have a shit. She could picture Joel rubbing his hands with glee as he told the editorial board what she was up to.

"When can you get here?"

Wow. That was easy. But then, Merry hadn't gotten to the disclaimers. Dolly might have second thoughts when she learned what her column was all about. The name "Don't Do What I Did" kind of said it all. "Well, I can leave pretty much anytime, but before you agree, I think you'd better take a look at the website and decide whether you're comfortable with the kind of exposure it'd bring. Oh, and my editor will want you to sign a release."

"It ain't some kinda *porn* site, is it?" Dolly asked warily. "I've heard porn's kind of a thing on the Internet. I don't have much truck with it—the Internet, that is—but that goes for pornography too. I don't want none of it going on at my ranch. We pride ourselves on running a family-friendly operation."

"Oh, gosh no! What I do is like a cross between *Dirty Jobs* and *No Reservations*," she explained, pitching it to Dorothy in almost the exact words Joel had used a couple of days earlier when cajoling her not to quit the magazine. "Except on a website instead of cable TV."

There was a silence. The kind of silence that said either "dropped call" or "I have no idea what the ever-loving fuck you are talking about but I'm too polite to tell you so."

"Anyhow, take a look at my website and get back to me," Merry reiterated. "If you're sure this is what you want, email me and we'll get the ball rolling. Sound good?"

"Sure, honey. I'll think it over. But I've got a good feeling about you, Merry Manning. I expect we'll be seeing you real soon."

"Oh, well, that's great! Incidentally, what would you recommend I bring?"

Dolly gave another laugh—surprisingly appealing despite sounding dredged from a riverbed. "Just the basics, child. Your Carhartt, your shitkickers, big ol' hats in both winter and summer weights. It's December overnight and July by midday here. Oh, and lots of layers, from flannels to woolens. Tourists never do take that seriously, no matter how many times I tell 'em."

My staple wardrobe, in other words, Merry thought, looking down at the ballet flats, Lululemon yoga pants, and Ralph Lauren silk top that was supposed to be a thigh-length tunic but didn't quite cover her butt. Her mother had sent the clothes, and Merry, strapped for cash, hadn't seen the sense in refusing Gwendolyn's latest "care package," despite the strong odor of reproof that, as always, permeated the clothing.

Don't disgrace me. Keep up appearances.

Gwendolyn would have blanched to the roots of her expertly colored hair if she could see how poorly the outfit fit Merry's outsized frame. God only knew what she'd say if she saw her daughter in the kind of getup Mrs. Cassidy was describing.

I'll probably look like the Marlboro Man in braids in that getup. Or . . . crap. Willie Nelson.

Sorry, Mother, Merry thought. *I'm about to embarrass you. Again.* She scrubbed a hand over her face. "Got it. Basics it is. Oh, one last thing," Merry said before Dorothy could hang up. "Do you mind if I bring my pet turtle? He's really very well behaved."

A sound suspiciously like a cackle tickled Merry's ears through the phone. "Honey, with the zoo we've got, I doubt anyone will even notice he's here." And with that, Dolly disconnected the call.

Merry picked up the sturdy little box turtle and stared him in his beady black eyes. "Ready for New Mexico, Cleese old boy? It's so sunny there, it's practically sunny at night! You'll be nice and toasty, soaking up those rays." It might have been Merry's imagination, but she thought she saw the little fellow nod. "Good. It's settled then. I think you're really gonna dig this one," she told the turtle with over-the-top enthusiasm.

No sense letting her loyal reptilian buddy know how little *she* was likely to dig it.

CHAPTER SIX

Aguas Milagros, New Mexico

*O*migod, *soooooooooo* CUUUUUUUUUUTTTTTTEEEEE!" *I squee'd.*

The second I got the car into park, unfolded myself from behind the wheel, and stretched my cramped legs (somehow I managed to get saddled with the only MINI Cooper in the West for my rental car), I caught my first glimpse of my new spirit animal. Standing behind a weathered post-and-wire fence, long ears cocked forward, rubbery lips twitching like a bunny, was a real, honest-to-goodness live llama.

He was cream and brown, sort of like a sheepdog, with a neck that was almost telescopic and eyes that were liquid and calm, the essence of good karma. The intelligent, friendly look on his smooshy-wooshy face drew me closer. I had to remind myself not to pinch the li'l fella's cheeks.

"Hey, pretty boy!" I cooed, approaching the fence perhaps a bit precipitously.

Ptttoooooo!

Thwack.

Oh my God.

Warm. Grassy. Globulous. Filled with whole universes of evil, vicious, human-monching germs.

I would have screamed, but even in this exigency, I realized that to open my mouth was to invite the unspeakable substance that now coated my face to invade my vulnerable interior.

Friends, I have been in a lot of intense situations, but never—not in the darkest throes of my weirdest fantasies—had I imagined I'd spend my thirtieth birthday getting spit on by an angry llama.

In North Bumblefuck, New Mexico.

I backed up fast, tripped over a root, and crashed so hard onto my fanny that a cloud of dust puffed up and settled upon the swanky new Burberry trench my doting mother recently sent me. Something told me it was now as besmirched as my face. (Sorry, Mother!) Huffing with horror, I struggled back to my feet, scrambling to avoid a narsty-looking draggle of cactus I'd been lucky enough not to discover with my ass. With nothing else for it, I was forced to use the sleeve of my formerly fantastic jacket to wipe the oobleck off my petrified puss.

"They don't like sudden moves," came a voice from behind me.

An amused voice—quite warm and slightly gravelly, if I'd been in any condition to notice.

"And I don't like sudden loogies!" I snapped back, spinning to face Captain Obvious, whomever he might be.

Oh my.

"Captain Obvious" was a demotion. He was Major Gorgeous.

Crouched by the side of the demonic animal's pen, wrapping wire around a fence post with some unidentifiable manly tool, was a guy who seemed to have sprung from the earth, fully formed, as the epitome of "Cowboy." A walking (okay, squatting) cliché in Wranglers and a dusty white Stetson, plaid work shirt beneath Carhartt coat rolled up to reveal sinewy forearms.

I had to wonder: Had someone up there found out about my forearm fetish? Had the god of clumsy travel writers perhaps planted this dude in my path just to delight me? (It was my birthday, after all.)

Major Gorgeous rose up from his crouch.

And rose.

And rose.

Holy hillbillies, Batman, *I thought.* He must be at least six foot five.

Forget the forearms, you guys: I'm a sucker for a tall drink of water.

He looked down at me—all blue eyes and chiseled features shaded from the slanting late-afternoon sun by that ridiculous Lone Ranger hat. Sun-streaked blond hair was caught in a leather thong at the base of his strong, tanned neck. And wait, was he... barefoot? Yes, definitely barefoot. A barefoot cowboy. Just the kind of little quirk designed to intrigue a red-blooded, redheaded woman like me.

"Pleased to meet you, ma'am," said the stud. "I'm Sam Cassidy, Dolly's nephew. We're right glad to have you here at the ranch."

⤝⤞

Merry stopped, fingers poised over the keys. *Now why did I write that?* she thought, mystified.

Sam Cassidy wasn't hot.

He wasn't particularly tall, either—probably at least three inches shorter than she was, if Merry was any judge. (And she had *become* one, early on, when her high school growth spurt had been so precipitous her parents had sent her to a pituitary specialist.) "Burly" might best describe Dorothy Cassidy's nephew, with the kind of bearlike physique that could equally have been beer belly or brawn beneath his oiled canvas work jacket. And his hair hadn't been some halo of golden sunshine, come to think of it—though thick enough, it'd been dry and straw-like, messily tied back and far too long for Merry's taste. Yes, his forearms were nicely corded—she'd seen that where his cuffs were rolled up. And yeah, he'd worn a Stetson. And okay, his blue eyes *had* been suitably piercing. But his craggy features could have been called attractive only by someone in a charitable frame of mind.

And Merry hadn't found herself in a charitable frame of mind. Because there was another thing Sam Cassidy wasn't. *Charming*.

There'd been no "pleased ta meetchas" from the surly man she'd encountered this afternoon. Instead, he'd eyed her with a distinct chill that told her that he was less than delighted to have Merry intruding upon his little corner of the world, not offering her any assistance while she sputtered and gasped after the llama had let loose, just watching as she reacted to its opening salvo. He'd almost seemed to relish her discomfiture, as a matter of fact, eyeing her with an expression that was practically a sneer. Nope, she'd gotten no warm welcome from Sam.

Dolly, fortunately, had been a different story.

⤞

I was still wiping llama effluvia off my cheek when our hostess joined the party. "You've met Buddha, I see," said a woman in an enormous straw gardening hat, striding from the shade of a shed I'd been too blinded by saliva to notice. "Sorry about that, hon. Most of our fluffies are better behaved, but Buddha here could use a few more spins on the karmic wheel." She cast an exasperated look at the perfidious beast, then stuck one hand out for me to shake.

I gave her my heartiest handshake in return. "I'm Merry," I said. "Delighted to meet you."

Mrs. Cassidy's eyes, every bit as piercing a blue as her nephew's, scanned me from the shade of both deep sun wrinkles and her prodigious hat. I was pretty sure she had me analyzed down to the DNA in five seconds flat, but she didn't drive me off with a stick, so I must have passed muster. "Dolly Cassidy," she said. "Welcome to the Last Chance, hon.

Here—you still got some Buddha-goo on ya." And she handed me a ker-chief from one of her voluminous pockets.

I have to tell you, my fabulous fans, that I liked my hostess from moment one. Mrs. Cassidy is a woman who gracefully inhabits her midsixties, sporting short, no-nonsense faded ginger hair beneath that prize-winning hat and a sturdy figure that told me she was no swooning lady of the plantation, but a real, salt-of-the-earth working farmer. It was clear to me that she is a woman of enormous confidence, humor...and a complete, total dearth of bullshit. I'm talking 100 percent bullshit free. She may run a ranch that's ankle-deep in what she likes to call "llama beans," but she will tell it to you straight every time. As witnessed by her next words.

"I can see you're a strapping gal, and lord love you for it, but are you sure you wanna be a ranch hand?" She gave me another probing look, not failing to take in my now-soiled white trench coat (in retrospect, a poor choice for my chosen mission) and flip-flop-clad feet. (I hate to drive in closed-toe shoes. Call me a weirdo.)

"If you'll have me," I assured her, inching another little bit away from the deceptively placid llama. "Just point to what needs doing, and I'll hop to it!"

"Let's save the hopping for the morning, hon," my hostess replied (rather to my relief, as I'd been driving all day). "Sun's gonna set before long, so grab your stuff from that bitty thing you're callin' a car, and I'll show you to your bunk. Sam, how 'bout you give our Merry here a hand with her bags," she suggested to her nephew, who'd been standing around looking studly all the while.

"Glad to help." He tipped his hat at me, then started gallantly for the MINI. I'll admit, it was no hardship at all to watch his easy gait in those snug Wranglers, nor the way his muscles flexed as he lifted my gear from the car. And then—as if he could sense my far-too-prurient gaze—he turned around.

And winked.

It was at that point, dear readers, that my knees developed a serious case of the noodlies.

⚘

What the...?

Merry took her fingers off the keyboard again and examined them for signs of possession. What was going on? What Sam had actually said was...well, he hadn't *said* anything. He'd merely grunted as if gravely put upon when Dolly had directed him to help with the bags. There sure as hell hadn't been any winking. And rather than weakening, Merry's knees—along with her spine—had stiffened with affront as he'd yanked her suitcases from the car's rear and stomped toward her accommodation. But somehow that wasn't the story she was telling her readers.

Maybe I should just go with it, she thought, an impish idea brewing in her brain. As a rule, she was scrupulously honest in her columns, if not 100 percent forthcoming. But this was a whole new gig, with a whole new mandate. Perhaps a little scrubbing up was what the surly Sam Cassidy needed, both to keep her audience hooked, *and* to keep Merry from wanting to kick the guy in his undoubtedly furry shins.

If I include any pics of him, I'll just have to take them from really *far away... or from the eyes up so no one will see that sour scowl of his*, she thought, snorting to herself. She suspected Sam wouldn't be keen on posing for the camera anyhow, and even less keen on having his image plastered all over some big-city travel writer's column. With that laconic mountain man act he exuded, he'd probably hate being mentioned at all.

Tough, she thought. *Joel wants me to milk this, so I'm gonna milk it.*

Merry went back to her keyboard, figuring she'd see where the little fib went. After all, this whole "Don't Do What I Did" thing was basically one big whopper, with her pretending to be all gung ho about mucking around in Fluffy-ville instead of confessing she wanted to flee for the comfort of the nearest five-star resort. *If the whole thing's going to be a fiction, I might as well give them good fiction,* she decided. At least her hostess didn't need much sugarcoating. Dolly Cassidy was a genuinely sweet lady.

∝

Dolly stepped in at that point, which was good for my continued vertical orientation. "C'mon, honey, let's get a move on before the aliens come to fetch their scooter back," she said, waving at the MINI Cooper as if it were a UFO rather than an overly design-conscious subcompact. "We hit the hay pretty early around here. 'Course, the fluffies are hitting it all day, the greedy little buggers, which is why we need a hand to keep them in feed and such." She offered up a smile that charmed me half out of the aforementioned flip-flops. "And speaking of vittles," she continued (to my great relief), "dinner's in an hour if you don't mind biscuits and sausage gravy. It ain't exactly local fare, but my not-so-sainted former husband was a Texan"—and here my hostess screwed up her face as if she'd pull a Buddha and hawk a wad—"and I kinda got in the habit of making up a mess of the stuff when I haven't got time for anything fancy. Tomorrow, I promise, we'll get you a proper plate of green chile huevos divorciados *to start the day. Girl like you will need a hearty breakfast, I'm thinking."*

Ouch.

Yet Mrs. Cassidy's expression was so kind, I couldn't truly take offense. Especially with the prospect of food in the offing.

And let me tell you, my friends, Dolly makes a mean smothered bis-

cuit. I've never eaten anything like it. (No, seriously, I had no idea smothered biscuits were a thing. Check out my Instagram account if you want a better look.) Anyhow, it was a dinner to remember, even if Studly Sam didn't join us (he had llamas to put to bed, he said, and I couldn't help envisioning him crooning llullabies to them in the night). Dolly suggested we save the shoptalk for the morning, so we just shot the Shinola for a while, until neither of us could conceal our yawns. And at last, we bid each other good night and I headed back to my coop to roost.

⚬

Merry sat back in her cabin's single creaky chair, staring into the laptop that rested on the equally creaky little table as if the computer could tell her what to write next. She rolled her shoulders to shake out some of the day's tension, but she couldn't shake the doubts that were plaguing her. Honestly, there wasn't much else to report to her readers just yet. All she'd really gotten to see so far was her lodgings—which her fans would undoubtedly want to know about, if she were going to set the scene for them properly. Yet somehow, as with Sam, Merry didn't want to share the unvarnished truth on that score either. *I know this is supposed to be a "Don't Do" mission*, Merry thought, *but if I trash-talk Mrs. Cassidy's ranch, I'm basically slapping her in the face, aren't I?* Her stomach felt queasy—and it had nothing to do with the delicious, if fattening fare Dolly had fed her. *I mean, I want this to seem rough-and-tumble, but . . . not like outright mocking the country bumpkins.* Her hostess didn't deserve that, no matter that her ranch was, in reality, closer to run-down than "rustic." Merry wanted to please Joel and the higher-ups at *Pulse*, to kick ass on this new assignment. But what did that even really mean? Was she supposed to make everything sound swashbuckly? Snarky? A combination of both? Joel hadn't been terribly clear.

But maybe that very lack of clarity was an opportunity, Merry thought. DDWID was uncharted territory. Virgin powder. And, damn it, they'd hired her for her adventurous instincts. It was time to trust them.

Let's just see what comes out, Merry thought, and set her fingers back to the keys.

⚬

That's right. I said "coop."

I'm staying in an adorable little outbuilding not far from the main house. Unlike the rest of the ranch, which is adobe, the cabin's made from clapboard, and apparently converted at some point from an honest-to-goodness henhouse. (The current coops are now just a hop, skip, and a peck farther past Dolly's house, and I can hear the soothing sound of clucking from my bunk if I listen closely.) The view of the Sangre de Cristo Mountains from the front step is gobsmackingly stunning, and my little bed had been made up with the most gorgeous hand-crocheted afghan I've ever seen. There are cute little rag rugs and burlap curtains too. Dolly tells me she makes them herself from old flour sacks, and she's promised to show me the knack of it if I want. (Hey, Brooklyn hipsters, let me know if you want me to hit Dolly up for a set of shades. You'll be the envy of all your friends.)

Weathered, cozy, with a raised front stoop (originally to keep the coyotes from digging under the hens' nests and snapping up their handiwork, Dolly tells me), the cabin is perfect—so totally the picture of ranch-hand habitation, it made me wish I had brought my Little House on the Prairie *omnibus for snug nights reading by the kerosene lantern. (Okay, she's got electricity, but that's about it.) Otherwise, just a cot, table, woodstove, a cou-*

*ple of pegs on the wall, and—you guessed it—an outhouse out back. (I'm
sure that'll be an adventure.) Showers are in the main house, and I'm told
there's a hot spring—for which the town is named—nearby if I want a long
soak. I'm really psyched for my time staying here, and so is my turtle!*

Ah, Cleese. Was there ever such a constant companion?

*First thing, I got the ol' boy out of his terrarium and made sure he
wasn't too carsick. (Those of you who are longtime followers know all
about my turtle, Cleese. He's a real trooper about travel, as you'll recall
if you read my Queen Elizabeth cruise series.) From the way he immediately started snooping around the cabin, I could tell he was a happy
camper.*

*And, folks, I think I am too. "Don't Do What I Did?" Well, per-
haps it's time we all do some of the things we shouldn't do, the things we
don't dare do normally. Because that's the stuff of life, isn't it?*

*Stomach and heart both full, I stand now on the cusp of a one-of-
a-kind adventure, and my friends, I'm glad you're along for the ride.
As the last light fades, I think I shall take my ease (and my turtle)
outside on my stoop and enjoy the cool of this quiet night at the Last
Chance.*

Bonne nuit *from the back of beyond.*

⚮

Quiet and *lonely*, Merry thought, saving her entry. Yet maybe,
just possibly, she hadn't been bullshitting her readers about looking forward to this adventure.

It wasn't your average thirtieth birthday, that was for sure.
No cake, no noisemakers and party hats, no razzing about being
"over the hill." But Merry wasn't keen on rites of passage and
"big birthdays" in any case. She'd purposely drifted away from
her old friends over the past two years—most of them had been

teammates or folks she'd met on the circuit, and she couldn't bear their awkward silences and pitying looks. Her parents had no doubt remembered—her mother kept track of other people's ages as assiduously as she denied her own—but Merry had found keeping her exact location from them to be a good rule of thumb, so there'd be no cards or presents from that front.

She told herself this was what she wanted—new experiences trumped sentimental remembrances. Still, for a moment she had a pang of longing—for what or whom she wasn't sure. Johnny? Nah. Johnny Black on a llama ranch made about as much sense as...well, as *Merry* on a llama ranch. Her brother, Marcus? Maybe. One of her big bro's comforting squeezes would definitely not go amiss right now. But Marcus, with his perennial puckishness, was not exactly a restful presence. No. Not the guy with whom you wanted to spend a quiet night on a ranch in the middle of nowhere.

Cleese would have to do. Merry rose from the table and reached for her boon companion. "C'mon, boy," she said, plucking the somnolent turtle from his travel habitat. "Let's go gaze into the abyss." She plunked herself down on the front step as the day's last lingering light faded from the sky, turtle on one knee and her elbow on the other, chin resting on her palm.

The abyss gazed back.

And it wasn't half-bad, Merry was surprised to find. She hadn't been exaggerating for her readers about the view from her little cabin. As she huddled into her sadly stained trench coat and curled her bare toes underneath her for warmth, Merry let her eyes go wide, her belly unclench, and just *observed*. It was a practice she'd developed this past year—turning off her brain and turning on her senses, trying to absorb the spirit of wherever she'd fetched up, trying to understand it, bond with it, even *be-*

come it for a brief time. It was what travel was all about, Merry had come to discover, whether sailing the Aegean in a yacht or making a pilgrimage to the pyramids of Giza. It was why—and how—she did what she did.

And now she'd do it in Aguas Milagros, New Mexico.

A rusty glow limned the horizon, silhouetting mountains that could rival the Alps for splendor if not for height. *Good skiing*, she thought before she could stop herself, the inevitable pang zinging her heart. A sharp crescent moon had already hiked halfway up the deepening indigo backdrop of the sky, Venus twinkling like a beauty mark just below and to its left. No city lights blurred the twilight; no traffic noise intruded. There was a poignant silence that stole Merry's breath, making her hesitant to exhale into the quiet and somehow shatter it. After the bustle of Chicago, and the clamor of Istanbul before it, she felt as if she could tumble into that silence, like she'd misjudged her footing and stepped off a curb unexpectedly. It was a rush, a sensation of being unsupported and alone, with no one to catch her. It was a feeling Merry had had many times over the years, on ski slopes and off, though never in quite this way.

The air was giving up the day's scents—hay and dust, piñon and wildflowers. And yes, a hint of manure, emanating from the goat pen between Merry's accommodation and the main house. (She'd made brief acquaintance with the passel of bleating, yellow-eyed beasties on the way to her cabin, though she wasn't sure quite what to make of them with their bearded, constantly chewing countenances and creepy, horizontal pupils.) The smell wasn't as bad as she'd have thought, and certainly no worse than the Arabians that Mother kept at the stable in Virginia...

The thought brought Merry up short, sending her tumbling out of the moment. Her mother would, no doubt, be mortified by this latest adventure. She hadn't told her parents about the new slant of her series, knowing they'd find out about it soon enough. She sighed to herself.

Wouldn't it be great if, for once, they were proud? Impressed?

Ah, who am I kidding? Merry thought. *There's pretty much just one way this can go. Straight to Hysteria-ville.* The only thing worse for Gwendolyn than knowing her daughter was gallivanting about, blabbing about her high-end travel mishaps, would be discovering that Merry was now elbow deep in excrement and shamelessly smearing these new down and dirty experiences all over the Internet—and destroying the last of her reputation in the process. Merry could picture the furrow of distaste that would be trying to carve its way through the Botox freezing her mother's brow, and her shoulders began to tighten in instinctive reaction.

Ixnay on the Endolyngway! she barked to herself. It was a mantra that, if childish, had nonetheless kept her mother out of her mind many times in the past. Merry didn't want to think about Gwendolyn Manning right now. *No. Tonight's not for the past. Tonight is for tonight, and for looking forward to tomorrow.*

As the stars winked on and the day breathed its last, Merry cradled Cleese in the crook of her arm and rose, heading for bed. She opened her laptop back up and added one more line to her entry.

I think I'm going to sleep really well.

CHAPTER SEVEN

Friends, I did not sleep well.

Why? Because the Last Chance Llama Ranch is haunted.

Of all the things I expected of my first DDWID mission (and the things I didn't, like llama loogies), a predawn spectral visitation in my converted chicken coop was, frankly, so far off the radar as to be astronomically insignificant. And yet, there you have it.

I, Merry Manning, have been touched by the other side.

More specifically, the other side stole my left sock.

The hell you say? Yes, that's what I said, among quite a few other choice phrases when I felt my crocheted coverlet being eased off my body in the dark, dead stillness of the night. It felt like I'd been asleep for only a blink, but I was wide-awake, if utterly disoriented now. A ghastly smell accompanied the unearthly movement, like brimstone and people who use mass transit in summer without availing themselves of deodorant.

I caught my breath in the eerily cold confines of my formerly charming cabin. I failed, however, to catch the blankie, which was whisked away out of sight. I thought I heard it ruffle to the floor at the foot of my bed, but I was too paralyzed with fear to look over the side. And then . . . and THEN . . .

The unseen force grabbed my left big toe!

It felt like pincers had hold of me—pincers from the great beyond. I wanted to scream but my voice had dried up and gone, quaking, somewhere deep into my lower intestines to hide from this terror. I felt a tugging. Was the infernal creature dragging me to a realm of eternal damnation?

No—not me. Just my footwear.

I'd worn my old REI performance socks to bed, it being a tad chilly in my otherwise adorbs accommodations. Apparently, the ultra-padded moisture-wicking foot cozies (which have served me well from Vail to Portillo and beyond over the years) were irresistible to the phantasm, because before I knew it, whoosh! *The admirable sock was no longer mine.*

A creak sounded from the other end of the cabin, and a crack of reddish light appeared before my still sleep-fuzzed eyes. My mind boggled. A portal to the fires of hell?

I didn't want to find out. I really, stupendously did not want to find out. But then I remembered my obligation to you, my fine friends, and I wrapped my courage around me in place of the afghan of which the demon had divested me. I must not quail before the supernatural, *I told myself,* lest I disappoint my dear readers, who are surely expecting more from their fearless heroine than to spend the next several hours gibbering beneath my bed.

So I set off to chase the specter back to the realm of the undead.

One-socked, I dared touch toes to floorboards and groped for my trusty smartphone, which, with handy flashlight app, did its electronic best to illuminate the small space. I quickly spied the only possible weapon in the cozy cabin (though what good such mundane armament might do against a phantom, I'm sure I don't know). A log from the small stack by the woodstove was in my hand before I knew it.

And with a "Hiiiiii-yaaaah!" that would have done Miss Piggy proud, I charged forward, toward the sullen slit of light that was all the spook had left in its wake, determined to dispatch the ghoulish garment thief. Charged . . .

Into Dolly Cassidy's front yard.

Dawn had come, I now discovered—the light I'd seen was not the en-

trance to the underworld, but the rising sun shining through the crack in my abode's inexplicably open door. And with the dawn's arrival, so too entered my hosts, who were emerging from a barnlike structure (presumably the barn) with pails in hand.

"*Hiya, honey,*" *said Mrs. Cassidy.* "*Sleep well?*"

"*Nice pj's,*" *said Major Gorgeous, giving my silken sleepwear the once-over with a glint in his eye.*

⚬

Merry paused over her keyboard, smiling at her own hyperbole. She had only a minute to finish typing up her supernatural sunrise experience, save it to send later when she found her way into town, and get ready to start the day. The nearest reliable Internet connection was, apparently, at a café down the road, and the personal wireless hot spot she'd so naïvely brought along would be useless unless she could get better cellular reception. Instead of bars on her phone, Merry had a dismaying little dot that indicated service was unlikely anytime this century. Her stories were going to start backing up if she couldn't upload them to *Pulse* soon, and she wanted to space them out in as close to real time as she could manage. That was what Joel was paying her for, after all. The more often she updated her column, the more eyeballs, and the more eyeballs, the more potential click-throughs—ergo, the happier the advertisers were. And Merry was all about happy advertisers . . . even if it meant taking certain liberties with the truth.

I appear to be quite fanciful, pre-coffee, she noted with a yawn. *I'm practically writing a gothic romance here.*

What Sam had *actually* said was, "You planning on working in that getup? Or should I ask, 'You planning on working *at all* today?' We've already finished milking the goats and gathering the eggs, Miss Manning." He'd shaken his head, his straw-blond plait swinging down his back. It was the most he'd said to her since she'd arrived. Curiously, though he looked like the Marlboro Man's homelier brother, he didn't have much of a western twang in his voice, not like Dolly did. His accent wouldn't have seemed out of place in New York or LA. His *tone*, however, was heavily laden with the universal language of disdain. "If you want to actually be of use instead of just exploiting my aunt for a story," he'd continued, "you'll have to get up a bit earlier. Ranchers rise before the sun, you know."

Merry had let the log drop through nerveless fingers, taken aback by Sam's hostility.

Fortunately, her hostess had stuck up for her. "Sam!" Dolly had scolded. "Give the gal a break. She just got here. She can't be expected to know our ways right out of the gate. Why, you were a newcomer here too, not so long ago." She plopped her hands on her hips and gave her nephew a reproving look.

Sam, Merry was pleased to note, actually flushed. "I'm just looking out for you, Aunt Dolly," he'd muttered. "I'm still not convinced hiring her on was a good idea. We don't know anything about this woman. She could just be using you as fodder for that blog of hers."

Merry took a breath, feeling a flush of anger as red as the ridiculous pajamas her mother had sent her. Irritation made her forget why she'd charged outdoors in flimsy nightwear and one sock. "*This woman*," she hissed, "is standing right here. And she may be a writer, but she's not a user. And it's not a *blog*, it's a magazine column. Yes, I'm going to write about this experience— Dolly already said she's cool with it—but I intend to pull my own weight while I'm here."

Sam looked her over again, not failing to note her broad shoulders and sturdy frame. "Well, if that's true, I guess you'll pull a fair bit."

Merry went scarlet. *Oh, so that's how we're going to play it?* Sam had already struck her as a bit of a butthole; now she suspected he might be an outright adversary.

I've faced worse, she thought. *Hell, my mother's mildest critique makes his snark look like flattery. No way I'm letting him blow my first "Don't Do What I Did" gig. Even if DDWID ends up meaning "don't kick your host's nephew in his hairy derriere."*

I. Am not. Quitting.

"We can't all be as low to the ground as you, Mr. Cassidy," Merry said through clenched teeth, channeling her mother's iciest voice. "Perhaps I'll be able to hand you down bales from the hayloft."

Sam scowled, as Merry had expected. But then something happened that she *hadn't* been expecting. As she studied her challenger, she saw it...one corner of his lips twitched upward. It was a smile so reluctant, so grudging, she'd wager it cost him a week's pay. It skidded across his craggy face, an unnerving sight, like watching a Mister Softee truck crash and burn while the cheerful jingle played on. And then it was gone. Merry wasn't sure if that evanescent smile had been disarming or alarming, but somehow she was glad she'd pierced his paranoid attitude, if only for a second. Underneath the prickly hedgehog exterior, maybe the grumpy galoot had a sense of humor?

"Touché," murmured Sam. Then louder, "Alright then, let's see what you can do. How about you change into something a bit more...appropriate...and we'll get you started."

Merry remembered the reason she'd run out into the yard *en déshabillé*. She opened her mouth to explain why she'd dashed out

of the cabin like a silk-swathed wraith, to blurt out the eerie encounter she'd had, then shut it with a snap. In the light of day—
which was beginning to spread spectacularly across the valley
in streaks of rose and gold—it seemed ridiculous to start rav-
ing about poltergeists. *They'll think I'm loony.* Some total stranger,
clearly a ranch noob, comes bumbling into their lives and starts
rambling about disappearing socks in the dark...? *No, Merry*, she
told herself. *Better save this story for the mag.* Sam might try to use
it as a reason to get Merry ousted from the ranch. He was obviously not pleased with her presence, though she'd done nothing
she could think of to warrant his instantaneous dislike.

Dolly obviously agreed. She harrumphed. "Who runs this
ranch, Sam Cassidy?" she asked acerbically. "Me or you? I assign
the work around here, at least with my alpacas. Why don't you
go see to the llamas while I give Merry here the lay of the land.
You've got a tour running this afternoon up at the preserve, don't
you? So why don't you go see if the boys are all set for their
stroll."

It wasn't a question.

"Yes ma'am," said Sam. He turned from Merry with an inscrutable backward glance—warning? Speculation? Merry decided she didn't care. She also decided she loved Dolly.

"All right then, Merry. First thing, shower. Then clothes.
Then breakfast," Dolly said decisively.

Yup. I love her. "Yes, ma'am!"

With that, Merry had dashed back to the cabin to write up
her post before the events of the morning could escape her. A hot
minute later, she arrived on Dolly's doorstep with her toiletries
and a change of clothes, jonesing for the promised shower and
some grub. Dolly was happy to grant both to her new hire. After
a shower just slightly longer than the hot water held out, clad

in a loose-fitting pair of men's jeans and a tank top worn under an Abercrombie hoodie that had been a present from her brother (swag from a recent catalog shoot), Merry eased herself down at Dolly's kitchen table. She allowed herself to look around again— last night she'd been too tired to take much in, and Dolly had kept the lights pretty low.

Home on the range.

"I love your kitchen, Mrs. Cassidy," she told the older woman. "Seriously, the whole hacienda is just...I don't know...*delicious.*"

Delicious was exactly the right word. While the rest of the ranch seemed a bit dilapidated to Merry, Dolly's home was snug and charming, with whitewashed stucco-over-adobe walls, *nichos* filled with dried wildflowers, and fluttering lacework curtains draping gauzily over old-fashioned wood-paned windows left open to catch the morning's cool breeze. Bookshelves stuffed to bursting with well-thumbed paperbacks of every stripe from pulp to Pulitzer winner lined most every wall. The ceiling was fairly low, supported by vigas—chunky, rough-hewn logs that ran right through the walls and protruded beyond the adobe exterior, log-cabin-style. Open-planned, with just a half-height wall and a couple of shallow steps up to separate the kitchen from the living room, one could see everything of the house from the dining table except the bedrooms and baths. Rag rugs warmed the knotty pine floorboards, and crocheted doilies adorned the arms of the somewhat saggy chenille-upholstered sofa. An antique spinning wheel sat nearby, a basket of new-spun wool at its feet. *Wow*, she thought. *People actually still spin?* A calico cat, fat and placid, occupied the house's sunniest spot, blinking sleepily at Merry from the rug by the sofa.

The older woman beamed. "Ain't you a peach?" She plunked two steaming plates of *huevos divorciados* down on the scarred, round wooden table that dominated the sunny little kitchen, poured satisfyingly dark coffee from an old-fashioned Chemex carafe into two earthenware mugs, then seated herself. "This maybe ain't the life I imagined for myself, but I've got the house fairly well the way I like it."

Merry was distracted into forgetting the astoundingly good smell of the food in front of her, though her stomach growled in protest at being denied the dish of fried eggs divided by a dam of refried beans and tortilla chips, one egg topped in *salsa verde*, the other in *salsa roja*. *This isn't the life she chose?* Dolly seemed so at home Merry could hardly envision her anyplace else. "Do you mind if I ask...?" she began. "I'd love to learn more about you. For the magazine, I mean. I mean, not *just* for the mag, but my readers would love to get to know you. Or," she paused, concerned, "do you need me to get a move on? I do really want to pull my weight—my considerable weight, as your nephew would say."

Dolly snorted. "Never mind Sam. Boy's got a bee up his butt this morning, though I don't know why. He gets ornery every now 'n' then, but that's his own business. Moody so-and-so." Dolly passed Merry a worn but scrupulously clean cotton napkin. "Eat up, hon. We can talk after we chaw. I wanna get to know you a bit too, and the fluffies can wait awhile—there's plenty of natural grazing right now with the good monsoon rains we've been having, and they ain't too high-maintenance, not really."

Five minutes later Merry had *divorciadoed* her *huevos* from the plate, and relocated the to-die-for dish to her stomach. "Oh, *man*, that's good," she sighed, patting her tum. "With food like that, you could make this place a major tourist destination if you wanted to."

Dolly beamed. "I do cook for the guests we take on overnight adventures," she said modestly. "And I send along picnic baskets for the 'lunch with the llamas' tours. Haven't heard any complaints yet."

Merry had seen the Cassidys' ancient, cringe-worthy website, so she had an idea what they offered tourists. But she—and her readers—needed to know more. "I'd love to hear all about it," she encouraged. "What you do here, I mean, and how you came to run the ranch."

Dolly waggled a finger at her guest. "Not without more coffee." She poured Merry a second cup of spoon-could-stand-up-in-it sludge, handing over the mug with a jerk of her head to indicate Merry should precede her out the door. Merry, who never messed with a woman who had perfected the secret to effective caffeination, did as bid and stepped out onto a porch guarded by a row of rattan rocking chairs.

Her breath caught in a totally wham-out-of-the-blue sob.

"Oh," she said, a bare wisp of sound. Merry's butt thumped onto the seat of one of the chairs. Her eyes filled with tears that didn't quite spill over, blurring the very sight that had started the waterworks. What she'd seen last night had been impressive enough. But out back...

Dorothy Cassidy had a million-dollar view.

A hundred miles of painters and poets' inspiration rolled and rollicked from Dolly's humble stoop all the way to the horizon. A field of rough southwestern scrub grass, saturated a rare deep mint from the recent monsoons, was rimmed on either side by stately cottonwoods, their boles wrinkly as Shar-Peis and their bushy canopies teased into music by the breeze. A little creek could be seen to one side, glinting in the morning light. And straight ahead? Heaven.

Even the clouds, gold-limned at the edges by the climbing

sun, couldn't steal the thunder of the vermillion sandstone bluffs and distant blue-purple mountains that created an abrupt and magnificent stop for the eye. It was like every western movie come to life, like God had painted his wisdom in stone and sand with the brush of time, wind, and water. Striations of cream, salmon, rust, and bloodred were set off by sagebrush and the occasional piñon, the whole flat-topped, with tall spires calved off the main mesa to stand like natural chimneys against the ever-blue sky.

The creak of the screen door told Merry her hostess was joining her.

"*Damn*, Dolly."

"I know." There was an understandable helping of smugness in the older woman's voice. "I get to grouching over my lot in life, I come out here and I shaddup."

Though she was loath to turn away from the stunning view, Merry angled her rocking chair for a better view of her host, who had settled into the seat to Merry's right. "Tell me about it," she invited. "How did you get started running the ranch?"

So Dolly told.

"My husband John and I bought the Last Chance about eight years back," she began, "thinking we'd run some cattle or just raise horses. John had some money from the oil fields, and I was ready as hell to leave Texas—I'm from Alamogordo, New Mexico, originally, and Texans ain't exactly our bosom buddies—so we came out here, figuring to spend our golden years. Only the years weren't so golden. Once we were out here in the ass end of Eden, John not off working and me with barely anyone to talk to, we started getting on each other's nerves. Imagine," she marveled, "a man who won't so much as read a Stephen King novel to pass the time. Pretty soon, he was passing the time with a

senorita from the village, and that was all she wrote. John vamoosed after about a year, leaving me with a pile of debts and
this little slice of picturesque pie. There was no way I was up to
wrangling a herd of beef on my own, and I couldn't afford to hire
a lot of help."

"That must have been scary," Merry said. Her own debts were
daunting enough. If she'd been left high and dry in a place as iso-
lated as Aguas Milagros, she'd have lost her mind.

"Nah, not scary, really," Dolly demurred. "But those were
tough times, I'll admit. And I made a few questionable choices,
let a few choose me." A smile lifted her lips.

"Oh, really?" Merry asked. She sensed the story was about to
get good.

"Yup." Dolly settled more comfortably in her seat. "I fell for
the fool alpacas around the time John lit out, and getting myself
a passel of them was nutty enough, but it was the damn llamas
that really sealed my fate. A *friend*," she said darkly after a sip of
her sludge, "saddled me with the first of them. What can I say;
I was feeling a bit vulnerable at the time." She shook her head
ruefully. "Well, let me back up." She took a deep breath, let out
a smoker's hack, and launched into her tale. "It began with one
particular llama named Mario, who turned out to be *Marianne*,
and who turned out to be pregnant, the sneaky so-and-so."

Merry lifted a brow—the more piratical one, since it was already higher than the other. "A sneakily pregnant llama named
Marianne?"

Dolly nodded. "I'd bought the first of the alpacas already—a
herd sire, a couple promising pedigreed females. Spent way too
much on them—this was before the great alpaca bubble of '09
burst, and back then us fiber farmers all thought we'd struck
woolly gold. I was still learning about spinning and grading

fleece—I've always been a keen crocheter, but I couldn't tell my grade one from the kind that's only good for stuffing and rug weaving, never mind guess the microns just by eyeball."

Merry decided an explanation of "microns" could wait. "Mm," she said encouragingly.

Dolly obviously sensed she'd digressed. "Anyhoo, I was just getting started with my alpaca breeding program, though they were mostly pets at that time. Then Needlepoint Bob swings by the hacienda one afternoon, all hangdog with those soulful brown eyes. He's hauling Mario behind him on a lead." She scowled. "And ol' Bob, he starts in with the sales pitch. 'Oh Dolly, you'll love him.'" She made her deep voice even deeper, imitating this oddly named mystery man. "'Llamas are great guard dogs. They're so low-maintenance. They carry your packs. And so friendly!'"

Dolly sighed. "Well, Mario *was* pretty cute, and Needlepoint Bob swore he couldn't keep him, since he was selling his acreage and moving into the trailer behind the café. So I said, sure, put him in the high pasture, and then Bob really turns on the charm. 'Mario's got a few buddies—just a couple!' he swears. 'They all grew up together, so it wouldn't really be fair to separate them.' As if they were kittens." Dolly shook her head, remembering.

"So how many was a couple?" Merry asked.

"Six." Dolly laughed ruefully. "And five of them pregnant, by the last. Didn't find out until eleven months later—they gestate for nearly a year, you know, and I hadn't thought to second-guess Bob on the subject of their sex. Now, they *were* good guard dogs, I'll admit—they'll set to stamping and squealing if any predator comes near. I've seen 'em scare off a mountain lion, if you can believe."

Merry had never seen a mountain lion in action outside of the odd National Geo channel special, but she guessed from Dolly's tone they were fairly fierce. "Wow," she said. "So what happened?"

"Once you get a reputation for being a llama lover, you're really in for it. Every Tom, Dick, and Harry comes out of the woodwork; 'Oh please, won't you take Tweedledum and Tweedledee?' 'Oh, Dolly, you're such a saint. Can't you care for this poor, broken-down boy my grandma left me?'" She sucked back the last of her coffee. "And what was I gonna say? They were all headed for slaughter if I couldn't take 'em in. So next thing I know, I got sixteen of the critters, all munching their weight in hay and looking to me to love 'em. Which I did, even though it wasn't doing my wallet any favors. I'd always thought I'd spend my later years traveling the world," she said with a wistful look in her eyes. "Had all the brochures ordered—Paris to the Pyramids, Thailand to Timbuktu—but after Bob stuck me with the damn llamas, well, all that went out the window, along with every spare cent I had. The money my alpaca yarn brought in couldn't begin to cover their keep. If it weren't for Sam coming to live with me just when I was about to go bust, and him coming up with the idea to run llama tours, we'd have gone under years ago. Least now the buggers work for a living."

Hearing the obvious love and pride in her hostess's tone, Merry began to see Sam Cassidy in a slightly more charitable light. *Slightly.* "You can't use llama fur for yarn?" she asked, leaning one arm over the porch rail, mostly empty coffee cup dangling from her hand.

"Wool. Not fur," Dolly corrected with a smile. "Oh no, hon. I mean, you *can*, but you wouldn't wanna wear a sweater made out of it. Maybe a wall hanging or a jacket if it had a thick lining. But a working llama's bred with the kinda coat that doesn't make great yarn—least, the ones I adopted are. And alpaca's just a whole 'nother ball game—once you go 'pac, we like to say, you never go back."

And it was at that moment that Merry learned why.

Something stuck its nose in her coffee cup.

And snuffled.

Merry jumped, the last drizzle of her coffee leaping from the cup... and onto the muzzle of one very innocent-looking alpaca.

"Oh. My. God," Merry breathed.

Want.

Want.

Want. Want. Want. Want. Want.

CHAPTER EIGHT

*B*oudicca polished off the last of my coffee with a slurp, then shook her head as if to say, "You coulda added some sugar." I apologized as best I could. After all, I didn't want to get on my new bestie's bad side.

Boudie is a little gray gal with an Afro, absurdly long lashes, and an attitude that plainly says, "I'm the cutest thing in three counties." And folks, she isn't wrong. Despite—or perhaps because of—a slight limp Dolly tells me came from a recent encounter with some stray barbed wire (the leg is now festively bandaged with bright pink stretchy tape), the lass stole my heart like a thief in a Hollywood heist movie... which is to say, with preternatural ease. Apparently, she didn't object to my company either, for she proceeded to escort me and my hostess for much of my first day, gamboling along at our sides and generally proving a worthy tour guide. I can only hope to do as well for you, dear readers.

So let me set the scene.

Now, a fiber farm is much like any other farm, except way, way cuter. One's first impression of the Last Chance is of just how vast, lonely, and unspoiled it is. Situated a little less than forty-five minutes' drive from the world-class skiing of Taos, and just about seventy from the state capital of Santa Fe (where I hear you can get some really tasty baked goods), the flyspeck of Aguas Milagros, NM, (named for some hot springs I'll be checking out ASAP), may not have traffic lights, or Whole Foods, but it has got a lot of Wild West charm going on. And the Last Chance, I'll wager, is its crowning jewel. Or sharpest spur, or whatever the appropri-

ate cowboy-town metaphor is. Nestled in a valley ringed with mountains that stay snowcapped practically all year round, the property spreads out in an unending carpet of seedy green grasses, scrubby sagebrush, and the occasional cactus, everywhere dotted by cotton balls that aren't cotton balls at all, but wool. And these cotton balls are quite curious about strangers.

The llamas had already gone with Studly Sam by the time we got out there, off to rendezvous with some tourists for a trek in the mountains. So it was just us and the alpacas, which suited me fine.

Because alpacas are The. Bomb.

Imagine you shrink a llama down mini, about, say, waist high to most women—or hip high on a Merry. (This is not including its ridiculously long neck, which makes it about shoulder height when it stretches to the fullest. Shorten its nose, make its ears stick out a bit more to the sides, and then you blow-dry the everlasting shit out of the critter until it turns into an Ewok/camel/sheep/Shmoo that is so foofy it can barely see out of its own woolly face.

I died. Like thirty times. One for each alpaca, I'm pretty sure.

And if that weren't adorable enough, get this: Dolly theme names all her beasties. Each year's "crop" of babies gets named after whatever idea takes her fancy—last year, since all the offspring happened to be female, it was Tough Women in History, so in addition to Boudicca, she's also got Anne Bonny, Catherine the Great (Cathy for short), and Hillary Clinton. The llamas and goats get their own themes too, I'm told.

Now, get ready for some research, kids. I looked a buncha this stuff up before I arrived, and Dolly filled in some blanks as we took our tour, strolling the pastures and getting the lay of the land. It's actually interesting stuff—shut up, it is! So let's get to it:

Both alpacas and llamas are classified as camelids, along with the vicuña and something called a guanaco that only abides in South America. While regular, humpy camels (like the one that nearly ran off with me that time in Abu Simbel) died out in the Americas umpty-bump

*millennia ago, these hardy, astoundingly useful critters have been do-
mesticated by indigenous peoples for centuries—llamas primarily as pack
animals, while alpacas are prized for their fantastic fleece.*

*Like its larger cousin, the alpaca has no upper teeth (and a good
thing too, as one cannot resist feeding the importunate little mooshy-moos
when they turn their pleading eyes up to you, and one doesn't want to
get nipped). Instead, as Dolly showed me, they and their llama buddies
have this weird bite plate for a palate and squarish bottom teeth that keep
growing continually and sometimes—eek!—have to be filed down. Like,
with a power tool. Anyhow, enough about their dental drama. Fact is,
they're cute enough to bring tears to your eyes, set your maternal instincts
kicking, and they're soft enough to sink your arm halfway up to the elbow
in their fleece when you pet them. Their wool is much coveted for the yarn
trade, about which I'm to learn quite a lot in the coming days, as my
hostess assures me.*

Best of all, I'm not even allergic.

*You've no idea how annoying it was to be a winter sportsperson when
you're allergic to most of the clothing you need. With the kindest of mo-
tives, people were always handing me woolen hats, woolen scarves, woolen
socks, sweaters, and ski masks. They've no notion they were essentially
handing me hives. Wool and I, you might say, have a contentious relationship. This caused me a certain degree of trepidation when first you
folks voted for this mission, but the heavens have heard my entreaties,
and, miraculously, it turns out that alpacas are hypoallergenic. You can
wear their wool all day long, and, due to the distinct lack of lanolin and
impressively long "staple length" that characterizes their fiber (you caught
me; I've no idea what "staple length" means), you'll experience only the
pleasure of excellent insulation and superior softness.*

Salutary animals, indeed.

*Under Dolly's direction, I discovered the joys of hefting hay bales
(each can weigh anywhere from forty to seventy or eighty pounds, so I*

*think I can safely let my gym membership lapse) and pumping spring wa-
ter into troughs for the fluffies to slurp (they can't live on coffee alone).
As part of my introduction to my new duties, we walked much of the
perimeter of the farm today, visiting with Boudicca's buddies and inspecting them for everything from burrs to birthmarks. Dolly tells me she has
a sort of sense for when an alpaca's "feeling poorly," but when she can't
figure out what ails them, she calls on her friend Jane, who is—I shit
you not—a holistic vet. I'll be meeting her soon, as it's "cria season" and
she'll be on hand to help with the births.*

*"Cria?" you cry? Yes, cria. That's what you call the even more un-
bearably adorable offspring of alpacas. I haven't been able to determine
who's pregnant or not due to the extreme fluffiness of the animals (I mean,
they're just about spherical, barring limbs, neck, and head), but Dolly
says there's a surefire way to tell. "How?" you howl? Well, they call it
the "spit test." Apparently all you have to do is put a male in with a
female. If they canoodle… not preggers. If she spits a wad at the poor
randy fella, she's had quite enough, thank you. Seeing as she'll stay pregnant for almost a full year, I can see where she might be a mite irascible
when Daddy comes looking for seconds.*

*Well, it's about time I wind down my tale for the day. And speaking
of winding, Dolly promises me I'm to learn all about fiber before my mission ends. Fleecy fun, my friends! She's got a shop full of fancy yarn she
spins herself, and she's even threatened to teach me to crochet. So stay tuned
for tangled times.*

*Anyhow, that was Day One of "DDWID," Farmer Merry edition.
Haulin' hay, sayin' howdy-do to the world's awesomest animals.*

How was yours?

$\mathcal{T}$hanks for being so patient with me today, Mrs. Cassidy," Merry said as they made it to the little cabin. It was going on five o'clock and the sun was still game to keep shining another few hours, but her hostess had decreed they'd done enough for the day. Merry couldn't help agreeing, if only privately. "I hope I haven't been more trouble than help," she said, swiping the back of one filthy hand across her sweat-stained forehead.

"How many times do I have to tell you to call me Dolly? And you did just fine, child," said Dolly, removing her gargantuan hat to ruffle the hair compressed within. "Just fine," she repeated, looking her new employee up and down with some concern. "Hope we ain't wearing you out. You look a bit peaked. How about I fix you some supper, then you can wash up and hit the sack."

"Thanks, Mrs.—sorry, Dolly—but I've really got to get to work."

Dolly's forehead wrinkled a bit with confusion. "Ain't that what we've been doing since sunup? I know you're gung ho and all, but you've got nothing to prove. You pulled your weight today, child."

Even through her haze of exhaustion, the compliment warmed Merry. "I meant for the magazine," she explained. "My editor's expecting me to publish my first pieces, like, yesterday, so I've got to get to that Internet café you mentioned and send them out. I figured I'd eat there and save you the trouble, though I would like to wash up before I go."

"I hear you," Dolly said, giving Merry a pat on the back as she propelled her gently toward the door of the cabin. "I could use a hose-down myself. Let yourself in through the mudroom when you're ready, and help yourself to the guest bath. Oh, you might see my nephew over at the café, since he eats there most nights. If you do see him, tell him we got two for the morning tour. I'll send you out to give him a hand with it tomorrow since the feed we laid down will keep the 'packies happy for a day or two."

Crap. More Sam? Merry wasn't up to sparring with that ogre again. Not after the day she'd had. And God knew gallivanting about with him in the wilderness all day would surely be a nightmare. But she just smiled and wished Dolly good evening.

Merry hung on to that smile for dear life as she watched Dolly depart. As soon as the door shut behind her, however, she let it, along with her screamingly sore body, slide down until it hit the floor with a thunk.

"Fuck," she swore.

It seemed to help, so she swore it some more.

"Fuck," she told her aching arms. "Fuck-fuck," she informed her abs. "Fuck, fuck, fuckity-fuck with a fuck on top," she told her spasming back.

To her leg, she merely said, "You are dead to me."

And then she cried, as quietly as she could manage.

There were many kinds of pain, and Merry had known most of them. There was strain-pain, where your muscles protested your inconsiderate overuse. And squishy, bruisy pain, that arrived when you decided to make acquaintance with solid objects better left to their own devices. Stabby pain, and thumpy pain, and even my-boyfriend-forgot-our-anniversary pain. But there was one kind of pain Merry wished she'd never met. And that was *damage* pain. The kind that said, *You ain't comin' back from this, sistah.*

The kind of pain she'd been married to since the day of the accident, and couldn't seem to walk out on, no matter how badly she wanted a divorce.

I can barely walk at all, she thought, digging her dirty fingernails into the rough pine floorboards as a wave of agony swept from the tip of her big toe all the way up to the third moon of Jupiter.

She'd hidden it from Dolly, she was pretty sure. They'd hoofed it what felt like miles circumnavigating the ranch, visiting each pen and pasture, getting to know the animals and their needs. She'd fed them, watered them, petted them, and been thoroughly gunked on by the smelly, if otherwise rather winning animals. She'd even managed to stay apace with her hostess, who, despite her claims of getting "past it," was admirably spry. She'd picked cactus off the hocks of patient alpacas, broken open ginormous bales of hay to feed them, even helped mend a fence or two. And all while walking what had to be miles under a sun that, though not blazing hot, was brighter and certainly burn-ier than most she'd encountered. Thank God Dolly had loaned her an old hat— one of her deadbeat husband's, as it turned out, but far more reliable than he'd turned out to be. She'd actually felt less silly than she'd expected in the brown, broad-brimmed cowboy chapeau, though she wouldn't be posting selfies anytime soon.

All in all, working the Last Chance *had* been pretty cool—for about the first half of the day.

Then her muscles had begun to sing German opera. And by the end of the day, there'd been *Carmina Burana* competing with the "Ride of the Valkyries" to express their thundering disapproval of Merry's unaccustomed activity. She couldn't imagine hiking in the mountains for hours tomorrow, trying to keep up with Sam Cassidy, who would surely brook no laggards.

For a moment, Merry was tempted to slink out to her car and head for the nearest airport. But then she pictured the look on Jimby's face, should he ever catch her committing such a colossal act of wussery.

Jim Beardsley, her former coach and dear friend, would never have let her get away with that kind of cowardice, neither before nor after the accident. Merry hadn't forgotten the gentle schooling he'd given her, when, months after she'd been discharged from the rehab facility, she still hadn't started returning phone calls, or, for that matter, bothering to brush her hair or put on anything snazzier than the moth-eaten bathrobe a previous tenant had left in the back of her condo's closet.

Merry had been lolling on her sofa, listlessly watching an old rerun of *Hoarders* on TV when Jimby rang her doorbell. Then pounded on the door itself, for a solid five minutes. Then yelled that he was going to call the gas company to report a leak if she didn't open up.

So Merry opened up. An inch, then a couple more when her eyes couldn't quite take in what she was seeing. Her coach, she saw with a dull sort of surprise, was struggling under the weight of an enormous rectangular package wrapped in what looked to be Hanukkah paper.

"It was all I could find at the store," he said, gesturing at the dreidel-adorned wrapping. He hitched the burden up gingerly with his leg to rest on one hip in a motion that clearly said, "Um, this ain't getting any lighter, here."

"Hey Jimby," she said, moving only reluctantly to allow him

inside her condo, and then only after it became apparent he wasn't going to take a hint and bugger off. "I didn't realize you were in town. If I'd known you were coming, I would have tidied up the place."

Jim's gaze skidded over the living room, taking in the coffee table strewn with pizza boxes, ice cream cartons, and crumpled cans of Diet Coke, the floor festooned with wadded-up tissues and candy wrappers. His nose crinkled at the funk Merry had grown so accustomed to she no longer could smell herself. "If you'd pick up the phone once in a while, you'd have known I was coming," he pointed out. "I've been leaving you messages for days."

Merry's phone had died of lack-of-charge-itis some days earlier and been jettisoned under the very sofa she was longing to get back to now. "Sorry, Jimby," she muttered. "Did you need something?"

"I need a landing place for this big-ass present I brought you, for starters."

The manners her mother had so painstakingly instilled in her kicked in. Merry ditched the roll of raw cookie dough she was holding in one sticky paw and limped over to help Jim set the package on her coffee table. Together they sat staring at it, while Merry maintained a sullen silence. She was not in the mood for one of Jim's chipper pep talks, and she had a feeling that was what this was. *I'm not going to ask. I'm not going to ask.*

Okay, fuck it, I'll ask.

"Alright, Jim. What is this?"

"Unwrap it and see."

Merry sighed and shredded Hanukkah paper.

"A *turtle?*"

"He's a metaphor," Jim said, hooking a strand of Merry's lank hair back behind her ear as they stared into the terrarium at the terrapin it contained. There was no hint of head, no tip of tail, nary a limb in sight. Just a shell.

Like me, Merry thought.

"It looks like a turtle to me, Jimby."

"Think more literary, less literal."

Merry shook her head. "I'm a jock, remember? Not an English professor."

"Please," Jim scoffed. "The girl who read James Joyce between time trials? The one who quoted Keats and Shelley on the plane to lull her teammates to sleep—"

"Clearly a useful hobby—"

"Merry, the rest of us always admired how you spent your downtime studying when you could have been goofing off. You think Annika Schimmerman reads Kafka on her off-hours? Sure's shit Mikaela Shiffren can't quote *War and Peace*, but I bet you can."

Merry could, but she couldn't see the relevance.

"Fine. I'm halfway literate. But I'm still totally clueless here. I give up. What's it mean?"

"Think Ancient Greeks."

"The unturtled life is not worth living?" Merry examined the greenish beast. "He doesn't look like a Plato to me."

"*Hellooooo*...Aesop?"

Merry drew a blank. Maybe it was all the cookie dough, or the crap reality TV, but her brain wasn't firing on all cylinders. "Aesop might make a cute name for it, but..."

"*Slow and steady wins the race*," Jim said, throwing his hands out in a "ta-da" gesture.

"*Ba-dum-pssh*," Merry said tonelessly. And then, to her great shame, her eyes had welled up.

She hadn't cried since it happened. Champions didn't cry. But

Merry wasn't a champ anymore. She was just a big, gawky crip-
ple with cookie dough on her bathrobe and no conceivable future.
Her voice broke. "Fuck, Jimby. What am I gonna do?"

"Oh, honey. It'll get better." He'd kissed her cheek and
wrapped his arm around her. "*You'll* get better. And like this little guy, you've got plenty of hidden chutzpah under your shell.
You'll find your way, sooner or later."

He'd sat there patiently and held Merry's shaking, sobbing
form, while on TV, they watched people with messier problems
than hers slowly dismantle the defenses of a lifetime. And ever
since, Jim had been a comforting presence, just as his gift, which
they'd named Cleese after their favorite Python, had turned out
to be.

Shit. Cleese. Merry looked around the cabin until she recalled
where she'd put his travel terrarium. He had to be hungry by
now.

Must. Get. Up. Must. Be. Responsible. Turtle. Mama.

Seven and a half minutes later, Merry had scraped herself
off the floor, fed and cosseted her pet, and managed to find her
strongest antibacterial soap.

Five long minutes after that, she made it to Dolly's place
to degunk. Twenty more and, freshly scrubbed, she crossed the
thirty feet to her car, ready to find that Internet café.

Please, God, let them have burritos.

CHAPTER TEN

Deadheads, rejoice! I have news. Your spiritual leader, much like Elvis, lives on. I know, for I have this very day met Jerry himself. He lives out his life quietly, modestly, in a wisp of a New Mexico mountain town. He swears his name is Needlepoint Bob.

And he makes a mean latte.

✂

Bob's café was part fifties diner, part general store, and all tongue-in-cheek. Merry glanced at the sign stenciled in flaking paint above the low adobe lintel. "*Café Con Kvetch?*" she murmured incredulously. "This I gotta see."

She ducked a net of draggling Christmas lights and headed inside what looked to be the only public building in Aguas Milagros that was actually open. "Town" was a generous description for the dusty streak of slightly less desolate high desert she'd nearly missed on her way in yesterday due to her need to blink once in a while. If she hadn't spotted the single faded sign for Aguas Milagros at the last second, practically obscured by a clump of cottonwood trees that lined the two-lane access road, she'd have cruised on by—all the way to Colorado, probably. From what she'd seen so far—primarily shacks that ran the gamut from "almost falling down" to "*Blair Witch Project*"—it

seemed as if the town might dry up and blow away like a tum-
bleweed any second. The tiny library-cum-visitors' center a few
yards down had a sign promising to "Be Back in 5," but judging
by the curling, yellowed corners of said sign, "5" was more likely
decades than minutes. A feed store looked lean and hungry across
the dusty street, and a defunct dollar store down the way didn't
make any cents.

But Bob's was quite the happening joint. Or at least, so the
many pickup trucks and battered SUVs parked outside, and the
music and laughter she could hear from inside would indicate. As
Merry swung open the door, her arrival announced by a chiming
bell, she was accosted with a wave of scents and sights that told
her, in no uncertain terms, that she was going to be *A-OK*.

Coffee, rich and bold.

Cinnamon, cocoa, and vanilla.

Nuts from hazel to pecan, emanating from pies and floating
from flavored frappés.

Fried foods both savory and sweet.

Chile, cheese, and refried beans; rice and posole, fresh corn
tortillas.

The ancient jukebox in the corner was playing the Four
Seasons' "Sherry," but thankfully at a volume that didn't cause
Frankie's falsetto to grate overmuch on the nerves.

Best of all, a little sign beside the host station/cash register
read: "Free Wi-Fi."

Tears welled in Merry's eyes, and she let out a hitching breath.
"Civilization!"

She hoisted her laptop bag higher on her shoulder, ignoring
the thrill of pain the motion brought to her hay-bale-challenged
muscles. Four Advil, a hot shower, and a great deal of teeth
grinding had provided a measure of relief, and Merry was ready

for her second wind. And firsts, seconds, and thirds on dinner. She couldn't remember the last time she'd been this ravenous. *Guess there's a reason for the saying "Hungry as a farmhand,"* she thought.

She looked around for a server, at last spotting a chunky, cherub-cheeked woman in an apron that had seen better centuries, and inky hair done up in a handsome knot of braids. Unfortunately for Merry's stomach, which was currently gnawing on her spine like a virulent zombie, the woman ducked by with her eyes averted in the universal waitress-who-thinks-you-can't-see-her-if-she-doesn't-see-you maneuver.

"Miss . . . ?" Merry began, intending to ask if she should seat herself. The woman just waved a spatula toward an empty booth by the back wall in a gesture that could have been anything from cordial to threatening, then hustled behind the pass and into the café's tiny kitchen. *Cook then, not waitress,* Merry decided. Or both? In a town this small, people probably wore a lot of different hats. Most of them Stetson.

"Okay then," Merry muttered, and made her way haltingly to the table in question, trying her best not to let her limp show. She passed several weathered-looking couples, all upwards of sixty, staking out the other booths, and a few men at the bar sucking down brewskis with their backs to Merry. She paid them little attention, sinking gratefully onto the patched vinyl bench and laying her computer beside her on the Formica-topped table.

Better. Now, if only I had a menu. And perhaps a small cadre of masseurs. An image of Sam Cassidy popped into her mind, for no reason she could possibly fathom. But this was Sam as she'd written him, handsome and gallant, waving a bottle of warm jojoba oil and an aromatherapy candle. Not Sam as he was.

Ha, she thought. *The real Sam would probably fire me for being dead weight if I let on how hard this is for me.* The image in her mind slowly shifted to reflect the rather disappointing reality of Mr. Cassidy. Stocky, scruffy, with rough-hewn features that had seen too much sun and too little laughter, and that stupid, scraggly braid down his back...

A braid like the guy at the end of the bar has?

Merry sucked in a breath and quickly flipped her laptop open, ducking her head behind the screen as best someone her height could manage. *Tomorrow is soon enough to deal with curmudgeonly Cassidy.* She powered up the computer and was relieved to see the antenna icon at the top register a network. Then she clicked on it, and chuckled. "FBI Surveillance Van," it read. Apparently the Wi-Fi provider had a sense of humor.

Someone plopped down across from her in the booth.

"Hiya, Merry."

Who else would know her name? Merry glanced up in alarm, but it wasn't Sam. It was...

The man saw her expression. "Nope! Not him," he said cheerfully. "Jerry's gone to that great acid-rock festival in the sky, I'm afraid. I'm Needlepoint Bob."

"Is that supposed to be more or less weird than Jerry Garcia?" she blurted.

"Well, I can't speak to weird, but it's more accurate anyway," said the man, whose salt-and-pepper hair waved wildly about his head. His bushy beard all but obscured his smile, but the humor twinkled plenty bright in his warm brown eyes. He pointed to a banner Merry hadn't noticed before, hanging over their heads.

𝔚𝔢𝔩𝔠𝔬𝔪𝔢 𝔱𝔬 𝔅𝔬𝔟'𝔰 𝔠𝔞𝔣é!

It was stitched in an exquisitely fine hand on a background of fanciful animals and trees. The sign looked like something out of a monk's illustrated manuscript, or a medieval tapestry.

"You made that?" Merry marveled.

"Yup."

"Cool! Where'd you learn...?"

"It's a long story," Bob said, "and I doubt you'd be able to hear it over the sound of your stomach growling. So let's save it for a less desperate occasion."

Merry blushed. "Um, yeah. I guess if you wouldn't mind sending over a waitress with a menu..."

"I'm your waitress," Bob said peaceably. "Your menu too. We don't like to set things in stone here. I find it messes with the metaphysics I'm trying to foster. Just tell me what you'd like, and I'll make sure you get it. After a day like you've probably had, Merry, I imagine you're ravenous."

He wasn't kidding. But Merry was puzzled. "How did you know my—"

Bob's eyes twinkled, if possible, even brighter. "My friend," he said, "there's about fifty-seven people—total—in this town. We tend to notice when the number clicks up to fifty-eight. Besides which, I recognize you from your past life."

For a second Merry wondered if Bob was talking karma, but then she realized. *He knows who I was...before the accident.* She squirmed at the realization. Once, she'd been accosted for autographs everywhere she went. Over the past year, however, that had died down, as other athletes had taken her place in the spotlight, and the public's fickle attention had waned. It had been a relief to feel those pitying gazes on her less and less as time went by. And somehow she'd thought that in a town this small...she might enjoy a measure of anonymity. *No such luck, I guess.* "I'm just a travel writer now."

"I don't know about 'just,'" he said, "but you're definitely grooving on that second career, Merry. I checked you out online when Jane told me you were coming. Fantastic stuff. That piece about the hamam? Man, could I ever relate. There was one time, back in '68..." Bob shook his head, reminiscing. "Well, I won't bore you with the story." He waved a mellow hand, and Merry wondered if he was still seeing tracers. "Suffice it to say, the whole town's buzzing over the travel writer who's descended on our little slice of heaven."

Merry looked around the café. Half the people in the place looked half-asleep, and the others looked all the way there. Her brow rose.

"Well," he allowed, "maybe 'buzzing' is stretching things a bit. But the news got around, and we're all very glad you're here. I know Dolly is, even if she won't unbend enough to tell me as much herself."

Merry put two and two together. *Ah, the great llama fob-off.* She could see how Dolly had been suckered into taking in Bob's livestock. The man had a definite charm about him. Unlike some others Merry could name...

"I don't think *he's* any too glad," Merry said, nodding over at the bar, where a certain mountain man was putting away a frosty one. "From minute one he's looked at me as if he thinks I'm here to piss in his coffee, or, I don't know...rip his aunt off or something."

Bob followed her gaze. "That one's a tough nut to crack," he said, looking solemnly at Sam. "'Where there is anger, there is always pain underneath.'"

Merry looked at him, bemused.

"Eckhart Tolle," he explained. "Guy's a bit of a charlatan if you ask me, but every once in a while he stumbles on something wise to say. I'll quote you Socrates next time if you prefer."

Merry smiled. Needlepoint Bob, it seemed, was a bit of a philosopher. "What I *prefer* is that Sam Cassidy give me a break," she said. "It's hard enough getting the hang of this ranching business without him giving me side-eye all the time."

"Side-eye?" Bob asked with a laugh.

Merry demonstrated, shooting him her best *Mean Girls* gaze.

"Ah." He laid his arms over the back of the booth, grinning. "I'm so glad you're here, Meredith Manning. I think I'm going to learn a lot from you in this lifetime."

"It's actually Meriadoc," Merry found herself saying. Instantly, her hands flew to cover her mouth. *Holy shit. I have never, ever confessed that in my life! Why would I tell a stranger...?*

"Cool," said Bob. "It suits you."

Merry blessed Bob's blasé reaction. "Just don't tell anyone, okay? Especially not..." She side-eyed Sam, who was engaged in what looked to be a crossword puzzle now, completely oblivious to her regard.

"No worries. Your secret is safe with me, Lady Hobbit." He winked and slapped the palms of his hands down on the table, as if to declare the subject closed. "Anyhow, let me get Feliciana working her magic on the grill for you. 'Licia can make pretty much anything New Mexican in about five seconds flat, and she does a mean green chile cheeseburger. What'll you have?"

Suddenly, Merry slammed face-first into her breaking point. Her mind was just...*done*...and she couldn't remember the name of her favorite ski wax, let alone favorite food. "I..." She dropped her head into her hands and peeked up at him with a wry half smile. "Honestly? I have no idea."

Bob took pity on her. "One of everything, then." He hefted

his comfortable paunch out of the booth, patted her on the shoulder, and wended his way on surprisingly light feet to the kitchen.

By the time Merry had gone through two days of accumulated email, updated her Twitter feed with a witty one-liner, and fired up her content management interface, Bob was back.

He hadn't come alone.

Plate after plate of glorious food plunked down on the table in front of her. Enchiladas. Rellenos. Burritos, and sopaipillas, and tostadas...just for a start. Green chile and red, tomatillo salsa and guacamole played sidekick. There were refried beans, and rice, and posole, all swimming in a lake of melted cheese.

Merry looked up to the heavens and whispered, "Thank you." And dug in.

"Well, that was a religious experience," she sighed to herself when she finally came up for air. Mere hunger alone couldn't account for how ecstatic her taste buds were. Unlike her muscles, which were still working through Wagner's Ring Cycle, they were offering up a rousing chorus of Beethoven's *Ode to Joy*. Feliciana might not be much of a hostess, but holy jinkies, that woman could cook. "Somebody needs to nominate that lady for sainthood."

"Martyrdom, more like." Bob had returned, beaming approvingly at the damage she'd done to the dinner. "At least, if you ask her husband." With delicacy, he settled a steaming cup in front of her. She looked down.

And goggled.

Merry had seen ferns, and even hearts painted in foam before, but this was...*a latte llama*? Yes, plainly and unmistakably, Bob had created a tiny, realistic portrait of the woolly beast within the confines of a wide china cup. With nothing more than steamed milk and deep, rich espresso, he'd performed a kind of enchantment. "I can't drink this," she said, looking up at Bob.

His twinkle faded. "Why not?"

"Because...because...I'll ruin it!"

The twinkle returned. "All things are impermanent," said Bob, folding his hands over his tummy and settling more comfortably into his beard. "Life, art, coffee...they all evanesce. So enjoy them while you can."

"Well, okay," Merry said reluctantly, "but not until I Instagram it. And do you mind if I post a picture of you with your creation for my magazine? My readers will have a spaz." She was already digging out her smartphone.

"A modicum of publicity would not go amiss," Bob allowed, making a peace sign as he posed with the latte. "And if a 'spaz' is anything like a thrill...I live to provide."

Merry snapped. And sipped. And groaned. Fuck, it was good. "Bob, can I give you a hug?"

"Of a surety."

So Merry did.

"I'll be back with your check in a bit. Meanwhile, relax and do what you came to do." He waved at her computer. "MacBook Pro? Fifteen inch?"

She nodded.

"I've got the new Air, myself. Wonderful device. Restores my faith in humanity."

And he wafted off, leaving Merry to her work.

The scant leftovers had congealed, as had Merry's restiffening muscles, by the time she was satisfied with her articles. She posted the pieces, along with an email to Joel letting him know they'd gone into the system and were ready for his review. Knowing how quickly he worked, and how little he slept, she'd no doubt they'd be live on the site by morning. Live, and waiting for her readers to enjoy . . . or loathe. They wouldn't be shy about letting her know which. With the web, she'd found, there was no such thing as middle ground. Or perhaps those who felt merely "meh" about one's work rarely chimed in. The extremists, on the other hand—the trolls—were vocal, prolific, and bred more of each other with each comment.

Well, I'll sink or I'll swim. And at least if I sink I can get out of this place soon.

But did she want to?

Merry was brought up short at the thought.

Yes, landing in Aguas Milagros was like traveling back in time. And yeah, it was weird as hell sleeping in a chicken coop and playing Farmer Fred with a bunch of woolly animals in the back of beyond. It was uncomfy. It was potentially hazardous. But at least it was new. And new meant *exciting*. Merry hadn't been a skier because she hated excitement. It was only after the accident that she'd learned to equate "excitement" with "danger." And "danger" with "no, thank you." Such discretion had seemed like the better part of valor—only an idiot failed to learn from her mistakes—but . . .

It's been killing me by inches.

She hadn't realized just how much she'd missed adrenaline until just now. Sure, the sleepy town of Aguas Milagros and its laid-back inhabitants might seem a strange place to find a thrill, but . . . there it was. Unmistakably. For the first time in two years, Merry felt energized. Excited to try new things, and immerse herself in this totally foreign experience. Excited to make that experience come alive for her fans.

Maybe I've just had too many enchiladas and a turbo-powered llama latte too late at night. But whatever. She was going to *crush* this assignment. If there was a Pulitzer for puff pieces, she'd own that shit. Because Dolly and her menagerie deserved her best. Bob and his wryly named diner deserved her best. And Sam...well, Sam could go fuck himself.

She turned back to her keyboard, intending to start a new post about how awesome this assignment was.

"Hoping the Last Chance will make you famous?"

Sam had not gone to fuck himself. Instead, he was fucking with *her*. She eyed him like a carton of week-old Chinese food she'd found in the back of a not-very-cold fridge. He was in jeans and a worn flannel shirt this evening, sans hat and, she noticed, sans shoes too. Come to think of it, she'd yet to see him wearing any footwear at all. Apparently Bob didn't have a no shirt/no shoes/no assholes policy.

"I've already *been* famous," she snapped before she thought better of it.

Sam looked at her, brow quirked. "I hate to tell you, but *in your mind* doesn't count, Miss Manning."

He didn't know? After what Bob had said, Merry had assumed Sam was aware of who she was—hell, that everyone in town knew. Merry Manning had been a household name, after all. A goddamn *Wheaties* box. The news media had been touting Merry's achievements for months before the Olympic trials, the sports broadcasts building her up into some sort of home-grown legend, America's great hope for gold. She'd done pretty well at her first Olympic games, but *this* was supposed to have been her year. All the races leading up to the big games, the national competitions and the World Cup...no one had been able to touch her. You'd have to have been living under a rock...

...or in North Bumblefuck...

...to avoid knowing.

"No, not *in my mind*. I was—" Merry stopped, reconsidered. *I really need to get out from under the giant boulder that is my ego*, she thought. *Not everybody cares about skiing. Even folks who live forty minutes from some pretty choice mountains.* Maybe Bob was the exception, not the rule, in Aguas Milagros. A flush crept over her cheeks. "Never mind," she mumbled.

Sam, arms crossed over his barrel chest and legs planted wide, continued to eye her. Or more accurately, he was eyeing the array of mostly empty plates that surrounded her laptop like soldiers laying siege to a castle. "They don't have food where you come from?" he asked, allowing the subject to shift.

"Not like this," Merry said, too distracted to bristle at Sam's sarcasm. She was busy digesting the realization that she was anonymous for the first time in a decade. It sat even better with her than the feast she'd just inhaled. *I can be anyone I want here.* "*No one* has food like this."

Sam's flinty gaze seemed to soften—just infinitesimally—as he glanced over at the kitchen, where the cook was now tidying up, off duty for the night. "Yeah, Feliciana's something, alright."

"Bob, too," Merry said. "I'm half-convinced..."

"I've heard him sing," Sam interrupted. "Couldn't carry a tune in a bucket."

"I'm sure there's quite a story there." Merry took a chance. "Quite a story with you too, Mr. Cassidy. Care to go on the record—give my readers a few details about the life of a llama wrangler?" She pulled out her smartphone and started tapping until she found the voice recorder app.

"Oh *hell* no." Sam reared back as if she'd offered him a shit sandwich. He pointed his finger at her. "Don't you dare put me in that blog of yours."

"It's not a blog—"

"Whatever the hell you're calling it, I don't want to be in it."

"Why, are you on the lam or something?"

"I like my privacy," he growled. "And I *don't* like my family being mocked for rubes by some big-city journalist."

"I would never mock Dolly!" Merry glared up at him. "Jeez, can't you even give me a chance? This is all new for me too."

Sam slouched back on one hip, brow raised. "I thought you were a legit writer. Now you're telling me you've never done this job before?"

Merry wiped her fingers on her napkin, stacking her plates neatly to make things easier for Bob. "No, it's not *new* for me, exactly. Just...well, this is my first DDWID mission."

"I have no fucking idea what you just said."

"'Don't Do What I Did,'" Merry said helpfully. "It's the name of my column. Didn't Dolly tell you?"

Sam shook his head. "And the 'don't do' part refers to working on a llama ranch?" His scowl was thunderous.

"The title's supposed to be tongue-in-cheek. If you check it out, you'll see it's really just meant to be me showing people how the other half live."

His face grew positively apoplectic. "The *other half*?"

Shit. "That's not what I meant..."

"It's what you *said*."

"I just meant...well, for crying out loud, you guys *do* live a pretty unusual lifestyle. I'm trying to show my readers a glimpse of something they may never get to experience on their own. It's meant to be charming! Read it for yourself if you like."

Oh, wait, no... If he did, he'd see she'd portrayed him as some sort of cowboy out of a Harlequin romance. But what were the odds that a guy like Sam Cassidy would even own a computer?

He probably lived in a yurt or something. If there was ever a guy who typified "off the grid," it was Sam.

"*Charming*," Sam said slowly, as if the word gave him heartburn. Merry contemplated offering him one of her antacids, then thought better of it. He pushed the sleeves of his oiled canvas jacket up, and Merry was momentarily distracted by the muscular forearms he bared. Hopefully not in preparation for strangling her.

"Yeah, you know...I show them what your daily life is like, tell them all about the animals, and how you take care of them. When I tag along on your llama tour tomorrow, I'll tell my readers all about that too. By the way," she hastened on before he could protest, "Dolly said to tell you you've got two people who signed up for the trek. My writing about it should be great for your business. I get like twenty thousand page views a day, and that's not counting my Twitter following. It's basically free advertising to exactly your target market, and I know Dolly's pretty keen to take advantage of that." Merry offered him the cheeky smile that had—at least before the evergreen had rearranged her face—won her countless hearts and no few sponsorship deals.

Sam seemed to respond less to the smile than the promise of publicity. Merry had gotten the sense that the Last Chance was hanging on by a thread, and whatever else Sam was, he wasn't stupid. She could do a lot for tourism at the ranch. "Well," he said slowly, "you *are* here to work. And Luke—that's our regular hand—did help out with the tours, so I suppose it's in your job description. If you're serious about doing this job—"

"I *so* am—"

"Then meet me out front of the barn tomorrow. No later than seven, or I leave you behind, got it?"

"I got it," Merry said stiffly.

"And Miss Manning?"

"Yeah?"

"Be prepared for some serious shit," he said, turning on his heel and stalking out of the diner.

Worse than the shit you just gave me? Merry wondered.

CHAPTER ELEVEN

𝒲ow. That is some serious shit," said Merry.

She was eyeing a flatbed truck of the sort that ranchers, she supposed, must use to transport livestock. Only this one had been customized for llamas. It was a bit like an army troop carrier, except that it was gated and had bars high enough that frisky fluffies couldn't hop out. *Do llamas hop?* she wondered, distracted by the image of the Last Chance's prized pack animals bounding fences like sheep in a mattress commercial. *One leaping llama... two leaping llamas... three leaping llamas... zzzzzzzz.*

They may not hop, but they sure do drop, she thought. The bed of the vehicle was awash with yesterday's llama leftovers. Leftovers Merry had been tasked with excising before they went out on their morning trek.

"Occupational hazard," said her new boss. "Shit, as they say, happens."

Merry didn't need the smirk that went along with that fatuous comment, but Sam Cassidy, it seemed, was giving them out for free this morning. Hat firmly in place, hair knotted back in a low, messy ponytail, his bearlike body clad in ratty overalls that could have come from the Dust Bowl era, he stood with arms crossed over his chest, bare feet planted wide in the dirt.

He was the very picture of rugged individualism.

Rugged, *asshole* individualism.

"And, um, after it happens, how does one dispose of it?" Merry slung her borrowed hat onto the passenger seat along with the satchel containing her laptop, and shucked off her sore-abused Burberry trench. She hung the latter over one of the truck's doors, far enough from the crime scene so that the still-mostly-white fabric wouldn't suffer further indignity.

Unlike me.

Sam unwound a hose from where it had been hooked to the side of the barn. "Start with this," he said, talking to her as if she were five, "and then you scrape off whatever's left with this." He pointed to what looked like a garden hoe leaning against the weathered wooden structure. "Lather, rinse, repeat."

Merry stifled the urge to flick a llama turd at Sam. Flinging poo at her boss on her first day working for him *might* start things off on the wrong foot—no matter how much his condescending attitude begged for it. "And what will you be doing while I'm in decon mode, may I ask?"

"Wrangling llamas, of course." Sam smirked again.

"Seems like you're getting the better end of this deal," she muttered, taking the hose from him while pointedly avoiding skin-to-skin contact.

"The front end, anyway," Sam acknowledged, looking not the slightest bit sorry. "You wussing out?"

"Not hardly!"

"Then get to work."

"Yes, *boss*." It took an enormous effort of will, but Merry did not hose her host down with freezing-cold water as he sauntered off, whistling for his llamas.

Setting her jaw, Merry hoisted herself painfully up into the bed of the truck, sluicing and scraping until the corrugated metal bed could once again be seen. Thirty minutes later, she was wet, cold, and caked in what was surely all the bacteria in the world. Mornings in the Sangre de Cristo Mountains were both chilly and breezy, and the blowback from her hose-down operation had not been pretty. As soon as this benighted expedition was over, she was going to boil the shit out of everything she was wearing, then take a quick dip in Betadine. Maybe start a course of antibiotics too. But the truck was about as decontaminated as anything short of a flamethrower could make it, and Merry was rather proud of her efforts. *I wouldn't want to eat off it, but I wouldn't stop Sam if he wanted to.*

She glanced over at her boss, and her gaze narrowed. He had four llamas haltered and hitched to the corral now, and four sets of bulging canvas panniers waiting loaded at his feet. He was leaning against the fence, loose as you please, chowing down on the breakfast burrito Dolly had made him. Merry had been too achy—and still full from the Café Con Kvetch dinner extravaganza—to take advantage of her hostess's generosity this morning, but now she was regretting it. *Not that I could eat with hands this filthy*, she thought. Somehow, seeing Sam blithely scarfing his breakfast while she *became* breakfast for a horde of rampaging germs only made her more annoyed. "Done!" she chirped, giving him her biggest, brightest smile.

He strolled over, tossing back the last bite of his breakfast and dusting off his enviably clean hands. He leaned over and took a gander at the inside of the vehicle. Then he pulled a pair of gloves out of the back pocket of his coveralls—why hadn't *she* been offered gloves?!—and put them on before brushing a llama bean she'd somehow missed over the side. He sucked on his teeth contemplatively as he walked around the truck, inspecting every inch, letting the moment go on until Merry could scarcely contain a growl. "Passable," he finally allowed.

"*Passable?! Mr. Clean* couldn't get that filthy fu—" Merry took a breath, seeing the amusement in his eyes. "Thank you *so* much for the lovely compliment," she bit off. "Do you have anything else you need me to do before we hit the road? I believe you said you've got two tourists meeting us at the trailhead, and I wouldn't want to keep them waiting."

"That we do. You know the drill?"

"Not really," Merry admitted.

"Well," he said, obviously enjoying her discomfiture, "these beginner trips, I like to take the paying guests up into the national preserve. The views are pretty stunning, and the trail's not too strenuous—only about seven miles. The llamas take most of the load so the tourists can enjoy the scenery without hoisting a pack. That's the appeal of these treks—well, that and the unique opportunity to bond with these very special animals." The sarcasm vanished from his face as he looked over his little herd. His expression was gentle, even loving, and it transformed his homely face into something halfway pleasing. *For a second there, Sam was almost…* *attractive*, Merry thought. *Almost.* He gave the nearest beast a scratch on its neck, and Merry could swear she heard it chuckle.

She could not share the humor, however. *Seven miles. Up a mountain.* Merry gulped. Levering herself out of her cot had been almost beyond her capacity just an hour ago, and while she had to admit the truck scrub-down had limbered her up a little, it was even odds whether she'd be coming back down the mountain under her own steam or strapped to the back of her llama. "Sounds great!" she enthused. "What do I have to do?"

"It's not rocket science, Miss Manning. Just hang on to your llama's lead and stay out of his way. They know what they're doing. When we get to the top, you'll help stake them out and lay out a lunch while I charm our trekkers."

Merry's jaw dropped. *Charm...? Sam...?*

He ignored her expression. "You better not hold us back, city girl," he warned. "Altitude gets above thirteen thousand feet up there and a lot of people can't hack it. Oh, and while you're saving your breath, that reminds me: I don't want you ruining their good time with a lot of reporter-type questions. They're here to relax and enjoy nature, not give an interview. So zip your mouth shut, keep up, and we'll get along just fine."

Merry would wager she'd spent more of her life at high altitude than Sam, though admittedly not recently. "Don't worry. I'll keep up."

He let out a *humph*. "Let's get loaded then." He let down the back ramp of the truck and took the first llama's lead. "C'mon, Paddington," he said, tugging gently. The beast, wearing a self-satisfied smirk much like his master's, swayed leisurely over to the ramp and ambled up it without fuss. "Now you, Miss Manning," Sam said, waving at the next one.

"You don't have to call me Miss Manning," Merry said, playing for time. Alpacas might be the bomb, but their larger cousins had yet to win her over. She looked askance at her charge. The critter in question was a dusty black, with a white blaze on its chest, a sweeping set of lashes, and banana-like ears. From its sulky expression, she gathered it was no more eager to make her acquaintance than she was its. "It makes me feel like a schoolmarm."

"Gym teacher, maybe," Sam drawled, giving her a once-over that made Merry feel every inch of her six-foot-three figure. "Now, you going to get cracking, or are we going to stand here jawing all morning?"

Merry sucked in a breath. *Do not slap your host. Do not slap your host.* "Right," she said, marching purposefully forward to grab a halter. "C'mon, little doggie. Let's get this show on the road."

"Miss Manning..."

"It's *Merry*!"

"*Miss Manning*, you might not want..."

Merry ignored him.

And paid for it.

Ptoooo!

A stream of sheer evil arced through the air.

Thwack.

Not again.

"Fuck!" Merry stripped off the flannel shirt she had on over her tank top, using it to mop her face where the fiend had doused her.

The next thing to hit her was Sam Cassidy's guffaw. It was loud. It was raucous. And it washed over her in waves of hilarity that just wouldn't quit.

When she was sure she wouldn't get any death-goo in her eyes if she opened them, Merry cracked them into slits just wide enough to skewer Sam with a deadly glare.

Sam had his back against the side of the truck, his head buried in his hands. He was shaking, and tears of mirth tracked down his cheeks. "Jesus, lady, you're about as subtle as a sledgehammer. Didn't I tell you not to make sudden moves around the llamas?"

"Fuck you, Sam Cassidy." The words were out of her mouth before she could call them back. *I've gone too far; I'm gonna get fired.*

But Sam was made of sterner stuff.

"Not in a million years, sister." Yet Sam was eyeing Merry with a curious light in his eyes.

Suddenly, Merry realized she had nothing on up top but a thin white racer-back tank. Her heart sank as she remembered. *My scars.* Her left arm was a horror show from her triceps to halfway down the back of her forearm, where the doctors had pinned the shattered elbow joint and forearm bones back together. The scar looked like a giant flesh zipper, faded now from angry red to pale pink, but still ugly. Her right hand flew up instinctively to cover the mess, but when she looked at Sam, dreading the revulsion she'd see in his eyes, she realized he wasn't looking at her elbow.

He was eyeing her *breasts*. Breasts which were now clearly outlined by the damp tank top, not to mention pressed together because of her protective gesture—*and* plumped up by the impractical lace push-up bra her mother had sent along in her last care package. *As if I were the lingerie type.* But beggars couldn't be choosers, and Merry had not been able to justify turning away her mother's gift when her own underwear budget was so under*whelming*. In the cold, her nipples had done the natural thing, and they were clearly capturing her host's attention.

When was the last time a man looked at my body and saw something other than my scars? Something about Sam's gaze told her that scars were the last thing on his mind right now. A warmth trickled into her belly. Flustered, Merry went on the offensive. "Eyes up here, buddy," she snapped, even as a blush spread across her llama-loogied cheeks.

"I'm not sure I can crane my neck that high," Sam shot back, nevertheless pulling his gaze up to meet her eyes. "C'mon, Wookiee. Stop scaring Severus and let's get these boys loaded."

"Severus?"

"Snape," he said helpfully. "You *have* read Harry Potter?"

"Of course I'd get the Slytherin," she sighed, but she moved forward gingerly and took its lead.

This time the llama, which appeared to have learned the art of smugness from its owner, allowed itself to be led up the ramp. *Out of ammo, probably.* The others followed suit and Sam slammed the tailgate shut.

"Up and at 'em, Wookiee," he said.

Merry, who was a veteran of unkind nicknames, had a pretty good idea when one was going to stick. *Could have been worse*, she supposed, though she wasn't sure how.

"Let me just wash up," she said, holding up her hands to show their grubbiness.

"Hate to break it to you, lady, but the trail's not any cleaner. Let's go already."

Merry balked. "Not until I've gotten clean enough to at least tie back this disaster," she said, pointing gingerly at the blowsy Medusa do that had replaced her usually quite delightful coppery mane. Her hair had slipped free of the clip she'd used to pin it up, and dangled now in unkempt ropes that clung to her cheeks, neck, and back in ways that made her want to scream like an Edvard Munch painting. Hell if she'd touch it with these farm-fresh fingers.

"Oh for Christ's sake," said Sam. He dug something out of his pocket, but before Merry could spy what it was, he'd already grabbed her and given her a one-eighty spin so her back was to him. A second later, his meaty paws were in her hair.

"Hey!" she squeaked, too shocked to move.

"Hold still." Something slid through her thick locks. *A comb?* Yes, unmistakably, a comb, followed by Sam's hands swiftly parting the tresses into three equal hanks. In seconds he'd formed a long rope of braid, twisting an elastic around the tail. "Done," he said, and shoved her away none too gently.

Merry felt the plait cautiously, forgetting for the moment her reluctance to contaminate her hair with the gunk on her hands. It was neat, tight, just the way she liked it. And amazingly, he hadn't pulled her hair even once. But she did *not* like it that he'd been so free with her person. "Hey, pal! Ever heard of personal space?"

"You wanted that mess out of the way? It's out of the way."

"You're calling *my* hair a mess, Mr. A-hay-bale-landed-on-my-head?"

Sam *almost* cracked a smile. "You want to compare coiffures or work the ranch?"

"Work," Merry grumbled.

"Okay then." Sam turned to go with a final infuriating smirk. "Let's go, Chewbacca." And he sauntered toward the driver's seat.

This time Merry *did* aim the hose at him, though she waited until she would only hit the closed door of the truck.

Next time I won't wait, she thought murderously. *Channel the llama, Merry. Channel the llama.*

Fifteen fraught, silent minutes later, Sam pulled the truck to a stop at the top of a campground sparsely dotted with tents and RVs. The drive would have been breathtaking had she been riding with anyone other than the surly llama handler. Even so, Merry couldn't help appreciating the scenery, which was all sheer gray cliffs and tall ponderosas intermixed with bright golden pops of aspen from the higher elevations. She'd missed mountains, she realized. More than she knew.

She rolled down her window and sniffed appreciatively of the evergreen-scented air. It was a glorious day, crisp and pregnant with that peculiar high-altitude clarity that made one feel the air like a spiritual caress against the skin. "Where are we?" she asked, looking around. "My readers will want to know."

Sam bared his teeth as if the notion of her readers irritated him.

"It's great publicity, remember?"

Sam sighed. "We're in the Carson National Forest. Takes up about a million and a half acres round these parts, and it's some of the most pristine wilderness anywhere in America."

"It's beautiful."

"Smartest thing you've said all day."

Merry was saved from having to dignify this remark by the appearance of a late-model Suburban that screamed "rental car." It hesitated, seeing their unusual truck bursting with woolly occupants. Then, as if deciding to man up, it pulled in two spots away, near the head of the trail. Out popped a white-haired Hansel and Gretel, geared up in hiking fleeces and walking sticks, mesh-roofed sun hats and fanny packs dangling everything from bear spray to extra camera batteries.

Thank goodness, Merry thought. *They're old.* She wouldn't have to worry about them bounding up the trail like the gazelles she most certainly wasn't.

"*Guten tag*," called the gent, and his wife waved. "Are these the ya-mas?"

Sam hopped out of the truck, beaming ear to ear as he swept off his hat in courtly fashion. "Hey, folks. Welcome! I can tell we're off to a great start because you even pronounced 'llama' the traditional way. Give the man a prize, Merry!"

Merry goggled at the stranger who had taken Sam Cassidy's place. "Go on," he muttered out of the side of his mouth. "Give them some feed for the llamas while I get everything unloaded." He thrust an old coffee canister filled with grain pellets at her, then moved to the back of the truck to retrieve his cadre of creatures and their gear.

Slightly dazed, Merry moved forward to shake hands with the two trekkers, who looked like they'd stepped straight off the cover of the Bavarian edition of the L.L.Bean catalog.

"Nice to meet you," she said, hesitating a second before giving her grubby mitt over to the care of the enthusiastic gentleman. She didn't want to give him hantavirus, but it would be rude to ignore his outstretched hand.

"*Ja, ja*, you too! We can't wait to climb with the ya-mas. They are friendly, yes? They don't spit? Birgit went on the Google from the hotel last night, and she read they sometimes spit."

"Oh, no, nothing like that," Merry said. With a wide, guileless smile, she held out the can of grain to the anxious Germans. "Here, would you like to feed them?"

CHAPTER TWELVE

As the sun spilled over the mountaintops, our llamas hummed hymns to greet the dawn and grace the day ahead.

To my mind, they are creatures of myth, magic, and considerable charm.

Our guests (two delightful Teutonic hikers of the elder set) were equally captivated. They cooed and petted the beasts' necks with gentle hands, heeding Sam's words about llamas' eyes, which, ever keen for predators, act as natural magnifying glasses. You don't want to appear suddenly in their field of vision by reaching to scritch behind their ears, for example, or grabbing hastily for their lead rope. (Lesson learned.) The couple fared better than I in their introduction to the boys, laying their hands flat, palms up to let the llamas snarf the grain from them as Sam instructed. I could tell they were smitten—and really, how could you not be? These dudes are like walking Shmoos. But the sun was climbing rapidly, and we couldn't stand around shmoo-zing all day. So, harnessed and packed with Sam's expert assistance, we hit the dusty trail, and soon found ourselves entering a pristine paradise of crystal-clean air, thick, majestic ponderosas, and sharp, high ridges of sheer stone that limned the horizon like the proverbial silver lining on a cloud. In the distance, as Sam pointed out to our awed guests, snowcapped Wheeler Peak rose; at 13,000-and-some feet, the tallest mountain in New Mexico. Can you believe I never skied it?

Well, today was for hiking it.

The trail was narrow, but not so narrow you couldn't walk two abreast—two meaning one human and one heffalump. The fun of the trek is (in part) leading your llama like the world's biggest puppy while it hauls your snacks, folding chairs, Gatorade, sweaters, etc., for you. This the boys did without complaint, ambling along on cleft-toed feet (not hooves, as Sam gently corrected Karl, our gentleman trekker).

And speaking of toes, get this, kids: Sam only hikes barefoot.

Bare. Foot.

Though as a journalist I have an obligation to investigate the mysteries of human behavior—and I bet you're dying to know what gives— somehow I hesitated to ask Sam about it. There is something oddly intimate about discussing one's decision to eschew shoes, particularly when one's feet are as . . . well . . . handsome as Sam's. (Feet can be sexy. Who knew?) Thankfully Birgit, Karl's intrepid wife, beat me to the question, exclaiming in a mother-hen voice that he was sure to injure himself on the stony trail without some form of foot protection.

"Walking barefoot brings me closer to the land," he told her. "I'm far more likely to get hurt if I lose my connection to the earth. Besides," he said with a twinkle (Sam is full of twinkles), "I've been going bare so long I really can't get comfortable when I'm confined."

Me and my fellow frau shared a blush. God knows why.

Blushing Brigit seemed relieved to turn her attention to Aslan, a beige beauty with a bit of a beard and flirty long lashes. In fact, she stared so deeply and lovingly into his limpid eyes I heard Karl clear his throat as he walked next in line behind her, squiring Paddington. Sam, bare feet and all, had taken point with Little Lord Fauntleroy, who naturally would allow no other beast to take precedence. I can tell you it was no hardship for either of us ladies to watch our guide saunter up the track in snug denim, sunlight glancing off his long blond hair (think Thor, gals). I was charged with rounding out the rear. Well, more accurately, Severus Snape was. But he seemed determined to catch me up or even pass me any second.

Now, I've always assumed "breathing down my neck" was a metaphorical saying. More fool, I. In a scarily accurate impression of Alan Rickman's character, my heavy-breathing pack animal whispered insidious spells into my shrinking ear all the way up the mountain. I would not have been surprised to turn and see him sporting a wizard's cloak or flickering a forked tongue. Nothing I could do would dissuade him from maintaining a snout distance of about six inches from my shivering nape.

Fortunately, the breath of a llama is surprisingly ungross. It's warm, and grassy—and, okay, a wee bit moist when it tickles the back of your neck—but not foul or satanic the way one might suspect. However, after about an hour, even the most excellent of exhalations become a hair less than welcome. Severus didn't get the memo. "Humph," hummed he, his rubbery lips a breath from my ear. "Hmmmm, hmmmm, snorkel-hmmm, hmm." I tried to teach him some Tom Waits, but he apparently doesn't appreciate musical geniuses. He kept up his refrain as we crossed tinkling brooks spanned with picturesque plank bridges, stopped here and there to sniff wildflowers (Sam telling the tourists all about the medicinal properties of the edible greens and occasional fungus as we walked), and generally enjoyed our nature hike. At last, however, Severus must have felt lunch was in order, for he traded his sweet nothings for a bit of a nosh.

On Dolly's ex-husband's hat.

Before you ask, no. No, no, no—I am not going to post selfies of me in that ratty old thing. While I have succumbed to the practical necessity of wearing cowboy couture for the sake of my fry-prone ginger-gal skin, I do not intend to put up with the indignity of having my picture in said hat plastered across the Internet. So forget it.

Well, unless you ask nicely in the comments.

Anyhow, Severus seemed to agree that le chapeau was not flattering, and he attempted to do me a service by munching it to death. But since *it was not my hat to dispose of, I had to deny him. I walked faster, trying to put some distance between his cud processor and my battered topper. Severus, that scamp, sensed the hunt was on and quickened his pace. The grassy breath laved my tender neck once more, and again I increased my pace. I was crowding Paddington's butt now, and even that mellow fellow wasn't appreciating such discourteous behavior, his stubby tail twitching with annoyance. Desperate, I decided to toss my hat up the hill ahead of me, hoping that by the time we crested it, Snape would have found a new preoccupation and I could retrieve it on the sly. With rather more gusto than I'd intended, I winged it like a Frisbee through the thin air, where it passed all three llamas ahead of me and landed just beside Sam.*

Friends, do not play Frisbee with a llama. Some of them like to fetch.

Severus shook off his air of insouciance and charged up the trail, pulling me along with him like a runaway dog on a leash (which I had not the presence of mind to drop). Bye, Paddington! Farewell, Aslan! And hello, Fauntleroy's tushie!

Oof!

I crashed hard into Sam as my llama lunged for the hat, coming up with it in his yap. A "Who, me?" look was on Severus's snoot as I shot him Evil Eye Number Forty-Five—a particularly potent blend of "You'll rue this day!" and "You don't fool me with that innocent expression, buster!" But I had bigger troubles.

I wobbled on the uneven ground. Teetered. Lurched. Reeled, and tumbled . . . right into my new boss's grasp. Instantly, strong arms wrapped around me, keeping me from toppling right into the steamy, shiny pile of fresh poop the llamas had used the pause in our trek to deposit. "Whoa there, gal!" Sam said, that inimitable twinkle in his eye. "You alright?"

Folks, I could scarcely summon the wits (and the wind) to stammer that I was. Those unholy blue eyes, the smile etched into his craggy features . . . be still my heart! "Y-yes, I think so. Thanks, Mr. Cassidy," quoth I, hand to my fluttering heart.

"Please, darlin', call me Sam."

"Sure...Sam." (Suave, right?)

"Alrighty then," he said, making sure I was steady on my feet once more. Then he turned to chide my beast. "Now, Severus, you behave with our Merry. You want her to have a good impression of our little outfit, don't you?"

As if there was any chance I wouldn't. My friends, I know we're calling this column "Don't Do What I Did," but I would urge you, if you're ever in the mood for a walk on the wild side, to check the folks at the Last Chance Llama Ranch out. A stroll through the stunning Sangre de Cristo Mountains, guided by the inimitable Sam Cassidy and accompanied by his magical beasties, is really bucket-list material.

And that was before we unpacked Dolly's lunch.

After a few miles of walking, gaining perhaps twelve zillion feet of elevation, we stopped by the banks of a stream to appease our appetites and rest our posteriors. (And, happily for me, wash my grody hands with the special easy-on-the-environment soap Sam carries.) A secluded, wildflower-dotted meadow unfolded before us, and Birgit took the opportunity to fling wide her arms and do a little Sound of Music *twirl I wish I'd captured on camera. The valley was ringed with glorious snow-capped peaks on all sides, and I could see our final destination silhouetted against the horizon, beckoning us on. Sam and I switched out the llamas' short leads for long, then tied them to some of the saplings that dotted the meadow so they could graze (which made for some interesting crop circles).*

Gals, take note. The sight of a long-eared llama kushing in a meadow is as one of those medieval unicorn tapestries is to a tween: the exact sort of thing you want a poster of on your wall. I must tell Dolly to stock some photos for sale in her shop.

When the four-foots were seen to, Sam settled Karl and Birgit around the remnants of an old fire pit, teaching them how to angle themselves into the V-shaped folding chairs the llamas had carried and fetching them some of the delicious Blue Sky sodas that one sees a lot of in New Mex-ico. (Try the pomegranate white tea flavor if you're feeling adventurous.) Meanwhile, I dug out a camp table from one of the panniers and endeav-ored to solve the quadratic equation that was its construction. At last, after I'd misaligned Pole A with Slot B for the fourteenth time, Sam am-bled over and offered to take the task off my hands. Whoosh! Done. So I laid out Dolly's lunch offerings upon it, and ... oh, man. Yum.

There was fried chicken, bathed in buttermilk and battered in fairy tales. More of her astounding biscuits. Peach cobbler that clobbered your diet while canoodling with your taste buds. A salad so fresh it made you blush, and even veggie portobello sammiches smothered in homemade goat cheese in case any of us was opposed to meat. The trek had whetted our appetites, and we all dug in with a will. Moans of delight and cries for the chef to be elevated to sainthood rang through the meadow, and Sam beamed, promising to pass the compliments on to his aunt.

At last, appetites sated, we settled happily into our camp chairs and got to know one another a little better.

"So," said Karl, "Mr. Cassidy, in Germany we would call you naturverbunden. A ... how do you say ... a true spirit of the wilder-ness."

Sam smiled modestly. "I wasn't always," he surprised me by saying. "I'm actually from New Jersey originally."

You could have knocked me over with a feather. Cowboy Cassidy, a Garden State native? I listened intently.

"Really? We have heard of New Jersey—we watched The Sopranos, *of course—but the guidebooks had very little positive to say about it, so ..."*

"Well, I didn't have much good to say about it myself," Sam said, smiling. (Sorry, Jersey folks—he said it, I didn't.) "I worked across the river on Wall Street for several years, as a matter of fact."

Forget the feather. A mosquito could have laid me out. My mind tried, but I could not envision our barefoot, weather-sculpted guide in a Brooks Brothers suit or Ralph Lauren tie.

"So how did you find yourself here?" asked Birgit, taking the words out of my mouth.

Those delightful lips twisted—delightfully. "It was time for a change. So I changed."

He would not say more. Damn it.

"And you, Merry?" Birgit asked. "Have you been with the ranch long? I could swear I know you from somewhere, but..."

I declined to bore the folks with my past history. "Sam's the real mountain man. I'm basically just a tourist like yourselves, along for the ride. So, Sam, how about you show us how you build a fire the old-fashioned way, or set snares for game? Something like that." (I was sure Karl and Birgit would love it—and you guys too.)

"We have everything we need right here," he demurred, extending his arms out wide to include our feast, the bubbling brook, the sun-drenched meadow. "Part of my job at the ranch is teaching primitive skills classes, and the first thing I tell my students is always, 'make only the minimum effort it takes to stay alive.' You want to conserve energy, and never waste resources in the wild. When I need it, I build it, hunt it, or gather it. When I don't... I just enjoy the bounty nature provides."

I blushed at my ignorance, but Sam wasn't judging. He is a teacher first and foremost, I am discovering, and he's most in his element when sharing his knowledge. I believe I'll be joining him on some of his survival skills classes soon, so do stay tuned!

CHAPTER THIRTEEN

A crumpled napkin arced over the top of Merry's laptop and landed on the keyboard, startling her half out of her wits. She looked up to see Sam standing over her, hands on his hips—or what she assumed were hips beneath the all-encompassing overalls he wore. For a second it surprised her to see him as he really was—a haystack sporting a scowl—instead of the dreamy fiction she was spinning for her readers. "Wrap it up, Wookiee," he said shortly. "We're getting ready to go. Your fans will have to wait a little longer for their next installment of 'How to Antagonize Llamas and Completely Miss the Point of Nature, with Host Meredith Manning.'" He turned and strode off to fetch the llamas without waiting for a reply, oblivious to the tongue she stuck out at him.

Too bad. That man is in dire need of a raspberry.

"My name's not Meredith, just so you know!" she called after him, but he didn't hear her. Probably for the best. Her sudden need to confess her true identity since she'd arrived in Aguas Milagros was totally inexplicable.

Karl and Birgit, she saw, were off looking for a stand of trees thick enough to hide the call of nature they were attending. (Sam had provided them baggies for the used TP so they could "carry out what they carried in.") Their absence was clearly all the permission Sam had needed to show his true colors...

Or was it only Merry who got his goat?

Talking to the tourists, he'd seemed relaxed, at peace...even happy. It was rather a stunning transformation. Without the dyspeptic look he wore around Merry, Sam's plain features were engaging, if not handsome. He looked younger, in his element. He radiated the sort of masculine confidence she'd often seen in her male counterparts on the ski team, though instead of competing to conquer the slopes, all Sam seemed to want was to share his understanding of the natural world with the people who signed on for his tours. Merry had had no cause to doubt his sincerity, or his obvious love of his adopted home. Everything she'd written about him, and their journey so far, was true.

Well, all except for his feet being sexy. And the dashing hero act when she'd crashed into him—which *totally* hadn't been her fault. Yes, she'd smashed into Sam. And true, he'd caught her when her damn leg had betrayed her by buckling. But instead of flirtation, there'd been a look of almost...*disgust*...in his eyes while he steadied her—at arm's length, certainly not in some movie-hero embrace. It was a look that had wounded Merry more than she liked to admit.

I know I'm big and clumsy, she'd wanted to scream at him. *I know I'm not exactly a supermodel. And yeah, I've invited myself into your world for my own gain, but, damn it, I* am *doing the work!*

Just not to Sam's satisfaction. Her efforts to get the picnic laid out had clearly not been fast enough. He'd nudged her aside brusquely when the table had proven tricky to set up and her exhausted, trembling hands had fumbled. He'd sighed as if pained when she couldn't get the llamas' harnesses switched out on the first try. And he'd snorted with derision when she'd almost tumbled into the brook trying to wedge herself into one of the infernal camp chairs after finally getting everyone served with Dolly's delicious food, the napkins, and utensils.

Speaking of which...Sam was expecting her to "pull her weight" and get their gear repacked. She saved her unfinished article and powered down the computer Severus had obligingly lugged up the trail for her (at least the beast was good for something other than just slavering all over her neck). It had been important to Merry to get her impressions down while they were still fresh, and besides, it had given her the perfect opportunity to eavesdrop while Sam had his guard down, chatting with the Germans. She'd have to finish the entry and post it when she got to Café Con Kvetch after the tour finished up.

If I make it to the end of this Bataan Death March.

Merry rocked, rolled, and wriggled her way out of the V-shaped seat, glad no one was around to see her flopping like a dying mackerel on the grass. The Germans were posing for one another by the stream now, snapping photos and generally having the time of their lives. As she watched, they trotted off to the meadow to catch up with Sam as he untethered the llamas. Even from twenty yards away, she could make out from their pantomimes that they wanted to get a picture with him.

"Wait, let me," Merry called, and started after them. *Damn well gonna pull my weight, and that means keeping the paying guests happy.* She sucked in a breath as her leg locked up, the lunch break having allowed lactic acid to build up in the damaged muscles. She *willed* the damn thing to obey her, breathing through her teeth, and it was with only a slight hitch in her step that she strode into the meadow.

"Here, guys, smoosh together with Fauntleroy in the middle, and I'll get you a souvenir your friends back in Bavaria will love." She took the camera from Birgit's eager hands, angling to give them a shot worth posting on social media. (Age not-withstanding, the garrulous Muellers were avid Facebookers, and they'd already promised to send her a friend request once they got home.) Sam gently tugged Fauntleroy into frame, then draped his arms across both beast and tourists in an encompassing embrace.

"Excellent," Karl beamed. "Say *käse!*"

"*Käse!*" At the last second Sam turned his face and gave Fauntie a smooch right on the cheek.

Merry checked the instant replay on the camera's screen. The animal was grinning fiendishly, as was Sam, and even she had to laugh as she handed back their camera.

"How about one with the two of you?" Karl suggested. "You make such a lovely young couple."

"Oh, we're not—"

"She's not my—"

Merry and Sam spoke simultaneously, and she saw his tanned face was so suffused with color his blue eyes fairly glowed by contrast. *Yeah, with devil fire*, she thought. She had a feeling her own blush was amply evident on her fair, freckled cheeks.

"No?" Birgit said, sounding surprised. Her gaze moved between the two of them, eyes narrowed shrewdly. "Well, maybe not yet, but I think soon, *ja?*" She gestured for the two of them to step closer together. "Kiss, you two. For the picture."

"I'd rather French-kiss Fauntleroy," Merry muttered, but she moved closer.

"Better him than me," said Sam, out of the corner of his mouth. He was careful to keep four hundred pounds of llama between the two of them, she noticed, and that was *just fine* with her.

"*Eins, zwei, drei!*"

Merry and Sam both moved to kiss the llama's cheeks. But Fauntie wasn't having any of it. He reared his head back...

And the tourists got a picture of a very surprised-looking Sam Cassidy and Merry Manning, kissing smack on the lips.

The only one grinning after that was his lordship, who hummed proudly at his bit of mischief and went back to munching grass as if he had not just dropped a nuclear bomb upon his human handlers.

Whoa. Merry's lips were tingling. *I need some antibacterial Chapstick*, she thought, *or maybe a visit to a Voodoo priestess. I'm surely hexed for life.*

Sam cleared his throat as if expelling some of that same bad juju. "Okay, guys," he said, clapping his hands together. He was still smiling for the benefit of the tourists, though it looked forced now. "Just a couple more miles to the top, and I promise you it'll be worth it. Everyone feeling refreshed and ready to go?"

"Ja!"

"Jawohl!" The couple trotted off to reunite with their llamas.

Um...no?

Sam wouldn't look at Merry. But he gave her orders just fine. "Wookiee, go make sure Snape's pack is strapped on securely while I finish breaking down camp. He likes to blow out his belly sometimes to keep it loose, and you have to let him think he's gotten away with it until he forgets and his guard's down. Just don't, for the love of God, get all up in his grille again. I already stowed the paper towels and I haven't got time for another spit-take."

"I'm not sure who's spittier, the llama or the wrangler," she groused. Which wasn't really fair—Sam's lips hadn't been at all slobbery. A bit chapped, maybe. And surprisingly warm...

Sam was scrubbing his hand across those warm lips right now, as if trying to erase all trace of their lingual collision.

"Just get Snape, would you? And do me a favor: Let's forget that...er...accident ever happened."

"Sure thing," Merry said. She found herself enjoying his discomfiture perhaps more than she ought. "Nothing worth remembering, anyhow. Here, Snapey! Here, Snape-Snape-Snape!" she called. "Jersey Boy over here says it's time to decamp." Hoping the slight hitch in her step looked more swagger than stagger, she headed back to their lunch site, where Severus was stripping the last leaves off the sapling he was tied to. She whistled a fair rendition of "Living on a Prayer" as she walked.

"Heard that, did you?" A resigned expression on his face, Sam followed Merry back to their camp, leading Fauntleroy in tow. The two animals chortled to one another in greeting, then parted to seek more tender shoots to nibble. Sam sighed as he wrapped the last of the long leads into a neat bundle and stuffed them into his animal's pannier. "I thought you were deep in cyber trance or I'd have been more discreet."

"There's no shame in being from the birthplace of Bon Jovi," Merry said, quirking her pirate brow and stuffing her tongue firmly in her cheek. *Yep. I'm loving Uncomfy Sam.* She located her sore-abused hat by the stream bank and stuffed it over her braid—the braid Sam had inflicted on her without so much as a by-your-leave—then busied herself checking Snape's pack straps. Despite Sam's warning, they seemed snug enough—though who could tell beneath three feet of matted wool? "Lots of people loved *Slippery When Wet*."

"I don't...Well, okay, I kind of *do*...but..." Sam stopped, smiling reluctantly. "Just don't post that on your blog, okay?"

"Column."

"Whatever you call it. I have a reputation to maintain."

"Sam Cassidy, Sullen Mountain Man?"

He looked up, blue eyes flashing in surprise. "Is that how you see me? Sullen?"

"If the shoe fits..." Merry didn't want to poke the bear too much, but really, did he think he was Mr. Cute-and-Cuddly? "Oh, wait, I forgot, you're too *close to nature* to wear shoes."

Sam scrubbed one leathery paw down his face. "I probably deserved that. I'm sorry, Miss Manning—"

"You can call me Merry already. We've practically swapped spit. And it's better than *Wookiee*."

"Merry then. Look, I'm sorry. I've been kind of an ass. It's just that, when I look at you, I can't help seeing every big-city princess..."

"Princess?"

"Would you let me finish?"

Merry nodded tightly. Much as she wanted to sock him in the jaw, she needed to know what it was about her that so chapped his troll ass.

"Maybe I got the wrong impression. But when you swanned your way onto our ranch in that prissy white coat that probably cost more than all my aunt's alpacas together, scaring Buddha and squawking like a chicken over a little spit—"

"A *little* spit? I've seen drier geysers—"

"Anyway, I got my back up, is all. I've known a few women like you in my time—"

"Women like me?"

Sam ignored her indignant sputter, setting his teeth as if determined to plow through a vicious headwind. "And I...well, maybe I overreacted. I can see you're trying, even if you *are* hopeless." He reached out, and for a breathless second Merry thought he was going to stroke her cheek, but he just snicked her hat out of the way of Snape's questing mouth.

I'm not hopeless, Merry wanted to say. *I'm crippled.*

Pride stopped the words in her throat.

"We'll see who's hopeless, Sam Cassidy," she said tightly, snatching back the abused hat and squashing its brim between white-knuckled hands. "This *princess* can take anything you dish out, and hand it back with ice cream on top. So if you're finished insulting me, I have a mountain to summit."

∞

Music from *The Good, the Bad and the Ugly* was playing in Merry's head. Not the theme song, but the part of the score that accompanied the scene where Eli Wallach drags Clint Eastwood, stumbling and half dead, across a wide and inhospitable desert. The music undulated, wavering from crescendo to low point as Merry trudged the switchbacks toward Wheeler Peak, single-mindedly focused on one thing. *Not being left behind.*

Step.

Ow.

Step.

Ow.

After a while the focus shifted from "not being left behind" to "not dying," but Merry didn't stop. She *would not* stop.

She wasn't pausing to admire the majestic trees flanking the trail, nor the clouds scudding across the achingly blue sky. She wasn't writing any odes to the chipmunks and Steller's jays that flicked in and out of her peripheral vision. Wheeler Peak was no more than a taunting mirage in the distance—glimpsed only in those few moments when she found the strength to glance up from the rock-strewn track—never seeming any closer than it had the last time she looked. She could hear Karl and Birgit's exclamations of awe and delight ahead of her like the twittering of birds—far away and hazy in some realm where people were having fun instead of suffering the torments of hell. Her heart was hammering somewhere at the base of her skull, and the thin air wheezed in and out of her laboring lungs. Worst of all, each breath, each desperate beat of her pulse sent a spiral of shame radiating through her mind.

How did I let myself get like this?

Mountains used to quiver beneath her feet. She'd been a freaking *Amazon* on the slopes. Over and over, Merry's agent had fielded requests for her to appear in magazines from *Sports Illustrated* to *Maxim* (though she'd politely turned down the latter's request to pose in just ski boots and a thong). She'd done countless interviews with top women's fitness magazines, had even been asked if she'd endorse some new exercise machine whose inventors had wanted to call the Merry-Go-Round. But now? Merry had to admit it wasn't just her injuries that had brought her to this nadir. It was the pathetic way she'd given up on any semblance of recovery, of ever being active again.

It's my own fault.

She'd gone through the required physical therapy after her accident. But once Merry was on her feet and it had become apparent that her skiing days were over, all motivation to keep fit had simply vanished. Her body had become a stranger, and a not-very-welcome one at that. Where once she'd been in peak condition, lifting weights, running, doing yoga to keep limber—and that was on top of the actual skiing, which occupied several hours out of each day—after the accident everything had changed.

So had the expectations.

That fact had been made exquisitely clear when she'd been

released from the final rehab center and, with help from her brother, finally headed home to the beautiful little condo she rented in Vail...

Only to find all her gear had vanished. From poles to goggles, boots to bindings, all of it was just...gone.

"Marcus, call the police!" Merry remembered telling her brother, as she'd crutched her way from the foyer to the living room. The hall closet, which had been bursting with skis, poles, and team jackets, was wide open and empty. The place on the wall above the mantel where she'd hung the set of skis that had taken her to a new record in last year's world championships—bare. The team jumpers, the sponsor-emblazoned clothes had all been removed from her drawers. And it wasn't just her equipment. Her medals were gone. Trophies, vanished.

"I can't believe this! I've been robbed!" Merry had hobbled all around the little condo, searching frantically, forgetting for the moment how much her injuries still hurt. *What the fuck?* Her iPod dock was still there. Her flat-screen TV, untouched. Jewelry—what little she wore—undisturbed in its box. Clothes, appliances, all good.

But every trace of her life as a skier had gone up in smoke.

"Why aren't you doing anything?! Jesus, Marcus, can't you see..."

But the look in Marcus's eyes had told her he saw more than she did. "No one robbed you, Sis," he'd said quietly, fine gray eyes brimming with compassion. "Mom and Dad were here while you were still recovering, and they cleared everything out. They thought...I guess they thought it would hurt less if you didn't have to see reminders everywhere."

The message had been clear. *You're not a winner anymore. You're nothing, just a hole where a winner used to be.*

After that, Merry found herself hailing cabs instead of walking, going to movies rather than out for hikes. Working out, painful in its own right, was worse because it reminded her that she'd never compete again. So she'd stopped.

What's the point, when I can never hope to win?

Merry paused on the trail, both to let the hammering of her heart die down, and to have a huge fucking moment of revelation.

That's my mother's voice. Not mine.

In her heart, Merry knew there was more to being a competitor than playing to win. And there was more to life than competition. *I mean, c'mon. What am I supposed to do now that I can't be the best? Crawl under a rock and die?* Gwendolyn Manning might not have objected—at least it would keep her daughter's shame out of the public eye—but, to Merry's surprise, she found *she* wasn't ready to give up quite yet.

Neither, fortunately, was Severus Snape.

Over the painful thrumming of her pulse, Merry could hear Snape's regular exhalations, feel them snorting softly against her be-slobbered neck. Having been so lost in her own misery, she was surprised now to find the llama had moved up beside her, crowding close to her left side instead of poking at her back. She tried to push him away, but when he wouldn't give ground, she looked at him—*really* looked at him.

Maybe it was her imagination, but she thought the llama bore a look of compassion. His ears were cocked forward, eyes liquid black and heavy-lidded. He twitched his lips, cocked his head, and shook his forelock. And then, tongue darting out, he gave her cheek a *sluuuurp!*

What the hell, I'm coated in black death anyway, Merry thought. "You're trying to help, aren't you, boy?"

Severus hummed, an inquisitive sound like a kitten assessing its welcome in a new environment.

"Blink once for 'You're crazy, lady.' Blink twice for 'Yes, I'm making nice.'"

Severus blinked slowly ... once ... twice.

Merry's eyes welled. She told herself it was just the exhaustion, the pain from her worn-out leg. She wasn't softening toward the spitty beast. She *wasn't*. But this time, when the llama leaned in to nibble her hat, she just snuffled a watery laugh and plopped the battered bit of felt atop Snape's head. She'd have to cut holes for his ears when she got a chance. "You win, my friend. Take it. Now, how about you give me a hand up this bastard mountain?"

By the time the switchbacks petered out and the gradient leveled out a bit above the tree line, Merry and Snape were old chums. They'd been through "99 Bottles of Beer on the Wall" and moved on to "The Banana Boat Song," Miley Cyrus's latest cry for attention, and even a little ditty she'd made up in her own fevered brain. By now Karl and Birgit had gotten so far ahead of her—curse their healthy Germanic hides—they couldn't have heard her even if she hadn't been singing in a half-delirious mumble. Sam, she assumed, must be up there with them, but she couldn't spare the energy to find out where.

Suddenly, Snape lollopped to a halt. Merry looked up, and her heart stopped. Snape flicked his ears back and forth, as if waiting for her to catch up mentally as well as physically. *Well, we're here*, he seemed to be saying.

And *here* was a glorious place.

How long had it been since she'd stood at the top of a mountain? *Duh, two years, dummy*, she thought. Once they'd been everything to her—from her first trip to the Alps with her family as a small child to the years she'd spent skiing the most extreme slopes her sport had to offer. High altitude was like a drug to her, the feeling of being above it all, able to see—just *see* everything, unimpeded—a fix she could not resist. It might be cheesy, but yeah, *hell yeah*, she felt like the queen of the world when she was up high. She'd talked about taking up mountain climbing when her skiing career ended—until it had ended the way it had. And *during* that career she'd tried every kind of skiing there was, from off-trail and out-of-bounds to heli-skiing, and not just because she liked the rush. She'd liked the scenery too.

Scenery like this.

Merry came to a halt at an outcropping of lichen-speckled granite. The Germans had gone on a ways, moving from one viewpoint to another to snap photos and exclaim over each new sight. Sam was helping them get a picture together at a likely looking rock ledge. But Merry was mesmerized right where she stood.

The world dropped away beneath her boots; the topsides of clouds were hers to explore. Wind—much colder up here than at the base of the trail—whipped about her and tried to tease her hair out of its braid. It stole moisture from her eyes, blurring her vision, but Merry blinked fiercely. She wanted to *see* this. In the distance, the sharp daggerlike edges of the smaller peaks in the Sangre de Cristo chain were blunted with a blanket of snow. The nearby slopes were a jumbled moonscape of barren stone challenged by hardy green tundra grasses, while the valleys, forests, and farmland of the surrounding area stretched out to the horizon like a banquet.

Her banquet.

"Fuck," she said softly.

And she started to cry.

Merry was not a dainty weeper. But now, standing at the summit of Wheeler Peak, was not the time for ladylike sniffles. Fortunately, she had a very absorbent friend. Severus stood stoutly at her flank, shoring up her weaker left side as she buried her face in his crusty wool and bawled.

"Jesus—Merry, are you alright?" A hand touched her back, and Merry jumped, spinning around and stumbling away from Sam. She knuckled her eyes, grateful once again that llamas were hypoallergenic.

"Give me a minute, would you?" she mumbled.

Understanding lit in Sam's eyes, and his gaze softened. "I had a similar reaction the first time I came up here." He fumbled in the pocket of his overalls and fished out a threadbare old bandana. "Here," he said almost shyly, proffering the cloth. "Catch up when you're ready. I'll get Karl and Birgit settled with some snacks meanwhile."

"I should help—" Merry started, even as she accepted the hankie.

Sam's hand curled over hers, patting. "Stay. It's just brownies and coffee. I can manage."

If he'd said one more kind word, Merry thought she might have dissolved into a puddle. Fortunately, Sam Cassidy had a rather limited stock of compassion. "Don't worry, Wookiee," he added. "I'll save you a brownie. Big girl like you needs to keep up your strength."

And he padded away on silent bare feet, leaving Merry unsure which she wanted more—to shove him over the cliff, or thank him profusely. Because, whether he knew it or not, Surly Sam had just given her back a piece of herself Merry had thought was lost forever.

True, things would never be the way they'd been BT (Before Tree). She'd never carve virgin powder at eighty miles an hour, or leave her competition spitting snow while she sliced the ribbon at the finish line. But she'd made it to the top of the tallest mountain in New Mexico under her own steam, damn it, and that was more than she'd ever expected to do again. (Well, Snape had helped.) Maybe she'd never own the slopes. Maybe she'd never stand atop a podium and listen while "The Star-Spangled Banner" played and gold was placed around her neck.

But I'm alive. I'm here. And I'm grateful.

"Let's go get some brownies, Snape," she said. "I think we've earned it."

ey, Lady Hobbit. How was the trail?" Needlepoint Bob, sitting on a stool behind the host station, greeted Merry with a
wide smile. In his surprisingly elegant hands, he held a canvas-
stretched hoop and a needle dangling colored thread.

Merry didn't have time to check out the design he was creating, or even answer his question. Other matters were more
pressing.

"Washroom. Stat." The words came out as a croak.

Bob chuckled, pointed down the hall with the hand holding
the needle. "Help yourself."

At the communal trough that served as a sink outside the toi-
lets, Merry washed. And scrubbed. Scrubbed again. But there was
only so much she could rinse away of this day. Gunk, yes, until the water ran gray down the drain. Emotional hangover? Not
so much. She was still quivering from the intensity of the moment when she'd stood atop that mountain, feeling all the loss
she'd spent the last two years trying to bury, run from, and ignore. Reeling with the knowledge that it was time to let go and
move on.

And speaking of quivering...every muscle in her body was
quaking like Jell-O. She stood clutching the lip of the sink,
breathing hard, sweat popping on her brow as her legs threatened
to give way underneath her. *We're the* Millennium Falcon, *remem-*

ber? she told her bad leg. *You. Will. Hold. Together.* She scrabbled in her satchel for her Advil. Percocet—or perhaps a keg full of Fentanyl—would have helped more, but Merry had broken with such medications the minute she'd been released from the hospital, determined not to descend into a habit that would take her even further down the rabbit hole than she'd already fallen. *The last of my self-preservation instinct, I guess*, she thought, running a brush through her hair and rebraiding it, then washing her hands once more after touching her dusty locks. She couldn't help acknowledging that Sam had actually done a better job of tidying her recalcitrant mane, though wind, llama love bites, and tree branches had since made a mockery of his ungentle ministrations.

Whereas his lips had made a mockery of her sangfroid.

For good measure, she gargled and spat before heading back into the dining area.

Taking the same booth she'd occupied the night before, Merry fetched out her cell phone and, seeing it had died the long, slow death of roaming disease, plugged it into the outlet she was happy to discover under her table. *Definitely gonna make this my regular booth.* She eased her laptop out of her bag and fired it up, plugging that in too. She figured she had just enough stamina to update her column before she lapsed into a catatonic state and Bob was forced to peel her out of the seat with a spatula to send her back to the ranch. She decided checking her email and reading the comments from yesterday's post could wait—right now it was more important to get the new stuff down while it was still fresh in her mind.

Her fingers—practically the only part of her that didn't ache—flew across the keys, and the rest of the world disappeared.

❧

*. . . Back at the truck, we thanked our beasts of burden with a hearty
helping of grain. (I fed Severus out of the hat he'd formed such an at-
tachment to, figuring that would be the best of both worlds for him.) Karl
and Birgit departed with many enthusiastic words of praise, a handsome
tip for each of us (I gave mine to Sam as I'm really just a freeloader),
and promises of positive reviews on TripAdvisor. As for my own review?
Yes, emphatically, you should try it. Live a little. Llama lot.*

'Til next time, I'll be . . .

On My Merry Way.

❧

Merry scanned her last paragraph, nodded with satisfaction, and
hit "Enter" to send the article out into the world. She found herself smiling, her memories of the day's outing the rosier for the
retelling. *I'm happy*, she thought, more than a little surprised.
Actually pretty happy! Then she uncrossed her legs and tried to re-
cross them in the other direction.

Lightning shot up her left leg, and she bit her lip to keep
the bolt from shooting out of her mouth. The diner was nearly
deserted at this hour of the afternoon, but the few folk who
sat nursing cups of coffee or toying with slices of pie probably
wouldn't appreciate a banshee wailing in their midst.

"I *hate* Germans," Merry groaned.

Bob, setting a steaming cup down in front of Merry, raised a
brow as he settled his comfortable bulk opposite her, needlework
at his side. "I'll admit some of their philosophical texts are a bit
dense, and World War Two wasn't exactly their finest hour, but
what brings this particular distaste on today?"

Merry's lips twitched as she saw the cup's contents—he'd
etched a fair rendition of *The Scream* into the foam of her latte. "I

should qualify that . . . I've known any number of Germans I liked quite a lot. I lived for months at a time in the Alps while I was in training, and my hosts were never anything but gracious. It's just these particular Germans *today* I resent."

Bob waited.

"Hansel and Gretel basically lapped me all the way up Wheeler Peak and back. They had to be about a hundred and sixty between the two of them, but those oldies could *hoof* it." Cautiously, she stretched her legs out, wincing as she rubbed the left one. "Even the llamas were winded before the end."

"It's true, Germans are the hardiest hikers. They come in here all the time, asking if we have any *hard* trails."

"From what I saw, they're *all* hard."

Bob smiled. "All a matter of what you're conditioned for, I guess."

"You hike?"

"Do I look like I hike?" He jiggled his Santa-style paunch, enrobed in a tee shirt that had once been black. Some wag had dyed the words *I Like Bleach*—in what was obviously bleach—across the front.

"I bet you hold your own," Merry said. Bob probably floated to the top of the local mountains on a magic carpet. She wouldn't be surprised if people flocked to him for wisdom once he got there. Merry sipped her latte, let out a moan of appreciation. If anything, it was even tastier than last night's. "Anyway, you'd think those two were reenacting the Teutonic invasion of Poland, the way they hustled. We were done an hour earlier than Sam usually finishes, he said."

"I saw him drop you off out front," Bob said.

You mean when he flung open the truck door and practically rolled me out while it was still moving? Merry grimaced. Sam hadn't said much after he'd handed her the hankie, though whether he was giving her space or disgusted by her display of emotion she couldn't say. Or maybe it was just lingering awkwardness from their accidental lip-whack. (She *refused* to call it a kiss.) In any case, he'd saved his conversation for the Muellers on the way down to the trailhead, and after they'd departed with many *danke, auf wiedersehens!* he'd said nothing, merely giving her a ride to town on his way back to the ranch. Merry had been grateful for the silence. She'd needed the time to process the shift that had taken place within her.

"Yeah, he told me he could finish up without me. I had a lot of work to do for the magazine, and I really can't put it off or my readers will get impatient."

Bob grunted understanding. "Speaking of which, I think your column is already having an effect on the local economy. Callie over at the motel told me she'd gotten a couple bookings through the Internet. Flustered her so much, I had to show her how to process them. And *I* actually had a call this morning asking if we took reservations." He grinned. "I think you're putting Aguas Milagros on the map."

Merry was absurdly pleased to hear it. *At least I'm doing* something *right.* "I hope that's cool with you," she said. "It can be a bit weird for small-business owners when they suddenly get noticed."

"Weird," said Bob, "is right in my comfort zone. And I don't think I'm in much danger of becoming overrun by—what's that you call them? Hipsters? Though come to think of it, it might be nice to talk Nietzsche with the younger set."

Merry smiled. "I'll have a muse-off with you one of these nights, Bob. Though I'm a bit rusty on my nihilist philosophers these days. I was always more partial to the French existentialists."

"Good deal." He swiped his needlework off the table and rose to his feet. "I don't want to keep you from your adoring public. Can I get you something to eat before I take my leave, Lady Hobbit?" Bob asked. "'Licia was going to shut down the kitchen for a few hours and catch a siesta but I think she's still back there."

"Oh, no thanks. I'm still stuffed on Dolly's picnic lunch." Besides, her body was wound so tight with pain she actually felt nauseated.

"Dolly's cooking *is* one of the finer pleasures of life," Bob acknowledged, "or so I recall from the days I was still welcome at her table." He put on what she was beginning to think of as his notable-quotable voice. "'If more of us valued food and cheer and song above hoarded gold, it would be a merrier world.'"

"Martha Stewart?" Merry hazarded.

"J. R. R. Tolkien. I'd have thought you'd know that one," Bob teased.

"I'm not at the top of my game just now." Merry sighed, scrubbing her hands down her face. "And I've still got a lot of correspondence to catch up on. Hopefully I can finish before my forehead makes forcible contact with my keyboard."

"Well, if you're full up with food but still out of gas, how about a shot of whiskey in your coffee?" Bob was looking at her with an all-too-perceptive expression, and more sympathy in his eyes than Merry could handle right now without breaking down.

A shot of whiskey would certainly jumpstart her coma, but Merry needed her wits about her for a while yet—after she finished here, she still had to check back with Dolly and see if her hostess had any final chores for her to do this evening. "Another time, and thanks."

"I'll leave you to it then." Bob picked up his needlework—

which looked to be a bust of Homer—and went back to his post up front.

✀

No sense putting off the inevitable. It was time to find out if she still had a job.

Merry opened a Skype window and dialed up her boss.

It was Sunday at three p.m. his time, so naturally Joel picked up halfway through the first electronic bleep. His face was unshaven, hair flattened on one side, and he appeared to be wearing his wife's (or possibly his mother's) pink-and-yellow flowered bathrobe, but his eyes were as alert as ever.

"Kid! What's the news from lla-lla land?" (Merry knew he'd thrown the pun in there because of the way he stretched out the l's, and because she knew Joel couldn't resist a good pun. Or a bad pun. Or, really, any pun at all.)

"Hey, Joel, got time to talk? I hope I'm not dragging you away from anything."

"Nah," he said. "Just catching up on *Call of Duty*." Behind him, Merry could see what had to be at least sixty acres of flat-screen television. The image frozen on it was a cartoonishly muscled supersoldier blasting something that looked like a glowing-eyed ghost with a weapon hardly smaller than himself. "What's the haps out west?" Joel leaned into the screen, giving Merry a magnified view of his stubbly cheeks as he peered more closely into the webcam, as if that would bridge the distance between them. "You look tired, kid. The farm folk treating you alright?"

Merry glanced around, but there was no one to overhear her except Bob, and he seemed completely engrossed in his stitchery. But it shouldn't matter; she really had nothing negative to say about her time in Aguas Milagros so far. "Oh, for sure," she told her boss. "It's amazing here. The animals, the scenery, the people...you can't believe it. I only hope I'm doing a good job capturing it for the column." Merry was fishing for compliments, but she didn't care.

"Have you seen your comments, kiddo?"

"No, I haven't had time to look yet."

"Well, look. I'll wait." Bob had already turned back to his video game, and the sound of machine-gun fire came faintly to Merry's ears from his living room. Merry switched browser windows to check out her column from yesterday, which was hosted on her own dedicated page on *Pulse*. A surprisingly strong feeling of pride hit her when she saw her first DDWID entries from "lla-lla land" in black and white, etched into the Internet forevermore. She scrolled down to the bottom.

Her eyes widened. There were *four hundred and eighty-seven* comments on her column. Her eyes scanned the most recent.

Blattypus: Holy, shizzle, Miz Merry...u weren't foolin' about the fluffsters! I died myself 4 or 5 times when I saw the pictures u posted.

KittyCamaro: I can haz foof?

TravelBiatch: Did you snog Major Gorgeous yet? We want Sam pics!

GrlyGrl: Srsly...I want a slice of Studly Sam.

MissPoppins: Dearest Merry, I wouldn't do what you did, but I love DDWID! Keep it up. I think I speak for everyone when I say, well done. We all love your new feature.

LeisureLarry: Don't speak for all of us. It's rude.

WhyKiki: Shut up, Larry.

GopherButt: This comment has been hidden for unhelpful content.

User46376: Is you're hair frizzy? Click here to recieve a free sampel of our miricle serum!

Merry sat back, stunned. She switched back to her Skype window. "Jesus, Joel. I've never had *nearly* this many responses before."

Joel hit "Pause" on his game and rose from his sofa to turn back to his laptop. His bathrobe gaped open for a second as he seated himself at what she figured must be his kitchen table, and Merry flinched. *I did not see anything. I most fervently did not just see my boss's junk.* "Did you run the analytics yet?"

"No—I'm sorry." Merry hung her head. How many times had Joel told her to check her stats first thing? "I literally just got back from escorting a couple of llama-loving tourists up a mountain, like, ten minutes ago."

Joel waved magnanimously. "No worries, kiddo. I ran 'em this morning. You're up eighty percent this column over last."

"What?"

"People are eating this 'Don't Do What I Did' shit up with the proverbial spoon, kid. Told ya they would."

"Wow." Merry sipped her latte, melting the last of the teeny scream into nothingness. "That's amazing, Joel. Are the corporate overlords happy?"

"Happier than a hedge fund manager screwing a subprime mortgage holder out of his life savings."

"That's pretty happy."

"You got that right."

"I was worried it wasn't 'Don't Do' enough," Merry confessed. "I didn't know if you were expecting me to make everything sound like a disaster all the time, or what."

Joel rubbed his stubble thoughtfully. "Well, a bit more falling on your fanny wouldn't hurt, though it seems like that Sam
character's been there to catch you whenever you're about to
crash."

Merry forbore to enlighten him on the truth of that little fiction. "So you're cool with the way it's coming out so far?" If he
wasn't, Merry thought, she might well be out of a job, and "Shit's
Creek" would be more accurate than she cared to consider.

"All I can say is Keep Doing What You Did, kid. And keep
pouring on the Sam stuff. Your numbers among women are
higher than ever, and you should see some of the comments from
the ladies. Made *me* blush, and I've seen it all, for crying out loud.
The guy's like cowboy catnip. You got a thing for him or something?"

"Um..." Should she tell him just how full of shit she was? Or
would that get her in hot water for poor journalistic ethics? "Or
something," she said lamely.

"Well, whatever. I'm not going to tell you to jump in bed
with your subjects. But if you *were* to, I can only imagine how
many hits you'd get..."

"I can assure you, Joel, I will *not* be jumping into bed with
anyone at the Last Chance Llama Ranch. I promised Dolly I'm
not a fuzzy-fucker, and I mean to keep that promise."

Joel cracked a smile. "Well, whatever. Just keep the Sam posts
coming."

"I've just finished another article," she told him. "There's
plenty of Sam in there."

"I'll check it right after I finish obliterating this zombie dirt-
bag." Joel was already fumbling for his joystick. "Need anything
from the world?"

Merry thought about it. "Maybe some Sani-Wipes."

Joel snorted. "Talk to you later, kiddo. Nice work." He severed the zombie's head, then severed their connection.

And suddenly, Merry felt rather cut off herself. Alone in a small town with virtual strangers, so vastly different from everyone and everything she'd ever known growing up. Aside from Sam, she'd been welcomed so far with open arms, but she was still very much alone in Aguas Milagros. Usually on her travels, she didn't mind being on her own—she was there to file a story and move on—but this mission was different. She was supposed to bring these people's daily lives to life for her readers, but she was still so much an outsider. She wondered if she'd ever truly feel a sense of belonging.

As if it had heard her thoughts, Merry's phone, now recharged, bleated the single *blat* that indicated she had a voice mail. She grabbed it, saw that the message had been sent earlier today. It was from Marcus. She smiled with genuine delight and hit the "Playback" button.

Thirty seconds of hideous howling and gibbering ensued. This only made Merry grin wider, as she recognized her brother's traditional rendition of "Happy Birthday to You." When the nightmare macaque noises wound down, his normal voice came on.

"Hey, Squatcheroo! Happy belated birthday. I would have screeched that stupid song in your ear sooner but I've been on location in the Seychelles and the damn director's kept me naked the whole frickin' week, lying on the beach with only a starfish to cover my junk and sand all up my ass. Fucking Vogue Italia. *Couldn't get near my mobile, and then I was caught up letting this sweet little chickie rub the local equivalent of aloe all over my poor abused body, and of course one thing led to another . . . yadda, yadda, yadda, and the time got away from me. Anyhow, just wanted to tell you I love you, Sis. Hope your day was great. Oh, and I read your blog—"*

"Column," Merry muttered at the phone.

"*—and I think the new stuff is frickin' awesome. Just a heads-up though, Sis. I don't think the parental units agreed. I'd think twice before opening your email.*" There was a sound of a woman's voice in the background, sleepily calling Marcus back to bed. *"Anyhow, gotta go, Squatchy. Try to duck the llama loogies next time!"*

Merry smiled fondly at the phone. "Love you too, Banana Hammock," she said to it. Then she sighed and logged into her email. She'd better get the inevitable parental rant out of the way.

And indeed, there it was.

To: MerryWay@pulsemag.com
From: MrsP_Manning@state.gov
Subject: It's Not Too Late

Meredith, this is your mother. Darling, are you alright? Your father and I were very much distressed to learn that you have found yourself in some sort of horrid backwater, forced to do manual labor amongst the beasts of the field. Darling, do you need money? Are they holding you against your will? Send us a sign if you're being held under duress. We can have you out of there within a day, two at the most. Simply say the word and Pierce will send his adjutant to make the arrangements. It's not too late to call off this ill-conceived stunt. I think we may still be able to salvage something of your dignity and your reputation if only you will quit now. Come home. We will take care of everything.

Your loving mother,
Gwendolyn Hollingsworth Manning

P.S.: Darling, you know the time is fast approaching for you to claim your inheritance, and you know what you must do to make this happen. Do not be foolish. Make your family proud and return to take up your responsibilities. It will be worth your while.

P.P.S.: Be sure to use that special toner I sent you for your face. One must always look after one's complexion, and that goes doubly for women unfortunate enough to have freckles.

"Hey, Bob?" Merry called. "I think I will have that shot of whiskey now, if it's still on offer."

"You got it, Lady Hobbit."

CHAPTER FIFTEEN

Pronk (v.): A stiff-legged bouncing up into the air that llamas and al-pacas occasionally demonstrate when playing with each other, or to scout and elude predators.

Author's note: Immature goats are also known to perform this gob-smackingly hilarious maneuver. Imagine Pepe le Pew when he's in love, leisurely skipping and bounding after poor Penelope Pussycat. Remove the reek—and the disturbing rapey-ness—and that's what you're seeing when an animal pronks. At least, that was what I was seeing when I came across the baby goats this afternoon. They were so excited to welcome their new playmate they couldn't contain themselves.

And after I met the object of their affection, I felt like I'd gained a new best friend too.

⧓

The goats were...swarming?

Yes, distinctly, if unbelievably, this was the case. A pile of bleating, baaing, pronking brown-and-white bodies had something down on the ground and wouldn't let it up.

That something, as it turned out, was a veterinarian.

A holistic veterinarian.

Jane Kraslowski, as a matter of fact.

And she was laughing so hard she couldn't catch her breath. "Help!" she squeaked. "Dolly, come get your fool kids off of me."

Dolly rolled her eyes at Merry, whom she'd been leading over to the goat enclosure. "Come, child. I want you to meet the Last Chance's guardian angel," she said. "We couldn't hardly manage a day without this lady, even if she is a goofball sometimes." She strode the last few feet to the fence, and Merry trailed stiffly behind, pasting a smile atop her pained wince. Neither the Advil nor Bob's booze-boosted latte had done much to eradicate today's ill-advised excesses.

"Hang on, Jane. Help's coming." Dolly let herself into the pen while Merry leaned against the outside rail, grateful to let it take the weight off her leg for a minute. Dolly reached into the pocket of the worn smock she wore over her jeans and chamois work shirt, rooting around. "Lucy! Ricardo! Ethel! C'mere!" she called. The goats ignored her, continuing their efforts to engulf the veterinarian.

"*I Love Lucy?*" Merry asked. She was watching the goat swarm with equal parts horror and humor. *So this is what being loved to death looks like.*

"Yeah. I named this year's kids after my favorite black-and-white-era TV characters."

"Niiiice. Keepin' it classic."

"I try," Dolly said. She moved toward her recalcitrant ruminants. "C'mon now, kiddies, leave the nice vet alone." Oblivious, the goats continued their scrum, leaving Jane half smothered in playful animals, rolling and squealing with merriment as they tried to lick her face. Dolly snorted. "I swear Jane must wash her hair in alfalfa-scented shampoo. Watch this," she said to Merry. "Never fails." She held up a fistful of grain pellets. "Treats!"

Boi-oi-oing! The baby goats bounced up and practically somersaulted in midair, turning their attention away from Jane and charging Dolly. Hopping on pogo-stick legs, ears flapping with excitement, they stretched their little necks up, bleating and sticking their tongues out for the feed Dolly held in her palm. The pellets were gone in milliseconds.

And I thought llamas *were greedy.*

"Jane, quit your foolin' and come meet our Merry. Merry, this is Jane, our resident vet and just about my best friend in the world," Dolly said.

Merry, safely on the outside of the pen, studied the woman. Probably in her late thirties or early forties, she was grinning ear to ear and plain as the day was long. She had buckteeth, wide-spaced eyes, and no lips to speak of, with hair cut short as a man's and of no particular color. And yet... her joy was so radiant she would turn heads anywhere she went. "Hi, Jane," Merry said, waving shyly.

Jane rose to her feet, expelling a few lingering chuckles, and brushed at her clothes. "Ah, the famous travel writer!" She strode over to the fence, sticking her hand out.

Merry shook the proffered hand. "I don't know about famous, but the writer part is true." She smiled politely. "Dolly tells me you're a..."

"A holistic vet. Guilty as charged. Certified naturopath but it's not as woo-woo as it sounds. I went through veterinary school same as any other vet. Got my large animal certification, but, well..." She looked fondly at the kids, who, along with their mama, had surrounded her and were currently testing her pants legs for numminess. "The more research I did, the more convinced I became that the first line of treatment for our four-footed friends should always be close to nature whenever possible. Natural sunscreen, natural nutritional supplements, that sort of thing." She spoke like a woman who was often forced to defend her opinions.

"Sunscreen? But aren't alpacas buried under, like, four feet of fur? Er, I mean wool. Sorry, Dolly."

Dolly waved off the apology.

"Oh, you should see the alpacas right after we shear 'em. With their crew cuts, their skin's all pink and tender, and quite vulnerable to the sun."

Merry tried, but she just couldn't picture a shorn alpaca. Q-tip? Show poodle? "Speaking as a certified ginger, I can relate," she said. She touched her cheeks with tentative fingertips. Yup, tight and hot. She'd gotten too much of that strong New Mexico sun today. "Maybe I can hit you up for some of that sunscreen. Snape kinda ate my sun protection this morning. Sorry about that, Dolly. I tried, but the rascal just wore me down."

"Eh, what the hell. I never liked that hat anyway," said Dolly. "Nor the head it rode in on."

Jane smiled that sunbeam of a smile. "Happy to," she told Merry. "I make a nice lavender lip balm too."

"You gals can talk beauty products later," Dolly said. "Now, come and meet Betty White," she urged Merry. "That's their mama. She's quite a scamp, but she gives the best damn milk in four counties. Half the cheese in Northern New Mexico comes from Betty."

"I'm good here," Merry demurred. The fence was pretty much the only thing holding her upright.

"'Sakes, child. Can't work a ranch without getting to know the goats. Betty and her sisters Bea and Rue need milking every morning, and the least we humans can do is provide a little polite chitchat before we wrap our hands around their nether bits. So come sweet-talk this little mama."

"Oh! Right, sorry." For a moment there Merry had forgotten she was here to work, not just gawk at the fuzzies from afar. "Coming." She let herself into the pen, walking slowly to hide her stiffness. And her apprehension. As far as she was concerned there was a good reason goats were associated with the devil. Their alien eyes alone were enough to give Merry the heebie-jeebies, and no amount of cute pronk action was going to dispel that dismay. "Um, howdy Betty...how's it..." She eyed the goat's bulging udder. "...hanging?"

"Bleh," said the goat.

"I feel ya," Merry muttered.

"Go on, give her a treat. She'll be your friend for life." Dolly shoved a handful of grain into Merry's tentative hand.

It's not going to steal your soul. Probably. Just get it over with. Taking a deep breath, Merry strode forward.

"Hang on, you might want to slow d—" Jane called, but it was too late. She'd spooked the beast.

Being a creature of nature, a goat faces only two choices when confronted by six feet, three inches of klutz. Fight, or flight. Apparently, Betty White subscribed to the "fight" school of thought. Her head went down, her hooves pawed the dirt...

And she butted Merry for all she was worth.

Smack on Merry's mangled left thigh.

Merry went down hard, but that was okay because she wasn't actually there for it. She was somewhere deep, and black, and swirly, about a thousand miles distant from her body.

When the stars cleared from her field of vision, Merry found three pairs of worried eyes staring down at her. Only two had round pupils—the third was Betty White, Satan orbs wide and innocent as if she hadn't just precipitated Merry's blackout.

"Bah," said Betty.

"To you too," groaned Merry, her ears still ringing.

She tried to rise, but Jane held her down with a hand on her shoulder. "Whoa there, cowgirl. You hit the dirt pretty hard. Let me check you out first before you try to move."

"I'm fine," said Merry, who wasn't. Pain was playing a violin solo all down her left leg, and not very expertly at that. The grating, shrilling thrill of it was making her nauseated, and chilly sweat had broken out all over her body. *Don't barf on the nice holistic vet, Merry. It isn't polite.*

"Slowly now," said Jane, wedging a strong arm beneath Merry's shoulders. "A bit at a time. We don't want you blacking out again."

Merry nodded and started to gather herself.

"You eat today, hon?" asked Dolly, face puckered with concern as she looked down at her fainting farmhand. She fanned Merry with her enormous hat. "I know you skipped breakfast. Sam better have fed you well at lunch, I hope."

Merry had burned off that lavish lunch surprisingly quickly, which was fortunate, or it might now be spewed all over the goat pen. Where she was currently lying. In the dirt. In the poop. *In hell.* "It's not that," she said, levering herself to a sitting position with Jane's assistance.

"What then? Hon, your eyes rolled back in your head like a porcelain doll's."

"Old war wound," Merry said, trying for flippancy. "No big deal." Teeth gritted, she managed to achieve her feet with Jane's help.

Jane looked at Merry more closely as she led the taller woman over to the fence, and recognition dawned in her eyes. She steadied Merry as they walked, taking a lot of her weight. "Wait a second...I knew you looked familiar. You're that skier, aren't you. The one that crashed?"

Merry rubbed a filthy hand over a face that was probably equally awful. "Yeah," she admitted. "The one that crashed."

Dolly looked puzzled, so Jane explained. "Remember a couple years ago, there was a story in the news about this big-shot skier, odds-on favorite to win at the Olympics, but she had herself a terrible accident during trials?"

Dolly shook her head. "Can't say I do, but then I ain't much for the news. Or sports. John always hogged the TV for his damn bowling tournaments...as if bowling ain't boring enough in person."

Jane grimaced at the truth of that. "Well, if I remember correctly, the woman was setting crazy records for herself all day long...seriously leaving everyone else in the dust. Then, on her last run...boom! She crossed paths with a tree instead of the finish line." Jane illustrated by smacking a fist into her palm, then fluttering her fingers as if they were debris from an explosion. "*Pshhhhh...splat!*" She looked over at Merry. "Is that about right?"

Shame curled in Merry's gut. "About."

"*Damn*, woman. I thought you were on life support in a coma in Switzerland or something."

"I wish," Merry muttered. It would save her the humiliation of this moment. *The great Merry Manning...felled by a goat.*

"How'd you end up here?"

"Funny story," Merry said. "Mind if I tell it from a chair?"

"Shit! Sorry. Let's get you sitting down."

Between the two women, they managed to support Merry back to Dolly's house, and get her seated on the sofa.

"Left or right, hon?" Dolly asked.

Merry, woozy from their jolting progress across the yard, didn't catch on right away. "Huh?"

"Which leg's gone gimp on ya?"

"Oh. Left."

Dolly eased Merry's dirty boots off and fetched a cushion, tucking it under her heel as the two women gingerly got Merry's left leg propped up on the chest that served as Dolly's coffee table.

"Let me take a look," said Jane, kneeling on the floor at Merry's feet between couch and coffee table.

"Um...no offense, but aren't you a veterinarian?"

"Physiology is physiology." She was already palpating Merry's leg through her jeans, ignoring her hiss of pain, but working as gently as a person could. "Dolly, hand me those pinking shears from over there."

Dolly went to her sewing basket.

"Wait—" Merry protested, but Jane already had her pants leg split halfway up her thigh. *Crap. Those were the only comfy jeans I owned. Now I'm going to have to wear the skinny jeans Mother sent me.*

When the thigh was fully exposed, both women sucked in a breath.

"Well, that ain't good," Dolly said.

The muscles had knotted around Merry's scars in fierce balls of protest, locked up tighter than a Swiss banker's vault at tax time. The scars were livid, and the damaged quadriceps twitched involuntarily around the worst of them. "Dolly, fetch me my bag from the truck, will you?" Jane said calmly.

"On it," said the older woman, out the door in a flash.

"You hiked seven miles on *this?*" Jane looked up at Merry with mingled compassion and exasperation.

"Well, it wasn't quite like this when I started," Merry prevaricated.

"*Damn*, woman," she said again. "Either you whacked your wits out when you crashed into that tree, or you're just plain hardheaded to begin with."

"Bit of both," Merry said, groaning as Jane gently rotated her leg and examined the scars more closely. She leaned back against the sofa's cushions, thinking of England.

"You're white as chalk, child," said Dolly, returning with a large, old-fashioned doctor's bag.

Jane took the bag and started rummaging around inside, clucking her tongue. "Why didn't Sam stop this? I can't believe he'd make you walk the whole way if he knew you were in this much pain."

Dolly snorted at Jane. "He'd sooner carry Merry down the mountain over his shoulder than let her suffer. And that boy could do it too."

The horror of such a scenario made the pain Merry was in seem more palatable. "I didn't tell him. And please, both of you, promise me you won't either."

"But why?" Jane asked. Her expression was bewildered.

Dolly spoke for Merry. "Pride. Pure, damn-fool pride." She waved a hand at Merry. "Look at her. It's about the only thing the girl's running on."

For the second time that day, Merry's eyes welled with tears, and it wasn't just from the pungent horse liniment Jane was rubbing into her leg. *That pride is getting in the way of Dolly's livelihood. She needs an able-bodied ranch hand...and I am anything but.* The realization hit her like a fist to the gut. "I'm sorry, Dolly. I never should have come here. But I really thought I could do this."

"Stop apologizing, child. You *can* do this, and you're gonna."

Had Dolly somehow missed the part where Merry had just

made intimate contact with the dirt? "But...you need a *real* ranch hand. Someone to lift heavy stuff, and...and...I dunno— put it on top of other heavy stuff."

Jane snickered, and Merry blushed, but Dolly patted her hand kindly.

"I'll see if I can't get little Joey from the village to pitch in and take over some of the chores until you're feeling better. That kid loves the animals so much I practically have to shoo him away with a broom, and he takes his pay in biscuits, to boot. But even if he does the sweaty stuff for a coupla days, I'm sure we'll find other ways for you to help out 'til that leg of yours calms down a mite."

Merry shook her head. "I can't let you do that, Dolly. You advertised for a ranch hand, and you deserve someone who can do the job properly." She made her voice firmer than she felt inside. "I'll leave tonight." Though where she would go, Merry had not the faintest clue. To save money, she'd sublet her condo all the way through the end of the year and tossed what little personal stuff she had in storage, planning to hop directly from the Last Chance Ranch to her next DDWID mission, whatever that might be. Now, it was looking less and less like there would *be* a next mission, since she was failing abjectly at her first, and the corporate overlords at *Pulse* were unlikely to cut her any slack.

"Last Chance" indeed.

"No one's leaving anywhere tonight," Dolly said firmly. "I don't know if it's the pain talking, or you're more of a drama queen than I pegged you for. But either way, I ain't letting you give up on me so quick." She marched over to the kitchen and opened her sixties-style avocado-colored refrigerator, coming out with a pitcher full of amber liquid, ice, and lemon wedges. Briskly, she poured three glasses of iced tea. She returned with the beverages on a tray, and shoved one tall, sweating glass at Merry. "Drink," she ordered. "I put lotsa sugar in there, which should help with the wooziness. Maybe it'll bring you to your senses too."

Merry took a swig of the tangy sweet tea. "Thank you, Dolly," she said thickly. "You've been more than kind. But if I can't do the work, I don't deserve the hospitality. I'd better get packing." Merry made to get up, then thought better of it as a wave of nauseating pain washed over her. She took another sip of tea, swallowed hard, beads of chilly sweat popping out around her hairline.

"Child, didn't you hear what I just said?" Dolly sounded exasperated.

"I—ouch!" Merry winced as Jane started wrapping stretchy bandage tape around her leg. It was, she noted absently, the same hot pink as Boudicca's had been. "I did, but..." She gestured toward the yard outside. "I know there must still be chores left to do. If I can't even finish out my first week properly, I've got no business imposing upon your generosity."

The failure rankled. Merry had *never* left a task unfinished. Hell, even that fateful day in St. Moritz, her unconscious body had somehow managed to slide past the finish line.

I'm terrible at this. She wasn't fearless, fun, or fabulous the way she'd portrayed herself in her column. No. She was facedown in feces and unable even to get up on her own.

Which, she realized with a start, *is exactly what my readers are tuning in to see.*

Merry sat back on the sofa, brain whirling. Maybe failing, in this case, was actually *winning*? Maybe being bad at this gig was exactly the point?

Duh. She could hear Joel's voice in her head, telling her the more falling on her fanny, the better.

But was that really fair to Dolly? "Are you sure?" she asked, glancing over at the older woman shyly. "I don't want to take advantage..."

"You just sit flat on your fanny and rest tonight, child," Dolly said, as if she'd heard Merry's thoughts. "Am I right, Jane?"

"Damn right, Dolly. This little chickie is roosting for the night. Doctor's orders." Jane threw the rest of the medical tape back in her bag, rose, and dusted off her knees. "Merry, if you so much as lift a finger for the rest of the day, I'm going to sneak up behind you and shoot you full of ketamine. You and Dolly can sort tomorrow out *tomorrow*. Tonight you rest, or I *make* you rest. You got that?" She waggled the black bag of doom in front of Merry demonstratively.

"Got it." Clearly, there was no arguing with these two when they banded together. A wave of relief washed over Merry—she wouldn't have to figure out what to do with herself *quite* yet. There was still a chance for her to figure out this DDWID stuff. A chance to succeed, whatever that might look like at the Last Chance Llama Ranch. "And again, I'm really, really sorry, Dolly. I never meant to be so freaking useless."

"Shut your flappy trap, child. You ain't useless. You did a great job for me yesterday, and Sam said you did just fine with the trekkers today. More'n fine. He said you were a big help."

"*Sam* said that?"

"Right enough. Said the tourists loved you. *And* he told me you managed to make friends with Severus Snape—something not many do. That scamp makes Buddha look like an angel." She clucked her tongue. "So you had yourself a bit of an unexpected sit-down at the end of the day. Big deal. You did what you had to do, Merry, and that's what counts. If you have to take it light for a couple days, well, we'll find another way for you to be useful in the meanwhile. Won't we, Jane?"

"I do recall you saying you've been meaning to do inventory in the shop." Jane scooched Merry over on the sofa and plopped down next to her, then dragged an afghan off the back of the couch and tucked it around Merry.

Merry looked down at the blankie, eyes moist. It was a stunning piece, a starburst of radiating earth tones ranging from cream to beige to deepest chocolate brown, with swirls of varying grays in between—courtesy of Dolly's herd, no doubt. She rubbed the supersoft wool between her fingers, petting it. "Inventory?" she asked shyly.

"Yeah. Only been putting it off for about the last seven years. Yarn's all over the damn joint, and I have no clue which goes where or how much is left of what batch." Dolly made herself comfortable in a well-worn armchair across from them, by the spinning wheel Merry had noticed the day before. She sipped her tea, looking at Merry over the rim of the glass. "You any good with numbers, Merry?"

"Stats, mostly. I had to keep track of a lot of them before…" Her throat closed. "Anyhow, yeah, I'm not bad with numbers. And I'd be happy to help however I can."

"Good. Tomorrow I'll put you to work. But tonight we veg."

"Music to my ears," said Jane, a grin making her plain features radiant. "It is *definitely* veg-time."

"So what does one do for, ah, veg-time out here?"

Jane looked at Merry like she couldn't believe she had to ask. "*Amigurumi*, of course."

And she tossed something soft and squishy into Merry's lap.

CHAPTER SIXTEEN

Allow me to spin you a yarn, dear ones.

Actually, in this case, I'll allow Dolly to spin it for me. For my hostess is, in addition to being one badass rancher, also an incredible craftswoman who can spin fleece into gold. The fleece in question being the fine outer coating of the Last Chance's prize-winning alpacas, and the gold being the fair market value of the fiber Dolly's wizardly fingers spins into soft-as-silk skeins of beige and white and speckled gray, chocolate brown, and rich midnight black.

I don't think anyone's clued our dear lady in to the true value of her handiwork, for you'll find the prices at the Last Chance Llama Ranch's charming little gift shop/yarn boutique brow-raisingly reasonable. Were I able to stitch as well as I bitch, I'd be driving home with a trunk full of balls of pure fluffy heaven. Instead, I'll be bringing back some rather unique souvenirs of Dolly's imagination. For, as charmingly rustic as Mrs. Cassidy's ranch is, she and her craft-happy friends are every bit au courant when it comes to trendy needlework.

Most notably, Japanese kawaii.

Ka-what now? You may well ask.

"Ami-roo-*who*-me?"

"Ah-mee-goo-roo-mee," said Jane, not for the first time. Or the second.

Or the third.

Housed in a converted outbuilding attached to the main hacienda, Dolly's shop was a spacious single room, with slants of late-morning sunshine beaming down from several skylights onto worn floorboards scattered with handmade woolen rugs. White wooden shelves reached from floor to ceiling on all four walls, stuffed with skeins of yarn in hues from sorbet to somber, while display tables featured finished pieces from shawls to hats and mittens...and amigurumi.

"Oh, give it up, Jane. Half the time I can't pronounce it either." Dolly, ensconced in an antique rocker, looked blissfully at home with a ball of yarn on her lap and her fat calico kitty at her feet. (The cat looked less sanguine, giving the rocker's runners a gimlet glare and twitching its tail well to the side.) She'd ceded control of their inventory after an hour of frustrated muttering and cursing, claiming she couldn't count past her fingers and toes anyhow. Merry and Jane, who wasn't on call at the regional veterinary clinic today, had taken over the job of tallying skeins, organizing shelves by dye lot and price, and sorting bags of roving—wool that had been cleaned, carded, and dyed, but not yet spun—by quality and color under Dolly's grateful direction.

Merry felt surprisingly...useful. After another of Dolly's delicious dinners, some girl talk, and a night's rest, she was almost back to her normal self today, though the leg would need to stay taped up for a while. The light work in the shop was just about her speed, and she was discovering she had a bit of a knack for it. After a quick, horrified look at Dolly's handwritten ledgers, she'd fired up her laptop and created a simple spreadsheet for her hostess to enter data in, and even Dolly had admitted she thought she could figure the "damn thing" out once Merry had walked her through it a time or two. She might even leave the Last Chance slightly better off than she'd entered, Merry thought—or at least not *worse* off. At the thought, a glow spread in her chest. It took Merry a moment to recognize her feelings for what they were.

Pride.

Satisfaction.

Self-respect.

Now, shelves organized, bags of raw wool stacked away and skeins priced and sorted, Jane and Merry were sacked out on the shop's rug-draped futon, taking a well-earned break. Dolly was still at work in her rocker across from them. Her fingers flew like birds tussling as she wielded hook and yarn faster than Merry's eyes could follow. In her hands, a figurine was taking shape. It looked like a tiny chinchilla, and it was achingly cute, with wide cartoonish eyes and a perfectly round body.

An ami-goo-thingie-majigy.

Jane had explained that *amigurumi* was a Japanese word for a type of crochet craft modeled after anime characters. It was, she said, part of a larger trend called kawaii, which meant "cuteness, lovability, or adorableness," and included everything from manga to fashion in Japan. And amigurumi dolls. Apparently, you could make just about anything as an amigurumi if you were determined—or weird—enough. Merry looked at the one Jane had lobbed at her last night.

It was Boba Fett.

Or perhaps she should call it Boba *Felt*. But whatever you dubbed it, the fluffy stuffed doll Jane had made was unmistakably bounty-hunterish. Merry turned it over in her hands again. From teeny blaster pistol to realistic jet pack, he was perfect in every detail. "Oh, man," she said, shaking her head. "My brother would totally flip his gourd for one of these."

"I didn't know you had a brother, Mer," Jane said. (Merry had graduated from Merry to Mer after less than twenty minutes of conversation last night.) "What's he like?"

"Total dork. Star Wars freak. Pain in my ass like you wouldn't believe." Merry was smiling. "Oh, and he's also a supermodel."

Jane rolled her eyes. "Doting sister, eh?"

"Oh, no," said Merry. "I shit you not. He's one of the top male models in Europe. Hell, pretty much the entire world. You can hardly open a magazine without seeing him half-naked, draped around some starving teenaged girl half his age. I keep teasing him that his shelf life is about up, but the magazines and designers haven't caught the memo yet. If you saw him, Jane, you'd seriously need a bib."

"A bib?"

"For the drool. He's that good-looking."

"Meh," said Jane, stretching her legs comfortably under the low coffee table that held several well-leafed-through copies of *Crochet Today.* "I'm not into handsome guys."

A thought occurred to Merry—one that perhaps wasn't polite to voice in front of her hostess. She shot a glance at Dolly, but the older woman was frowning intensely, absorbed in the skein of yarn she was attempting to untangle, while her cat, somnolent until now, suddenly discovered delayed kittenhood and did his best to undo her handiwork. "So, um, if that's true, why haven't you and Sam ever hooked up . . . ?" she asked quietly. "Or, er . . . have you?" She flushed, horrified at herself. Why Merry had assumed Sam was single, she didn't know. Maybe he and Jane were married, what the hell did she know? If so, she'd just insulted a woman she was already coming to consider a friend.

"Oh, *hell* no," said Jane, though she spoke low enough for just the two of them to hear. "If there's anything worse than a handsome guy, it's a *broken* guy. Not that Sam's unattractive, if you ask me. He's got a certain je ne sais quoi. You know...like, man-juice or something."

Merry choked on a laugh. *Man-juice?* "Um, sure," she said, giving Jane a minidose of side-eye. "He's got *something* going on, alright."

Jane shrugged. "Anyhow, Sam's not really my type. I like confident guys. Homely, confident guys."

Sam, not confident? To Merry, he was the picture of self-sufficiency, the proverbial island. She raised a brow. "Isn't he, like, a certified survival expert? That's what Dolly told me anyway."

"Oh sure. Primitive skills, he's got 'em in spades. People skills, not so much. Sam's the guy you want to be holed up in a cave with in the dead of winter when you get lost in the woods. But not the guy you wanna trust with your tender feelings." She leaned closer to Merry. "I think someone did the tarantella on *his* feelings, once upon a time."

Merry could see that, now that she thought about it. Sam had a bit of the guarded attitude you saw in guys who'd had their hearts trampled pretty good. She remembered Bob's quote from the other day. *"Where there is anger, there is always pain underneath." Not that it makes me like him any better*, she thought. *Dickbag is still dickbag, whatever the backstory.*

Thinking about Sam Cassidy was harshing her wool-induced mellow. "Are you going to show me how to make one of these am-um-um-mumbles?" she asked, holding up the amigurumi again. "These little guys are almost *obnoxiously* cute." She examined the little doll from all angles, then petted it fondly on its helmeted head. "My readers are gonna do spit-takes in their Star-

bucks when they get a load of the crazy things you two make."
She waved around the shop's display shelves, where cartoonish
kittens stalked catnip-stuffed mice, Teddy bears taunted yarn
unicorns, and wide-eyed owls hooted at lop-eared puppy dogs.
And of course, crocheted alpacas and llamas were everywhere. "I
bet they'd make great Christmas ornaments if you put a little
loop on the top to hang them from. Do you think I could learn
to make one of them by the holidays?"

It would certainly save Merry money on presents for her
family. *Maybe a tiny figure skater for Mother . . .* She pictured Gwendolyn's reaction to receiving such a homely, handmade gift from
her daughter. *Maybe not.* "It would be really cool if I learned to
knit—"

"Crochet!" shouted the two women.

"Sorry—crochet, while I'm here. What, is knit versus crochet
like some kind of Red Sox/Yankees thing?"

"It's more like an alpaca/llama thing, or a cat person/dog
person thing. You prefer one or the other, or you're not a true
devotee," Jane explained, and Dolly nodded.

"'Zactly."

"But you have both here at the ranch, Dolly," Merry pointed
out. "Not just alpacas and llamas, but your herd dogs and this little guy." She nudged the spotted butterball with her toe, and the
cat happily started bonking his head against her alpaca-socked
toes. Dolly had insisted Merry put on a pair of the shop's signature hand-knit footwear, which her friend Rebecca from the
village made using Dolly's finest wool. Her handiwork was on
display at the front of the shop, and Dolly claimed they were
her best-selling items, even if they *were* knit rather than crochet.
"Best-selling" must be a relative term, Merry thought, as she had yet
to see a single customer enter the shop. However, that was a sit-

uation she hoped to rectify, if "Don't Do What I Did" had any influence at all.

"Ha!" cried Dolly.

Merry started. *What, did I say that out loud?* Her face reddened. *Is it so laughable that my writing could actually be influential in some way?* An unwelcome thought crept in. *Mother would certainly agree.*

"Sorry, just finally got that bitch of a knot sorted out." Dolly held up her skein triumphantly. It was a gorgeous natural graphite color, speckled with lighter gray. "Boudie makes a beautiful ball of yarn, but she'll tangle on you if you let her."

"That's Boudicca?"

"A year's worth of her," said Dolly, showing Merry a basket full of similar skeins.

Merry had an idea. "You sell the yarn by the alpaca? Like, each ball comes from just one?"

"Not all the time, but yeah, for the natural-colored wool I like to keep like with like. It's kinda like a dye lot, if you get my drift."

Merry did not, particularly, though this morning had been a real education in esoterica like gauge, handspun versus mill spun, and fiber quality. "What if you put a little picture of each alpaca on the label of the skein? And a minibio of the beastie? Like those stuffed animals you see at zoo gift shops, that have the tags that tell a whole tale about their habitat and backstory."

Dolly looked thoughtful. "Think folks would like that?"

"*Like* it? I think you'd sell out of Boudie and her besties in five minutes flat. And if you sold these little arigoofoofoos—"

"Amigurumi!" chorused the two women.

"—*amiguwhatnots* on your website, I think you could really make some nice money."

Dolly's smile faded.

"What?" Merry asked, concerned.

"I ain't got a website for my wool," Dolly said—a bit sheepishly, Merry thought.

Merry was scandalized. "No website? I don't understand, Dolly. Didn't you tell me the yarn is a big part of your business? Without online advertising, how can you stay afloat?"

"You're assuming I *do* stay afloat," Dolly said with a wry twist of her lips. "I don't advertise because I figured no one who wasn't local would have the slightest interest in my shop," she went on. "But since yesterday, well, I might be coming around to the idea of casting a wider net."

"Why, what happened yesterday?"

"It was the darnedest thing, Merry. I got three big phone orders for my yarn, from people I never even heard of before! They said they got wind of me through what you wrote on your blog—"

"Column," Merry corrected automatically.

"—and they were trying to order through the Internet, but couldn't because I didn't have a proper site. It got me thinking, if that magazine of yours can get the word out to more folks, well, maybe that's no bad thing, and maybe it's time I got with the times myself." She paused, looking at Merry almost shyly. "You think you could see your way clear to showing me a thing or two about the Internet?"

"Of course! Dolly, of *course* I'll help. I'm happy to tell my readers all about your products and how to get them. Hell, I can build you your own virtual storefront." Merry had learned quite a lot about the Internet this past year, and to her surprise, she'd found she had rather a knack for web development. Not something she'd ever imagined herself doing during her ski-racing days. "The least I can do is get you going with an Etsy store."

"A what now?"

"Never mind, I'll show you." Merry made to rise.

"Later, hon," Dolly said. "I've about exhausted my ability to absorb new things for the day. That Extol spreadsheet pretty much wiped me out."

Merry shared a smile with Jane.

"You mean Excel?" Jane asked.

"Excel, expel—whatever. It about maxed me out in the learning department."

"I hear that," Merry said. "Speaking of learning new things, how long did it take you guys to learn to crochet?"

"Oh, I've always known how," Dolly said. "Pretty sure I came out of the womb with a hook in my hand." She paused thoughtfully. "Might be that's why my mother liked my brother best." She laughed that rumbling smoker's laugh.

"I learned to crochet in vet school," Jane put in. "Got pretty boring when I'd be on call to keep watch over a high-risk birth all night, and I needed something to occupy my mind. Plus, crocheting keeps the fingers nimble, so it's great practice for suturing too. I can teach you, Merry. Just let me get my implements of destruction." Jane started rummaging in the same doctor bag she'd carried yesterday, but today she wasn't looking for liniment. She came out with a sheaf that looked like a chef's knife sleeve, unrolling it with a flourish to display a row of slender metal sticks.

"Those are the needles?"

Jane rolled her eyes. "Hooks," she corrected. "The uninitiated never get that."

"Give the gal a break. Our Merry was a skier, not a crafter."

She patted Merry's knee, and Merry experienced a flush of warmth in her cheeks at the word *our*. It felt nice to be claimed. "Do *you* know your downhill skis from your cross-country, Jane?"

"As a matter of fact I..."

"*Anyhow*, Merry," Dolly interrupted, "you don't have to know anything at the beginning, except how to be patient." She came over to the futon, plopping herself down so that Merry was wedged between her and Jane, then reached across Merry to un-sheathe the largest of Jane's hooks. She snagged the topmost ball of yarn from the pyramid display Merry had carefully stacked not an hour earlier, unraveled a few feet, and wrapped the end around the hook, tying it off tight against the metal tool.

"First you make some chain stitches," Dolly instructed, her fingers looping yarn until she had about six inches of yarn chained. "And then you build off them from there. We'll start you off with a simple single crochet, and save the hard stuff for later." She demonstrated, dipping the hook, wrapping yarn, dip-ping again. "Ta-da! You got yourself a row, Miz Merry!"

Dolly handed Merry the yarn, and Jane, leaning in from Merry's other side, helped position her hands correctly around the hook and fiber. Merry was pretty sure if she twitched so much as a finger, a bomb might go off, or a busload of school kids fly off a cliff. "Um, guys...I don't think I can both hold all this stuff *and* make stitches out of it."

"Patience, child," Dolly said again, adjusting Merry's death grip. "You'll get the hang of it."

There was quiet in the shop while the women worked. Dolly's amigurumi chinchilla gained little feet, a tail, and adorable whiskers. Jane began whipping up a Princess Leia action figure to keep Boba Fett on his toes. And Merry...? Well, Merry did a great job getting started on an ulcer. She scowled down at her yarn, or what had *been* her yarn before her clumsy fingers had mangled it. *This has to be good for the soul, right? Because it sure as hell is not good for my mood.* Getting yarn to do what you wanted was right up there with Zen Buddhism and quantum physics—theoretically possible, but unlikely to be mastered in one lifetime. *At this rate, global warming will have made this scarf pointless by the time I get it done.*

As hobbies went, crocheting was not for sissies.

Back and forth. Dip and yarn-over. Chain one, turn. Merry could once again hear *The Good, the Bad and the Ugly* music undulating in her mind. Sweat popped out on her brow, and her tongue ached from being gripped in the vise of her teeth. Still, Merry had to admit to a certain satisfaction when she'd gotten ten whole stitches off her hook successfully. *Hey! Maybe I'm getting the hang of this crafty business after all!* she thought. Then she looked at what she'd wrought.

Fishing nets had fewer holes.

"Argh! Dolly, I think this hook is defective. Can I try another?"

"I started you on the biggest one, hon. That's the size I use to teach kindergarteners on, down at the schoolhouse."

"Great. Another thing I suck at." The string snapped under her frustrated grip. "Damn it!" Merry pitched the sweaty ball of yarn across the shop.

The skein sailed through the air, unwinding as it went. It arced through the half-open door...

And thwapped Dolly's nephew in the face, just as he started inside the shop.

The fine fiber clung for a moment to his stubble before gravity sent the skein tumbling away, the end of the string still held loosely between Merry's surprise-slackened fingers.

There was a pause while a peculiar expression worked its way across Sam's face. It looked to be equal parts chagrin, irritation, and humor. On seeing the source of the projectile, however, his features reassembled themselves into their customary grouchy expression. In a move more balletic than his bulk would indicate, Sam scooped the yarn off the floor and started winding it like a kite string toward the end Merry still held, walking toward the seated women as he wrapped. "Drop something, Wookiee?" he asked as he flipped the ball back into her lap. "Or are you farming Tribbles now?"

"Way to mangle your sci-fi metaphors, Sam-o," Jane said, surfacing from an intricate series of stitches that were shaping up to be Princess Leia's teeny cinnamon bun hair rolls.

"At least I'm not mangling the merchandise," he said, looking pointedly at the crap-fiesta that was the scarf Merry had been making.

Merry winced. Her store of goodwill with Sam—scant as it had been—seemed to have dried up overnight. Atop his frayed flannel work shirt and shapeless jeans, he was armored with a heavy coat of animosity. *What's pissed him off now?* she wondered. *Llama crap in his coffee?*

"Something you wanted, Sam?" Dolly asked. "Or just stirring up the heifers like an ornery ol' bull today?"

Sam flushed. As usual, his aunt's presence seemed to recall him to his manners. "I just came in to see if you needed anything before I headed out to check on Dashiell."

"Dashiell Hammett's one of Dolly's pregnant alpacas," Jane whispered to Merry. At Merry's raised eyebrow, she added, "Dolly was so deep in her noir detective novel phase when li'l Dashie was born, she didn't much care that 'he' was a 'she.' You should really take a look through Doll's pulp fiction collection sometime, Mer. Pretty sure she's got first editions of every story that guy ever wrote." She turned her attention to Sam. "I'll tag along with you on that welfare check if you like, Sam-o," she told him. "Don't think Dashie's gonna drop cri for a couple weeks yet, but I'm happy to give her another look-see if you're concerned."

Sam shrugged, as if uncomfortable being caught fretting. "I'm sure she's fine, but seeing as she took it so hard when she lost her cria last year, I want to make sure she's got plenty of that enriched feed blend you mixed up for her, and some good fresh hay for bedding so she's comfortable. The mutts are already keeping her company at night. I think they know she's due pretty soon."

Merry felt a pang. *It's supposed to be my job to feed the fluffies.* "I can do it," she said, starting to rise. The not-entirely-*un*-scarf-like object in her lap slid to the floor. "Just point me to the right paddock."

Dolly caught Merry's shoulder and set her firmly back on the futon. "You're right where you're supposed to be today, child," said Dolly. "Sam can see to Dashie just fine on his own." She gave Sam a level glance. "Ain't that so?"

"Of course I can." His gimlet glare was laser-focused on Merry. Something about her seemed to be agitating him . . . a lot.

"What?" Merry demanded, flustered.

His glance skittered away. "Nothing."

But Merry saw his eyes dart in her direction once more—and this time she followed that gaze . . .

Below the belt.

Understanding dawned. *The skinny jeans.* When she'd shifted to get up, she'd dislodged the needlework in her lap, exposing the tragically hip designer denim her mother had so thoughtfully included in Merry's last care package. For a wonder, the pants were long enough, but they sure as hell weren't generous in any other respect. *Will Mother* ever *stop mistaking me for someone stylish?* she wondered. Round here, fashion sense would get her precisely nowhere. More to the point, it was becoming eminently clear that Sam Cassidy was no fan of fashionable ladies. At the sight of the stupid stretch jeans, his homely brow had crinkled with disapproval, his lips—those lips she'd crashed into not twenty-four hours earlier—thinned with what looked very much like anger. She could practically *see* the thought bubble above his head.

City girl.

Spoiled little rich girl.

Useless.

Merry's throat tightened and her eyes stung with unexpected moisture. *Maybe he's right. Maybe I'm just a broken chick, with a busted bank account, hiding out at a llama ranch.*

A broken chick staring up at a broken cowboy.

Who did not seem best pleased to be sharing his little corner of the Wild West with the likes of Merry Manning.

Well, tough shit, Sam Cassidy, she thought, suddenly angry. *I may be nobody special anymore, but I ain't your whipping boy either.*

"Is there a problem, Mr. Cassidy? You seem rather fixated on my...nether regions."

"Don't flatter yourself, Wookiee," Sam snorted, crossing his arms across that barrel chest. "If I'm staring, it's only because I'm concerned for your circulation."

And he smirked.

Oh no you didn't.

Visions of schoolyards in six countries swamped Merry—the same snotty kids in every private school, boarding school, and diplomat-brat farm her parents had ever shunted her off to, always eager to make fun of her for her size, her social awkwardness; hell, even her damn Raggedy Ann freckles. *Look at the freak!*

Is it a boy or a girl? I wouldn't touch that chick with a ten-foot pole. Dude, she IS a ten-foot pole! Ha, ha, ha-ha! And so it had gone. Across Europe and all the way to Hong Kong, Tokyo, and Berlin. Taunts and ostracism, until Merry had taken the only refuge open to a girl who didn't fit the usual mold. Sports.

Which weren't an option anymore.

Like Betty the goat, Merry was left with a single choice when a big, braying menace got up in her grille. A red haze misted her eyes, and she forgot her hostess for the moment, forgot Jane at her side watching the two of them square off with humor fading to concern in her kind brown eyes. The only thing in Merry's mind was *knock the bully down before he senses your weakness.* She didn't know exactly what she had in mind—only that she wasn't about to let the insult slide. Merry rose, wanting the advantage her superior height would give her.

And she had it too—for as long as it took to round the coffee table. But the high ground was lost as her sore leg locked up.

Abort! her nervous system screamed. *Abort!*

Merry had been sitting too long. And she was about to pay for it—spectacularly.

While a small, resigned part of her mind looked on with detachment, Merry's body pitched forward. Her arms windmilled, but there was nothing to break her fall. She toppled...

Right into the pyramid of yarn balls she'd spent half the morning setting up.

Visions of bad sitcom grocery store snafus danced through Merry's head as she sent skeins scattering every which way.

"Merry!"

"Child, are you alright?"

Jane and Dolly spoke almost simultaneously.

"I'm fine," she muttered, facedown in fluff balls. "Just gimme a sec while I muster up some self-esteem." *At least the wool cush-ioned the fall some*, she thought. Yet nothing could cushion the embarrassment as she looked up and saw the expression on Sam's face.

Klutz, it said.

Hopeless, it said.

But—small mercies—he didn't say any of it aloud. He simply stretched out a hand.

Merry didn't want to take it, in the worst way. She'd rather have sucked snake venom straight from the fang, as a matter of fact. Dolly and Jane were watching, however, and it would have seemed churlish to spurn Sam's gesture. So she surrendered her hand into his enormous, callused paw, and a second later she was flying.

Straight into his arms.

"Oof!"

There came a very peculiar instant when time wobbled, and, of its own volition, Merry's circulation took itself a breather. Sam's arms instinctively clamped around her back as she wavered on her feet, and Merry's senses could detect nothing but man and muscle for a long, disconcerting moment. A woodsy, musky odor swamped her scent receptors, and Merry suddenly remembered Jane's words about Sam's je nais sais quoi earlier.

Man-juice.

Despite topping him by a good three inches, in Sam Cassidy's arms, Merry felt suddenly, bewilderingly petite.

Which, all precedent to the contrary, was *not* a way Merry wanted to feel.

"Would you *please* remove your hands, Mr. Cassidy?" she hissed, trying to keep her voice down so their wide-eyed audience wouldn't overhear.

"Sorry," he grunted, shoving her away from him as if she were coated in six types of oobleck. "Don't get any ideas in that Wookiee head of yours," he continued, as low as she. "I'm not asking you to the prom. I just overestimated the force I'd need to budge a woman your size."

Who's the klutz now? Merry thought, more than her old injuries stinging. She opened her mouth...

But Dolly beat her to it. "Sam Cassidy, that was a mean thing to say!"

His homely face reddened. "Didn't think you heard that, Aunt Dolly."

"Whether I heard it or not ain't the point, now is it?" Dolly shot back. "You shouldn't have said anything like that either way."

Sam reddened. "I'm sorry, Meredith," he said stiffly.

"It's Merry," she said, "and it's fine."

"It's no wonder you locked up, Mer," Jane said, coming to Merry's side—as much, Merry guessed, to defuse the situation as to prop her up. "After yesterday...you better let me check that le—"

"No!" Merry interrupted. "Everything's fine. I'm just clumsy, is all." She shot Jane a "remember your promise" glare, and Jane subsided, holding up her hands in a gesture that said, "You wanna act like a crazy lady, who'm I to stop you?"

"Thank you for helping me up, Sam," Merry said stiffly. "Did you need me for something? Some poop that needs scooping, perhaps?"

"No thanks. I've had about enough of your crap for one day."

Merry's jaw dropped. *The hell did I do to deserve* that*?*

Apparently Dolly and Jane were wondering the same thing.

"Samuel Cassidy!"

"Whoa there, Sam-o!"

The two women leapt to Merry's defense, but Sam was already in retreat. "Aunt Dolly, Jane, I'll see you soon." He tipped his hat, already turning on his heel to go. "Miss Manning, the less I see of *you*, the better."

Taint!

Taint in the face!

Hairy, scary taint, mere inches from my appalled eyes!

Friends, the things I do for you.

But let me back up—as I wish Steve Spirit Wind would have—and explain myself.

How, you ask, did I come to be perilous breaths from the perineum of a naked, shame-free hippie?

Well, it's Aguas Milagros, my dear ones. And apparently, the miracle is that anyone surfaces from the waters with any simulacrum of their dignity intact. For the eponymous "AM" is a nude-only spring.

Not nude-optional. Nude-mandatory.

Apparently, something about the chemicals people wash their swimsuits in pollutes the pristine waters, and so bathing costumes have been banned.

Gulp.

The bare butt-ery is not, IMHO, what I would call a selling point. But in Aguas Milagros, it's just one of the little "extras" that really make your soak memorable. And, oh yes, my friends, whether you like it or not, the locals will ensure you experience the full package.

And by "package," you can guess what I mean.

The moment a very naked, very close-talking gentleman by the name of Steve Spirit Wind asked if he might "sage smudge" me, I knew I was a fish in the wrong kind of water, but I had my obligation to you, my dears . . . and so I soldiered on. But I can safely say—Do NOT *Do What I Did today.*

∞

"'Miracle waters,' eh?"

"That's right," Jane said. She unhitched her seat belt and reached into the back of her pickup's extended cab for the two towels she'd tossed there on their way from the ranch. She sized Merry up as she slung the towels over her shoulder. "From the looks of things, you could use a miracle right now."

"At least one," she gasped as she half hopped, half dissolved out of the vehicle and wobbled on noodly legs. "I think sitting all afternoon actually made the leg cramp up more than if I'd stayed on my feet." She shook her head ruefully. "I haven't been this sore since the time I took on the Austrian cross-country ski team."

"Why, what'd they do to you?" Jane's eyes were twinkling as she came around the vehicle and linked arms with Merry.

Merry shut the truck door behind her and leaned on Jane more than her pride would have preferred. "I bet them their event wasn't as hard as mine."

"And that was a problem?" Jane asked.

"Yeah. It's *harder*."

"Ah." Jane nodded as if understanding had just dawned. "No gravity assist?"

"Something like that." Merry winced and rubbed her leg through the fabric of the skinny jeans she'd just as happily have tossed in the nearest pile of llama beans. *Maybe Dolly's got some old slacks I can borrow for tomorrow,* she thought, *though they'd be more like Bermuda shorts on me. I certainly ain't looking to get into Sam Cassidy's overalls anytime soon.* "Suffice it to say it was a painful loss."

"Well, don't worry, Mer. You're gonna be feeling a lot better in a few minutes, I promise. Our springs will fix you right up." Jane steered them toward the head of a faint trail that disappeared into the mixed evergreen forest. It might once have been marked with a sign for a natural spring, or a warning of nuclear radioactivity, or a memorial to pioneer settlers forced to eat one another for sustenance. Now, all that remained was a wooden pole with half a weather-beaten board drooping dispiritedly from it by a single rusty nail. Nothing could be read of the words except, "...HOT!" and "...OWN RISK!"

Not going after the tourist dollars, I guess, Merry thought. As a town, Aguas Milagros appeared to be woefully—or perhaps willfully—ignorant when it came to the art of attracting visitors. *Considering how close this community is to drying up and blowing away like one of their ubiquitous tumbleweeds, you'd think they'd want to advertise* any *selling point, no matter how small.*

"How long's it been since you pushed your body as hard as you've been doing since you got to Dolly's spread?" Jane asked, interrupting Merry's musings.

"Probably BT," Merry admitted with a wince.

"BT?"

"Before Tree," she explained. "So, like, two years ago."

Jane abruptly left Merry's side.

Jeez, I know I'm a lame-o, but you don't have to abandon me in the creepy forest just for being a slug.

The vet darted into the crepuscular woods, and Merry could hear branches snapping and leaves crunching beneath her boots. A moment later, her head popped back out of the trees, followed by a big stick. *What, is she gonna beat me for being out of shape?* Merry wondered. But Jane just handed her the shoulder-height staff she'd salvaged. "Here. You look like a woman who could use a good walking stick."

She's too kind to call it what it really is, said Merry's inner voice. *A cane.*

Well, if the stick fits...

"C'mon, Mer. We'll have you limbered up and bouncy as a newborn kid in no time."

Merry wanted to bounce, alright—back to her condo in Chicago. But she'd committed to DDWID, and that meant trying everything Aguas Milagros had to offer. *So suck it up, Merry,* she told herself, *and do what the nice vet lady says.* She followed her new friend up the primitive, stone-strewn trail into the mixed conifer forest.

"You never tried skiing again?" Jane asked over her shoulder as she skipped up the slope.

Merry's throat closed. Even if her parents hadn't done a complete NSA cover-up job after the accident, making all Merry's equipment vanish as if it'd never existed, she doubted she'd have strapped on skis again. After the effortless rush, the fierce exultation of owning every slope she faced, limping down some bunny slope, falling all over herself, would have driven her crazy with grief...and shame. "No," she said tightly. "After the physical therapy was over, I figured it was best just to get used to the new normal."

Jane looked back sharply. "New normal?"

Merry stabbed her staff into the dirt. "Well, I was never going to compete again," she said, shrugging uncomfortably. "I was lucky to walk, or so they told me. My athletic days were over, so I decided to try out life as a civvie."

"As a lady of leisure, you mean," Jane corrected, looking at Merry levelly. "When the going got tough, you went on a cruise."

Merry sucked in a breath, feeling as if she'd just been sucker punched. "That was my *job*," she protested.

"Uh-huh. And it's a great job, Mer. Honestly," she said, eyes earnest. "It just seems like...I don't know...like you left a lot of yourself behind along the way."

Jane was far too nice a person to say things like "fuck you" to, but Merry was tempted. She gritted her teeth. "How much farther is it to the hot spring?"

Jane let the moment pass, shrugging. "We're just about there. Take a sniff."

Merry sniffed. "Mm, rotten eggs," she enthused.

"Medicinal minerals," Jane corrected, disappearing over a ridge Merry was not at all happy to see. But she slogged up it, leg protesting all the way. And found...

A mud puddle.

Full of hippies.

The steaming, rock-outlined fissure harbored a woman with a serene face and long gray braids, bobbing neck-deep in the bubbling-hot water. A man with identical braids floated at her side, one arm wrapped about her shoulders. He had a feather tucked behind his ear, and a necklace that looked like it was made from every item in a kitchen junk drawer tangled in his abundant gray chest hair. Clouds of steam swirled about them, the whole scene reminding Merry of the hags from *Macbeth*. *Except there were three of those*, she reminded herself.

But wait...For a second, Merry thought she glimpsed another body somewhere in the depths of the pool, but the vapors were thick enough that, in the fading afternoon light, it was hard to see all the way across. *Just my fevered imagination*, she told herself. *This place is creepy as hell.*

"Yo, Lady Jane," called the gent, distracting Merry from her spectral suppositions.

"Peace, travelers," said the woman, who could have been his twin or his wife, holding up her fingers in the universal two-fingered salute. The crepe-like skin of her arm was dyed from fingertip to elbow with a multitude of intricate henna patterns.

"Hey, guys," said Jane, unslinging her towel from her shoulder and looking around for a place to hang it. "Nice to see you." To Merry, she said, "That's Steve Spirit Wind, and Mazel Tov, his woman."

"Who's your pal?" the man asked before Merry could do more than raise a brow at this. His voice was rich, languorous, as if his tongue couldn't be bothered to get up in the morning and show up for work. He tilted his head to study them both, squinting at Merry through the steam. "Don't tell me—you're the travel gal, right?" He didn't wait for an answer. "Hey, Mazel, check it, baby; it's the lady who's writing about Aguas Milagros!"

The woman—apparently really named Mazel Tov—put her hands together in prayer position. "The peace of this place be upon you, dear one."

"Um, thanks," said Merry, clutching her stick. She thought she might need it.

"Thought we'd grab a soak, if y'all don't mind," Jane announced. "I told Merry that this was one experience she really shouldn't miss while she's in Aguas Milagros."

"Be welcome," Mazel said, the corners of her eyes crinkling as she smiled up at them. "There's always room for those of good intent. And," she added in a less lofty tone, "I promise, I haven't fed Steve beans in at least three days. These bubbles are all products of nature."

"Hey," said Steve, pouting at his woman. "My bubbles are all-natural too, baby!" To Jane and Merry, he said, "C'mon in, gals. Join the party!"

"I'll just catch the next one," Merry murmured, backing away slowly. She hadn't realized she'd turned to flee until Jane grabbed her arm.

"No wussing out, Mer."

"I'm not *wussing out*," she hissed. "I'm letting discretion be the better part of valor! And besides..." She gestured lamely. "The pool appears to be occupied."

"Bah," Jane scoffed. "We fit five times this many folks in here last New Year's, and we're all still friends! There's plenty of room."

Yeah, if you want to play footsie with Mr. and Mrs. Free Love.

"We'll make room for ya, Merry-Bo-Berry," said Steve, waving her in.

Merry gulped. "Um...I just remembered I didn't pack my antifungal powder," she hedged, "and, I'm, like, *really* prone to catching athlete's foot. Seriously...they used to call me Funky-Foot Manning, back on the team." She started to back up.

Jane set her fists on her hips and eyed the taller woman, shaking her head sadly. "These springs are naturally antifungal, and antimicrobial too. You're wussing out, Mer, plain and simple."

Merry felt Jane's words hit home. She was right, damn her. *Since when did I become the kind of woman who "wusses out"?*

Since *never*. "Show me to the changing rooms," she said, steel in her voice.

Jane rolled her eyes. "Changing rooms? Look around you. Where do you think we are, the Ritz-Carlton?"

Merry looked around.

Right. A mud puddle. In the forest.

"If you're shy, go behind a tree to shuck trou," Jane suggested. "Though I can't see the point. There's nothing to change *into*. It's not like we're gonna be wearing swimsuits."

"Um . . . we're not?"

"Nope," Jane said cheerily. "National park rules: The chemicals we wash clothing in contaminate the waters. Ergo, no clothing."

"Ergo, I'm not going!"

"Suit yourself," Jane said with a shrug, "but I've got the car keys. You can sit here and sulk while I rest and rejuvenate."

I'm not a wuss. I'm not a wuss. And I sure as hell don't sulk.

"Last one in is a rotten egg," Merry gritted, blasting Jane with a dose of Death Ray Number Ten, which should have incinerated the vet where she stood. She "shucked trou" with about as much enthusiasm as one would display for a full-body prison delousing. Merry stood there defiantly, scars exposed, just long enough to prove she *wasn't* a wuss, then made to slosh into the pool.

Except there was a hippie in her way.

"Before you can accept the gift of this healing spring, you must be purified," said Mazel Tov, blocking the crude stone steps that led into the spring. Her pendulous breasts bobbed at the surface of the oily-looking water. "Steve will be happy to oblige; won't you, dear?"

"Oh, for sure, Merrilicious," said the Spirit Wind. He tossed his braids back in preparation for exiting the pool, moving his woman aside with a gentle pat on her shoulder. "Hang tight, ladies. I'll just get my smudge bundle, and be right back." Rising like the Swamp Thing, he sluiced water off his body.

His very *naked* body.

Oh boy. Merry caught a glimpse of a rather unfortunate piercing before Steve padded away toward the tree line to rummage inside an enormous macramé satchel hanging from a bough.

Jane, eyes alight with mirth, divested herself of her own clothes and waded into the pool, Mazel making way for her like an aquatic guard dog welcoming her master home.

"Hey, why do *you* get to go in and I don't?" Merry demanded, crossing her arms over her breasts and trying to pretend the rest of her body did not exist. Once, she'd been rather proud of that body, despite its unfortunate height and the Viking warrior-maiden comparisons it had invited. But that had been when she was in competitive condition, when she'd been working out eight days a week and strong as an ox. When she had been *whole*, not looking like the aftermath of a bad slasher flick. Now…it was nothing but a source of shame, an announcement of her failures.

"Oh, I've already been purified," Jane told her. "A couple years back. It's a blanket blessing."

A blanket would be a blessing right now, Merry thought. She turned her death ray up to eleven, but Jane only smiled wider, dipping her hair in the water and shaking it out sassily. For a healer, she seemed to have a serious streak of sadism.

"Darn it! Mazel, where'd I put the premium blend?" Steve muttered, elbow deep in the bag.

Merry edged farther away from Steve.

"It's next to the Udder Butter, sweetie," Mazel called.

I feel faint, Merry thought.

"Right. Here we go!" Steve cried triumphantly. He raised his arm, at the end of which was a foot-long bundle of bound-up brush. He brandished a Bic, flicking it alight and holding the flame to the bundle, watching until it caught. "Comin' at ya, Mer-Ber," he said, suiting actions to words as he fairly skipped to her side. Merry squeezed her eyes shut, trying not to see anything that jiggled. "Now, hold still. Won't take but a sec!"

Steve proceeded to smudge her.

It did not take "a sec."

Performed by Steve Spirit Wind, the ritual of sage smudging appeared to have a great deal in common with the acrobatics of a ground controller guiding a plane to a safe landing in foggy weather. He swooped and waved, flourished and swirled, smoke billowing and sparks spinning from the burning baton under his enthusiastic ministrations.

I definitely feel faint, Merry thought, *and it ain't the sage.* She was blushing from stem to stern, six feet three of pure, agonized embarrassment. *Please, let this be over soon*, she begged the god of hapless travel writers.

"Sage smudging is an ancient practice," Mazel informed Merry as she oversaw her man's efforts. "Make sure you get the smoke everywhere, dear," she chided.

"You got it, babe." Steve waved the bundle lustily, then, with spastic flaps of his hands, encouraged the resulting fumes to envelop Merry. "Cup the smoke," he told her, panting from his efforts, "and wash with it."

"Ah . . . wash with it?"

"Here, watch me. I'll show ya."

Steve began to pantomime using the sage stick like a shower brush. Under the arms. Over the head. Between the toes. Behind the knees.

And betwixt his legs.

Bending over nearly double, limbs akimbo and tush aimed right at Merry, Steve passed his smoldering rod dangerously close to his *other* rod, encouraging the herbal effluvia to invade every one of his body cavities.

Hole-y smokes...

He straightened up, beaming, then made as if to give Merry the same treatment. "Now you!"

"It's okay," Merry squeaked. "I think we're all pure here!" She backpedaled furiously, but Steve would not be deterred. He advanced, waving his wand, fairly chasing Merry around the rim of the pool. Out of the corner of her eye, Merry just had time to register Jane, biting her fist and crying with silent laughter before her heels met only thin air. She hurtled backward...

And found the third hag.

With her ass.

A series of kaleidoscopic impressions hit Merry, one after another.

Scalding blue water.

A scalding blue glare.

A steaming cauldron.

A steaming-mad man.

Naked flesh.

Naked fury.

"The fuck!?" Suddenly Merry found herself hoisted skyward, in defiance of all the laws of gravity, then just as quickly plummeting back down with a tremendous splash—three feet from a simmering Sam Cassidy.

Water dripping down his brick-red cheeks, sun-bleached hair tied in a messy bun atop his head, Sam's expression was thunderous and shocked at the same time. *The outraged virgin, ogre edition.*

Merry's own mouth made a perfect O of surprise, and she blinked stupidly. "Um, hi?" Trying out a queasy smile, she pushed sopping hair back from her face and looked around the pool for a quick exit. Jane, she saw, was nearly hysterical with laughter now, face buried in her hands and shoulders shaking, while Steve had rejoined his woman in the water, a pleased-as-punch expression on his face as he cuddled her close by the shallow end. "Now our circle is complete!" cried Mazel.

My humiliation sure is, Merry thought, backing away from Sam as fast as she could in the sulfurous, neck-deep spring. Or at least, it would be neck-deep on *most* of its occupants. On Merry, she'd have to stay crouched to keep her boobs from breaking the surface. *Fuck, did he see me naked?* She hadn't seen *him* through the steam, so maybe she'd dodged the bullet there. But it hardly mattered, she realized. *He's* felt *me naked.* The sensation of his slippery flesh sliding against hers was indelibly burned into her nerve endings.

"Nine-point-six from the Russian judge," Jane hooted. "With bonus points for artistic expression."

Merry shot her the Death Star of all dirty looks, even as she crab-walked over to the vet for safety. She wanted to get out of troll territory as fast as humanly possible. "It's not funny, Jane!"

"You're damn right it's not," Sam snarled, slapping the water with his palm and spraying everyone, including the now-open-mouthed hippies. "But I can't say I'm surprised. You've been throwing yourself at me since the moment you got to Aguas Milagros!" He slapped the water again, drenching them all a second time. "You want a gander so bad? Well, get it while the light's good, Wookiee." With a lunge, suddenly Sam was airborne, launching himself up with stiff arms to clear the water and land with surprising lightness on the patchy moss and ferns covering the ground around the spring. He threw his arms wide, drops of water flying in all directions.

"There. Look your fill, if you're so hot and bothered. But let's be clear—a look is *all* you're gonna get." He twirled like Stevie Nicks—once, twice—gave a sardonic curtsy, then swiped his towel off a nearby tree branch and tied it around his waist with jerky motions. "Thanks for spoiling another otherwise beautiful day in paradise, Wookiee," he growled, and strode—some might say *flounced*—off down the trail. They could hear angry mutters and snapping branches for some time after he had disappeared.

"Um...wow," said Jane. She flapped a hand to fan her face as if to cool her heated cheeks.

"Wow is right," said Merry, her pirate brow making friends with her hairline.

Because Sam—naked Sam—wasn't an ogre at all.

What *might* have been beer belly beneath the enveloping overalls he usually wore was a barrel alright—of pure muscle. From broad, deep chest to arms every bit as steely as she'd only suspected earlier when he'd caught her in the store, he was primal male in its most honest form—muscles built by nature and hard work rather than hours at some gym where they swapped the towels out every hour and blared Bloomberg Business news from every treadmill. And it didn't end above the waist. His legs were solid columns of brawn, surprisingly shapely for all their strength. And that ass...

Good on 'im, Merry thought, pursing her lips. Nice, round buns, not flat—or God forbid, furry—like she might have suspected. She had seen world-class athletes who weren't in as good condition as Sam Cassidy. But it was when he'd done his final flourish that Merry *really* had to give it to him. *Whoa*, she marveled. *And that's with shrinkage?*

"I think Sammy-whammy needs another smudge," said Steve. "The negative energy is really funky on him today."

CHAPTER EIGHTEEN

*W*hile the days in Aguas Milagros are idyllic, the nights can be a tad chilly.

Whoops. I mean, chill-ING.

Just when I was snuggling down under my lovely crocheted blankie, tuckered from an honest day's work and an eye-opening evening of soaking with the locals, a movement on the ceiling of my cabin caught my attention. A cobweb, *thinks I.* Surely no more than a breath of wind tickling the spider streamers in the eaves. *Never mind that it didn't move like any cobweb I'd seen before.*

Cobwebs, in my experience, don't scurry.

And they don't fall out of the sky and land on your face.

After which they most certainly do not race, with one hundred horrifying legs, down your neck and disappear—all six inches of them— beneath your covers.

Where they very adamantly do not dive into your pajamas and attempt to make a home for themselves in your navel.

As one might imagine, there came after this a spate of quite understandable hysterics. There were screams, dear reader. A number of screams that carried on for an indeterminate period of time that I'm guessing lasted anywhere from thirty seconds to thirty thousand years. There was the throwing back of covers. The Olympic-caliber leap from an unfortunately unspringy cot. The tearing off of nightwear. Much thrashing, and slapping of various body parts that might potentially be harboring the

beast. There was stomping. And whimpering, and perhaps even a wee bit
of gibbering.

And that's when Sam Cassidy busted down the door.

With an axe in one manly fist.

ℝ

Merry was naked and panting when next she saw Sam Cassidy.

Her desire, however, was not for him but for a flamethrower, a suit of seamless, impregnable armor, and the phone number of a reliable exterminator.

"*Yeeeeeeeeeaaaaaaaaaaahhhhhhhhhhh!*" she howled, rending garments, hair, and the quiet of the night with equal abandon. She spun in circles, pajama top torn open, hair flying about her like a flaming copper cape, hopping and recoiling at every shadow. A slithering in the seat of the silk pj's made her shriek again, loud enough that the very windowpanes shivered, and she kicked the bottoms off as if they were afire, leaving her lower half clad in only panties. "Cleese!" she screamed. "Save me!"

"Who the hell is Cleese?"

Merry spun again to find the source of the furious voice. She gasped. Standing silhouetted in the doorway of the cabin was a burly, vaguely manlike shape with a huge-ass woodcutter's axe braced on its shoulder, like a character out of a fairy tale. But was it Big Bad Wolf or hero come to save the day?

Then the figure flicked on the light switch. Merry blinked in the sudden light.

Definitely Big Bad Wolf.

"The hell are you doing, Wookiee?" Sam's sun-bleached brows were beetled, and he stomped into the room with his axe at the ready, looking for trouble. "I could hear you wailing like an air-raid siren from six acres away." His chest was rising and falling as if he'd been running—which he probably had, if he'd been that far away when she'd started caterwauling. Finished scanning the room and obviously finding nothing worth axe-murdering, he eyed her up and down. A strange expression crossed his face. It was almost...*mortified*? "You got a guy in here?" His gaze darted to the cot in the corner of the room with its rumpled covers.

Merry shook her head, still trembling. "There was a...a..." She paused, gulped. "I don't know what it was. A creature of some sort. It fell..." She swallowed again, shuddering. "And landed..." She gestured toward her face and neck. "And ran..." She waved down her chest, oblivious to the fact that her pajama top was gaping open. "And it tried to..." She made a swirling motion of her finger around her navel. "And then it..." She made walking gestures with her finger down her leg. "And now I don't know where it is!" She spun again, toes curled in terror of the floorboards.

"And you were expecting some guy named after a Monty Python actor to save you?" Sam lowered the axe, but he didn't look any less murderous.

Merry waved her hand absently at the cabin's tiny table, where her pet had taken up residence. "Cleese is my turtle," she said, still peering anxiously into corners.

"Oh, well then," Sam said, looked at the travel terrarium with a jaundiced eye. Inside the enclosure, Cleese appeared to be sleeping soundly. "Guess you don't need rescuing after all."

Broadsided by the sarcasm, Merry looked at Sam—really looked at him. Her eyes widened. Her jaw hinged open.

The man was wearing nothing but a faded red union suit. An honest-to-goodness, pioneer-era onesie, saggy ass-flap and all. Beneath it, his feet were bare as usual, and up top, his hair was a wild nimbus of bed-head—if one were in the habit of bedding down in a barn. Merry gaped stupidly for a minute at the sight of his ridiculous getup, then abruptly realized she herself was wearing only panties and the torn-open top of her red silk pajamas, which covered precisely *none* of the important bits.

Shit, she thought. *The leg!* Her scars were on full display. Merry dove for her coverlet, then paused, struck by a terrifying thought. What if the mutant creature that had just creeped years off her life had gone to ground in Dolly's intricately knotted afghan? She had no idea what the horrid thing had been, but one thing was sure—she didn't want it anywhere near her naked flesh again. But then again, she didn't want Sam's gaze anywhere near her naked flesh either. She snatched, flapped, and wrapped the fabric around her with record speed.

Maybe if she went on the offensive, Merry thought, he'd forget how offensive the sight of her mangled body was. "Um, what's with the Miner Forty-Niner costume?"

"*You're* giving *me* sartorial snark? A woman wearing half a pair of Frederick's of Hollywood pajamas?"

"Shows how much you know," Merry snapped. "My mother wouldn't go near a Frederick's of Hollywood for all the tea in Ceylon."

Sam scrubbed a hand over his face. "Lady, sometimes I don't even think we speak the same language. Do you have an emergency or not? Because if not, I'd like to go back to bed. You're lucky Dolly's a heavy sleeper, or you'd have given her a heart attack with your histrionics. I heard you hollering from halfway across the ranch."

"Well, gee, Mr. Cassidy, I'm sorry my abject terror got in the way of your beauty sleep. It's clear you need all the help you can get." The words were out before Merry could call them back. She knew it was a cheap shot. Someone as looks-challenged as herself had no business throwing stones. But she was too damn tired of taking crap from Sam—and, hell, too damn tired in general—to worry about fairness right now. The contemptuous look he'd shot her in the store this afternoon when she'd fallen, the way he'd flung her from him in the spring this evening as if she were poison...enough was enough! "What is your *problem* with me?" Merry demanded. "You've been a total prick from the moment I met you. Then, just when I thought you *might* be turning into a human being on the hike yesterday, you get all weird again today. And I don't even know *what* that shit was at the hot spring tonight. You'd think I was carrying seventeen kinds of swine flu, the way you've been acting."

Sam puffed up like a bullfrog, axe still held across his flannel-covered chest. "And you'd think *I* had catnip in every pocket, the way you've been sniffing around me!"

"*What!?*"

"C'mon, lady. Fess up. You've been angling to get naked in front of me since the minute you got here. Falling all over me in those skintight jeans, the *accidental* slip at the springs, and now..." He waved at her blanket-wrapped form.

Merry drew the cover more tightly around her, hoping the elegant pattern might lend her some dignity. "You have *got* to be kidding me. I mean, I know your ego's half the size of New Mexico, but even you have to know you're not exactly..." She trailed off, waving demonstratively at the threadbare union suit.

"'Major Gorgeous'? 'Thor in snug denim'?"

Merry's mouth gaped open in an excellent impression of a deep-sea bass. Then it snapped shut. "You've been reading 'Don't Do What I Did.'"

"I have," he said, laying the axe atop the table next to Cleese's terrarium and glaring at her in a way that made Merry glad he was no longer armed with a handful of highly honed steel. "Bob gave me a look this morning, and imagine my surprise. Hate to break it to ya, but you, Miss Manning, are barking up the wrong tree if you think we're gonna have some kind of Crocodile Dundee–style romance while you're here."

"Wait. Back up a minute. You thought I was *serious*? That I see you as some sort of Marlboro Man with a string of llamas instead of mustangs?" An incredulous laugh burst from her throat.

Sam suddenly looked less sure of himself. He folded burly arms across his barrel chest—a chest Merry now had cause to know was 100 percent muscle. "Well, what would *you* call 'Studly Sam'? A friendly nickname?"

"Dude," she said. "I don't know if they have mirrors in your yurt or dugout or whatever it is you live in, but there's a *reason* I'm only photographing you in silhouette for the column."

"You've been photographing me?" His scowl was thunderous.

"I've been photographing the goat shit too, Llama Boy. Don't let it go to your head."

Now it was Sam's turn to gape. For a second, a corner of his mouth curled up. Then he smothered the nascent smile in its crib. "So what was all that 'Oooh, Sam's so dreamy' horseshit?"

"I was *trying* to do you a favor," Merry said. She attempted to plant her hands on her hips, but it wasn't exactly easy when one was wearing nothing but a blanket and the ruins of an eight-hundred-dollar pair of La Perla pj's. "If I wrote you the way you've really been behaving, it wouldn't exactly reflect well on Dolly, would it?"

Sam looked like she'd just planted the axe right through the top of his skull. He backed up until his rear hit the chair behind him, then availed himself of it, all the wind gone from his sails.

Merry pressed on, relishing the chagrin on his face. "It wouldn't do much for tourism at the Last Chance if I told my readers how singularly rude and unwelcoming you've been from the moment I got here. How many people would be signing up for llama tours if they knew their guide was going to insult, demean, and debase them the whole time?"

"So . . . you haven't been trying to get in my pants?" Sam asked slowly.

Merry snorted. "Believe me, if I wanted to seduce you, I sure as hell wouldn't be naked."

Sam turned his head sideways, like a dog eyeing a particularly vexing house cat. "You wouldn't be naked," he repeated slowly, "if you were trying to seduce me." His expression was baffled. "Lady, are you *completely* batshit?"

Merry crossed her arms defensively. "You've seen the mystery meat," she muttered, gesturing to her leg. "Not that I was ever anyone's idea of a supermodel, but *that* hot mess, combined with the rest of the package . . ." She waved up and down the length of her tall figure and face. "If I were at the post office, they'd stamp me 'damaged goods.' "

Sam squinted at her as if reassessing the situation. "You know," he said slowly, "I'd give you shit about that ridiculous statement, but I'm starting to get the idea somebody's *already* fed you a whole heap of bullshit." Arms crossed over his flannel-clad chest, he eyed her solemnly. "Who did a number on you, Merry Manning?" His tone was gentler now, and his scowl had faded to a more open, inquiring expression.

Merry's eyes stung, suddenly, and her throat seemed to be trying to swallow a tennis ball. His abrupt switch from sparring partner to confidant had her scrambling to shift gears. "I don't know what you mean," she mumbled, looking away.

"Well, someone's obviously got you convinced you're some sort of . . . hell, I dunno, a Frankenstein's monster or something."

"And you're telling me that's *not* how you view me?" Merry crossed her arms once more, tightening the blanket around her shoulders. Her leg was throbbing again after her frantic attempts to evade the alien slither-monster, though the hot springs *had* loosened her up some earlier. (Once Sam had gone, she and Jane had been able to relax for an hour or so with Steve and Mazel, who were actually pretty nice once you'd passed the smudge test.)

The last thing I need is to take another header in front of Sam. Still cocooned in the blanket, Merry hobbled to her cot before her muscles could give out. "I saw how you looked at me in those stupid jeans earlier today. Obviously, I'm nobody who should ever attempt fashion."

Sam sat back in the chair. His fingertips drummed against the axe haft. "You thought I was looking at your pants because I'm some sort of Tim Gunn fashion police?"

Merry's eyebrow rose. *He knows who Tim Gunn is?* "Weren't you?"

"Merry," Sam said slowly, like a teacher explaining basic arithmetic to a particularly dense student, "I was looking at you because you were a six-foot Amazon in painted-on jeans. What man wouldn't look?"

"Six three," Merry mumbled, her cheeks going scarlet. Well, that put this afternoon in a different light, didn't it? "And I'm well aware I was a freak of nature even *before* I got run through a wood chipper, so you don't have to feed me a bunch of crap just to make me feel better. I know guys get all wiggy when a woman's taller than them. Believe me, I've been dealing with that shit since I was seven years old."

"I don't care if you're seven feet tall. That doesn't make you a freak."

"Says the guy who calls me Wookiee!"

Sam looked abashed. "I didn't realize you'd be so sensitive about it. I was actually referring to your hair—which at the time was doing a fair Chewbacca impression."

"Says the guy who ran headfirst into a haystack!"

Sam's shook his head, letting his rough-and-tumble mane fly where it would. "It's true, I haven't been down to the mayor's office for a haircut in a while," he acknowledged, baffling Merry. "Anyhow, my point is, any man worth his salt isn't going to be put off by a woman just because she's taller than he is. If he is, he's not worth your time anyway. He's probably an asshole with a tiny schlong."

Merry's blush went nuclear. *Well*, she thought, *Sam has the asshole part down pat*...Still, from what she'd seen at the spring this evening, his schlong was something to schling home about. She looked away. "Whatever, Llama Boy. I'd really prefer not to get in a measuring contest with a dude in footie pajamas."

"I take offense at that categorization," he said, crossing his legs at the ankle and gazing fondly at his broad, callused—and very bare—feet. "I'm a big believer in letting the tootsies breathe. And while we're on the subject of gnarly things, why are you so hung up about a couple of scars anyway? A scar is just a record of where you've been in this life, not a source of shame."

Shows how much he knows, thought Merry. Her career-ending injury had been the ultimate humiliation. Winning had been Merry's whole reason—and frankly, her whole *justification*—for being.

Suddenly, Sam looked stricken. His eyes widened and he sucked in a breath. "Wait...is *that* why you've been such a klutz?

Why you had so much trouble keeping up on the llama trek? Your injury?"

Merry looked away and didn't answer.

"Well, hell."

He stood up abruptly, strode over to the cot, and helped himself to a seat on it. The bed dipped under his solid bulk, and Merry's body lurched close to his. Suddenly her senses were swamped with that warm, slightly musky Sam scent, and she scrambled to the other end of the cot to get some distance. She pressed her back to the wall and gazed at him with something close to alarm.

"I really am an ass, aren't I?" he said, seeing her reaction. "But Jesus, Merry, why didn't you tell me you were hurt?"

"I'm not hurt. I'm *crippled*," she snapped, then clamped her mouth shut, embarrassed by the admission. Her eyes were suddenly blurry, but that only made her madder at Sam. *Damn it, I. Will. Not. Cry!*

"What are you talking about?" he asked, genuine puzzlement in his voice. "You shoveled shit, you baled hay, and you helped get the Muellers all the way to the top of Wheeler Peak and back. You were slow, sure, and you stumbled a bit, but you made it. Nobody could ask more from you."

My mother could ask more, Merry thought.

"Merry, I'm sorry I've given you such a hard time. I guess since you got here, I've just been afraid you were trying to take advantage of my aunt. But you aren't, are you?"

With so little space between them, Merry could see the gold flecks in his blue irises. *Pretty*, she thought, before his words sunk in. "Of course I'm not! I'm trying to help! I've been doing everything I can to portray the ranch in the best light possible— and honestly, aside from *you*, I haven't had to fudge a whole lot to make it look good. The Last Chance really is a pretty magical place. And so is what I've seen of the rest of Aguas Milagros. I want to do the place justice for my readers—and I was hoping maybe that might do you guys some good, tourism-wise. I don't know if I'm physically capable of doing all the heavy lifting I signed on to do, but I'd like to be of use while I'm here, if you'd only stop trying to run me off at every turn."

Sam sucked thoughtfully on his teeth, giving her a sideways assessing glance. "I guess I can see that now. I just thought... hell, I dunno. I thought all that over-the-top 'Cowboy Sam' crap was you making fun of us country bumpkins—that, or you were wearing some serious rose-colored beer goggles." His lips twisted ruefully.

"No beer goggles," Merry said. "But maybe I have a career as a romance novelist in my future if I've managed to sell *you* as a leading man." Relenting a bit, she allowed a small smile to cross her lips.

Sam matched it with his own, then allowed the smile to grow into a full-fledged grin. It transformed his homely features into something that made Merry's heart grow warm.

At least she told herself it was her heart.

"You're gonna tone that down now though, right?"

"Am I?" Merry arched her brow. "No, I don't think I am. I could stand to stretch my fiction-writing wings."

"I'm not going to start having groupies, am I?" He sounded alarmed.

"You might, if the comments on my columns so far are any indication."

"Oh, sweet Jesus," he muttered. A look of consternation crossed his face. "Maybe *that's* why..."

"Why what?"

"Well, Aunt Dolly told me she's started getting a surprising number of bookings for the tours the last couple days. All of them from women."

Merry had to laugh at the chagrin on Sam's face. "Maybe you'll get to play swashbuckling hero after all, Mr. Dundee."

Sam changed the subject, clearly uncomfortable. "If you don't mind me asking, how did that happen?" He waved at her leg.

Merry hesitated. It would be so easy to let her guard down, but she wasn't actually sure she *liked* this new Sam. Or more precisely, she wasn't sure she liked how easily he might get under her skin. Bantering about his fictitious sex appeal was one thing— it was awesome to watch him squirm—but she wasn't about to swap confidences with a guy who got his jollies calling her "Wookiee." His sudden about-face was just that—a little *too* sudden. She wasn't sure how he'd react once he learned who she had once been.

"I *do* mind," she said shortly. "It's not something I care to discuss with ogres who come galumphing into my bedroom in the middle of the night, brandishing battle-axes."

Sam snorted. "I don't 'galumph,'" he informed her, letting the issue of her injury drop. "And it was a wood axe."

"Whatever. We're not getting all buddy-buddy, *buddy*, so if you don't mind, it's time for you and your pilgrim pj's to shove off." Suiting actions to words, Merry gave Sam a shove on his thigh with her foot.

It was like trying to dislodge a boulder from a riverbed with a spork.

A hot, muscular boulder. "Move it, Llama Boy. This Wookiee needs her shut-eye."

"You're not worried about the so-called monster you think you saw anymore?"

"I didn't *think* I saw it, it landed splat on my face! And believe me, Mick Dundee wrestled *crocs* that were smaller than this beast."

"Uh-huh."

"I'm serious!"

"I'm sure you are, Wookiee," said Sam, getting to his feet and dusting off his faded red flannels. "I'm sure wherever you're from, mosquitoes seem like ferocious wildlife to you too."

Merry started to sputter a tart rejoinder at the unfairness of this, coming from a Garden State native, but a movement in her peripheral vision had her catching her breath. "Oh my God, there it is!" she hissed, pointing to the pile of firewood beside the woodstove. "I think I just saw it disappear between the logs!"

"Just a centipede, probably," Sam said, not bothering to investigate.

Just a centipede? The thing was enormous! "Aren't you going to slay it?"

"I doubt it'll bother you again," he said. He shouldered the axe and turned, giving Merry a gander at the fireman's flap of the buttoned-up union suit. "If we're all done with the girl talk, Wookiee, I'm gonna head back to my bed. I gotta be sure I'm properly studly in the morning for your readers."

Merry ignored the snark. "But...you can't just leave me here with that thing. It's horrible!"

Sam shrugged, heading for the door. "Lots of things are ugly at first glance. Doesn't mean they don't have a place in nature. And I certainly don't want to be the one to kill the poor bugger just because it had the poor judgment to dive into your skivvies. I didn't try to murder *you* when you tried to dive into mine, after all."

Merry was too terrified to get huffy. "At least leave me the axe," she pleaded.

"I don't think so, Wookiee. You're accident-prone enough as it is."

"Some hero," she groused, squinching herself into a tight ball at the head of her bed. "Won't even leave the distressed damsel the means to defend herself. Be careful, or I might have to tell my readers the truth about Studly Sam."

Sam shrugged, as if unconcerned with such trivialities as public opinion. "In your case, fiction is stranger than truth. *Hasta mañana*, Merry Manning." Then he paused at the door, looking thoughtful.

"Tell you what. We've got some very special guests coming in for an overnight experience in a couple days, and if you're serious about sticking this out, I'll want your help with them. I think you might learn a few things about perseverance. And who knows: Maybe you'll have something to teach them too. Unless..." A look of challenge lit his blue eyes. "Unless you're giving up on the Last Chance?"

"I'll be there," Merry said tightly. *If I'm not in the gullet of a monstrous insect by then*, she thought.

"Alright then," he said. "Sweet dreams." And he sauntered out, swinging the door shut behind him and leaving Merry to wish it had hit him on the ass. She settled back in the cot, cranky and out of sorts. Had they just formed some sort of truce? Or was this only the beginning of a whole new phase of weirdness, Sam Cassidy–style?

And he didn't even save the day, she thought grumpily. *Some Marlboro Man.* Her eyelids grew heavy at last—it had been one of the longest days in recent memory—and Merry started to doze off.

Crunch!

A loud, carapace-munching sound came from across the room.

Merry looked up just in time to see her very pleased-looking box turtle snarf the tail end of an enormous centipede, then drop back into his terrarium to savor his victory. If she didn't know better, she'd *swear* she heard a tiny belch.

"My hero," she said, drawing her covers up with a smile. At least *someone* on the ranch understood chivalry.

CHAPTER NINETEEN

I started to feel like Ebenezer Scrooge, for I had another spectral visitation the next night. Round about three, perhaps four, or whenever the witching hour is witchiest, I heard a creak, and a draft of air cold as the crypt washed over me. On this moonless night, there was not a speck of light, and the ranch might as well have been resting on the bottom of the ocean.

There came a noise: Clatter-clop, clickety-tromp.

Jacob Marley's chains dragging against the floorboards? The centipede's kin seeking revenge? No, too loud for the latter. I held my breath, burrowing beneath the coverlet, and stayed as still as a quivering wreck of a woman could manage. I was too terrified to reach for my phone's flashlight app, lest it pinpoint for the phantom exactly where I lay. Yet despite my precautions, the sound came closer—and with it came an infernal reek. A reek mixed with . . . lavender?

I heard the sound of snorting, as if Beelzebub himself had popped in for a bedtime story, and I tried to breathe as shallowly as I could. But just as I thought I would perish from sheer fear, I heard the thing move off again, into the night. Another creak, and the draft stopped. I lay there, panting with horror, until at last my tired body gave up the ghost (or more precisely, gave up on the ghost) and I fell back into an uneasy doze.

This morning when I set feet to floorboards, I found a bouquet of fragrant wildflowers at the foot of my bed.

Apparently, this ghost wants to be friends.

CHAPTER TWENTY

To: MerryWay@pulsemag.com
From: J_Jonas@ChicagoManagementLTD.com

Subject: Urgent: Your Garage Space

Dear Ms. Manning,

It is my unfortunate duty to inform you that your vehicle was towed from its assigned garage space in the building this morning. The attendant who witnessed the incident tells me that the gentlemen who towed it were repossession specialists (I believe "repo men" was the term he used), and they had the proper documentation to authorize the removal of the car. I've attached a scan of the paperwork for your convenience.

Please note: You will still be required to pay for the space so long as you are a resident of the building. Perhaps your subtenant will be interested in utilizing it?

Sincerely,
Jonathan Jonas
Managing Agent

"Fuck," said Merry, "a duck."

That car had been just about the last material possession she could call her own, aside from a few sticks of furniture currently being "utilized" by the tenant she'd gotten to take over her lease. *Probably should have gotten my mail forwarded*, she thought. She'd undoubtedly missed more than a few bills since she'd been in Aguas Milagros. Well, "missed" wasn't really the word to use, she thought ruefully. *Dodged* might be more accurate. But even if she'd received the notice saying her car was about to be repossessed, there wasn't much she could have done about it—except take the old CDs out of the glove box and say a tearful good-bye. She had nothing in her bank account with which to pay off the title loan. It was only because *Pulse* was paying for her rental car that Merry was able to keep the MINI while she was here at the ranch. It would have to go back the minute this assignment ended. Leaving Merry up shit's creek for real.

"Fuck," said Merry to no one in particular, "two ducks."

Fortunately, Bob's diner was devoid of ducks this morning. It was just her, and her laptop, and the unfortunate connection to the world it provided.

Well, while she was facing unpleasant things, she'd might as well get it over with and rip off the Band-Aid. She'd been putting it off for the past several days while she settled into ranch life and her leg started to heal up a bit. But she couldn't ditch this responsibility any longer.

It was time to scan the comments.

Nooooooooooooooo, she thought, as she always did before she undertook this most loathsome portion of her job. *No, please God, spare meeeeeee!*

But there was no help for it. Merry needed to see how her fickle fans were responding to her column. The first DDWID installments had done remarkably well, but that was no reason to go ahead and think the Internet had sprouted daisy-covered rainbows overnight. When you worked as an online journalist, you were only as good as your latest post, only as safe as the trolls were magnanimous that day.

How had the hot-spring hippies gone over? Had they liked her story about the trek up Wheeler Peak, and her descriptions of Sam, Dolly, Bob, and the other Aguas Milagros locals she'd been interviewing? Had the bit she'd done about the amigurumi bored them, or were they anxious to see how crafty she could be with a crochet hook? For the past several days since her encounter with Sam (and the centipede), she'd barely had time to do more than post and run—or rather collapse—given how busy ranch life had been keeping her, but Merry had to remember the Last Chance wasn't her real job. Or her real home. Reality couldn't wait any longer.

Maybe it'd be better to check the back-end analytics before subjecting herself to the soul-slashing callousness of the World Wide Web. Merry clicked and typed, clicked some more, and was soon in the bowels of the content management system *Pulse* staff members used, perusing site stats for her column.

What she saw made her sit back and reach a shaky hand for her latte—this morning's design was of a sunrise over the mountains—and slug back a swig. *"Hot damn,"* she breathed, and not just because Bob's coffee was just short of scalding. The bar graph said it all. Where her numbers had been chugging along respectably for months (though dipping more than she'd liked before Joel had done his bait-and-switch with her column), suddenly there was a spike that sent her into a whole other stratosphere.

The kind of spike that said *viral*.

Viral. The great white whale of Internet commerce. The elusive, ineffable, and utterly unforeseeable quality that took a story from "hey, cool," to "you gotta fuckin' see this" on social media.

Merry switched over to Twitter, where her handle was @merryway. The feed was slow, because Bob's Wi-Fi was still barely out of the twentieth century, but she could see she'd gained an amazing number of new followers in the past several days, some of whom were even not horny Russian teenagers eager to please. Her message box was awash with spam, lewd offers, and requests for follow-backs—nothing new there—but it was the sheer volume of traffic that set Merry back on her heels.

Scarcely able to believe her eyes, Merry went back to the CMS and delved deeper, clicking through charts and site referral numbers. Yup. Her shares, likes, and retweets had all grown exponentially. More important, they'd grown *organically*. Which meant people were interested enough in what she'd been doing enough to post about it, reblog it, and share it with their friends all over the world.

Which meant happy sponsors getting mountains of click-throughs on their ads.

But did it mean the *readers* were happy—or laughing their asses off at her?

Enough dithering. Time to check the comments and find out.

Except there would not be *time* to check all the comments. Not if Merry wanted to meet Sam at his house this morning as she'd promised.

There were twelve hundred and forty three of them.

It was near triple the number she'd done on her best day before.

"Ho-ly..."

"Want some eggs and toast with that coffee, Lady Hobbit?"

Bob swung by, fishing an order pad from his apron and a pencil from his frowsy hair. "Maybe a pinch more nutmeg on your latte?"

Merry gave him a look that was half baby bird, half woozy travel writer. "No, thanks. Dolly's got me bringing a picnic brunch over to Sam's in a bit, so I'll skip the chow and the nutmeg, but maybe you can spare a pinch on my arm to wake me up? I'm pretty sure I'm dreaming right now, because I am just *not* that lucky." She nodded to her laptop.

Bob peeked around her shoulder to see her screen. His eyes darted as he scanned the page, and he nodded wisely. "People have good taste."

Merry followed his gaze to the topmost comment.

CawfeeKlatch: Does the latte maestro take requests? I want Smaug in my next cappuccino.

Bob stroked his beard. "I don't know about a cappuccino, but if I used a bit of cayenne for the flames, I bet I could make a Mexican hot cocoa dragon," he mused.

Merry smiled, mouth already watering at the idea. Then she snorted when she saw one of the replies to the comment.

I want Steve Spirit Wind in my next cuppa, wrote PennyPetticoat from Brixton, UK.

"Way ahead of you," Bob said to the screen. For the first time, Merry noticed the tray Bob held in one hand. Two wide-mouthed coffee cups rested atop it, and in each one, a mound of stiff foam had been sculpted into the shape of a tiny person, arms draped over the side of the cup, as if bathing in a hot tub. The detail was perfect, down to the chest hair on Steve, and Mazel's long braids. "Gotta get these to our friends over there before the magic melts," Bob said, nodding over his shoulder. Merry followed his gaze and saw that Steve and Mazel Tov had taken the booth two down from hers, and were pulling out bottles of stevia and assorted vials of spices from Mazel's macramé bag.

"Oh no," Merry whispered. "They haven't seen the bit I wrote about..."

Bob's beard parted to show his smile. "Oh, we've all seen it," he said. "It's getting to be quite a thing, to come over my way of an evening and check out the latest from our esteemed guest."

Merry shrank down in her seat, but the two hippies had already seen her. They waved enthusiastically, and Merry waved back, half apologetically. *They don't* look *mad*, she thought. But she'd better start remembering that Aguas Milagros was a *small* town. She'd be bound to see the subjects of her articles daily, and she needed to keep that in mind when she wrote about them.

"Speaking of evenings at Café Con Kvetch," Bob said, breaking into her thoughts, "you coming to the happening this weekend?"

"Ah...'*happening*'?" Hippies and "happenings" could be a lethal combination.

"Music, poetry, dancing; that kind of thing. Pretty much the whole town's going to be here," Bob told her. "Might make great material for your column," he added.

Merry noticed Bob never said "blog," and she loved him just a little bit more for getting it right. And he was correct. It sounded like exactly the sort of thing her readers would relish. *And terrify me*, she thought. Parties weren't exactly Merry's forte, to her Mother's endless exasperation. "I wish I could," she said, not quite honestly. "But I promised Dolly I'd join her and some of her friends for this craft night thing they do." *That is, if I survive this "experience" Sam's got cooked up for me today.*

"No need to split Schrödinger's cat," Bob said. "The two are not mutually exclusive."

Merry looked up at him, pirate brow raised.

"Dolly's troupe does their stitchery over here at the café," he explained. "It's the most central location for the ladies. Unlike Dolly, some of 'em live really far out in the rural areas, and this is the only chance they get at enjoying a spot of civilization. All the better for everyone when craft night coincides with our local talent slam."

Merry smiled. *Dolly's ranch is* not *considered rural?* She could scarcely picture Aguas Milagros' idea of "far out." "Cool," she said to Bob. "Two birds—or quantum zombie cats—with one stone, I guess. Catch you later?"

"You got it, Lady Hobbit. I better let you get back to your work, and get back to mine as well. Mini Mazel's melting from the heat." He hefted his tray of foam-born hippies and headed for the real hippies' table. "Don't let the rascals grind you down today!"

And on that baffling note, Bob left Merry to her own devices. Specifically, her laptop. She scrolled back to the entry she'd done on the hot springs, and smiled to see one of her top commenters had left her a note filled with her usual enthusiasm.

GrlyGrl: Best trip everrrrrrrrrrrrr! I'd totally get "tainted" with you, Merry!

So how'd things end with Steamy Sam? another commenter wanted to know. *Don't leave us hanging!*

Merry wasn't surprised her readers were falling for him—she could fall for the fictitious version of her host herself, if she hadn't had the reality to keep her firmly fed up. But she had to admit, Sam *had* shown a softer side lately—*slightly*. Why, he'd been *almost* decent to her these past few days, keeping the razzing, snarking, and sarcasm to a dull roar as Merry learned her way around the ranch. But it hadn't been all that hard to stay civil— he'd mostly stayed out of her way since their axe-wielding en- counter, leaving Merry to work with Dolly and Jane while he guided guests on overnight excursions with his llamas.

Today, however, she'd be one of those overnight guests. If she ever finished catching up with her correspondence.

Merry slugged her rapidly cooling coffee and hunched over her computer.

❧

Twenty minutes later, laptop safely stowed in her satchel and sufficiently fortified with caffeine to face anything—even beard- ing Sam Cassidy in his den—Merry rose and tossed a tip roughly double the pittance Bob had charged her for her coffee on the chipped Formica. But she wasn't getting away that cleanly.

"Hey, hey, Merry-Berry," Steve called, waving her over to the booth where he and his woman were up to their braids in chiles and cheese, their cappuccinos drained to thin films of froth on the edges of Bob's capacious cups.

"Come gift us with your inner light," invited Mazel.

Merry hesitated. *So close . . .* she thought, looking longingly at the bright sunlight just beyond Bob's diner door. But she owed the hippies their chance to give her hell for her post about them. Despite their smiles, she couldn't quite believe they were cool with their portrayal on DDWID.

Until Mazel got up from the table, sliding from the booth

with the grace of a true flower child, and engulfed Merry in a full-body, patchouli-redolent hug.

And Steve clamped himself to her other side and made panini di Merry.

"You're not mad?" Merry asked.

"Mad?" Steve's face was a mask of incomprehension.

"About the whole, um..."

Steve let loose with a guffaw that shook dust from the ceiling fans. "The taint thing?" He laughed.

Merry blushed.

At his side, Mazel Tov grinned, answering for him. "Steve's been tellin' me his junk's newsworthy for the past forty years. He's pleased as punch to rub my nose in it now."

"Rub *everybody's* nose in it, according to Mer-Ber," Steve said, waggling her in his embrace as if trying to unscrew her from the earth. His eyes were alight with pleasure.

"Oh, well, um...I'm glad you weren't offended..." Merry extricated herself with the deftness of someone who'd once had groupies.

"Takes a whole lot more than that to offend Steve," Mazel assured her.

"Hold on now," Steve interrupted, pasting a cunning expression over his delight. "What if I *was* offended? How would you make it up to me?"

"Well, I..." Merry was at a loss, but she sensed Steve already had a few ideas up his sleeve. "What would you suggest?"

His grin widened. "Mazel and I just so happen to have a bit of a side business going on. A hobby, you might say, but we think people would really dig it—*if* they heard about it." Steve fiddled with the end of one of his long gray braids, and if Merry hadn't become intimately familiar with his complete dearth of self-consciousness, she might have thought he was feeling shy. "Me and the old lady, we were talking about it the other night, and we wondered if maybe you could help us spread the word? Like, maybe you could mention it on your blog?"

"*Column*," Merry mumbled.

"Right on," Steve said, clearly not appreciating the difference.

"Our product makes a perfect holiday gift," Mazel put in brightly. "But really, it's great for any time of year."

"What is it?" Merry asked, wondering if she'd regret it.

"Come by our pad some night, dear, and we'll give you a demo."

But Merry had another pad to visit first.

Or yurt, or tipi, or earthship or whatever, she thought. Sam's lair was sure to be something out of this world.

CHAPTER TWENTY-ONE

In a hole in the ground there lived a Cassidy...

⚬⚬

"I should have known," Merry sighed.

Sam Cassidy had himself a gen-u-ine hobbit hole.

Into the banks of the cottonwood-lined creek that bordered the far side of Dolly's property, Dolly's nephew had dug himself a Tolkien-worthy den, complete with round wooden door and sloping turf roof. Merry looked down at Cleese and sighed.

"Well, boy, shall we see what quest awaits?"

The turtle, along for the ride in its clear plastic travel terrarium, nodded slightly. He seemed more ready for their excursion than Merry was. She hadn't wanted to leave him to his own devices overnight, though the truth was she didn't know what might be in store for the terrapin—or for herself—on this mission.

"Alrighty then." And Merry grasped the brass knocker set into the middle of the green-painted door. It swung open upon the first strike, all of its own accord.

"Oh, for the love of literature," she sighed. "First Tolkien, now Lewis Carroll?"

For a bunny stood, nose twitching, at the door of the hobbit hole. A plain brown bunny, with one lop ear, rather fat.

"Aren't you going to invite me in?" asked Merry—as she thought, facetiously.

"Come in already," it boomed.

Merry staggered backward, unbalanced both by the enormous picnic basket Dolly had sent her over with and by the travel terrarium she carried. And, oh, yeah, by the rabbit that had just talked to her.

"Are you deaf? I said get in here. Time's wasting."

What was it with bunnies and time? She searched for evidence of a top hat or pocket watch, but the rabbit was pretty ordinary, not counting its powers of speech. It turned and hopped back into the house, and, bemused, Merry followed.

Cassidy (presumably the actual source of the irritable command) was nowhere to be seen, but that was okay. Merry needed time to take in his habitat. She gaped around her. The great room's central feature was a *tree*. A huge, knobby-barked tree—a cottonwood, Merry thought—whose ancient branches, no longer living but no less imposing for that, arched toward the ceiling, while a clever spiral staircase climbed its bole. At the top, what looked to be a loft bedroom had been nestled into the fossilized tree's crown, and hanging plants trailed down from the railings that bounded the little aerie.

Rough-hewn *latillas* wove chevron patterns along the ceiling, while thicker beams of gnarled wood with the bark still on supported walls of whitewashed adobe that had clearly been plastered by the loving hand of an expert. Free-form archways made from more plaster-and-tree-branch construction led off in several directions toward what looked to be a kitchen, a bathroom, and storage closets. The living room sported padded benches tucked against the thick-paned passive solar windows that made up one whole wall of the house, offering views of the creek, the not-so-distant mountains, and the rolling, alpaca-dotted pastureland of Dolly's ranch.

It was Wonderland meets Middle Earth.

"Hoooo, boy, Cleese," she muttered to her turtle. "We are *not* in Kansas anymore."

Merry could swear the turtle snorted. *Sorry, boy. Too many metaphors, I know.*

"Where've you been, Wookiee?" Sam appeared in the doorway of what looked to be the kitchen, judging from the copper pots hanging from a ceiling rack behind him. His ever-bare feet were so quiet on the packed-earth floor she hadn't even heard him approach. He was wearing a shabby pair of Oshkosh overalls over a faded yellow western shirt that had what might once have been tiny flowers or horses or cowboy hats printed on it. His hair formed a nimbus of I-don't-give-a-fuck around his head. He had the bunny in the crook of one elbow, and he was stroking its lop ear absently as he scowled at her. "Half the morning's gone already."

Merry ignored his surliness, too amazed by his abode to let him rile her up. "Holy crap, Sam. How on earth did you ever find such a house? Was the ranch built around it? Did Peter Jackson film a scene from *LOTR* no one knows about here?"

Sam eyed her as if he couldn't tell whether she were complimenting or insulting him. He shook his head. "I didn't find it, I made it," he mumbled.

"Like, *made it*, made it? With tools and all that?"

He rolled his eyes, but he still looked a bit shy, as if nervous about her reaction to the home. "With tools and all that," he confirmed.

"*Daaaamn*, Llama Boy." Her pirate brow rose. "You've got some seriously hidden talents."

He snorted. "Seriously hidden, or seriously talented?"

"Bit of both," Merry said, her lip curling up.

Sam let the bunny down gently at his feet and crossed his arms, but he was only reluctantly scowling now. Merry didn't fail to notice how his biceps and pecs stretched the fabric of his shirt. He turned and gestured for her to follow him through the house, bunny hopping at his heels as if carrots would sprout from them. *They might too*, thought Merry. Sam swiped his hat from a hook on the wall and smashed it over the haystack on his head. "C'mon, we'd better get out back and greet our guests. I've already kept them waiting too long because of you, and they're probably getting hungry."

She hefted the substantial wicker basket as she hurried after him. "Who're we feeding today anyway, a pack of ravening wolves?"

"Pretty much," Sam said. "Come meet them."

And he led the way through the kitchen, past the mudroom, and out the back door. Where the hungry wolves awaited.

Merry's guts went cold.

CHAPTER TWENTY-TWO

When confronted by wild adolescents, make no sudden moves. They can smell a fogy a mile away. And woe betide the fool who betrays uncoolitude for even a microsecond. For she shall be heaped with scorn such as the world has never known...

☙

Teenagers.

She was surrounded by teenagers.

Sullen, scowly teenagers.

Is there any other kind? Merry thought. Her feet had grown roots in the doorway (appropriate enough, given that the doorframe was practically woven from roots). But Sam was having none of her hesitation. "C'mon, Wookiee, the kids are waiting," he said, and shoved her out into the sunlight.

Merry barely had time to take in her surroundings—a well-tended vegetable patch, with a lattice of climbing grapevines overhead providing shade for the motley crew who stood, in various poses of studied nonchalance, under it. Five sets of eyes narrowed on her. Five sets of arms crossed over chests that ranged from underfed to overstuffed. Five chins lifted, and five mouths made moues of distinct disdain.

"Whoa, Sam. Where'd you find the Brienne of Tarth look-alike?" asked the meanest, nastiest, snottiest-looking one. Merry, who'd endured more than her fair share of bullying, zeroed in on the source of the snark unerringly. It was the lone girl who had spoken. She had piercings in lips, ears, and nose, and a purple-dyed ponytail shellacked up high on her head.

Merry shot a glance at Sam, uncertain that it was her place to tackle this offensive, but he just gazed back, blasé as could be. *Thanks for throwing me to the wolves*, she thought. Of course, he probably didn't watch *Game of Thrones*—she'd seen no TV inside the hobbit hole—so he'd have no cause to catch the reference. *Not that he'd be likely to come to my defense anyhow. Nope, I'm on my own here. So what would Brienne do?*

She'd face her opponent head-on, is what she'd do. With a broadsword. Merry took a deep breath, pasted on the most engaging grin she could dredge up, and stood up to her full height, facing the teens. The boys, she saw, were all snickering, following the example of what was obviously their ringleader. All except one, a runty-looking kid with dark circles under his eyes and acne scars, probably about sixteen. He was staring at Merry with particular intensity. No, with *recognition*.

"Hey," he said, venturing forward hesitantly. "Aren't you...?"

"Hagrid?" one of the other boys quipped, flashing a look at the girl for approval. She high-fived him.

"Naw, more like Optimus Prime," said another. More snickering. But the skinny kid shook his head, peering up at Merry with something close to awe. He shot his compatriots an impatient glare. "Don't you dweebs know anything? This is *Merry Manning*."

Blank looks and sneers.

"Duh. She was in the *Olympics*."

Well, just the once, Merry thought. She shifted uncomfortably under the teens' scrutiny, aware as well of Sam at her side, looking at her with baffled interest.

The kid was gazing up at her with mingled adoration and astonishment. "Right? You were that skier, who won all the medals a few years ago?"

For a second, caught in the spotlight of all those adolescent eyes—and worse, Sam's—Merry was tempted to deny it. Dealing with fans—or anything to do with her now-faded fame—had always been the worst part of Merry's former career. But she sensed the kid was low man on the totem pole, and his peers would turn on him in a heartbeat for any perceived weakness.

"Yes, that was me," she said, ratcheting up her smile to professional strength and striding forward with the entirely fake confidence her mother had drilled into her. She extended her hand to shake the boy's. "It's nice to meet you. What's your name?"

The kid looked starstruck, and it seemed to be going around. The other boys—including Sam—were looking uncertain. Even Purple Hair had lost her sneer. "I'm Joey," the kid said bashfully.

"Hey, Joey. It's nice to meet you," she said again. "And how about you guys?" She spread the smile around to the rest of the group, watching their faces transform from hostile to halfway human.

Sam came forward, gathering the kids together with a gesture like a mother goose chivvying her goslings into order. "Survivors, let me introduce you to our temporary ranch hand, Merry Manning. She's visiting from..." He paused, looking at Merry with a certain chagrin. "Uh, I guess I never asked where you're from, did I?"

No, you didn't. That would have required pleasantries. Merry had grown up all over the world, and didn't particularly identify with any one place. "Chicago, most recently," she said.

"Right, Chicago, and she's a travel writer. She's working on some stories about the Last Chance for her online magazine." Another pause, more chagrin. "You kids cool with being in a magazine article?"

Their eyes widened. Sam's narrowed as a thought occurred to him. To Merry, he side-mouthed, "Ah, do I need to get release forms or something?"

"Only if I use their pictures and their real names. We can ask their parents afterward."

"That might be tough," Sam said quietly. "These kids haven't got the most, um . . . involved . . . families." He turned back to the teens. "Why don't you introduce yourselves to Ms. Manning—"

"Call me Merry, *please*, for the love of God." Merry pulled a face. "I feel ancient enough in present company, *Mr.* Cassidy."

One or two of the teens cracked a smile.

"Right. Say hello to Merry."

"Yo. I'm Thaddeus." This came from a tall, budding lothario with overly gelled hair and an attitude that said he knew he was irresistible. He had the sleeves of his white tee shirt rolled up to his shoulders to reveal arms that were corded with muscle, which he was flexing at the magenta-hued girl with no particular subtlety.

"Hi, Thaddeus," said Merry.

"You could call me Thad if you want," he said gruffly.

"I'll do that," Merry said with a smile. She turned to the next boy. "And you are?"

"Mikey." He was a plump, sandy-haired kid with more smudges than clean spots on his oversized tee shirt and torn jeans. He couldn't have been above fifteen.

"Hey, Mikey. Pleasure to meet you."

The boy colored, staring down at his feet. Merry let him off the hook. "And who's our curly-haired friend?"

"I'm Bernie." The kid was a born charmer (now that he was no longer scowling), with wild, corkscrew curls and chocolate brown eyes like a Labrador's. "You can call me Bernito, or Beebs, or B-Bomb. Anything but *Bernardo*. Cool?"

Merry nodded, smiling her promise to the boy. She looked expectantly at the last of the group.

A pause, but eventually the girl gave it up. "I'm Zelda." Her crossed arms trumpeted just how impressed she wasn't, but her toe, tapping in Chuck Taylors that had been graffitied over with markers into a colorful abstract painting, showed she was nervous in Merry's presence. "So, what, like, you used to be like on TV and shit?" She shot a glance at Sam, then amended, "I mean, and stuff."

Merry darted her own glance at Sam, whose expression was approving of the girl's belated retraction. Interesting. Prickly as they were, the kids seemed to worship Sam.

"She used to be on the US Ski Team," Joey volunteered, seeming to enjoy being the possessor of proprietary information.

Captain, actually, Merry thought, but saying so would have been blowing her own horn a tad too much. "It's true, I was," she said. "But I don't ski anymore. Anyhow, today's not about me. It's about you guys. So, Sam"—she turned the smile up to blinding—"what's on tap for us on this excursion?"

Momentarily, Sam seemed knocked off kilter by the wattage of the smile. Then he shook off his bemusement, hooking his thumbs in the pockets of his overalls and rocking back on his callus-crusted heels like a proper rancher. "Right! I promised you guys last time we'd be going balls to the wall this go-round, and I mean to keep that promise."

There were some smothered grins at his choice of phrase, but Sam kept on going. "I don't care what you may have heard outside of this circle, what people tell you at home or around town. You guys are badass. I don't call you 'the Survivors' for nothing. You've made me proud these past few months, and I think you've proven you're ready for just about anything I can dish. Am I right?"

"*Fuckin' A* right!" yelled Thad.

"You know it, dude," Bernie said, ruffling up his hair into a lion's mane and making fearsome faces at the other boys.

Mikey flashed gang signs and assumed a pose of supreme confidence. Joey just smiled shyly.

Zelda rolled her eyes at their antics, but Merry noticed her cheeks had flushed at Sam's praise.

"Alright. So, *since* you're such badasses, I figured you're not going to freak out if I really challenge you this time. I'm talking a twenty-four-hour *immersive experience*." He paused to give them each a lingering look, as if measuring their mettle. The teens stood up straighter. "Today's survival scenario is all about roughing it, like you'd do if you were caught out lost on the woods and had to make it through the night with no time to prepare. Now, did you all bring your overnight gear with you?"

There was some shuffling around, and Merry noticed a pile of packs at the feet of the teens. Most of them were beat-up old school book bags, scribbled over with band logos and anarchy signs, ripped and torn. One was the same magenta as Zelda's hair. The kids nodded.

"Did I *tell* you to bring overnight gear?" Sam's eyes were alight in a way Merry had rarely seen. *He loves these kids*, she realized. *Loves 'em like his llamas*.

Bernie spoke up. "Well, no, but dude, you did say we were gonna be out all night..."

Mikey cut in. "And, like, it's barely fifty overnight."

"I brought my old man's camp stove and sleeping bag," Joey said softly. "I'm sure he wouldn't mind."

"Well, dump it all in the house, guys. You aren't going to need it."

"I don't travel without my eyeliner," Zelda informed them loftily. "Girl's gotta have standards, amirite?" She glanced shyly at Merry as the only other female present, but, seeing Merry wasn't wearing any, seemed to deflate.

"Eyeliner too, Zelda. You can get reacquainted with your cosmetics tomorrow."

Huge sigh. But she trooped into Bag End with the others, tossing her knapsack with a distinctly teenaged thunk onto the mudroom floor. Before the kids could return, Merry gave Sam a skeptical look. Eyeliner might not be de rigueur for a camping trip, but she was pretty sure blankets and flashlights and s'mores were. "Um, Sam? Is it wise to go without any gear up into these mountains? Like the little guy—what was his name, Mickey?— said, it gets pretty darn cold up there overnight."

Sam scowled. "Mikey," he corrected. "Are you questioning my judgment? Do you seriously think I'd endanger these children?"

"Well, no, but..."

"We all have hidden depths, Ms. I-failed-to-mention-I-was-in-the-Olympics. You weren't always a writer? Well, I wasn't always a llama wrangler—*or* a Wall Street shill, for that matter. Before I came to Dolly's to help her run the ranch, I was a certified survival instructor. I've taught kids *and* adults primitive skills for years, and I've never lost a student yet. I don't intend to now."

Merry felt a pang of conscience. Not because she'd questioned Sam's judgment—she'd be happy to do that all day long—but because she hadn't done her research. A professional journalist should have done more thorough background on her subjects. Not that Sam had been any too forthcoming about his past with her—or welcoming in any way whatsoever—but still. *I'll do better from here on out*, she promised herself. *My readers deserve it.*

"Anyhow," Sam added grudgingly, "I'm not going to starve them." He gestured to the enormous picnic basket Merry had laid at her feet. "With my adult excursions, we go without the smorgasbord, and just eat what we can forage. But you can't do that to teenagers unless you want a riot on your hands. Besides, while the idea here is that they learn something that helps them become more self-reliant, some of these kids already know more about deprivation than you or I ever will."

Merry thought of how skinny Joey was, how Mikey's clothes seemed to have come straight from the rag bin. Her heart ached. "So what's the plan?"

"You'll find out when they do, Wookiee," he said.

The teens trooped back out to surround them again before Merry could flip him the bird he so richly deserved.

"So, dude, what're we s'posed to do without our shit?" Thad said, forcing his voice into its lowest register. "You want we should cuddle together for warmth?" He grabbed Zelda around the waist and made humping motions while the other boys howled with laughter. Merry started forward, but Zel was way ahead of her. She snatched hold of Thaddeus's ear and gave it a twist that had him yelping and crying uncle.

"Thaddeus, we talked about this," Sam said sternly. "We do not dry hump our fellow survivalists."

Bernie fell out laughing, his snorts and giggles contagious.

"Except Bernie. You can dry hump him."

"Hey!"

"Alright, enough, you reprobates. Daylight's burning, and we've got miles to cover before we make camp."

"What's a reprobate?"

"Look it up in the dictionary, Thaddy-puss," Mikey advised. "You'll see your ugly face staring back."

"I'll show you ugly face, you little..."

Zelda snapped her fingers in Thad's face and said one word. "Chill."

Thad chilled.

Merry hid a smile. *She has that boy wrapped around her little finger, and hoo-boy-howdy does she know it.*

"If you're finished clowning around, Survivors, circle round and I'll give you the equipment that's gonna save your life tonight." Sam grabbed a box that had been on the ground beside his bare feet. A box... *of lawn and leaf bags.* He whipped one out with a flourish and handed the slippery black plastic to Merry, who accepted it with all the enthusiasm of someone receiving a dead fish. Then he proffered the box to each of the teens in turn. "Here's your gear, guys."

"What're we supposed to do with this? Tidy up the forest like Yogi Bear?" Bernie flapped his trash bag open, looking hopefully inside as if he might find a nice propane stove and some hot dogs.

"I'd never ask you to clean anything, Beebs," Sam said on a smile. "Badass you may be, but every man has his limits, and tidiness is clearly beyond you." His gaze rested on Bernie's wild-and-woolly hair, and the boy grinned and shook his head to send the mass even higher.

Merry noticed Sam hadn't subjected Mikey to the same teasing, and her estimation of him rose, for clearly Mikey's dishevelment had more to do with his home life than his personal habits.

Sam scraped his own hair back under his hat and settled it

more firmly on his head, obviously eager to get the show on the road. "We're learning the art of self-reliance here. With just this one tool, and the skills I'm going to teach you, you'll come through in great shape. So stow those bags in your pockets, tighten those shoelaces, and hit the bathroom if you need it. It's the last chance before it's all leaves and squatting in the bush for the next twenty-four hours."

Zelda looked faint. Merry didn't blame her.

Sam wasn't concerned for their tender sensibilities. "Merry, would you please go fetch Snape from the pen over yonder?" Merry gave him a goggle-eyed glance for this unaccustomed politeness, but he just waved out past the vegetable patch, up a dirt track, where, now that she put her ears to it, Merry could hear the unmistakable hum that was Severus's morning warm-up song. *Glad he's treating me with a bit of respect in front of the kids, at least.* "He's already haltered up and waiting," Sam informed her. "Just don't be drawing any fire this time, you hear me? We haven't got time to hose you off again." He flashed a grin at the kids. "You wouldn't believe how much the llamas love to lob loogies at our friend Merry here."

"It's true," Merry had to admit. "I'm a loog-magnet." The boys made "ew, gross" faces that made them look, suddenly, very young and sweet. Zelda just shuddered.

"Zel, why don't you help Merry load up Snape's panniers with the picnic basket Dolly sent over, and make sure you secure those four-gallon water canisters too. Don't forget to distribute the weight equally or our lunch is gonna get mighty dusty dragging on the ground. Once we're loaded up, we'll get moving on up the mountain. Oh, and Merry, make sure the tincture of iodine's still in the small pouch at the front, okay? We'll probably be sucking stream water by morning."

Ew, gross indeed.

"Can Snape carry that much?" Merry asked as Zel took off up the path, towing the picnic basket and leaving the far heavier water jugs for Merry. Her new friend was doughty, but that was a heck of a lot of food and water...

"He's a *llama*. He could probably hump half those kids up the mountain and not break a sweat."

"Oh." Suddenly, Merry remembered. "Um, in that case, is there room for one more?" She held up Cleese's travel terrarium.

Sam's lip twitched. "You brought your turtle?"

"What? He gets separation anxiety. I didn't want him to languish in my cabin while I got to have some fabulous adventure. And I can't leave him at your place now. He might get in a race with your rabbit, and who knows what sort of tesseract of bad literary metaphors they could create in there without supervision."

The lip twitched some more. Then he sighed. "Fine, pop him in there. The kids will love him. But if he gets llama-sick, *you're* cleaning it up."

⚬

Sam gathered the flock to him and off we trooped, Von Trapp–style, into the pristine wilderness for our overnight adventure. Now, Sam's charges—whom he calls the Survivors—are no children of privilege like the adorable Austrian warblers. In fact, these kids are a lot hardier—and harder up. For the truth is, charming as Aguas Milagros is, New Mexico can be a tough place to grow up. Poverty is pervasive, the education system sucks (at forty-ninth in the country in terms of success, I'm told the state motto is, "Hey, at least we're not Mississippi!"), and alcoholism and drug abuse are rampant as well.

Tight-knit as this community is, some of the kids fall through the cracks.

Sam catches 'em.

∞

Sam walked alongside Merry and Snape, the kids ranging ahead of them up the trail with an energy Merry envied. Her leg seemed to be holding up better as the days at the Last Chance went on, but she was still struggling not to limp in front of Llama Boy. He might show a softer side around the kids—and Merry wasn't going to argue he was awesome with them—but she had no such faith he'd stay Mr. Mush when they were alone.

She eyed him warily.

He eyed her back.

Merry increased her stride, but he kept pace with her effortlessly on those bare feet of his.

He said nothing.

He said it a lot.

"*What*," she finally snapped.

"What, what?"

"I know you're dying to ask, so just get it over with."

"Alright then," he said. "So, you weren't just blowing smoke up my ass with that whole 'I've already been famous' thing?" He gave her a searching look. "Like, really famous?"

"Well, I'm no Kardashian, but yeah, if you think of athletes as famous, I wasn't exactly hiding under a rock."

"You're under one now," he pointed out, gesturing to the dusty track that wound up into the mountains. "No cameras here, no adoring fans."

"Yeah, well, your fans stop adoring you pretty fast once you stop spreading butter on the mashed potatoes and start spreading your guts across the finish line."

"Butter on the mashed potatoes?" His face was a mask of incomprehension.

"Yeah, you know. Carving the gnar pow. Thrashing the sickey poo. Shredding the cheddar."

"Either you're hungry, suffering intestinal distress, or you're teaching me ski slang."

Merry allowed a smile to escape. "The latter. Well, and the first one too. Not so much with the intestinal distress, but if you're going to be forcing me to drink water that needs iodine to make it safe, I can't promise that won't come later."

Sam studied her face, then ran his gaze down her body to rest on her left leg. The one he'd seen the night of the centipede attack and knew was covered in scar tissue. "So what happened?"

"I crashed."

He sucked on his teeth meditatively, nodded. "Bad?"

"Yeah. Bad."

He let that sit awhile as they hiked up the track, Severus pacing between them. "I'm sorry, Wookiee," he said at last.

Her throat tightened. How many times had she heard the same, from how many well-meaning people? Yet somehow, coming from Cassidy, the words felt both simpler and more sincere. "I'm fine now," she said gruffly. "Long as it's cool if I co-opt your llamas for crutches once in a while." She patted Snape's neck, and the beast responded by whuffling her neck...and then attempting to steal her well-monched hat. "How did you get involved with the fabulous five over there?" she asked, changing the subject. "It's obvious you mean the world to those kids."

Sam shrugged uncomfortably, reaching into the pocket of his overalls for a carrot to feed Snape. He wiped the resulting drool off on the denim, ignoring Merry's wince. "It started with Joey," he said, nodding to the littlest of the bunch, who was fending off a Star Wars–style stick incursion by Bernie and Mikey with a stick lightsaber of his own. "I noticed this scrawny slip of a kid was hanging round the ranch a lot, at odd times of the day, when he should have been at school. He was so skittish I could barely get him to say hello, but he loved the animals, and honestly he didn't seem to have anywhere else to go. Came to find out, Dolly had been feeding him on the side, like a stray cat. His mom didn't seem to notice, or care, and his father . . ." Sam shook his head, eyes gone stormy. "Better that asshole stays gone."

"Mm," Merry said. Her eyes softened as she watched the boy try to keep up with the others. "Poor muffin."

"He holds his own surprisingly well," Sam said. "Sometimes I worry more about Thad, to tell you the truth."

"Really?" Merry examined the tall, well-built boy, but he seemed without a care in the world, trotting backward up the trail so he could talk with Zelda, who was just behind him. *Kid like that's probably the most popular boy in his class*, she thought. "Why?"

"Thad was the second of my strays," Sam told her. "A lot smarter than he looks, but he's dyslexic, and no one intervened early on. Or pretty much at all. He's basically illiterate, though he hides it well. His folks are migrant fruit pickers, so he stays with his grandmother out here a lot of the year, and she doesn't speak English, so she hasn't been able to help much. She has some health issues too. Thad takes care of her as best he can, but he doesn't have a lot of prospects and he knows it. Makes him a mite prickly, but underneath it he's sweet as they come. He just needs someone to give him a chance."

Merry looked at the stiff way the tall teen held himself, the branch he held out of the way for Zelda to walk under. The fact that Sam had seen through the boy's façade made her look at Sam's own façade a little more closely.

Where there is anger, there's pain underneath.

Bob was wise. Maybe someday she'd learn what made Sam so prickly around her too.

"And the others?"

"Mikey and Bernie are local kids who come from generations of government assistance. Good kids, but they don't get much example of what it's like to work hard for what you want. There's a lot of malaise and hardscrabble living round here—and to tell you the truth, there aren't a lot of jobs for those who want 'em. When they heard I was starting up a program for at-risk youth, their folks sent them to me for a chance to learn something new."

"And Zelda?"

Sam's lip twisted. "She's one tough nut I've yet to crack. Showed up one morning and told me 'no more sausage fests, Mr. Cassidy. I want in.' She doesn't attend the local school with the other kids. Lives somewhere near Taos, but I've never seen her parents. They either homeschool her or...well, I'm honestly not sure. She doesn't like to talk about herself, that much I know. She usually hitches a ride out here, gets dropped off over by Bob's. Maybe you'll get more out of her than I can," he said. "She seems to look up to you."

"Everybody does," Merry said wryly. "I wouldn't put much stock in it."

Sam laughed—a good, honest laugh, with no mockery in it.

"Listen, Sam," Merry said, "I can see what you're doing here is important for these kids. I just want you to know that no matter what, I won't slow you down or ruin their experience today."

Sam's blue eyes were keen as he looked her over again. "I've no doubt. Seems to me a woman who climbed a mountain on a bum leg can probably handle herself."

Merry found herself warming all over, despite her resolve to keep him at arm's length. "Why, Sam Cassidy, are you telling me I'm not 'hopeless' after all?"

His cheeks flushed darker than his perma-tan could cover. But his tone was light. "There may be hope for you yet, Ms. Manning."

CHAPTER TWENTY-THREE

The outing with Sam and his teen-tastic charges turned out to be a big, fat nothing.

"What?!"

I can hear your disbelief from here. "How can anything Studly Sam does turn out to be a dud?" Well, I didn't say dud, now did I? I said, "nothing."

Which was exactly all Sam Cassidy allowed us to bring on our overnight adventure.

Okay, I hyperbolize. We were each allowed one huge-ass garbage bag.

Like, whoopee.

Now, I don't know if you know anything about the mountains of Northern New Mexico, but there's one thing they ain't, and that's warm at night. So when I tell you that the aforementioned waste receptacle was intended to serve as duvet, pillow, and mattress to boot, you may infer that there were a number of pouts round the campfire last night. Some of them even came from the teenagers.

But let me start from the beginning. Which in this case was the Stone Age. For, once we arrived at our campsite, a lovely little spot among the aspen and scrub oak by a babbling brook, what followed was a great deal of bashing of rocks against other rocks, a vast whacking and smacking engaged upon with a fair degree of zeal by our young charges, and a deal less enthusiasm by yours truly, who has rather more regard for her thumbs.

∞

"Ow! Fu— uh, fudge!" Merry hissed, casting a sheepish glance at the kids, who were smacking rocks together as Sam had taught them. "Making discoidal knives," he'd said. Discordant, more like, if the banging was anything to go by.

Most of the teens seemed to have caught the hang of the exercise. Flakes of sharp stone piled up at their knees where they knelt in the shade of the rustling aspens—primitive knives formed from nothing but force and physics, and a little of Sam's expertise. But not everyone had caught the knack—or knap—of it.

"How you doing over there, Mikey?" Sam, who was kneeling near Merry, called to the boy. The towheaded kid looked up, tongue wedged between his teeth. In his pudgy hands he held two rocks he'd salvaged from the streambed, one big and rounded, the other a wedge shape, as Sam had taught them.

"I can't get it to flake like you showed me," he said. His cheeks were red, and Merry could see moisture in his eyes that told her it was more than just the noonday heat that had him flushed. Frustration oozed from every pore, and shame hung like a cloud around his head. *I feel ya, kid*, she thought. Her own inadequacies—especially since she'd hired on to be the worst ranch hand in the world—often made her want to curl up under a rock and hide. But somehow, seeing Mikey struggle, the only thing Merry felt was compassion.

Sam obviously felt it too. "Come over here and I'll help you." Sam patted the bare earth between himself and Merry. The kid knee-walked over to them and plopped down in jeans that were nearly as dirty as the earth beneath them. *Someone has not been doing this kid's laundry*, Merry thought, aching for him all the more. Whatever struggles she'd faced over the years, she'd never had to worry about the fundamentals the way Mikey and the others did. Even now, deep in debt and facing an uncertain career, she knew she'd never starve so long as she could swallow her pride. These kids had no such safety net—and yet they were out here, trying their best. It was humbling. As was the quiet love and guidance Sam gave the teens.

"See now, all you have to do is find the sweet spot, that little acute angle." Sam's callused paws engulfed the boy's littler ones, adjusting his grip gently. "Relax your arms, let the swing come naturally, and allow the stone to tell you where it wants to flake."

Mikey took a halfhearted swipe, but the rocks just rang dully together, the bottom one developing a scratch but refusing to give up the goods. Mikey's lip trembled, and his face reddened even further. "I suck at this. I don't want to do this anymore." He threw the bigger rock into the trees, scrunching into himself miserably.

Wow, that sounds familiar, Merry thought, feeling as if the stone had hit her square in the forehead. How many times had she said the same? *But it sounds so harsh when* he *says it*. She wanted to comfort the boy, but it didn't seem like her place to do so, just an hour after meeting him.

Thankfully, Sam had the situation in hand. He gave Mikey a minute, and then handed him his own striker rock to use, curling the boy's hand around the stone. "Don't sweat it, Mike. You got this. Just do exactly what Merry *isn't* doing, and it's in the bag."

Mike cracked a reluctant smile, and, the moment he relaxed, he cracked the *rock* in exactly the right place. A perfect oval of stone flaked off, sharp as could be. "I did it!" he cried.

Yes! Merry thought. She exchanged a grin with Sam, who sat back on his bare heels, beaming with quiet pride. *Like a proud papa*. Her cheeks went rosy for no reason she could fathom, and she looked away quickly.

The others looked up at Mikey's yell. "Give Pig-Pen a medal," Thaddeus snorted, scooching closer to Zelda and looking to her for approval. But she just curled her pierced lip at him and tossed her ponytail huffily. "Rock on, Mikey," she called over to the sandy-haired boy.

Hm. Maybe Zelda's not just the pack leader. She's a bit of a den mother too. Merry's heart warmed to the girl.

Bernie dissolved in giggles that made Merry revise his age down to perhaps thirteen, but his humor wasn't at his compatriot's expense. "Rock on? Get it, *rock* on?"

Zelda allowed a smile to replace her sneer. "You laugh like that, people are gonna think you're *stoned*."

Even Thad smiled at that.

Mikey just pocketed his blade with care, looking about two feet taller than he had before the exercise.

"Alright, Survivors. I think we've got enough knives. Now let's start getting our fire and shelter sorted out. Gather up the best flakes and let's head for the stream banks for those dogbane reeds I showed you earlier."

About making hand drills and reverse-wrap dual-ply cordage, I will say only this, dear friends: extremely useful skills, very hard to describe on paper. Check out my photos for the exemplary results of our intrepid team's efforts!

Within hours, we had chosen a lovely little spot close enough to a stream to provide water, but not so close as to add wind chill and "convection"—the dangers of which Sam was adamant about, along with a whole host of other things to avoid. (Wiping keisters with poisonous plants being high on my personal list.) Suffice it to say the selection of our campsite took the best part of an hour, and the grooming thereof another. This, we only knew after Sam showed us how to count time by measuring our fingers against the sky, for our cell phones and watches had been packed away as contraband. (I was allowed to keep an old camera only because of my reportorial duty to you, my friends.) Lean-to built, fire pit dug, and kindling kindled (we pretty much reenacted Tom Hanks's performance in Cast Away, *screaming "I ... have made ... fire!!!" when we'd made fire), we stuffed our trash bags and our shirts full of roughage in preparation for the drastic shift in temperature that was to come.*

By the time all was in readiness for the night, the Survivors were glowing with pride at their accomplishments, and Sam was looking over them like an indulgent (and hot-as-hell) papa.

Me?

Well, hell. Not to get too maudlin here, gentle readers, but the honest truth is, I was totally humbled by the gumption of these kids today. They have spirit, they've got stick-to-itiveness, and they're funny, smart, and brave as all get-out. And most of all, they remind me that it's not where you come from but what you make of yourself that really matters.

⸎

"Duuuuuuude," Bernie groaned. "These leaves are crunching all up in my crack. How'm I supposed to sleep in a bed of raisin bran, brah?"

"At least you *got* leaves," Mikey said. "All I could find was some straw. At least I think it was straw. It feels like shish kebab skewers."

"It's not so bad," Joey said softly. "I slept in worse places."

"That's because your daddy drank away your double-wide, dorkus." Thad, huddled in his threadbare jean jacket across the fire pit from Joey, tossed a twig at the smaller boy. He'd been getting progressively more irritable as the day went on. Though he'd excelled at all the primitive skills Sam had shown them, easily outshining the other kids with his instinctive knack for woodcraft, even his successes only seemed to make him angrier and more withdrawn. Now he had Cleese's terrarium out and was fiddling with the catch at the top. He reached in and extracted the turtle with hands that, to Merry's eyes, seemed just a bit too rough, and set Cleese closer to the fire than Merry liked. "You don't know from real beds, Joey," he jeered. "But I bet your mama does."

The camp went dead silent, except for the collective sucking in of breath.

Even in the fading light of dusk, Merry could see Joey had gone pale.

Sam caught Merry's arm before she could intervene—either for the sake of her turtle or her young admirer. "Give them a minute," he said softly at her ear. Merry's lizard brain couldn't help noticing the strength of the hand that gripped her biceps, and the warmth of his breath against her nape. But then again, it was a lizard, and couldn't be expected to have good taste. "Part of this experience is to give them space to let them work everyday conflicts out on their own," Sam continued.

"But—" She didn't want roast turtle for dessert. Yet even less did she want to see little Joey bullied by the bigger boy.

"Trust me, Wookiee. I know these kids."

Merry subsided reluctantly.

Joey had jumped to his feet, his slight frame vibrating with fury. "You take that back!"

"You gonna make me?" Thad rose too, dwarfing the younger boy, and stripped off his jacket to reveal his bulging muscles.

Out of the corner of her eye, Merry saw Zelda's hands reach

out and quietly retrieve the turtle from the fireside, settling him in her lap and zipping her purple windbreaker around them both. The girl snicked a bit of lettuce from the sandwich at her side and fed it to Cleese.

Joey paused, swallowed audibly. "Yeah," he said. "Yeah, I am." His fists were clenched, and his chin trembled in the twilight and the wavering light of the fire.

Merry's heart clenched at his bravery. "Sam," she whispered, "are you sure . . . ?"

"I'm sure." Squatting next to Merry, he rested his hands loosely at his sides, eyes unwavering on the two boys who were squaring off.

He wasn't the only one riveted by the confrontation. Mikey had drawn up his knees under his ratty tee shirt, squinching into himself and watching nervously. Bernie's sweet brown eyes were filled with worry as he looked on. "Ultimate fighting cage match is that way, boys," he said, pointing down the mountain. "This here is a low-T zone. Well, as low-T as a bunch of badasses like us can manage, ha, ha."

The two ignored him, eyes locked on each other's. The space between them crackled in a way that had nothing to do with the fire they'd built to keep the night at bay.

"You know I could kick your ass from here to next Sunday, right, dweeb?" Thad's eyes had narrowed with something akin to puzzlement, as if he could not comprehend the idea of someone as small as Joey standing up to him. "You really want me to do that in front of everyone?"

"I don't care," Joey said resolutely. "You're gonna take it back, or we're gonna get into it, right here and now."

"Why you wanna defend that drugged-out whore anyhow?" Thad demanded, shifting his feet a bit. "She never did shit for you—except leave you out in the cold while she bones some meth dealer for her next hit."

"At least my mom's *around*," Joey said. A single tear spilled over his cheeks, but he held his reedy voice steady. "She didn't just dump me with some old lady and take off like *your* folks did."

"They're *working*," Thad said hotly. "You know, that thing your daddy never figured out how to do?"

Joey looked at the bigger boy in silence, clearly measuring more than his muscles. For a minute, to Merry, he seemed the taller of the two. His stance changed from scared puppy to something almost...confident. Like he'd figured something out about his foe, and suddenly...well, maybe he wasn't an enemy after all. "Yeah, they're working," he said. "Same as a lot of folks around here. But do *you* really want to pick fruit all your life too?" To Merry's ears, the question sounded less like an insult and more like a challenge. "'Cause that's where you're headed if you keep blowing off school and getting in trouble, Thaddeus. I know it, you know it. Everybody here knows it."

Thad looked around the fire; shame, fury, and defensiveness radiating from his body. Merry found herself barely breathing, and at her side, she could feel Sam was wired to step in, watchful. He put his hand on her knee, but it was hardly less edgy than she was. "Hold steady," he said quietly, his eyes darting between the boys. "I won't let anything happen."

Somehow, Merry believed him.

"And, what? You think farting around in the woods like a bunch of fairies is going to change things? Make your daddy stop beating on you and your mom every time he comes around drunk?" Thaddeus rounded on the other two boys. "You think rubbing sticks together and building Boy Scout shelters is gonna get you the hell out of this one-horse town? Get you into college?

Find you a job?" He laughed bitterly. "Dream on, you morons. None of us is going anywhere."

"Then why are you here, if you think that?" The question came from Zelda. "Nobody's forcing you."

"Maybe I just came for a chance at your sweet snatch," he said, leering.

Zelda's mouth dropped open, a flush blooming across her cheeks. Merry sucked in her breath in shock.

"Enough," Sam said. He'd risen to his feet so quietly Merry hadn't even heard him. "Apologize to Zelda. Right now."

Next to the still-sprouting Thaddeus, Sam was like a boulder, immutable, immovable, and just as rock steady. Thad seemed to shrink down in size until he was just a boy again, unsure of himself and aware he'd gone too far. He looked from Sam to Zelda, whose arms were crossed defensively inside her windbreaker. Tears of anger and hurt trembled on her mascara-clotted lashes.

"Sorry, Zel," he mumbled. "That wasn't cool."

"Fuck you, sleazoid," Zelda sniffed, but she tossed her hair in a way that told Merry she'd already half forgiven the boy.

"Now how about Joey, while you're at it?" Sam prompted. "I think you owe him an apology."

"For what? Telling the truth?" Some of Thad's belligerence returned. "Everyone knows his mom's the trailer park hoochie."

"That's not true. My mom's *not* a whore!" Joey insisted hotly. "She just...she just..." His voice broke, and he started gulping air. "She can't help how she is. And if people like you didn't give her such a hard time, maybe she could get better."

"Hate to break it to you, Joe Blow, but people like her *never* get better. Sooner you realize that, the better off you'll be."

"And what about people like *you*, Thaddeus?" Joey was steaming, even though his cheeks were wet with tears.

"What's that supposed to mean? People like me?"

"Illiterate people." Joey crossed his arms and lifted his chin. "Everybody here knows you can't read anything harder than *Goodnight Moon*."

"You're gonna regret that—" Thad started around the fire, pushing past Sam.

Mikey stuck a foot out.

Thad went down—thankfully into the pile of leaves they'd gathered for insulation, and not the fire. He sprawled out in an undignified tangle of arms and legs, sending leaves scattering in all directions.

No one laughed.

"Who did that?"

"Musta been a tree root," Bernie said. "That or you're a total klutz, brah."

The redness in Thad's face was evident even in the waning light of approaching nightfall.

Joey stepped forward before Thad could jump back to his feet, quicker even than Sam, who had moved to intercept him. The slender kid stuck his hand in front of Thaddeus's face. "Take it or break it, Thaddeus," he said quietly. "But either way I'm not backing down."

For a moment Merry thought Thad would choose the latter, and she bit her lip, thinking how little fun it would be to cart the kids down the mountain in the middle of the night in search of medical attention—and perhaps the aid of law enforcement.

Then Thaddeus cracked a smile. It lit up his face and showed Merry for a second what a heartbreaker he was going to be when he was fully grown. "Good for you, Joe." He took the smaller boy's hand and let him help him to his feet, though the assist was clearly not needed. "Maybe you aren't a total pussy after all."

"And maybe *you're* not a total asshat, but the jury's still out," Joey said.

The two other boys loosened up visibly. Zelda, stroking Cleese's shell, was smiling at Thad in a way that told Merry she was no more immune to his charms than he was to hers. "We could teach you to read, you know," she said. "All of us could take turns. We'd never tell anyone."

The other kids looked solemnly back at Thaddeus, nodding.

Now it was Thad's turn to have tears in his eyes, though he scrubbed them away before they could fall. "You'd do that for me?"

"Dude," Bernie said. "We're like the Three Musketeers. Or five, or whatever. Anyway, we stick together when it counts."

"We'll sort you out, Thad," Mikey said. "Just stop acting like such a jerk, okay? It's really uncool."

Thad scooped up a pile of leaves and tossed it at Mikey, but he was smiling. "Deal."

"Hey, Sammy," Bernie called, "all this chest thumping is hungry work. Did Dolly pack any dessert?"

∞

With a lean-to built of branches tied with dogbane-husk cordage to keep the warmth of our fire at least ostensibly from escaping, we bedded down at last between a layer of scrounged-up leaves and our garbage bag comforters. However, precious little comfort was to be had as the stars wheeled into view, and all trace of warmth stole away like a thief in the night.

Actually, a thief in the night would have been welcome, so long as he was willing to spoon.

There's one piece of advice I will share about overnight outdoor survival, dear friends, and that is: Do not be the outside penguin.

Remember March of the Penguins? *Where all the roly-poly emperor penguins huddle in a big stinky circle on an ice floe in Antarctica for like, ten hundred months? Well, some unlucky bastard has to be the outside penguin. And since I couldn't very well cuddle up with a bunch of teenaged boys (this is a* PG *magazine column, after all) and I was busy keeping dear Zel from a frozen grave by being "big spoon" to her little, yours truly played OP for the night. Even Snape stood me up, content to kush all by his lonesome closer to the stream. (Honestly, he farts, so I wasn't too broken up about it.)*

But what of Studly Sam? Wouldn't his arms have made the perfect haven of warmth and security a girl dreams of in a dark forest echoing with the cackles of coyotes and screeching of owls in the night? Well, perhaps, but our fearless leader had to stand sentry, did he not? Lay wakeful through the night to feed the fire and keep us all safe?

Indeed. Sam took that bullet for us, and, cold posterior notwithstanding, I was most grateful.

❧

ZZZZZZZZZZZZZZZZZ—GNUP!

Haaaaaaaaaaaawwwwwwwwwwwwww—shwishwishwi!

The sound of someone sawing logs with a wood chipper made of pure Satanism woke Merry. And not for the first time. Throughout the course of this most miserable night of her life, someone—namely the rather *un*studly Sam—had been snoring fit to wake the dead. The pile of leaves he'd burrowed under for shelter fairly shuddered with the force of his stentorian snores. Or perhaps they were his defense mechanism—no woodland beast in its right mind would disturb anything making such a monstrous ruckus.

Merry, who had slept approximately one third of a wink,

scrubbed her hands over her face and gave sleep up as a bad job. The trash bag full of last year's leaves may have served Sam's intrepid young squirts fairly well, but a six-three Amazon wasn't getting much coverage from a contractor bag. And *damn*, it was cold out here overnight. Merry had plowed into snowbanks that felt less chilly. Of course, in those days she'd been clad in space-age fabrics designed to keep competitors in peak condition, not the remains of one woefully insufficient Burberry windbreaker and a pair of skinny jeans she was coming to loathe with a passion fiery enough that it probably *should* have kept her warm. At one point, Merry had even tried to climb *inside* her leaf-stuffed bag instead of just using it as a blanket, but the resulting fiasco was worse than what little she cared to remember of prom night—all wrestling, rustling, and ultimately, disappointment.

Sam obviously had no such struggles. After the evening's dramatic confrontation, he'd made sure the kids dropped off to sleep okay, then tromped off to his own private pile of leaves, declining even a trash bag, as he'd been "training his mitochondria" for over a decade to keep his temperature optimally regulated, he said, and never felt the cold.

Bully for you, Sam Cassidy.

She snuggled deeper into her personal mulch pile, putting her arm back around Zelda to keep the girl warm. At least one of them should get some rest, she thought. *I'll just lie here and dream of Mother's Austrian goose-down feather beds, the ones at the winter chalet where we spent so many Christmases pretending to get along.* Merry started to slip back into some semblance of slumber.

This time it wasn't Sam's attempts at New Age nasal symphonics that woke her. "Um, Miss Manning?" A voice piped up in Merry's ear.

Surely the voice would go away if she ignored it. Surely the gods would not be so cruel as to snatch this last chance of rest from her, just as she was so close to achieving it?

A finger poked at the arm Merry had wrapped around her young charge. Tentative, but insistent. "Miss Manning?"

Merry said a silent prayer for generosity of spirit. "Wassup, kiddo?" she asked, scrubbing a hand over her weary face again. She looked down at the kid she'd been spooning. Zel had rolled over on her back, her dyed hair looking black in the faint light.

"I, um...that is, I have to..." The girl nibbled on her lip piercing. "Would you come with me to the bathroom?" she blurted. "I'm scared of, um...everything. Plus," she added with more spirit, "I don't want those pervs staring at my ass."

Merry felt a little bit flattered to be needed, even for so basic a function. *Sleep can wait.* "Sure, Zel. I don't know about a bathroom, but I can probably scope out a suitable tree. And I'll totally keep those pervs"—currently sleeping angelically like a pile of puppies across the fire—"from gawking where they shouldn't." With a repressed groan, she rolled stiffly to her feet, every muscle a scream after the night spent in frigid temperatures.

Zel bounced up with enviable grace, ponytail swinging as she headed out from camp. She'd found a suitable thatch of cover and had her jeans down before Merry even caught up. *Somehow I don't think she needs my help*, Merry thought. *At least not with pissing in the woods.*

When in Rome...Merry found her own bush and attended to nature's call a few feet away.

"So, ah, Miss Manning..." Zel said from her hiding place.

"Please, Zel, call me Merry. Once you've peed in the trees with someone, formalities seem a bit absurd." Merry pulled out some of the velvety wipe-safe leaves she'd stashed in her pockets and did the necessary, hoping her skin wouldn't have some horrible delayed reaction.

"Um, okay . . . Merry. So, like, I had a question. Can I ask you a question?"

Merry zipped up. "I think you just did."

"Um, like, another one?" Zelda rustled around, finishing up her own business. Her footsteps were muffled on the leaf duff as she tromped over.

Merry left off teasing. "Of course. What's on your mind?"

Zel leaned her back against an aspen tree, whose trunk barely shone white in the predawn light. She shivered, but Merry thought it was more nerves than the temperature. "So, like, you probably had a boyfriend or two, when you were younger?"

Ouch, kid. "Well, back in those days, it was all arranged marriages between us knights and damsels," she quipped. "Of course, gals like me and Brienne of Tarth, well, we weren't exactly hot commodities, but I did have one or two suitors vying to carry my favors in the lists."

Zelda colored, but wouldn't be deterred by Merry's teasing. "Yeah, um, right. So, like, what do you do if you like a guy, but he's kinda . . . I don't know, like . . . not in your same league?"

Merry's lips quirked. *Well, that's one I know plenty about,* she thought. When you were bigger and stronger than 90 percent of them, somehow that tended to have a paradoxical effect on your league stats with men. But Zelda—zesty, conventionally pretty—she'd be unlikely to have the same issues. "I don't think anyone's out of your league, sweetheart," she said to the girl. "Just in one day of knowing you, I've seen enough to know that. You're smart, you're lovely, *and* you're kind—a lot kinder than I bet you want people to know."

Zel blushed at the compliment, but she brushed it off. "Not

that kind of league," she said, with an arrogance that made Merry smile inwardly. She tossed her hair. "I mean *money*."

"Ah," said Merry. She knew a lot about that too. Having come from more wealth than she knew what to do with, she'd met her share of guys who felt intimidated by her family's fortune and prestige. She hated to think of Zel feeling that way. "I'm sure no one would judge you for not having a lot of money, Zelda—" she started.

"No, I mean, I *have* money. Like, a *lot* of money. And he doesn't."

"Ah," she said again. Merry looked the girl over, noting belatedly how her hair's dye job, even as punked-out as it was, had been done with an expert hand, and her clothes, while as trashed as the others', looked to have been deliberately demolished by a designer's fashion-conscious hand. Even her body jewelry was obviously quality, now that Merry looked. "I'm guessing you don't want him to know."

"I don't want *anyone* to know." Zelda kicked the dirt at her feet, sending leaves scattering. "Money ruins everything," she said. "My PUs are, like, these tech meganerds who made a zillion in some dot-something bubble thing way back in the nineties, and they're, like, totally clueless."

"PUs?"

"Parental units," Zel said, as if it should be obvious. "They moved out here to the middle of nowhere to 'retire' and they dragged my ass with them. I'm supposed to be in school in Taos right now with the other kids whose parents are, like, movie stars and oil billionaires and shit, but I ditched 'cause I can't stand their whiny bullshit, and how they look down on the people who *really* live here."

"Like Thaddeus?" Merry asked gently. "That is who we're talking about, right?"

Zelda colored nearly as purple as her hair. She crossed her arms tightly over her chest. "Maybe," she muttered.

"Oh, kiddo. That boy's so head over heels for you, you could be the queen of England and he'd still pull on your pigtails to get your attention."

"Pull wha—?" Zelda looked alarmed.

"Never mind. It's just something we used to say back in the dawn of time, where I'm from. It means he likes you."

"Oh. Um, cool." Zelda blushed again. "But, like, wouldn't he get all tweaked if he knew? I mean, he's worried about *real* stuff, like whether he can get his grandma her medicine. All I have to worry about is which college my folks are going to donate a library to, to get me in. Should I try to help his family out? Give them some money...or would he hate that? I thought maybe, with all those ski bucks you have, you'd know what to do."

Ski bucks. Ha. Ha-hahahahahaha. Ski bucks. But Merry did know plenty about family money, and the perils thereof. "Well, honey. I think you're right to be cautious about that kind of thing. Your boy Thad is obviously very proud. I think just being his friend is probably the best thing. What you did earlier, offering to help him with his reading...that's the kind of thing friends do for each other." *And of course, we all know what happens when teenagers study together*, she thought with an inner smile. "If, after a while, you want to let him know about your circumstances, let it come out naturally."

"You think he'll be cool?"

"Yo, Zel, you get chomped by a bear or some shit? We're about to break camp, so get your sweet butt back here!" Thad's voice, shouted through the trees, was full of energy and enthusiasm once more, as if the events of the night before had never happened.

"Yeah," Merry said, grinning. "Somehow I think he'll be cool. C'mon, let's get back to the others and see what Sam's got in store for us this morning."

They turned to head back, but Zelda stopped before they could enter the campsite, pulling her ponytail higher and tighter atop her head. She looked back at Merry with a shy gaze. "I'm sorry for what I said before. About the Brienne thing. I can be a real bitch sometimes, like, when I'm nervous or something. You're actually pretty cool, for a grown-up." She trotted down the trail to catch up with the others.

Merry smiled. *I am, aren't I?*

∽

She wasn't the only one who had a scintillating experience camping with the kids.

When Merry unpacked the terrarium from Snape's pannier upon returning to the ranch that afternoon, she blinked in disbelief, turning her turtle this way and that. "Oh, sweet Jesus," she murmured, biting her lip.

Someone had bedazzled Cleese.

His shell sparkled with tiny rhinestones set in star shapes, hearts, sunbursts, and flowers. Even his tiny toes had received an expertly done pedicure—a *purple* pedicure. He cast a forlorn look at Merry, as if to say, "the things I put up with for you, woman."

"Zellllddddaaaa!"

CHAPTER TWENTY-FOUR

The Last Chance Llama Ranch is, you might say, about second *chances as much as anything else. My overnight outing with the inimitable Zel, Thad, Joey, Mikey, and Beebs was some of the best fun I've enjoyed in all my time as a travel writer. While I will say spending the night in the mountains with nothing but a trash bag to keep your buns toasty definitely falls into the "don't do what I did" category, if you gotta do it, you really wanna find yourself in the company of Sam and his crew, who'll teach you how to make it through the night with aplomb, if not camping gear. You can find Sam's class schedule on his website (linked here), and he'll be happy to arrange a little adventure for you and any teens you might have in tow.*

The takeaway, dear readers, is this: Whether you're a llama that's been left out in the cold, or a kid who just needs a little extra love and attention, you'll find what you need to thrive and survive in Dolly and Sam Cassidy's little slice of paradise. Come on by, friends. They'll take care of you proper.

⌁

TravelBiatch: That got me right in the feelz! Someone's been chopping onions again, dammit.

GrlyGrl: Inorite? I think we should do something nice for those kiddos. Who's with me?

Borgormeister: I'd like to *get* with you.

GrlyGrl: Dream on. Now shut up, I'm trying to be altitudistic.

Grammahnazi: You mean *altruistic*?

GrlyGrl: Whatevs! Sheesh! Can we just focus on the point here?

Schwingbat: What *is* the point?

GrlyGrl: The point is, these kids deserve a break!

TravelBiatch: They deserve better than a damn trash bag anyway. Studly Sam loses points there, IMHO. What, he couldn't give them a tent, some sleeping bags? SOMETHING???

HansBlowHole: I got an awesome Tauntaun sleeping bag on ThinkGeek. But I'm keeping it.

Schwingbat: Nobody wants to know about your sleeping arrangements, dorkus.

GrlyGrl: That's *it*! Let's get them a gift certificate to L.L. Bean or wherever for some real camping gear. And maybe matching "Sam's Club" tee shirts. Because awesome!

Grammahnazi: Um, there's already a Sam's Club, Grly. I do not think it means what you think it means.

GrlyGrl: Grammah, did you forget your anti-troll tea? Coz someone's got a gnarly case of the b*tchies this morning.

TravelBiatch: Hey, I resemble that remark!

HansBlowHole: Done and done. While you kittens were busy being catty, *I* just started a Kickstarter. Check it out, I've already tweeted the URL and started a FB page. Now let's fund this thing and go home.

CHAPTER TWENTY-FIVE

*O*pen *mic night at Café Con Kvetch is something to see.*

Actually, it's the only thing to see, on a Friday night in Aguas Mi-lagros. But don't worry. If you come with your ears, your mind, and your heart open, you'll leave happy.

❧

Merry was filled with dread.

Pure, unadulterated dread.

When she arrived at Café Con Kvetch, courtesy of Dolly's pickup truck, where she'd been wedged inescapably between her hostess and a very voluble Jane Kraslowski, there was scarcely a parking spot to be found. The three women ended up hoofing it from halfway down Main Street—the sign for which, Merry noticed, some wag had crossed out and replaced with "Only Street." Merry was serenaded along the way by a toe-tapping country duet that leaked out the wide-open windows of the diner-cum-general store, and her path was lit by the glow of light spilling from the propped-open door. It was brisk, she noticed, with a chill in the air that said autumn was well and truly set-tling in. It was getting darker earlier too, reminding her that Thanksgiving was fast approaching. With the golden aspen and cottonwood leaves skittering down the road in the twilight juxtaposed against the warmth of the inviting café, Aguas Milagros was the very picture of small-town conviviality tonight, exactly the sort of thing her readers would eat up with the proverbial spoon.

Merry would prefer to stab herself in the eye with said spoon.

Though she'd said nothing to Dolly, she was not what one would call "pumped" for tonight's events. "Rather face a firing squad" might more accurately describe how Merry felt about the festivities ahead.

"Darn it," Dolly said, breaking into her apprehension. "Forgot my bag o' tricks in the pickup." She turned back for the truck.

"I'll fetch it for you," Merry offered, a bit too eagerly.

"No need." Dolly was already tromping back to her vehicle. "You-all head inside and I'll catch up."

"Right," Merry muttered. And didn't move.

Jane rolled her eyes. "Let me guess. Crowds make you nervous."

"Yup." One or two people at a time she could deal with, and still make like she was a normal, functional adult, but whole bunches tended to overload her limited stores of social grace. Gwendolyn had tried for years to beat Merry's introversion out of her—being comfortable in society was second only to being impeccably dressed in Mother's book—but it was just one of the many ways Merry had proved a disappointment to her mother.

"Didn't you used to compete in front of thousands of people?" Jane asked with some asperity.

"Yeah, but I was wearing a helmet. And goggles. And whizzing by them really, really fast."

Jane snorted. "Seriously, woman, you need to get a grip. The Happy Hookers are harmless. What do you think a bunch of middle-aged broads are gonna do to you?"

If they were anything like her mother's circle of harpies—er, friends—these "middle-aged broads" would find fault with every aspect of Merry from her height to her personality and everything in between. She shrugged, fiddling with her satchel as if it might contain some excuse to bail. "Um...I think I left my yarn back at Dolly's. Maybe I should skip—" She started back for the truck.

"Liar. You've got it right here." Jane flipped back the flap of Merry's tote, exposing the ball of scrap yarn ("crap yarn," Dolly called it) she'd been given to practice on. The fiber and the hooks she would no doubt use to mangle it rested securely atop her computer and smartphone. If the ladies allowed, she'd be documenting the event, and maybe even live-tweeting it for her Twitter followers too. *If only real social interaction could be as easy as Twitter*, Merry thought. *One hundred forty characters and you're out of there.*

"And even if you didn't," Jane continued, "collectively, the Happy Hookers have got about a Hobby Lobby's worth of wool in their purses tonight. Pull it together, Mer, before Dolly catches wind that you're not looking forward to meeting her friends. She's been beside herself talking you up to them."

Oh, great. More expectations.

Merry sucked in a breath. *C'mon, woman. You befriended the terrifying teens. You can deal with a few old broads.* "Right," she said briskly. "Lay on, Macduff, and damned be him who first cries, 'Hold, enough!'"

Jane rolled her eyes. "Alright, Shakespeare, let's get a move on." She tucked her hand into Merry's elbow and drew her forward as Dolly rejoined them.

The joint was hoppin'.

Café Con Kvetch was packed floor to rafters with what had to be all fifty-seven official residents of Aguas Milagros, plus at least

a dozen more from the outlying areas. Couples in matching cowboy hats squeezed in by the bar. Kids fidgeted while their parents
talked animatedly with their friends, or shushed them so they
could pay attention to the performers. Steve and Mazel Tov had
grabbed a little table right in front of the "stage" (really just a
few shipping pallets stacked together at the rear of the restaurant,
with some lamps clustered round to shed a bit of light). Their
toes were tapping and their arms were uplifted as if conducting
the music. Merry suspected they might be seeing tracers.

Onstage at the moment were a couple of codgers playing
bluegrass banjos with rather more enthusiasm than talent. White
grizzled beards tucked into their shirts to keep them out of the
way, cowboy boots thumping the worn floorboards to mark the
beat, they were in finger-pickin' Nirvana. Each time one would
riff off the other, the first would get so tickled with delight he'd
stop, slap his friend on the arm, and chortle with appreciation
before trying to one-up him. It was hard not to grin along with
them, even as they lost the rhythm more than once, dissolving
into mirth (no doubt helped along by the impressive collection
of empty beer steins and shot glasses littering the floor by their
instrument cases).

From his perch behind the host station, Bob presided over all,
his beard and hair neatly combed and tied back, a magnificently
tie-dyed top gracing his portly form. The hubbub being too great
for prolonged hellos, he just nodded over to them, waving the
women inside. As they passed within, Dolly raised her chin and
sailed by without a how-d'ye-do for Bob, while Jane rolled her
eyes and shrugged apologetically at their host. Merry gave him a
little salute.

Toward the back, Merry caught sight of Sam's Survivors, clustered together in a booth, looking excitedly at the screen of a

purple-sheathed tablet that could only be Zelda's. Bernie happened to look up and see Merry, and he elbowed Joey, who elbowed Mikey, who blew his straw wrapper at Thad. Thad scowled until he saw where the others were pointing, and then his face broke into an endearingly boyish grin. Zel looked up from her beau to see who'd earned his smile, and cracked one of her own as she caught sight of Merry. The little crew waved enthusiastically at her, and Merry waved back, amused to see Thad using the opportunity to ever so casually drape his arm over the back of the booth (and not so incidentally Zelda's shoulder).

"Come on, hon. I want to introduce you to the gals." Dolly steered Merry toward one side of the café, where a group of ladies who could not be other than the Happy Hookers sat by the fire. "Now, don't let 'em scare you off—they may be crude, but they're a close-knit bunch."

"Get it?" Jane asked, chucking Merry's shoulder. "Close-kn—"

"Oh, I get it," Merry said. She pasted on Professional-Strength Smile Number Three as Dolly urged her forward.

"Gals, here she is, just like I promised!"

"Pleased to—" Merry started, but they were having none of it.

"Dolly Cassidy, you are *late*! Get your ass in this-here chair right now, and bring the new blood!"

⚬⚬

The Happy Hookers consider Dolly their madam, their mistress, and spiritual leader, and it's easy to see why. Dolly enters their midst to cries of delight, genuflections, and calls for advice on certain "knotty" dilemmas, and she takes it all in her stride like the queen bee she is.

Café Con Kvetch pulls out all the stops for the hookers' get-togethers. Despite his ongoing feud with Dolly (a shame, as anyone can see they should be the best of friends), Needlepoint Bob arranges sofas, chairs, and side tables in a circle by the cozy kiva fireplace, and starts blending margaritas the minute the first hooker sashays in, tools of her trade in tow. I was roundly welcomed, provided with ample libation, and treated to a show of feminine solidarity that warmed my heart to no end.

⌾

"You brought us a new initiate, Dolly dear?" A woman with an old-fashioned coronet of braids wrapped round her head smiled as she looked up at Merry from her seat by the fire. Merry noticed that what was holding the heavy weight of her hair in place appeared to be a vast assortment of artisanal wooden crochet hooks, knitting needles, and even a pair of snipping scissors. She was, Merry saw, in the midst of making what might well be the world's tiniest sock out of rainbow-dyed wool.

"New *victim*, is more like," another said. By far the youngest of the bunch, and up to her eyeballs in steampunk accoutrements, she had taken over half a love seat with her frothy full-length skirt, a pair of brass-and-leather mad scientist goggles perched atop her extravagance of auburn curls. Over a flowy white poet's shirt, she wore a Victorian-esque vest that nipped in her waist and accentuated a very buxom set of breasts. A veritable Mr. T's worth of pocket watches and iron key pendants nestled in the woman's cleavage. She had an enormous set of circular knitting needles in her lap, from which some sort of fantastically intricate and totally unidentifiable project dangled in shades of silver, pewter, and gold. "I'm Sage," she said. "I'm a fashion designer, when I'm not immersed in the fiber arts. And the pincushion over there? That's Rebecca. She's our town archivist."

"Hi ladies," Merry said shyly.

"You'll have to do better than that if you wanna hang with us hookers," said a third woman. She was halfway into a huge margarita, and about two-thirds of the way into a positively Whovian scarf Tom Baker would have been proud to sport on the classic BBC show. "I'm Randi. Randi with an *i*, so get it right when you put it in your blog." She emphasized her point by stabbing her crochet hook in Merry's direction. "I got me a sheep farm, not too far past the springs. Glad to know ya, Merry Manning. Whatcha working on?"

"Huh?" For a moment Merry thought the woman meant her next column, which was already coalescing in her mind. Then she realized Randi with an *i* was talking about yarn. "Oh. Well, tonight I thought I'd just watch you all, and take notes for my bl—I mean column. If that's alright with you all."

"Well, it's not alright." This came from a stick-thin woman about Dolly's age, who had more wrinkles than a Shar-Pei, a long ponytail of faded red curls, and a stack of crocheted granny squares piling up in her lap. "I'm Pam, and I'm here to tell you, you hang with the hookers, you better get those fingers flying. We all take it real serious. Even my Sage over there"—she nodded to the steampunk goddess—"has got herself a sideline in sci-fi outfits for the weirdos—'scuse me, *'alternative set.'* Does pretty well for herself over in Taos and as far away as Santa Fe. Got a woman named Hortencia she sells to down there, at some fancy-pants yarn shop. To earn your seat with us, you better be one crafty lady."

"Get it? Crafty?" Jane elbowed Merry. Merry groaned. "Come sit next to me and I'll get your chain stitches set so you can at least pretend to be making something."

"Rest of you gals, go ahead and introduce yourselves to Merry," Dolly urged. The remaining three hookers looked up from their projects and smiled a hello.

"I'm Marie."

"Susan."

"Lupita."

"Hey, ladies," Merry said shyly. "Thanks for letting me crash your party." The women—comfortable older ladies dressed in slacks or broomstick skirts for the most part, with scarves and shawls and all manner of stunning handmade sweaters layered on top—waved her into their conclave with welcoming smiles. Merry allowed herself to be tugged over to a bench while the women on either side of them made room. Between the music, the noise of the crowd, and the heat of so many bodies, she was feeling a bit dizzy, and more than a little overwhelmed. Yet this was nothing like the interminable cocktail parties and diplomatic events she'd been required to attend with her parents. It was nothing like the team events where athletes spent as much time measuring each other up and courting corporate sponsors as they did making friends.

This was ... fun?

Merry found herself next to Sage, who grinned up at her while Jane did as promised and got Merry's stitches started. "So, you're a writer, huh? And a skier too? I heard the kids running around earlier telling everybody how they spent the night camping with this famous skier."

"I guess that is me," Merry acknowledged. "But I'm really here to learn about *your* stories, not bore everybody with my background."

"*Bore* us?" Randi snorted. "You're talking to a woman who lives fifty miles from the nearest human being and spends most of her evenings having conversations with her cats just so she won't forget the English language. Woman, you're the *least* boring thing to happen in Aguas Milagros since the meteorite splashed down in Wayde Williams's water tank, and that was seven years back!"

"It was really just a little meteorite," Rebecca said primly. "Barely made a ripple."

"Well, if we'd had a newspaper, it would have been front-page news around here," Pam said with some asperity, and Jane nodded in agreement.

"His cows wouldn't give milk for a week. Finally had to give them udder massage, but I think it was my singing that brought 'em back to themselves."

Randi rolled her eyes. "Do *not* let Jane get notions of grandeur in her head. And do *not* let her up on that stage to sing!" She reached over to pat Jane's knee. "I'm sorry, Janey. But while you're a woman of many talents, no one wants to hear your caterwauling."

And speaking of caterwauling...The duo onstage finally wound down into such a fit of hilarity they could no longer keep their banjos straight. Cordial applause ushered them off, and Bob stepped up to usher *on* the next participant.

"Ladies and gentlemen, I'm delighted to introduce this next act, which promises to tickle your ears while it expands your consciousness. Please welcome, direct from the yodeling championships in El Paso...Maxwell McCoy!"

A man in a ten-gallon hat that might have actually fit twelve or fifteen trotted up, to a thunderous welcome of woo-hoos and a few amateur attempts at yodels from the crowd.

What followed made Merry wish fondly for Ricola commercials.

"You might want to stuff these in your ears," Dolly advised. Her clever fingers plucked a wad of unspun wool from her bag and rolled it into two little balls, then made as if to toss them to Merry.

Merry grinned, but she wanted to keep her ears sharp, despite the assault from the stage. "Thanks Dolly, I'm good."

"Suit yourself." Dolly made use of the makeshift earplugs herself, then withdrew a length of fine-gauge yarn from her bag. In moments, she was deeply engaged in whipping up what looked to be a tiny alpaca figurine.

"Amazing, huh?" Jane said, unfolding a sheet of paper filled with arcane symbols and laying it on her lap. "How she does it without even using a pattern, I'll never know. Me, I always have to use a book or download instructions from Ravelry.com." She dug out a half-made woolen Wookiee from her bag and went to work. "In your honor, my friend," she said with a wink.

Guess Sam's as good at giving nicknames as he is at taming llamas, she thought. Of the man himself, there was no sign tonight, and Merry wasn't sure whether to be sorry or relieved. Because what she'd seen of him with the Survivors? Snoring aside, he'd been...

Let's face it. He was amazing with those kids. There's no other word for it. As softer sides went, Cassidy's was positively cuddly. And it wasn't just her readers who had eaten it up. Merry had found herself looking at him with new eyes—eyes that could *almost* justify how thick she'd been laying on the "Studly Sam" schtick in her column.

Better not get all moony, Merry, she warned herself. *He might not be giving you as much shit as he was, but he's still obviously not interested in getting with some half-mangled has-been. Don't you dare start digging him. You'll be leaving soon, and the last thing you need is to bring home a suitcase full of heartache.*

At the thought, her heart did give a pang, but it wasn't all about Sam. Her short time at Dolly's ranch, and in Aguas Milagros itself, had made Merry feel more at home than all the legendary palaces, Ritz-Carltons, and pleasure cruises she'd visited over the last year working for *Pulse*. And of course, during her years on the circuit, there'd been no such thing as home; just an ever-rotating series of sports clinics and ski resorts and team hostels in cities all over the world—anywhere there was powder to carve. She'd loved that life, but it was nothing she'd ever call home. Hell, home was where she'd felt *least* at home. In the Manning household, every move she made had been scrutinized, judged, and disapproved of. You could never just relax, hang out in your pj's, shoot the shit. You had to be *on*, and heaven help you if you were less than socially acceptable.

Here . . . everybody was a bit of a weirdo. And nobody seemed to mind that Merry was a weirdo too. Even the Happy Hookers seemed to be taking her in stride.

Realizing she'd been woolgathering too long, Merry shook herself and looked over at Sage, whose project was truly out of this world. "What is that?" she asked her. "It's really, um . . . wild."

Sage grinned. "I modeled it after Katniss's outfit in the second *Hunger Games*." She held up the piece, which was some sort of free-form cowl made to look distressed though it wasn't even off the needles yet. The effect was somehow very chic. *Maybe Sage can make a male version for Marcus, and he can wear it on the runway during Fashion Week. It's better than half the stuff his designer friends put out.* The woman would be up to her eyeballs in orders. "It's part of my postapocalyptic young adult series," Sage went on. "I've also got snoods, and fingerless gloves, and skirts . . ."

"It's fantastic! Mind if I snap a shot of it to post with my next article?" Merry looked around the greater circle. "And how about you ladies? Could I maybe feature you and your pieces too? And contact info so people can get in touch with you in case they want to place orders for your stuff?"

"Are you kidding?" Randi said, slugging her drink. "Woman, we're counting on you to put us on the map!"

"I wouldn't mind," Rebecca said with more dignity. She felt around in her braids and found the needle she needed by touch. "I do fairly well selling my socks at Doll's shop, but winter'll be along soon and I wouldn't say no to more work to see me through the long snowy nights."

Merry felt a surge of excitement. Now *here* was something she could do to pay her membership dues in the hookers' circle. "I think—now, I don't want to promise anything, but I think I may be able to really help with that. I don't mean to brag, but a fair number of people are tuning in to my column lately, and they really seem to like what they're seeing of Aguas Milagros. I haven't been as much use as I'd have liked over at Dolly's, but hopefully I'll be able to earn my keep a little this way. That is…" Merry stumbled to a halt, embarrassed by her own torrent of words. "That is, if you'd like me to."

The women all looked at one another, and for a moment Merry's stomach clenched. *They don't look pleased*, she thought.

"Hon," said Dolly. "We're all glad of the publicity, and we'll take you up on it for sure. But you need to know…you don't have to do anything to be welcome here. Just relax. Take a load off. You're off the clock—hell, we all are. So hush with all that 'earning your keep' crap, will ya? We're trying to have fun."

Merry's eyes got a little misty. "Okay…yeah, okay, thanks, Dolly. Sorry, I didn't mean to…"

"Shut up and stitch, woman," Jane advised. She handed Merry a set of perfect chain stitches and a hook.

Bob wafted by just then with a pitcher of margaritas in one hand. "Ready for another round, ladies?"

"Need you ask?" Randi drawled. She slugged the remainder of her glass down and held it up for a refill. The others—including Merry—took libations gratefully from their host. At last Bob and the pitcher came round to Dolly.

"Doll, care for a tot?" Bob asked.

Dolly sniffed. "It's Mrs. Cassidy to you. And no, thank you. I don't accept drinks from deceitful, two-faced llama fobber-off-ers."

Merry saw Bob wince, but he quickly pasted on a smile. "True forgiveness is when you can say, 'thank you for that experience.'"

"Whoever said that never had to feed sixteen hungry rumi-nants!"

"I believe it was Oprah Winfrey," Bob said mildly.

"Well, *Oprah* has enough staff to care for half the llamas in Peru," Dolly snapped. "Sam and me have to look after ours our-selves. Not that you give a damn."

Bob's air of Zen cracked again. "You're really still holding that against me, Dolls? Can't you forgive me? It's been near eight years."

"'Everyone thinks forgiveness is a lovely idea until he has something to forgive,'" snapped Dolly. "Or so C. S. Lewis tells me."

"'Always forgive your enemies; nothing annoys them so much,'" Merry put in.

"And what genius said that?" Dolly wanted to know.

"Pretty sure it was Oscar Wilde."

"Well, alright then." Dolly subsided back in her chair, swiped Jane's margarita glass before the vet could protest, and held it up for Bob to pour. "I always was partial to his books. I've got a cria named Dorian Gray. And I am a mite parched, so I'll take a margarita. But that doesn't mean I want you in my sewing circle, Bob Henderson!"

"Desolate as I am to hear that, Dolly, I'm afraid tonight's festivities preclude my enjoying the pleasure of your company in any case. I've got emcee duties, and thirsty customers too." He hefted his pitcher. "I'll leave you ladies to your needlework. Next time, however, I intend to work on that new sampler!"

And so I was introduced to the world of women who have mastered the abstruse art of making string into . . . things. As we sucked back several spectacular margaritas and enjoyed the acts on the stage (more about these in a moment), I watched baby blankets, socks, hats, and even something Sage referred to as "dystopian knitwear" spring from the fingers of these talented ladies.

Me? Well, I actually managed quite a decent set of stitches, which one might charitably call straight. But I was far more interested in the goings-on around me than I was in learning a new life skill. For the folks here in Aguas Milagros have any number of odd and intriguing talents, and they're not shy about showing them off.

The yodeler had been followed by an aspiring snake handler— quickly ushered offstage by Bob with the help of a couple of local cowboys—and a blood-stirring flamenco number by a dapper Spaniard named Federico Rios y Valles. Now Steve and Mazel rose to the occasion, waving for silence.

"This oughta be good," Jane whispered in Merry's ear. Several rounds of excellent margaritas had blurred the edges off her consonants and added a mischievous tinge to her already cheerful voice. "They always come up with something spectacular."

"Really?" Merry set aside her stitchery and reached for her smartphone, which was already filling up with candid shots of the night. Her Twitter feed was awash with commentary and retweets of her photos and blow-by-blow commentary under the hashtag #DontDoWhatIDid, and she could hardly keep up with her followers. "Spectacularly good, or spectacularly awful?"

"Depends on your point of view," Sage said, overhearing them. "Personally, I'm a fan, but then, I'm all about the drama."

"Shhh!" Rebecca said. "It's about to start."

Merry turned her eyes to the stage.

Mazel, with great dignity, was unbinding her braids. She shook them out into knee-length ripples of gray cascading down the back of the flowy white goddess dress she'd worn to the event. She ascended to the creaky little platform with deliberate steps. She inhaled deeply, waiting for the crowd to hush.

"Stronger than lover's love is lover's hate. Incurable, in each, the wounds they make," intoned Mazel, henna-adorned arm upraised to the gods.

"That's Euripides," Merry murmured. "I'm sure of it!"

"You know it?" Jane raised a brow.

"Yeah, it's from *Medea*. I studied it in…well, during one of my boarding school adventures. Always loved the Greeks."

And then Steve joined her.

In a sheet.

"Escape, O woman, your ungoverned tongue!" Steve struck a pose that threatened to send his improvised toga to Tartarus.

Merry's eyes widened as the hippies launched into the famous scene where Medea harangues Jason for spurning her. Mazel railed, wept, rent her hair and her blouse. Steve, as the unfaithful Jason, pleaded for understanding, then turned sullen, prideful, and at last angry. Spittle flew from impassioned lips. Breasts were beaten, gods called down to witness vengeful vows. The bedsheet flapped, swished, and flashed glimpses of Steve's nether regions. The crowd was riveted.

"But nothing good can please thee," Steve railed, in his guise as the beleaguered hero. "In sheer savageness of mood thou drivest from thee every friend. Wherefore I warrant thee, thy pains shall be the more!" With regretful backward looks, he hitched up his bedsheet and trudged off the stage, disappearing in the direction of Bob's restrooms, where presumably he'd hop back into his regular hemp attire.

Mazel stood alone in the spotlight. "Go," she thundered after her husband. "Thou art weary for the new delight thou wooest, so long tarrying out of sight of her sweet chamber. Go, fulfill thy pride, O bridegroom! For it may be, such a bride shall wait thee—yea, God heareth me in this—as thine own heart shall sicken ere it kiss!"

She let the promise of vengeance hover in the air of the over-crowded café, in which a pin drop could now have been heard. Then Mazel's withered lips broke into a grin, and she curled her fingers in front of her face in the unmistakable gesture of drama majors everywhere. "Annnnnd—*scene*!" she cried.

Bob led the uproarious applause that followed, sweeping up to the stage to usher her off with a bouquet of wildflowers that she accepted with a diva's grace. Merry noted no few people swiping tears from their eyes before calling for fresh drinks from the bar. Feliciana and her husband 'Nesto were swamped with orders, sweat beading on their brows as they served up beers, shots, and platters of nachos for the café's hungry patrons.

"And now for something completely different," Bob said with a smile when the clapping had died back. "Before their bedtimes roll around, we've got a couple young folks who'd like to do a number dedicated to our own honored guest, Merry Manning!"

Bob called for the lights to be dimmed. Merry looked around the café, wondering what in the world...

And Destiny's Child strode out onto the stage.

∽

Few things, in my experience, can top the sheer contagiousness of a pop empowerment anthem. When it's sung by a purple-haired, pint-sized Beyoncé and four blinged-out backup dancers, there's truly nothing to compare. For five of the funnest minutes of my life, I watched as Sam's Survivors—with the aid of someone's old boom box and a lot of cheering from the crowd—performed a truly spectacular rendition of a song that could not be more apt.

"I'm a survivor. I'm not gon' give up! I'm not gon' stop..."

Well, you know the tune. I think I'll let this little video I took speak for itself.

∽

When the kids wound down, sweaty and exultant from their exuberant performance, there wasn't a booty left unshaken—or in a seat. Dolly, Jane, and the whole horde of hookers were all up and clapping. Everyone from cowboys to kitchen staff was woo-hooing and giving thumbs-ups. Even Steve had managed to wrestle free of his toga and was applauding from his place beside his woman.

Merry finished snapping pics and whistled through her teeth. "Rock on, dudes!" she yelled. "You nailed it!"

Thad bowed like a born showman, arm around Zelda. Mikey and Beebs mussed Joey's sweaty hair and bowed as well. But it was Zelda who took the mic. "Thanks, everybody! And thanks, Miss Manning for what you did for us. We really appreciate it." The other kids nodded.

What did I do for them? Merry wondered. She looked at Jane and Dolly in puzzlement, but they just shrugged. Merry blew them a kiss, and they waved happily and clambered down from the stage. Merry saw Bernardo and Mikey being taken under the wings of their parents and ushered out into the parking lot. Thad, meanwhile, hooked his arm around Joey's neck and noogied him fondly as they headed back for their booth, Zelda following with a fresh round of soft drinks.

Speaking of which... Merry had had quite a few beverages herself. She excused herself and headed for the lav.

⚬⚬

Zel caught up with her before she could get there. "Seriously, it meant a lot to the boys," she said, beaming up at Merry. "*I* couldn't have done it without hurting their pride, but this way they get what they needed without all that weirdness. Joey especially. This is going to do him a *lot* of good." She raised up on tiptoe and pecked Merry on one very surprised cheek before skipping off into the crowd.

"*What* will?" Merry called after her, but Zel was just a ponytail disappearing into the throng.

Alrighty then, she thought. *I'll sort that one out later. Right now, I gotta pee.*

When Merry pushed the door of the stall open a few moments later after seeing to her business, she got whacked in the face.

With the blues.

The guitar sang, it wept, it scraped the bottom of the Mississippi delta and came up for air carrying with it the souls of generations of master bluesmen. Just a guitar, no vocals, but it spoke to her all the same, cutting through her buzz and tugging at something central to the core of her being. Merry stood stock-still for a moment, just listening, until the person behind her in line for the bathroom nudged her gently into motion. She smiled an apology, shaking her head to clear it of the spell. As she washed up in the communal trough-style sink outside the loos, Merry encountered Dolly. "Whoever that is playing is frickin' *amazing*," she marveled, flapping her hands dry. She thought recognized an old John Lee Hooker tune, but while the music came clearly to her ears, it was impossible to see from here who was performing on the stage.

Dolly beamed. "He is, isn't he?" Dolly ushered her back toward their seats, and Merry's gaze followed the soulful music to its source.

It was Sam Cassidy. Of course it was.

He sat alone at the center of the stage, perched on a stool with one leg dangling, the other propped on a rung to keep his guitar braced upon his knee. His head was bowed, ear to the belly of the instrument as if it were whispering secrets to him. His hair had been scraped back into what was, for him, a neat braid, and he'd switched out his customary overalls for a pair of well-worn jeans and a whisper-soft white cotton button-down that wrapped lovingly round his muscular torso. His feet were, as ever, bare.

Not bad, Sam. Not bad at all. Merry surreptitiously snapped a photo with her phone, thinking that with the soft lighting and his head down like that, her readers would see the "Studly Sam" she'd been telling them about all this time. And maybe he wasn't so bad looking in truth, she admitted. She already knew he had a killer bod beneath the unflattering clothes he favored. And his face, plain as it was, was beginning to grow on her.

Fungus grows on you too, Merry told herself. *They make medications for that.*

The crowd had quieted, seduced by the music. Couples kissed, singles stared wistfully into their beers. Merry found herself drifting into a reverie that was half margarita, half melancholy as she watched Sam's fingers pluck the strings with unerring skill. What else might he strum so well? she wondered. The hookers had all stopped stitching, she noticed, and several had similarly faraway looks in their eyes. Merry smiled, thinking Sam had quite a coterie of female fans. *A man of many talents indeed*, she thought. She leaned her head against Jane's shoulder, feeling warm and fuzzy, and remarkably content.

I like it here, she thought. *I like these people.*

I like Sam.

Oh, shit.

Merry grabbed the nearest margarita and guzzled. Then she grabbed another one and chased it down.

We do not need to be reenacting Shrek, New Mexico—*style*, she told herself. *Especially considering we're both the ogres, and I don't think I'll be changing into a princess anytime soon.* Still, she couldn't help watching how completely present Sam seemed as he spoke to the guitar, and made it speak for him. Here was a man with no pretense, no bullshit, and who would accept none from the people in his life. He could be fierce. Abrasive. Totally off-putting, as she had good cause to know. But he was alive and unafraid in a way Merry herself could only wish to be. The way she'd once *thought* she was, when she competed, but now realized she'd never really managed. She'd used competition as a way to gain acceptance.

But no matter how many medals she'd won, she'd never really accepted herself.

This man has, Merry thought.

Face intent, almost tender, Sam wrung the last notes of the song from the instrument. There was a communal sigh, and a respectful silence, but he didn't stick around for the applause that followed it. He slipped offstage and over to the bar with barely a nod of his head to acknowledge the whistles and cheers. Aguas Milagros seemed to understand his need to keep a low profile, and the crowd went back to eating, drinking, and making merry without much fuss.

Except, now they were making a fuss *over* Merry.

"Mer-RY! Mer-RY! Mer-RY!"

"Um, why are people chanting my name?" Merry asked Jane. Her head was snuggled against the vet's shoulder. Jane smelled like lavender and liniment, and the sister she'd never had.

"'Cause it's your turn, lushy girl." Jane patted Merry's hair fondly.

"Turn to do what?" Merry wanted to know.

"To get up on that stage and wow us with your hidden talents, of course."

Merry blinked owlishly. "But I don't have any hidden talents," she protested. "I don't even have any *obvious* talents. Not anymore, anyway." Suddenly her good humor took a margarita-fueled dive.

"Oh, please," Randi scoffed. "Everybody can do *something*."

"Yeah, like, I can tie a cherry stem in a knot with my tongue," Sage said. She stuck her tongue out and swirled it demonstratively.

"I can tell cat fur from dog fur just by feel," Jane offered.

Merry had a *Breakfast Club* flashback. But she didn't think taping people's buns together or applying lipstick via her cleavage was really wise in front of half the Aguas Milagros population. *Gotta maintain my dignity*, she thought. And hiccupped.

"Mer-RY! Mer-RY! Mer-RY!"

Bob was holding out his hand. "The masses are calling," he said, waving her up to the stage.

"You better get on up there, hon, and show you're a good sport," Dolly advised. "You don't want folks to think you're too high and mighty to go up against the local talent."

High and mighty. Yeah, right. But that gave Merry an idea. "Alright, alright," she shouted over the chants. "I'm coming! Keep your shirts on." For no reason she could fathom, she was smiling, and it wasn't all about the margaritas. She stumped up onto the rickety wooden pallets, to much whistling and applause.

"Show us what you got, girl!"

"Shake your moneymaker!"

"Make us proud, Mer-Ber!" (This last was from Steve Spirit Wind.)

Merry held up her hands for silence. She found, to her astonishment, that she was rather enjoying being in the spotlight. For the first time since skiing had been taken away from her, she was actually relishing attention. Because these folks weren't judging. They were just having fun.

And, maybe, so can I.

"Here's a little trick I learned at my mother's knee," she announced, discovering her inner ham. "Does anyone have a nice, big book?"

Bob dug a hardcover copy of Thucydides's *History of the Peloponnesian War* from inside the host's stand. "Will this work?"

The tome was at least seven hundred pages long, not counting appendices. "I would think so!" Merry laughed, gesturing for the book. Bob brought it to her, eyes twinkling.

"Now, how about a cup of tea?"

"I got a shot of Jameson over here," shouted one of the blue-grass banjo players. "Better speak quick though, or it's going in my cake hole."

"That'll do."

The shot was passed up to Merry, who set it on the stool at her side.

"Whatcha gonna do, Merry?" Randi called out. "Read us a bedtime story?"

"Watch and see." Merry stood up to her full height, straightened her back, and set the book on top of her head. She bent at the knees—daintily—and picked up the shot glass with thumb and forefinger, pinky extended, before placing it with great deliberation atop the book.

Then she took a stroll around Bob's café.

∝

It goes without saying that my estimable mother, the gracious, elegant, and always entertaining Gwendolyn Manning (hi, Ma!) did not have parlor tricks in mind when she required me to practice deportment with a tome and a tot of hot tea upon my head. She knew that, with my general Goliath-itude, I would be tempted to slump. "Mannings don't slouch, Meredith!" she would say, and, thanks to her instruction, I shouldn't dream of it to this day.

Well, the good people of Aguas Milagros were "right glad" of your home training tonight, Mother dear. I treated them to a display of Swiss boarding school's best, and I never spilled a drop! But while I daresay I didn't embarrass myself overmuch when it was my turn to take the stage, it was Sam's appreciative response I most cherished when I'd taken my bows (and drunk my shot). His applause made me blush like the school-girl I most certainly no longer am.

∻

Merry received her fair share of good-natured applause when she'd finished her perambulations around the restaurant and stepped back up onto the stage. Thucydides and the Jameson still precariously perched atop her noggin, she curtsied deeply, not even feeling the twinge in her left leg as she did. Then, with a whoop, she plucked the shot glass from atop the book and drained it, to the cheers of the audience. Flushed with pleasure (and the shot of whiskey), she soaked it up. A sense of love and acceptance suffused her.

Until someone started a slow-clap.

Clap.

Clap.

Clap.

Into the silence in the wake of her performance, the derisive sound echoed like thunder, like a slap to the face.

Clap.

Clap.

Clap.

Merry squinted into the dim interior of the packed café. It took a moment, but when she saw who was mocking her, it felt like an ice-cold dagger to the heart.

By the bar, Sam Cassidy stood, hipshot, mouth twisted with contempt as he gave her the sarcastic salute. Merry went red all over, her pleasure shattered. She gathered herself and started to slink off the stage. But then she stopped. *Why should I run away?* she thought. *I've done nothing wrong.* He's *the asshole.*

But why is he being an asshole? I thought we were past all that.

She hopped down and stomped over to Sam. "*What*," she demanded, staring down at him deliberately from her superior height. "What did I do now?"

He didn't back down. If anything, he puffed up to meet her belligerence. "Just giving her majesty her due, Miss Manning."

Not "Merry." Not "City Girl." Not even "Wookiee." *Ruh roh.* Merry's buzz—and the fact that he was stealing the first real moment of acceptance she'd felt in far too long—made her bold. "What did I say? Did I put too much Studly Sam in my latest article?"

"You put too much of *something* in there, all right. I think we call it Rich Girl Privilege."

Merry's jaw dropped. "Did you really just say what I think you said?"

"Damn right," he snarled. "You think you can just swan into our town and make fun of everyone in it for your own amusement? Make us look like jackasses—or worse, charity cases—for ratings?"

"I wouldn't . . . I'd never!"

"You *did*," Sam said savagely. "And the worst of it is, you used my kids to do it."

"What are you *talking* about?"

"Sam, maybe you should dial it back a notch," Jane advised, coming to stand at Merry's side. "Here, have a brewski, take a break." She tried to hand Sam a longneck.

He ignored her and the other Happy Hookers, who were staring at him, mouths agape. He was laser-focused on Merry.

"What am I talking about? How about using a bunch of kids

who've already got it harder than most for your own selfish purposes. You know, I actually believed you cared for them. The way
you were with them…you really seemed to give a damn. I guess
I should congratulate you on your acting skills." He shook his
head in disgust. "Exploiting those kids was beyond anything I
could have expected, even from a woman like you."

"Wait, what?" Merry gasped. "'*Exploiting*' them? And what
the hell do you mean, 'a woman like me'?"

"A selfish, thoughtless prima donna who cares for nothing but
her own fame." Sam's eyes were incandescent blue. "I want you
off the ranch by morning. If you need help packing I'll be more
than happy to help—by tossing your shit in the creek!"

"Samuel Cassidy!" Dolly snapped. "First of all, it ain't your
ranch to go tossing folks off of. You may be my heir and my
blood, but as long as I'm still kicking, the Last Chance is my
place, and in my place my rules go. Number one being, 'don't
be an asshole.'" She pointed her crochet hook at him like she
might shove it up his nose. "I got rid of the last asshole when
I sent my husband packing, and I'll be damned if I let 'em
start sprouting up like mushrooms, even if they are my own
kin. And second, you better explain why you're throwing out
accusations like a crazy person all of a sudden, because not
even a whole *pitcher* of Bob's margaritas could account for your
ill-mannered behavior right now." Dolly crossed her arms and
glared at her nephew.

Sam gritted his teeth, obviously trying to rein in his fury out
of respect for his aunt. "Because of *her*, they're treating the kids
like charity cases!"

"Who is?"

"They! The Internet!" Several sets of brows rose, and Sam
gestured impatiently, flapping his hand into the ether. "Merry's

macchiato-sipping hipster audience. The 'Don't Do What I Did' fans. They started up some kind of fund drive for the kids, to buy them *camping gear*."

They did? This was news to Merry. Maybe that was what Zelda had meant a few minutes ago, and why the kids had been so excited looking over Zel's tablet earlier. Merry hadn't had time to check her comments since she'd posted the column this afternoon. She whipped out her phone and started the app that took her to her page on *Pulse*, squinting booze-blurred eyes to bring it into focus. Sure enough, there it was in the comments. Someone had started a crowd fund campaign for the kids. She clicked the link provided.

Ho-ly...

It already had something like three thousand dollars in it. And REI had promised to match the funds, plus provide tents and sleeping bags with each of their names monogrammed on them. Merry blew out a breath. She'd never expected this, never imagined her column could provoke such an instantaneous reaction. Never dreamed people's lives could be affected in any real way. It was sobering. But also exhilarating. "Damn," she breathed, and Jane grabbed her phone to look.

The vet whistled. "That's a lot of camping gear."

"So they got some tents and such. What's wrong with that?" Dolly wanted to know.

Sam clenched his hands into Hulk-like fists. The veins in his neck bulged. "The whole point of what I teach is *self-reliance*!"

A tiny, margarita-induced laugh escaped Merry's lips.

"You think it's funny? You think embarrassing those kids in front of the whole world is some big *joke*?"

"No, of course not! I would never...I don't think they're embarrassed, are they?" She looked over to the booth where Thad and Zel were still canoodling. Joey was engrossed in Zel's tablet, ignoring the two. None of them looked upset to Merry.

"They'd hardly tell you, would they? You're the 'famous athlete.' The 'visiting writer.' They're half in awe of you. But that doesn't mean they aren't being exploited and objectified for your own glorification."

Merry had had enough. Liquor stoked her bravado and she got in his face, enjoying her height advantage for once. "Oh, come on, Sam. It's camping gear! It's not as if I started a telethon for 'Sammy's Kids.' One of my readers started a Kickstarter campaign, is all, and I guess it took off. I had no way of knowing it would happen. I didn't suggest it, or even have anything to do with it! I wasn't deliberately trying to make them look hard up. But sometimes..." She shrugged. "The Internet has a life of its own."

"So you're saying you bear no responsibility for what happens as a result of your writing?" If he'd seemed angry before, now Sam was apoplectic.

"Sam, they got *camping gear*. And maybe couple of girls friended Thaddeus on Facebook. It's not like I put their pictures on milk cartons."

"You really don't get it, do you? You can't even see your own entitlement, you're so far up your own ass!"

Now, in the course of any given social occasion, there will be times when a natural hush just happens to fall. Total silence will simply settle over a crowd, at random, as if everyone's train of thought had been interrupted at the same time. And no matter how crowded the venue, during such a moment, one can hear a flea sneeze.

That moment occurred just as Sam hollered *"up your own ass!"*

Sixty pairs of eyes swiveled toward them, and Merry went

beet red, then blanched so white her freckles stood out sickly, even in the cozy lighting of the café. She took a step back from Sam. People were whispering, pointing, staring agog. It was every nightmare moment of rejection and public humiliation she'd ever feared, rolled into one.

No, it was one particular humiliation. One she'd never forget as long as she lived.

Merry was sixteen years old. *Exactly* sixteen, as a matter of fact. She was also, to her chagrin, dressed in the tea-length Oscar de la Renta cocktail dress her mother had picked out, in a soft peach hue that was, admittedly, fairly flattering to her skin. It was less flattering to the bruises and abrasions all over her body, and the knee brace that encased her left leg.

The whispers of her peers made this all too apparent to Merry. The gaggle of girls from the UN school, with their shiny, swinging locks curled just so, their designer dresses and expertly applied makeup, were all staring and whispering behind their hands. She could feel their eyes on her, raking her from stem to stern and seeing every flaw. The broad shoulders that made mockery of the dress's dainty straps. The sturdy legs, strong from years of near-constant skiing; the bulky brace; the flats she'd worn because, even if she could have negotiated the waxed marble floors of the chateau's ballroom with her bad knee, she'd have looked like a transvestite in any kind of heels. The scrapes, bruises, cuts from her recent encounter with the barrier wall of the course she'd crashed.

"She's a *freak*," Merry heard one girl titter to another.

"So pathetic," her friend agreed, rolling her eyes. "Why does she *bother*?"

Merry bothered because her mother made her. This whole party, this excruciating, naked-in-the-schoolyard nightmare of a party—had been Gwendolyn's brainchild. She'd been planning it for months, and none of Merry's pleas, threats, and tantrums had had the slightest impact. She was stuck with a sweet sixteen, whether she liked it or not.

Merry did not.

She could see Gwendolyn, glittering in a vintage Yves Saint Laurent gown, standing beside her husband and son, Pierce the picture of dignity as he chatted with some of the other dignitaries whose offspring attended the school, Marcus effortlessly sporting black tie and looking like the budding god he was already well on his way to becoming. The girls weren't giggling over *him*, Merry thought, except perhaps over who might score with the gorgeous twenty-four-year-old. His clutch of friends, home from college or starting careers in their family's footsteps, were eyeing the nubile girls and nudging one another. None of them was looking at Merry, of course.

Which was fine with her. She preferred being invisible to being mocked.

Then Merry saw her mother whispering to one of Marcus's friends, her hand on the arm of his dinner jacket. The young man looked dazzled, nodding at whatever she'd said. He started across the dance floor, headed straight for Merry.

Oh no. It was Paolo. Paolo, who Merry had been crushing on since she was thirteen, and who had never so much as deigned to notice she was alive before tonight. He was bearing down on her now with a look of resignation that Merry knew all too well. Her mother had coerced him into partnering her. *You'd think she'd have given up after the fiasco at my junior debutante presentation last year,* Merry thought.

Paolo arrived at her side, a pleasant expression tacked on his face. He looked up, and up, and up into her eyes. He was probably a good six inches shorter than she was. *Mother couldn't find a taller sacrificial lamb?* Merry thought bitterly. Paolo took a deep breath, obviously steeling himself. "Would you care to dance, Meredith?" he asked, his Italian accent utterly sexy.

"No!" Merry blurted.

Loudly.

One of those awkward silences fell. The band had just finished one song with a swoop and a flourish, and the next had yet to begin. The ballroom was suddenly as quiet as the grave. Except for the sound of Merry's humiliation.

She couldn't take the hypocrisy, the pitying look in his eyes. "No, Paolo. You don't want to, and I don't want to, so let's just skip it and you can ask someone you *really* want to dance with!" She turned and clomped off the dance floor, tears blurring her eyes. Still, she could *feel* the scandalized delight of her peers as she fled for the ladies' room as fast as her knee brace would allow.

She shut the door and collapsed onto the brocade-covered couch in the lounge of the ornate restroom. She breathed heavily, trying not to cry. The flounce of her dress had caught in the hinge of her knee brace, and she yanked it out, not caring as stitches popped.

The door swung open. Merry didn't look up. She knew who it was; she could smell the Chanel No. 5. A cool hand alighted on her shoulder, stayed there in silence. Finally, Merry found the courage to look up, seeing her mother's face reflected in the gold-framed vanity mirror, her perfect lips pursed in a way Merry knew all too well. "Why can you not just *fit in*, Meredith?" her mother sighed.

"Why can't you just let me *not* fit in?" Merry cried. Her fists clenched and tears spilled from her eyes. "I never wanted this stupid party. I never *asked* for it. I wanted out of it so badly I crashed on *purpose*, Mother!"

Gwendolyn went ashen. "What did you say?" Her hand dropped away from Merry's shoulder.

Merry gestured to her bruises, the knee brace. "I wanted out, Mother. And you wouldn't listen. It seemed like the only way. But I guess I didn't crash hard enough to get you off my back."

Little did she know how, twelve years later, the universe would mock her for tempting fate.

And how two years after *that*, she'd find herself once again failing to fit in.

Merry felt the tears start as she stared at Sam, who quite clearly thought she had no place in Aguas Milagros.

The patrons at Bob's café suddenly became extremely interested in their beers and burritos, but Merry could still feel eyes glancing surreptitiously at them. She found herself trembling. She was beyond embarrassed, she was *mortified*. The look of disgust in Sam's eyes was more than she ever wanted to see. Maybe he was right. Maybe she *was* thoughtless, entitled. Maybe she *had* swanned into this town and used its inhabitants for her own ends.

"I... I don't know what to say..."

"You didn't have that problem when you were writing that column, did you?"

"Sam," Jane warned. "Cool it."

Dolly stood up next to her. "You're out of line, boy. And you're embarrassing me and Merry both."

Bob wafted up to the group. "Sam. Buddy. I'm all for self-expression. It *is* open-mic night after all. But if you're going to be a dick about it, I'll ask you to do your expressing outside."

"You're taking her side on this? All of you?" Sam's eyes darted from one to another, taking in the disapproving expressions of his friends and family. He looked wounded, betrayed.

Bob patted his arm. "As Christopher Hitchens once said,

'There can be no progress without head-on confrontation.' And in the interest of philosophy and truth, I'm down with a little contention now and again. I just like to maintain a certain vibe in my place of business. And, frankly, my friend, you're harshing everybody's mellow."

Sam breathed deliberately through his teeth. "Fine. You know what? I'll take my harsh home and leave you all to your mellow. But you, Miss Manning . . . I don't want to see your face again until you *fix this!*"

He shouldered his guitar and stomped out into the night.

Guess our truce is over, Merry thought. It hurt more than she'd expected.

A lot more.

CHAPTER TWENTY-SIX

Last night I had a rather unpleasant dream, dear readers. In it, I lay paralyzed in my cot while over and over someone whispered in a satanic voice, "Baaaaaaaaad news. Baaaaaaaaaad news."

When I woke I would have thought nothing of it were it not for a strange and disturbing fact: The door of my cabin was open a crack. And that hellacious smell I mentioned from prior nocturnal visitations? It had returned.

To the list of "Don't Do What I Dids," I may now with authority add, "Do not overimbibe margaritas, no matter how delicious, if you are subsequently to be haunted by the world's smelliest ghost.

Because feh.

Your friendly neighborhood hungover travel writer,
Merry Manning

⚬⚬

To: MerryWay@pulsemag.com
From: MrsP_Manning@state.gov

Subject: Leave me out of it

Meredith,

If it was your intention to wound your father and me with your latest forays into "journalism," all I can say is, job well done. I have never been so mortified in my life. It's bad enough that you choose to caper about like a court jester for the amusement of strangers. But to make your own mother the object of ridicule…well, it doesn't bear speaking of.

We shall, however, have much to discuss over the holiday. I would call it Thanksgiving, but I hardly see much for which to be thankful, just at the moment.

Your mother,
Gwendolyn Hollingsworth Manning

P.S. About that "selfie" you posted. Do they not have hairstylists in New Mexico?

To: MerryWay@pulsemag.com
From: P_Manning@state.gov

Subject: You know how she gets

My Dear Girl,

Your mother is, perhaps, a bit histrionic. But she isn't entirely wrong. Best to keep her name from your online escapades in future, don't you think? She feels it reflects badly, and things are delicate right now, what with fundraising season at the foundation coming up, and my meetings with the State Department and all.

Glad you're having fun though, sweetheart. Be safe and watch out for centipedes.

Your loving father,
Pierce Manning

P.S. Thanksgiving is still on, I hope. Time is running out and your grandmother's estate must be settled.

To: MerryWay@pulsemag.com
From: BananaHammock@MeMail.com

Subject: Hidden Depths

Squatchy!!!

Crocheting!? Troubled teens?! Talent shows? My God, you're a wild woman!

Seriously, I didn't realize you still had it in you, Li'l Sis. And I'm so frickin' glad you do. Was worried for a while there.

Save me some of those sweet-sounding biscuits the old lady makes, okay? I need something to give my trainer fits about.

Your way hotter brother,
Marcus

Oh, and P.S. That Sam guy treating you right? Sounds like you got the major hots for that dude. Lemme know if he needs beating up or anything. Can't risk this pretty face myself (frickin' insurance, you know?), but I know a couple guys...

P.P.S. I don't know how much longer I can hold off the 'rents. You'll have to see them sooner or later. Turkey Day?

Some days it doesn't pay to check email. Merry scrubbed a hand over her hungover face and hunched down in her booth at the café, which Bob and his helpers had magically put to rights overnight. A cheese-and-chile-smothered breakfast burrito sat next to her laptop, daring her to test her queasy stomach, and a latte with a tiny foam skull and crossbones floating in it steamed at her elbow, promising sweet succor for the margarita-and-shame-induced headache that throbbed behind her eyes.

Café Con Kvetch was as quiet this morning as it had been hopping last night. *And thank God for that*, she thought, fighting the urge to slap shut her laptop and crawl back to her cabin at Dolly's. But like it or not, she was going to have to face this day. She'd tossed and turned all night over Sam's very public diatribe, wondering how much truth there was to it, and what, if anything, she could do to set things right.

She'd grown up with more than most people ever dreamed of having, and she knew it. She'd never wanted for anything, from educational opportunities to financial support. Her parents had enthusiastically backed her in her quest to win Olympic gold, paying for her training, flying her all over the world to compete. She'd had everything a kid could want—unless it was accep-

tance one wanted. She'd certainly never been through the kinds
of things Joey, Thad, and the other Survivors experienced on a
daily basis.

*Was I insensitive? Am I so used to getting things my way that I'd
bulldoze those kids for the sake of a story?*

The truth was, Merry didn't know. She'd never given much
thought to the effect her articles might have on their audience—
or their subjects. She'd simply never considered herself that influential. Of course, in her competitive days, she'd been conscious of
her responsibilities as a role model, and had kept her nose clean.
But now?

Does anyone really give a damn what I do?

If I want to know the answer to that, she told herself, *I'd better
see how the column is doing.* She'd been posting as the evening
went along last night—she refused to call it live-blogging—but
she had no idea how the little experiment had gone over. She
switched her attention back to the laptop.

Then groaned again as another email caught her attention.

To: MerryWay@pulsemag.com
From: J_Jonas@ChicagoManagementLTD.com

Subject: Urgent: Your apartment

Dear Ms. Manning,

It is with regret that we must inform you that the tenant
you selected to sublet your apartment has not paid
the agreed-upon rent. He has, however, been using the
premises as an unauthorized Airbnb hotel. There have
been reports of unapproved guests coming and going

at all hours of the night, upsetting many of the building's residents, who have made formal complaints. The
terms of your lease are very clear, and you are in viola-
tion of several provisions.

We have asked your tenant to find other living arrangements, and we will also expect the same of you. At
your earliest convenience, please provide an address to
which we may ship the belongings in your storage bin.
It goes without saying that your security deposit is forfeit.

Sincerely,

Jonathan Jonas
Managing Agent

"You've got to be kidding me!" Merry yelped.

And just as she was digesting that one, another email popped
up. It was from her editor, and it said only one thing:

Call me, kiddo.

CHAPTER TWENTY-SEVEN

I've got good news and bad news, kid," Joel said.

The bandwidth at Café Con Kvetch was as sluggish as Merry herself this morning, causing his face to freeze on the Skype session so Merry couldn't read his expression properly. Her own image, captured in the unfortunate little inset window, was scary enough. Despite her attempts to tame it, her hair seemed determined to escape her pounding headache by standing out all around her head. Her skin was pallid, and dark circles—whether caused by guilty conscience or ghostly visitation was a toss-up— ringed her bloodshot eyes. *Way to be a professional, Merry*, she thought with a wince.

"Which am I going to want first?" she asked the tableau of Joel with half-closed eyes and unhinged jaw. She saw what she feared was egg salad in the depths of his mouth, and shuddered. Her screen jerked and jumped. Her stomach lurched.

A smile burst full blown across his chubby features, then vanished just as quickly. "Good news," he said definitively. "That'll make *me* feel better, anyway."

"Okay then...hurry, lay it on me before the connection cuts out." *Or before that burrito I just finished comes back to visit.* Merry could see Joel lean back in his chair, propping his feet on his desk and very nearly knocking over the takeout container from his lunch. He was wearing a shiny new pair of wingtips, she noted;

the cool-kid Converse he'd been sporting last time nowhere in evidence. The red sweater vest he had on over his usual rumpled oxford even looked clean, as if he was posing for a Christmas card photo.

Merry found herself very uneasy.

"Good news is, Don't Do What I Did is now certifiably a thing! Hashtag and all." Joel paused to let that sink in.

Merry's mouth dropped open, until she caught a glimpse of how unflattering that looked on Skype, and shut it. But . . . *Ho-ly wow!* Becoming "a thing" on the Internet was a Very Big Deal, as Merry had learned during the many social media lectures she had been required to attend during her tenure at *Pulse*. Like going viral, it was nothing one could control, and every bit as desirable. Because once you were *a thing*, people didn't forget you. If #DontDoWhatIDid was trending, it meant it had made it into the vernacular. "You're shitting me," she said, hardly able to take it in.

Joel shook his head. "I shit you not. The data is in, and readers are lapping up those llamas like you wouldn't believe. Your numbers are through the roof, and your click-through rate on the ads has half of sales out of the office with celebratory hangovers."

"That's great! Well, not the part about the hangovers, but you know what I mean." Merry had a lot of sympathy for hangover victims just at the moment, and even some for their sales force.

Joel smiled indulgently. "Knew ya could do it, kid. And I knew I was a genius for creating Don't Do What I Did in the first place."

Merry let him have his moment of self-congratulation. She was having one of her own, if more discreetly. "I'm so glad," she said. "I really think this place is something special. The minute I got here, I knew people would love Dolly and the ranch."

"That Sam dude is going over even better," Joel said. "You should read some of the comments after that picture you posted of him playing guitar last night." He tsked his tongue. "Filthy minds you ladies have."

I've got no one but myself to blame for that little fiction, Merry reminded herself. Sam would no doubt go through the roof if he found out she'd snuck a picture of him into her column. Not that it was likely possible to make him any angrier than he already was. "Yeah, well," she said, "that all sounds fabulous. So what's the bad news?"

Joel was silent long enough that Merry nearly reset the connection.

"Well, kid. Bad news is, you're fired."

CHAPTER TWENTY-EIGHT

Sorry, Joel, My connection must have cut out. Can you repeat? Heh, heh. You won't believe what I thought you said." She couldn't tell if the screen was frozen again, or if Joel just looked like an axe-wielding executioner all of a sudden.

"I said you're fired, kid."

"Shit, Joel. I think I better call you back from a landline. I keep mishearing what you're saying. It's so hard to get a good Wi-Fi connection out here!"

"Kid," Joel said.

"Yeah, Joel?"

"You didn't hear wrong."

"But...what about what you just said? About how great DDWID is doing? I mean...*a thing*! You said it's a thing!"

Her editor sighed, reached for a takeout cup and tipped it to his lips. He made a face that said, "Ew, sour milk" and tossed the container in the general direction of his wastebasket, which, like everything else in his office, was filled far beyond its capacity. A small, disconsolate thunk accompanied its dismissal.

A lot like the noise my soul is making, Merry thought.

"It's nothing you've done, Merry. Thing is, *Pulse* just got bought out, and the new owners aren't keen on a lot of our old content."

"New owners? What the hell, Joel?! I hadn't heard anything about a buyout."

"Well, I'm guessing Bloomberg Business isn't part of the cable package out there in North Bumblefuck," Joel said drily. "Anyhow, word only just came down from corporate last night. Mandate's changed."

Merry wasn't of a mind to enjoy his attempts at levity. "Who are the new owners?"

"Good Word OmniGlobal," Joel told her. Even with the poor connection, Merry saw his wince.

"The right-wing Evangelical Christian conglomerate?" Merry noticed that her voice had gotten all funny and high. She swallowed.

"The very same."

That explained the wingtips and the sweater vest. "But...Joel, why would they want *Pulse*? I mean, we're not exactly their speed." Merry frowned, bewildered.

"Anything with seven million page views a day is their speed," Joel said with a sigh. "They're gobbling up sites like the Rapture's tomorrow. And if they don't like the content, they just... *rebrand* it."

"Can't they rebrand *me*?" Merry asked. "Joel, I promised Dolly. I can't just leave in the middle of my gig..." *And without a home. Or money to rent a new place.*

But it was more than that. She was just getting to know the people of Aguas Milagros. And the longer she stayed, the more she felt their lives deserved better than a few tongue-in-cheek features on the Internet. "I feel like...well, like the story isn't *finished*."

Joel shook his head. "Afraid it is, kid—at least at *Pulse*. You didn't make the cut. Something about 'swimming in llama shit'

didn't sit well with OmniGlobal. They're sanitizing all our features. You should see what they did to Allison's 'Advice from an
Active Alcoholic.'" He reached into his desk drawer and pulled
out a bottle of bourbon, though it couldn't have been later than
eleven in the morning in Chicago. Not finding a glass handy, he
scrounged around at his feet until he found the Starbucks cup and
shook the last of the contents in the vicinity of his garbage pail.
He poured a couple of fingers of Maker's Mark into the container
and slugged for all he was worth.

"Anyhow, I couldn't save you this time, kid. OmniGlobal
plans to make 'Don't Do What I Did' a cautionary column about
underage sex and the perils of rejecting Jesus as your personal
lord and savior. Nothing I could do to dissuade them. I'm halfway out the door myself. If I can't get current with Evangelical
megachurch culture within the week, I'll be out on my ass."

"But, Joel, what am I supposed to do? My place in Chicago
just kicked me out, and I've got bills like you wouldn't believe. I
can't go home, and I can't afford to rent another place either."

"What about your family? Aren't they insanely rich?"

"Yes," Merry said through tight lips. "Also insanely insane."

Joel made a sympathetic face. "Heard that. Family's the worst.
Can you believe my wife threw me out last month? Said I was a
slob." He rolled his eyes.

"I can't imagine what possessed her," Merry murmured.

The look on her editor's face became thoughtful. "What
about...can you stay with the woolly folk awhile longer?"

Merry shrugged. "I'm only meant to be here another week or
so, until their regular hand comes back from his honeymoon." *Besides*, she thought, *I dunno about Dolly, but I've sure's hell worn out
my welcome with Sam.*

"I'm sorry, kiddo. I managed to get you a couple weeks' severance, and we'll pay you to write one final column, but that's about the best I can do. I'm sure you'll land on your feet."

Merry gulped. *I'm not exactly known for landing on my feet. Not since the accident, anyway.*

Joel's "buck up, kiddo" mask slipped into something much closer to sincere. "Listen, Merry. You've got a lot of talent, and this assignment has shown me you've got grit too. We hired you because we thought readers would enjoy the novelty of a badass skier and we could capitalize on your name recognition. But this past year, you've proved you're a badass *writer* too. You've got solid journalistic instincts. You say there's a story still to be told out there. So if it was me? I'd follow the story."

"But . . ." Merry protested. "Without *Pulse*, how can I?"

"People can't get enough of your dispatches from llama-land," Joel said. "So screw OmniGlobal. Direct your fans onto your own site and do whatever the hell you want with 'em. They love you, Merry. You've got a voice that makes readers want to cuddle up with you and rub your feet. They want to eat pie with you and braid your hair at slumber parties. So take that, and make hay with it."

I can't eat hay, Merry thought. *Maybe my alpaca friends can, but I need a bit of lettuce, myself.*

"I'll think about it, Joel. And thanks, I guess."

"Chin up, kid. If you ever need a reference, you can always hit me up. That is, if I'm not editing the Koch brothers' corporate newsletter by then." Joel gave her a salute, then cut the connection.

Leaving Merry stranded deep in the heart of North Bumble-fuck, and facing, once again, a very uncertain future.

She bolted for the bathroom before the burrito could make its second appearance.

CHAPTER TWENTY-NINE

*W*hen she emerged, Bob was there to greet her. He had a damp dishcloth in one hand and an icy can of soda in the other. "Forehead," he said, waving the cloth. "Back of neck." He waggled the frosty can. Before Merry could protest, he led her back to her booth and applied both as directed.

Merry let him.

Normally, she hated to be fussed over. She hated to be seen in moments of weakness. But right now . . . she was on empty, and it wasn't just her roiling stomach.

"Breathe," Bob advised. He took on his notable-quotable voice. "'When we pause, allow a gap, and breathe deeply, we can experience instant refreshment. Suddenly, we slow down, and there's the world.'"

Merry endeavored to follow the advice. "Who said that?" she asked after several deep inhalations.

"Pema Chödrön. Or at least, her social media manager. I saw it on her Facebook page."

"I'm not sure I'm ready for the world," she confessed. The cold can on the back of her neck was helping; she no longer felt as if she might faint. Quaking, however, was still very much on the menu. "I guess you heard all that?" She gestured to her laptop.

"It's a small café," he acknowledged. "Sounds like you've hit the end of the line with that website you work for."

"Yeah. With a splat." Merry scrubbed a hand over her face, feeling the screws under the skin. Right now the titanium felt like about all that was holding her together. "I don't know what I'm going to tell Dolly. She was so excited about me bringing in new business for the ranch through DDWID."

Bob looked thoughtful. "You know, I really dig your column, Lady Hobbit. But have you ever thought of doing more with your writing?"

Merry shrugged. "Not really. I'm still pretty new at it. I don't even know what I'm doing most of the time. My editor was always teasing me about trying to write the great American novel when I should have been pleasing Five-Second Sally."

"Well, *that's* interesting," said Bob. He scratched pensively at his beard. "I don't know who this Sally chick is, but seems to me you could give her a run for her money."

Merry's lips twisted ruefully. "That's sweet of you, Bob. But I'm not a real writer. Most of the time I'm just pulling stuff out of my ass."

"My dear," said Bob, "most of life is 'pulling stuff out of your ass.'"

"Who said that?"

"I did."

Merry gave him a wan smile.

"Seriously, why don't you try it? You could write a book about life with the llamas."

"Like, a novel?"

"Could be." He shrugged. "But I was thinking maybe you could take what you've already been doing—your profiles of the town and the people here—and turn the whole thing into a book. Like one of those travel memoirs. *A Year in Provence*, or *Wild*. That sort of thing. Be good for tourism," he said, gazing around at his near-empty establishment. "And the Buddha knows we need more of that around here."

The wheels started churning in Merry's mind. A sense of hope, of excitement, uncurled in her gut. What she'd said to Joel was true. Aguas Milagros was worth more than just a couple of throwaway pieces posted on the Internet. It was a corner of the world unlike any other she had visited. A place that made you want to stay, get to know folks. Even set down roots. "You think anyone would be interested in reading a book like that?"

"I think..." Bob rested one warm hand on Merry's shoulder. "I think with a book like that, you could make a real difference in this town."

You *make a difference*, Merry thought. Aguas Milagros could hardly survive without Bob and his unique café. *Dolly makes a difference. Jane makes a difference. And hell, Sam, sour as he is, makes a difference here. But how can I?*

What does this town need?

A draft of autumn air swept Dolly into the café.

"I need Merry." The screen door slapped shut behind her with a bang, and she caught sight of Bob, standing by Merry's booth with his dishcloth in hand. "Don't think I'm speaking to you just because I'm speaking *near* you, Bob Henderson. I only came looking for my redheaded ranch hand." Her eyes lit on Merry. "Ah, there you are. Child, I am pure overwhelmed, and I need you back at the ranch. We've got to get prepped for the Wool Festival at Taos next weekend, and I'm about up to my eyeballs with everything that needs doing."

"Um, Dolly... there's something I have to tell you. Can you sit for a minute?"

Dolly plunked down opposite her in the booth, giving Bob the hairy eyeball as if daring him to challenge her right to be there. "What is it, child? You look worse than even Bob's margaritas can account for."

Bob's lips tightened, though he pretended not to notice the jibe, heading back to the counter and his prized cappuccino maker. The sound of steam could be heard, coming, Merry thought, as much from his ears as the machine.

In as few words as she could, Merry filled Dolly in on the situation. Bob busied himself refilling Merry's coffee cup, and brought over a cappuccino for Dolly as well. Merry noticed Dolly's had a Medusa head drawn in the foam. Dolly sipped at it, then scowled when she realized she'd accepted Bob's hospitality. She didn't seem to notice the Gorgon she'd slurped.

"So, Don't Do What I Did is basically kaput, though I'll try to keep it going on my own website and see if I get any traction," Merry finished. "I can keep doing my best for you around the ranch until Luke gets back, but I won't have the same readership I once had. All that publicity I promised you and the Happy Hookers...well, I don't know that I can deliver on that anymore." She hung her head.

Dolly patted it, stroking her chapped fingers through Merry's hair in a motherly gesture. "Don't get your knickers in a twist, hon. You've done plenty for us already, and it ain't like I'd have gotten a ranch hand I didn't have to pay if it hadn't been for you coming here. Worry about yourself right now. Didn't you tell me you planned to head straight on to the next gig after you were finished here, and your place was rented out meanwhile? You got somewhere to go after this?"

"Ah...I haven't exactly figured that out yet."

"Well *I* have, and it doesn't take much figuring. You'll stay at the ranch 'til you sort yourself out." Dolly thumped the table decisively. "Looks like Luke's taking his sweet time down in T or

C anyhow, canoodling with his new bride. Might be a while before he makes his way back up our way, and with autumn settling in like it is, we're gonna need someone handy with the 'women's work' we do in the colder months. Spinning wool and such. Dyeing yarn. I can't pay much, but I can keep your butt in biscuits 'til you figure out your next step."

Merry gulped. "Uh, Dolly, you do know I'm not exactly..." She made crocheting motions with her hands.

"I know you aren't. Not yet anyhow. But you'll learn. That is, if you think you're up for it—and you aren't too proud for such homely stuff."

"Dolly, I'd do just about anything for you. I hope you know that." Merry's throat tightened. "It's only, I don't want to let you down..."

"So don't."

Just like that, eh? Merry smiled wryly. A sense of relief washed over her at the thought of staying awhile longer. Relief, and something stronger. "Okay, but what about Sam?" she asked. "Last night he didn't seem any too keen to have me sticking around."

"You let me worry about Sam. Anyhow, he's gone off on one of his legendary sulks as of this morning, and it may be a while before we see hide or hair of him again. Now, we finished jawing? I got about a truckful of yarn needs sorting, labeling, and packing up, a half-dozen prize alpacas waiting on a good grooming before we can show 'em at the festival, not to mention about ten hundred amigurumi need boxing and price tagging. So shake a tail feather, child, and let's get a move on."

Merry got to her feet, took Dolly's hands in her own, and, with tears in her eyes, gently kissed the older woman's weathered cheek. "Yes, ma'am!"

❧

Once, they called me the redheaded renegade. (That might have had something to do with the way my skis went out from under me from time to time, but shush, we're not talking about that.) Anyhow, now I'm going rogue once more, dear readers, and this time I invite you to join me. Aguas Milagros has been too damn much fun to leave behind. So I'm not going to leave it behind. I may be parting ways with Pulse, *but I think I'll stay with Dolly and her llamas awhile longer. I invite you to stick around too, and see what transpires. Find me at OnMyMerryWay.com.*

CHAPTER THIRTY

*T*he theme from *The Exorcist* poured out of Merry's back pocket. She arched her butt up to retrieve her phone, looked at the screen, and winced. There were six missed calls from her mother, not including this last one. "Take a hint, woman!" she told the device.

"What's that, hon?" Dolly looked over at Merry. She had one hand on the steering wheel of her battered old pickup, the other arm out the open window, and an inquisitive expression on her face as the wind teased her gingery hair. She was taking the winding road to Taos with the ease of someone intimately familiar with it.

"Oh, just my mother." Merry stuck the phone back into her jeans pocket and unconsciously smoothed her unruly brows. "She'll call about twenty-five times more, until I pick up. It's never anything urgent, unless you consider the shameful state of my wardrobe or my skin-care regimen an emergency."

Dolly cracked a smile. "You two not too keen on one another?"

"Oh, she's keen on *me*," Merry said. "Keen to change everything about me, that is."

Dolly laughed. "Had me a mother like that. Wanted me to be a beauty queen, if you can believe it. Took me traipsing all over New Mexico trying to enter me in two-bit kiddie pageants. Me! I was practically born in a pair of shitkickers."

Merry knew the feeling. If she had her way, they'd bury her in sweatpants. "So what did you do?"

"Got so bad, I started faking I was sick the morning before we'd set out on one of those stupid auditions. But it wasn't 'til I hit upon the idea of drawing spots on my face that she finally took the hint. I only meant to dab on some chicken pox, but I used a Sharpie marker 'cause I didn't know any better. Wouldn't come off for about two weeks, and the whole time I was looking like Raggedy Ann." She chuckled. "That was the end of *that*."

"I wish it were that simple for me." Merry sighed. "At least back when I skied I could get Mother off my case a little."

"Is that why you did it?" Dolly wanted to know.

"Skied, you mean?"

Dolly nodded.

Merry looked out the window, letting the question settle in as the dramatic scenery sped by in tones of rust and sage and sand. She wanted to say yes. Her mother had pushed and pushed, and had as much as come out and said that Merry was only satisfactory as long as she could bring home gold. But she couldn't honestly claim her whole career had been about making her mother proud. She'd made *herself* proud too. There'd been nothing like the rush...the feeling of her body obeying every command, of being powerful, graceful, even *fierce*...instead of just a freak. Since she'd first picked up poles when she was three years old, nothing had ever made Merry feel so at home, so *herself*, as skiing.

No. She hadn't done it for her mother. She'd done it for her own satisfaction, and if it got Gwendolyn off her back in the process, so much the better. "Let's just say it was a point of commonality," Merry said, "and once it was gone...well, these days we have fewer and fewer safe subjects to discuss."

Merry's phone played *Tubular Bells* again. She ground her tush into the car seat as if that might shut her mother up.

"You gonna keep ducking your ma forever?"

Maybe I can claim to be out of range for a little while longer. Or fake like I fell off a cliff. They were, after all, driving along the rim of the very steep Rio Grande gorge at the moment. But as much as she might fantasize doing a *Thelma and Louise* to escape reality, that would probably fly about as well as a '66 Ford Thunderbird. "I'll have to deal with her sooner or later," Merry acknowledged. "There's some family business that needs deciding, and they want to see me for Thanksgiving."

"You should invite them out to the ranch," Dolly surprised her by saying. "Might be nice, getting to meet your folks, and we always make enough food for an army."

Merry choked on a laugh. The image of Gwendolyn Hollingsworth Manning at the Last Chance, surrounded by Dolly's menagerie, was beyond absurd. And her father...Pierce would be gracious, of course, but she couldn't really see him sitting down at Dolly's kitchen table and tucking in to one of her homely meals.

Marcus might like it though. Merry smiled at the thought of her suave supermodel brother kicking back with a bunch of farm animals...and Sam Cassidy.

"That's kind of you, Dolly. But I wouldn't dream of imposing"—*inflicting* was more like it—"on you or Sam that way. You've already been so hospitable, and I'm sure I'll have found my next gig by then." She changed the subject before Dolly could insist. "Oh, hey, looks like we're coming up to Taos!"

CHAPTER
THIRTY-ONE

*A*guas Milagros might be Merry's new favorite hangout, but Taos was a pretty magical place too. With the bigger ski destinations of Aspen, Vail, and Telluride not far away, she'd never had cause (or time) to visit the funky little town, though she'd heard good things about the skiing here. Turned out Taos had a lot more going for it than just slopes.

Especially during the annual Wool Festival.

The town was painted in a palette of soft browns and faded greens, all beneath a sky so blue and wide the clouds that hung suspended from it seemed designed to reassure you that you weren't just going to float away into forever. The city center was a surprisingly sophisticated mix of chichi shops, hotels, and restaurants, Merry saw. Tourists strolled the narrow sidewalks, popping in and out of coffeehouses or window-shopping at the many galleries showcasing both modern and traditional Native American arts. While the architecture was similar—all quaint one-story adobe construction—the vibe in Taos couldn't be less like sleepy Aguas Milagros, Merry thought. It was a town for the well-off, the tourist, and the aspiring artist.

In the distance, she could see the ski valley and Kachina Peak looming over the little city, promising steep runs the likes of which she'd once thought nothing of tackling. Now, she'd rather not think of them at all. Merry turned her gaze back to the road as Dolly wound their way toward Kit Carson Park, where the festival was already under way. Dolly's pickup rumbled and groaned, towing behind it a horse trailer full of slightly queasy but extremely well-groomed alpacas and one unamused llama. Merry had managed to load up Snape and his smaller cousins this morning without so much as a drop of saliva being slung her way, and she was quite proud of that fact. Now she was all eyes, straining to see everything around her from the adobe-fronted shops and galleries to the snowcapped mountains visible through the funnel of the little city's streets. "Is that the park?" she asked, pointing. *Duh*, she thought. The enormous "Taos Wool Festival!" banner spanning the entrance and the people streaming in and out of the green space were a bit of a giveaway.

"They better not have given away my slot," Dolly grumbled. "Paid extra for a good one by the entrance too."

"We're not late, are we?"

"Nah. I just ain't willing to get my ass in gear as early as some of these fanatics. I mean, it's great to see everyone, and I sure appreciate the chance to show off my handiwork, but some of the MAVWAs are plain gaga for this shindig."

"Mav-*wha's*?"

"Mountain and Valley Wool Association people," Dolly explained. "Mostly it's the same vendors every year. It's not like there's an unlimited pool of idiots ready to beggar ourselves raising hay burners. You gotta love it pretty fierce to keep doing it year after year."

"Don't you?" Merry asked, surprised.

"'Course I do. But that doesn't mean I wouldn't jump at the chance to take a hiatus... say about five years long. I think I could pretty much see all I want to of the world in that kinda time. But Sam can't run the ranch all by himself, and I can't afford to go gallivanting all over God's creation anyhow. I barely scrape by as it is. The festival's a good opportunity to get the word out about the Last Chance, sell some wool and whatnots, and even get my babies the recognition they deserve in the competitions, which doesn't hurt when I sell off a cria or two. Always helps the price when you can say they're sired by a blue-ribbon winner." She jerked her thumb toward the trailer they were towing. "That's why we got the fluffies all floofed up. Hope this year Greta and her coven of witches play fair and give us first prize like she ought to've the last five years running. She's been favoring her cousin Beth's sorry beasts too damn long."

Merry had seen the extreme cuteness of Dolly's little herd, whom she'd helped wash, brush, and blow-dry over the last few days. If they weren't the epitome of alpaca-dom, she wasn't sure what would be. Even Severus was looking dapper, flicking his banana-like ears and stepping high as if to show off his extra-petable pelt. "I'm sure they'll kick ass, Dolly."

"If they don't, I'll kick *her* ass. And I don't mean any damn donkey either."

⚬

The Wool Festival at Taos is a three-ring circus, where the rings are full to bursting with woolly goodness. On one side of the wide, grassy Kit Carson Park (apparently, ol' Kit was a resident of these parts), there are pens for the show animals waiting on the judges' decisions, a petting zoo, and even a bit of horse—er, sheep, goat, and alpaca—trading. Then you've got your booths full of fantastically talented folks selling hand-knit ponchos, cowls, mittens, booties, hats, sweaters, scarves, and just about anything warm and fuzzy you can wear on your bod. There are play areas for kiddos, and tents selling treats from fry bread and

Frito pie to sandwiches of shaved goat meat (a bit disconcerting consider-
ing the goat's cousins are bleating not far away) and cheeses that can be
traced back to the very sheep from whence they sprang.

A terrier in a sweater trots by. Not unusual, perhaps, except that he's
trailing the loose end of the yarn used to make it, and behind him is a
woman frantically trying to stop him from unraveling. A toddler feeds
a lamb, and squeals as he gets slobbered on. There are hand-spinning
demonstrations using fibers from vicuna to dog hair (ew). Weavers work
their looms. Dyers dip and knitters purl. And fiber fanatics of every stripe
find themselves in seventh heaven.

And I? Well, your newly freelance heroine spent the day manning the
Last Chance's little booth, selling balls of yarn and adorable amigurumi
to connoisseurs of the craft.

To sum up... it's loud, it's zany, and it's where Dolly Cassidy truly
shines.

❧

Dolly had her fingers six inches deep in Fred Astaire's beautiful
beige pelt and was extolling the virtues of the alpaca's "well-
organized fleece" to the panel of three judges who were visiting
their booth when a voice brought her up short.

"Finally bred yourself a show-worthy herd sire, did you?
Didn't think you'd manage it, Dolly-my-girl."

Merry saw Dolly's spine stiffen, and her expression grow
almost... horrified? Yes, there was no "almost" about it. She was
really, truly horrified. Merry turned to see what could possibly
have the fearless ranch owner blanching. And came face-to-face
with Sam Elliott's doppelgänger.

Lush, lip-obscuring white mustache? Check. Craggy, lean-
and-handsome face? Check. Twinkling blue eyes? Yup. He even

had on a dashing cowboy hat with an eagle feather trailing jaun-
tily from it, a denim shirt tucked into form-fitting Wranglers,
and alligator-skin cowboy boots that only needed spurs to complete the look.

The man was a total silver fox.

Dolly could not have looked more repulsed had she been popping llama beans in place of chewing gum.

"Why, John Dixon, what in blazes are you doing here?"

This did not come from Dolly. It came from one of the judges,
a middle-aged lady named Greta wearing an enormous pair of
spectacles that did nothing to obscure the prurient interest in her
eyes. "Dolly, you never said your husband was back in town!"

"That's because he *ain't* my husband. And as far as I'm concerned, he's on his way *out* of town as soon as can be arranged—
on a rail if I have anything to say about it!"

"Now, is that any way to greet your long-lost love, Dolly
dear?" The tall, handsome cowboy looked indulgently down at
Dolly, whose face was apoplectic—*much like Sam's gets when he's
pissed at me*, Merry thought. She took a step closer to Dolly to back
the older woman up, but Dolly was holding her own just fine.

"A thing ain't lost if you never go looking for it!"

The man chuckled as if she'd said something terribly quaint.
Merry bristled on Dolly's behalf. "Dolly, is this man bothering
you?"

"Only for the last eighteen years," Dolly said drily. "That's my
no-account ex," she told Merry. To the no-account, she growled,
"What are you doing here, and what the hell do you want?"

"Do I have to want something to come say hello to my wife?"
His twinkle turned aggressive. "Now that ain't kind."

"*Kind?* The only kindness you ever did me was running off
with that senorita seven years ago!"

The judges tittered. "We'll leave you to your lovers' quarrel," Greta stage-whispered. "We can come back later to look over your other animals, Dolly."

Dolly only nodded tightly, not taking her eyes from John. *Like a scorpion that might strike at any second*, Merry thought. "What. Do. You. Want?" Dolly repeated. "You got about five seconds to tell me before I sic ol' Snape on you, and he packs one hell of a loogie!"

John's jolly demeanor slipped a notch. He crossed his arms and puffed up his chest. "Knew you'd be at the festival, and I figured I'd be less likely to get a shotgun in my snoot if I found you here instead of at the ranch," he said. "I came for what's mine, Dorothy."

"I ain't yours!" Dolly was scandalized.

"Well now, that's not exactly true," he drawled, stroking his epic mustache in a way that made Merry think of penny-dreadful villains. "Thing of it is, I never actually got around to filing those divorce papers."

"What?!"

Dolly's mouth gaped open in pure disbelief, but John barreled on before she could demand an explanation. "Still, handsome as you are, Dolly-my-dear, I ain't actually talking about you. I'm talking about the ranch." He smiled through his mustache. "Long as we're still hitched, it's still half mine."

Dolly fumbled for the counter behind her and leaned against it as if all the stuffing had gone out of her. Merry put her arm around Dolly's shoulder. "You okay, Dolly? You want me to go find a security guard?"

"It takes more than a snake in the grass to spook me," Dolly told Merry. To John, she said, "Even if that were true—and I don't for one minute accept it—you've never shown the slightest bit of interest in the Last Chance all these years. Why come after it now?"

"Well now, that might have something to do with this tall drink of water right here," said John, leering at Merry.

"Me?" *Oh, no*, Merry thought. *He doesn't mean...*

"Imagine my surprise when I come to find out the Last Chance is all of a sudden famous 'cause of some writer on the Internet." He shook his head, clicked his tongue. "Never imagined folks would get a kick out of Aguas Milagros. It never held much to interest *me*, and the ranch sure's heck wasn't no prize. I was happy to leave you to it, Dolls...until I got a better offer." He looked over his shoulder, and the two women followed his gaze.

What met their eyes was rather unexpected.

The cowboy had brought along his lawyer.

The gentleman, stiff and sweltering in a blue pinstripe suit on this unusually warm November day, shifted foot to foot in his polished wingtips, as if afraid of stepping in dung. Which, Merry thought, was a pretty reasonable fear considering the venue. His thinning hair was plastered to his head with sweat, and he was clutching an attaché case as if it might shield him from attack by wild animal. Snape, picketed by the side of the booth, stared at him from under his long forelock, flicking his banana ears in a way Merry had come to know meant a loogie was a definite possibility.

John aimed his thumb at the suit. "This-here fellow says he'll give me four hundred grand for the ranch, kit and caboodle."

The man stepped forward, seeming relieved to get to business. "That's correct, Mrs. Cassidy. I represent a company called Massive Euphemistics, based in Denver. And we'd like to talk to you about buying out your ranch."

"What the hell for?" Dolly straightened up from the counter, stiffening her spine.

Seeing her expression, the lawyer took an involuntary step back. "Well, Mrs. Cassidy, our morale department feels it would make a perfect location for a retreat and conference center." He shrugged, as if the idea were beyond his personal comprehension. "Running team-building workshops, llama therapy exercises... that sort of thing."

"You have a *morale department?*" Merry muttered incredulously.

"*Llama therapy?* The hell is that?" Dolly demanded. She moved nearer to Snape, as if to shield him.

The lawyer consulted a sheet of paper from his briefcase. "Well, I'm not fully up to speed on all the details, but, ah, I believe the idea is to allow our management leadership to express their core values and explore their initiative in a rustic environment, and to interact with the animals in a way that's conducive to freeing their inner creativity and adding value to the collective."

Dolly's chest heaved.

"You know. Like a dude ranch."

Dolly's eyes grew wide as saucers.

"Like that movie *City Slickers*," he added helpfully.

Merry stepped in before the man could lose an eye. "Listen, Mr...."

"Watts. Cyril Watts."

"Mr. Watts. I think you're barking up the wrong tree here. Mrs. Cassidy runs a small fiber farm and llama rescue. It's not set up for large groups of guests. What would some big corporation want with it?"

"Well, Ms. Manning... you are Merry Manning, aren't you? The writer?"

Merry nodded tightly.

"I thought you must be. Can't be too many women fitting your description, I imagine. As it happens, it's actually your reporting that caught the eye of our company's morale manager. Your"—he looked down at the paper again, clearly reading from a script—"charming blog about Aguas Milagros made management think it would be the perfect spot for our retreat center. With a few tweaks, naturally."

"Tweaks?!"

The man's gaze darted back and forth between the two women, settling on Dolly as the more outraged of the two. "We'd be open to the possibility of you staying on, Mrs. Cassidy, in some capacity. Perhaps as a hostess, or an animal consultant—"

"Animal consultant?!"

"It's all laid out here, in our proposal. The buyout offer, the terms and conditions." Watts waved a binder with a glossy cover embossed with the corporation's logo and the phrase, "M.E. and You: A Winning Combination."

"Maybe you should give Mrs. Cassidy a minute here, to digest what you're saying," Merry suggested. "It's a bit of a shock for her—"

"'Shock' ain't the word I'd use," Dolly muttered, glaring at her not-so-ex-husband and Mr. Watts with equal venom.

"—And obviously, she'll need a little time. Why don't you leave your proposal with her, and she'll look it over when she's ready."

"I ain't *ever* going to be ready for no 'dude ranch,'" Dolly growled.

"Ready or not, woman, this is happening," John warned her, crowding in front of the lawyer and wagging a finger in her face. "No way I'm letting you get in the way of my payout."

"I knew you were a weasel, John Dixon, but this is beyond

even your usual capacity for callousness! Never mind what you'd be doing to me and Sam, kicking us out of our only home. What'll happen to the animals?"

John didn't look any too worried. He waved a casual hand. "They said they'd provide for 'em."

"Like hell. Some of our llamas are so far out to pasture they need bifocals just to spit at you. You think some money-grubbing corporate hack won't look at them and say, 'bad for the bottom line,' and send 'em off to slaughter?"

"That ain't my problem, Dorothy. No one asked you to encumber yourself with a lot of broken-down beasts that ain't good for anything but burning hay. It'll be a mercy on most of 'em anyhow."

"I'll show *you* mercy!" Dolly made as if to charge her ex, but Merry wrapped an arm around her shoulders to calm her down.

"Perhaps Ms. Manning is right, Mr. Dixon," said the lawyer, putting a nervous hand on John's denim-clad arm as well. "We've presented the proposal. I'm sure your wife is a reasonable woman—"

"Ha!" scoffed John.

"—and she'll see what a great opportunity this is, given time."

"Not too much time," John said. "How long did you say this offer was on the table, Twat?"

"It's *Watts*, Mr. Dixon." The lawyer looked pained.

"That's what I said. How long before she's gotta get off her high horse and sign the papers?"

"We'd like to set the wheels in motion before the holiday season. So by Thanksgiving, let's say."

"How's *never* work for you? Because that's when I'll roll over and show my belly to you, John Dixon!"

John swiped his hat off his head and slapped it against his thigh. "You won't sign? Fine. I'll just stay at the ranch until you see reason."

"I'll see you six feet under before you step foot over my threshold!"

"It's my property as much as yours, woman. I got every right. Ask as many lawyers as you want. I can outstubborn you any day of the week, and you know it. Unless..." He stroked his mustache again. "Unless you got the money yourself to pay me as much as they're offering. In that case, you'll see the back of me, fast as you like."

Dolly looked sick. Her bravado wavered. "How...how much did you say it was?"

Watts stepped forward. "We're prepared to offer four hundred thousand. That includes everything on the ranch. Animals, structures. Of course, they'll want to demolish the main house and build something more suitable for their important guests."

Dolly gasped. "That hacienda's near two hundred years old! Chief Manuelito stayed there during the Indian Wars! You can't just come with a bulldozer and knock it down!"

"It's not up to me, Mrs. Cassidy." The lawyer shrugged. "But I'm sure any historically significant items will be properly preserved."

Dolly didn't look sure. She looked furious.

"And if I fight it?"

"That's your right, of course. If you and your husband—"

"*Ex*-husband!"

"Yes, of course. If you and Mr. Dixon cannot come to an agreement as to the disposal of the property, that will be for the courts to sort out. Massive Euphemistics takes no stand on personal matters. But I do believe that a costly legal battle is not in anyone's best interests. Such a case could take years to wind its way through the judicial system. Of course by then M.E. would have rescinded its offer. Right now management is very excited to take advantage of the word-of-mouth provided by Ms. Manning's articles, so we're willing to offer far above market price for the ranch. But years from now, without a buyer like us...well, it's very likely that the actual value of the ranch would have been eaten up by the cost of legal representation."

"So if he wants to sell, but I don't..."

"Both of you lose. Yes."

Dolly had gone pale. So, for that matter, had Merry. Seeing her friend so cornered made her want to do battle on the older woman's behalf. Yet it was her own fault that this battle had come to Dolly's door.

"Try to see this in a positive light, Mrs. Cassidy. We really believe it'll be a net gain for the economy of your little town," Watts said. "In previous acquisitions, we've found that once we establish a presence in an area, all the amenities of civilization soon follow. Highways, Walmarts, Olive Garden restaurants. That sort of thing."

Dolly wavered on her feet. Merry felt a surge of nausea. She'd wanted to help bring commerce to Aguas Milagros, but not at the cost of the town's very soul. Bob, Jane, the hookers... and especially Steve and Mazel...There'd be no place for them in such a sterilized, strip-mall cultural wasteland. They'd hate it...and worse, they'd hate *her* for bringing it down on their heads.

And Sam? Merry couldn't bear to think of his reaction.

"Admit when you're licked," John said, settling his hat back on his head. "Take the buyout, or I'll take you to court for what's left of your golden years, and you'll end up with nothing."

Dolly snatched the proposal out of Watts's hands. "I'll look it over," she said grudgingly. "Now both of you, get out of my sight before I lose my lunch."

"I'll be back for your answer by Thanksgiving, woman. If you ain't got the money to buy me out by then, we're taking the offer from these Eugenics people—"

"*Euphemistics*, Mr. Dixon—"

"That's what I said, Twat." He turned to go, then shot over his shoulder. "'Less you got the cash, we're taking the offer, and that's that!"

❧

Merry led Dolly to a folding chair at the rear of the booth, putting the cross-stitched "Back in Five Minutes" sign out on the counter. She patted the older woman's shoulder, as if that would make it all okay. "I'm so sorry, Dolly," she said, and once she said it, she couldn't *stop* saying it.

Eventually, Dolly's expression went from empathetic to exasperated. "What're you sorry for? You ain't my evil ex. And it wasn't you who dropped the ball on the divorce settlement. It was me who let things lie instead of checking to see that scorpion didn't sting me on his way out the door."

"But he wouldn't be here now if it weren't for me! Massive whatever-the-hell wouldn't be interested in the ranch. Everything would be just the way it's always been."

"And everything hasn't always been rosy either," Dolly said. "I haven't liked to say, but . . . well, the truth is, we're not 'just scraping by' like I claimed earlier. We ain't scraping by hardly at all." She took a kerchief from her pocket and swiped at her sweating face. "I haven't even told Sam this yet, but the fact is, the Last

Chance is about two mortgage payments away from kickin' the bucket."

"Oh, Dolly," Merry said. "And you've been carrying around this burden on your own all this time?"

"I don't like to worry folks," she said tiredly. "Once, I might've talked it over with Bob, but he and I don't see eye to eye anymore. Besides," she said with more asperity, "it's half his fault I'm in this mess, what with his orphaned-llamas-on-the-doorstep bait-and-switch."

Merry got the feeling this was more a source of sorrow for Dolly than she let on. *They would make a great couple*, she thought, if only Dolly could see her way clear to forgiving the man. But while Dolly might not forgive Bob, she was going all too light on Merry. "I'm so sorry, Dolly. I never should have come. First I couldn't do the work properly, and now my very presence is endangering everything you and Sam have worked for all these years."

"Child, I hate to break it to you, but you ain't *that* influential. Something always comes along to rock the boat, if you float down the stream long enough. If it ain't one thing, it's another."

In my case, Merry thought, *if it isn't one thing, it's my mother*. "Yes, but..."

"Child, *stop*. Right now, I ain't got the energy to comfort you *and* deal with this nasty business. So, if you really want to help, take your head out of your rear and help me come up with a solution."

Merry reeled as if slapped. *God, she's right. What a time to make everything all about me. Dolly doesn't need mea culpas. She needs help.* "I'm so—"

"Say sorry one more time, child, and I'll set Snape on you," Dolly warned, but she patted Merry's cheek to soothe the sting.

"Put on your thinking cap and help me figure out what I'm gonna do so John doesn't go smirking all the way to the bank and leave me without a ranch."

Right. Get a hold of yourself, woman. A thought occurred to Merry. "Are you sure you actually *do* want to head this off?"

"What do you mean?"

"Well, maybe this isn't all bad. You did mention you wanted to take some time off; travel the world. Might this not be your chance?" Merry asked hesitantly. "I mean, your half of the buyout would be two hundred grand, and that kind of money buys a whole lot of suitcases."

Dolly sighed. "It's a great flight of fancy. I've got a stack of brochures a foot thick, full of places I've wanted to see. Only, who'd look after the fluffies? That stuffed shirt?" She waved in the direction the lawyer had vamoosed. "Some fool from back east who doesn't know his alfalfa from his fanny?" Dolly shook her head. "And what about Sam? This is his home too. Where's he supposed to go, if I sell out?"

Merry couldn't imagine Sam happy anywhere else on the planet. Maybe he hadn't grown up here—his mysterious past on Wall Street still seemed unimaginable to her—but caring for his llamas, hanging out in his homemade hobbit hole—this was where Sam belonged.

This is my fault, she thought. *There's no two ways about it. I brought these creeps down on them with my column. Like Sam said, I don't think about the consequences of my actions, or take responsibility for the fallout. That's got to change.* She swallowed hard.

"What if—hypothetically now—what if someone else *did* come along with a better offer? Enough to pay off your ex-husband, more than those Massive assholes were proposing?"

Dolly sighed. "Like who? I ain't exactly been fending off buyout offers with a stick. Nobody's gonna pay as much as them for a struggling ranch in the back of beyond, no matter how charming it sounds when you write about it. Anyhow, I'd still have the same problem. Someone needs to look after the animals, and nobody takes in llamas these days. They'd all be for the slaughter, if I didn't give 'em shelter. Plus, me and Sam still need shelter ourselves."

"What if you didn't have to leave? If the new owner wanted you to stay on, and run it just like you always have? Like, they'd just be a silent partner or something."

"And who would that new owner be—hypothetically?"

Merry took a deep breath. "Me."

CHAPTER THIRTY-TWO

*A*n eyeball squinted at Merry from the Skype screen. It was bloodshot, but otherwise an excellent example of male pulchritude. "Squatchy?" It blinked. "Do you know what time it is here?"

Merry didn't even know where "here" was for Marcus. He could be anywhere from Brazil to Bombay, for all she knew. "No idea. Do you?"

Marcus adjusted his phone, effortlessly finding a flattering angle that allowed Merry to see that he was lying on a rumpled bed, which looked to contain several other sleeping occupants. "Cute," he said, ruffling his hair up with one hand and making himself look even more like he'd just tumbled out of a Calvin Klein ad. "So what's up?"

Merry swallowed, suddenly missing her brother fiercely. "I think I'm coming home, Uglymug."

"For T-day?" Marcus stretched elaborately, pulling his white tee shirt taut over his tanned torso. "Cool!"

"No, I mean, for good. Or ill." She waved irritably. "You know what I mean. Permanently."

"You're kidding! What about all that 'My turtle and I would rather starve in our garret' stuff you were spouting a few weeks ago?"

"Well, it's not just me in danger of starving anymore. It's

Dolly, and it's my fault." Quickly, Merry sketched out what had happened, watching her brother's face as it ran the gamut of reactions from sympathetic, to scandalized, then back to worried. "So, I was thinking, if I made peace with Mother, she'd give me my inheritance, and I'd have enough to buy the ranch away from Dolly's husband, so she'd own it free and clear."

"And Mother would own *you*," Marcus pointed out.

"I know." Merry nibbled a hangnail, then remembered that she'd spent her morning handling barnyard animals. *Won't be too much of that in my future if I run back to Mother*, she thought. The realization hurt, despite the prospect of being permanently poop free. "But what choice do I have? I can't let Dolly's life be ruined. Nor her animals. Not even Sam. They've done nothing wrong, and this would be catastrophic for them."

Marcus looked skeptical. "Well, that's super noble of you and all, Squatchy, but are you sure this is the right thing to do?"

"I'm sure it's the *right* thing to do. I'm just not sure if I can bear to *do* it."

One of the other bodies in the bed began to stir. A hand crept out of the sheets and began to caress Marcus's pecs. There was more rustling, and another hand joined it—wearing, Merry saw, a different color nail polish. Marcus casually plucked the hands away, but a third—this one distinctly masculine—began to fondle his ear. He ignored it. "Well, don't be too hasty, Little Sis. This is a big decision. I'd hate to see you do something you'll regret for the rest of your life."

"Wow, Banana Hammock, you almost sounded sincere for a minute there. Don't hurt yourself."

He smiled, unoffended. "Well, you know how *I* handle the situation with the 'rents." He held up his wrist, from which dangled a stunning white-gold Rolex. "Might as well be golden handcuffs," he admitted. "But then again, a bit of bondage never really bothered me. You…" His expression grew more serious than was his wont. "You've always had more character than I do. You stand up to them—stand up for what matters to you. Don't give that independence away unless you're really sure you won't regret it."

Merry's eyes welled, and she sniffled. "Roger that, Uglymug. And thanks for listening. I love you."

"I love you too, Squatchy. You'll be fine, whatever you decide to do."

One of the hands groped for Marcus's phone, snatched it from his grasp, and tossed it across the room. The sounds of squealing, romping, and gasping ensued.

Merry left him to it.

∞

Merry trudged back to Dolly's booth as if she were walking the green mile to the electric chair. Her steps were resolute, and if there was any hitch in her gait, she told herself it was just her bum leg, and not the psychic shackles she could already feel clamping around her ankles. She plastered a smile on her face as she approached the older woman, hoping to hide the heaviness in her heart.

"Jesus H. Christ on a buttered biscuit, child. Who crapped in your cornflakes?"

Guess that worked out well. Merry smiled wryly. "Thanks for giving me some time to make that call, Dolly. I just had to check in with someone back home before I could fully commit."

"And now that you have?"

"I'm standing by my offer." Merry plunked her hands on her

hips and took the plunge. "Dorothy Cassidy, I'd like to buy your ranch."

Dolly stroked her hand across the back of the nearest alpaca— Ginger Rogers, if Merry remembered right. The alpaca tele-scoped its long neck to give her a nose bump, and Dolly rubbed its face fondly. "Well, hon, that's nice to know. But I ain't sell-ing."

"What? Why?"

"You haven't said much about your situation back home, but I'm assuming that death-sentence look on your face has a little something to do with that. What aren't you telling me? Where are you getting the money? I thought you said you were broke?"

"Well, I am...and I'm not," Merry hedged.

"Usually it's one or the other," Dolly said drily. "'Less you're one of Bob's philosopher cats."

Merry sighed. "Well, I'm broke if I want to live life on my own terms, and I'm, er...rather well off if I want to go along with Mother's ideas of how a Hollingsworth Manning ought to comport herself."

"Uh-huh. And exactly how well off is 'rather well off'?" Dolly asked.

Merry named a figure.

Dolly whistled. "You know how many ranches you could buy for that kinda money? Hell, you could have the whole town and half the inhabitants of Aguas Milagros for that much scratch."

Merry looked away, uncomfortable. "So you see, it really wouldn't be so much of a hardship for me to be your silent part-ner, while you continued to run the ranch as always. Of course, I'd probably rarely get to see it, if ever, since I'd be so busy with Mother's foundation...But still, it's not going to break the bank, if you know what I mean."

"Maybe not, but it *would* break your spirit, wouldn't it, child?"

Merry blinked and breathed hard. *Don't cry. Don't cry.* "I don't know what you mean."

"Sure you do. You got access to all that dough, and you're running so hard from it you land up on some crazy lady's llama ranch half a world away from your family? Something bad's got to be attached to it, to set you against it so hard."

"Not bad, so much . . . just . . ."

Banal. Phony. Soul killing.

Merry shrugged, not wanting Dolly to see she'd hit the target dead-on. "It's not so bad, honestly. Mother might have certain expectations for what I do with my life from now on"—*demands* were more like it—"but I know she'd let me do this for you at least. Honestly, it's a drop in the bucket for her, and if it would stop me from 'airing our family's dirty laundry all over the Internet,' she'd consider it a small price to pay."

"But it's not a small price for you to pay," Dolly said shrewdly. "It's everything."

"The Last Chance is everything to *you*," Merry pointed out.

"Yes. It is. I won't deny it. But here's the thing, child. The Last Chance is where people go to find refuge, a place to belong, not to give up hope. Not to roll over and let others run their lives." She stared up at Merry, her eyes fierce. "Running home to Mama? The way I see it, that's the *easy* way out. And I'm not going to let you take the easy way out. What I want is for you to find your *own* way. A way that doesn't do disservice to the things this ranch stands for, and that you and I can both live with. So no, I won't take your money, Merry Manning. But I will take what you're best at."

Merry found herself snuffling back a sob. "What's that?"

"Inspiring others."

Merry's mouth gaped open. "Um, Dolly...have you *met* me?"

"Yeah. I have. And here's what I see when I look at you. I see a woman who never quits. Who never lets hardship slow her down. You take your licks and you hop back up, Merry. I've seen it. Jane's seen it. Sam's seen it, whether or not he likes to admit it. Your grit's why your fans tune in, not for flowery language or a laugh once in a while. They're *rooting* for you, Merry. And so am I. I know you'll find another way to help me save this ranch."

Merry let her tears slide freely down her face. In her mind's eye, she could see her coach Jimby smiling and pointing finger guns at Dolly, as if to say, "Listen to this lady; she knows what's what."

"I won't let you down, Dolly. I don't know how, but I'm going to find us a way out of this."

Dolly patted her arm. "First go find us some chocolate. We can't be expected to brainstorm a way outta this shitstorm without sugar."

CHAPTER THIRTY-THREE

*O*f all the booths at the festival selling fantastical fiber arts, trinkets, and tools of the trade, there was one that drew Merry like no other. Like a lodestone, the smell of baked goods sent her salivary glands into overdrive, and she was helpless to resist.

"Bliss," read the hand-calligraphed sign at the top of the tent. And Merry had no doubt that was exactly what the purveyors provided. Rows of exquisite chocolate confections and cupcakes covered the counter, seeming to shimmer like a mirage before her eyes.

"Can I get, like, eight dozen of whatever's most fattening?" Merry asked the black-haired sprite behind the counter. The woman had to be a foot shorter than she was, and at least six months pregnant.

"That bad?" asked the woman, dimpling.

"Oh yeah. And then some."

"Then I recommend these." The woman pointed to something that looked like a cross between a cupcake and a benediction from God.

"If it's got chocolate and it'll send me into a stupor, I'm sold."

"I think this will fit the bill," said the woman. "I'm Serafina, by the way."

"Merry Manning." Merry shook Serafina's outstretched hand.

"Oh! You're the one who's been writing about that llama

ranch over in Aguas Milagros, aren't you? The travel writer? My
aunt-in-law Hortencia told me about you. She buys from one of
the women in Mrs. Cassidy's stitch-n-bitch club."

Small world round here, Merry thought. "That's me. Or, that
was me until a few days ago," she amended. "Now I'm not sure
what I am, or where I'm headed next. Hence the need to induce
food coma."

"Been there," said Serafina. "Hoo-boy-howdy, have I been
there." She helped herself to one of the miniature cupcakes, with
frosting shaped to look like a ball of yarn and two chocolate
knitting needles poking out the top. She plucked out the chocolate sticks and stuffed the whole cake into her mouth, grinning
around it. "Trying to get the little one into the family business
early," she said when she'd swallowed, rubbing her baby bump.
She picked out a pink-frosted cupcake and handed it to Merry.
"On the house."

"Oh no, I couldn't." The woman's confections were so exquisite, she could obviously charge a premium for each morsel.

"It's not wise to look a gift cupcake in the mouth," said a voice
with an intriguing accent. Merry turned to see one of the most astoundingly attractive men she'd ever encountered coming to lean
against the counter. (And, as an athlete surrounded by well-built
men in the prime of their lives, not to mention the sister of a supermodel, she'd seen a *lot*.) Tall, blond, and craggy featured, he
was everything she'd been telling her readers Sam was. And he
had eyes only for the woman at his side.

"This is my husband, Asher," Serafina said.

"Lucky you," blurted Merry, then turned as pink as the cupcake in her hand.

Asher smiled and wrapped his arm around his wife's shoulder.
"I'm the lucky one," he said.

"Hey, hot stuff!" an older woman's voice called from behind the flap of the tent. "Get your buns back here and bring these buns out there!"

Asher smiled indulgently. "Coming, Pauline."

"That has to be about the most jaw-droppingly handsome human being I've ever seen," Merry sighed when he'd gone. "Good on ya."

"He makes an atrocious omelet though," Serafina replied, eyes twinkling. "Guess no one's perfect. So, what has you seeking succor in sugar this fine afternoon?"

Somehow, Merry found herself spilling her guts to this woman who'd been a stranger not two minutes ago. "I think I may have inadvertently ruined my hostess's life with my big mouth."

"How's that?"

Merry's lips twisted. "It's complicated. But suffice it to say, if I don't find a way to fix the situation, I doubt I'll be welcome at the Last Chance Llama Ranch much longer. Hell, there may not *be* a Last Chance Llama Ranch much longer."

"Wow. That's pretty heavy."

"Yeah. I have to wonder if they wouldn't be better off if I hightailed it out of town before my blundering around causes *more* trouble."

Serafina looked at Merry speculatively. "You know, if there's one thing I've learned, it's that sometimes you have to face the things you least want to—to 'clear away the wreckage of the past' as they say, before you can find your way to the life you've dreamed of."

"Looks like you've found it for yourself, if you don't mind my saying."

"I don't mind," Serafina said frankly. "And I *have* been incredibly lucky. But I wasn't always in such a good place. I blew up my life once in a pretty spectacular way. If I could put myself back together after the mess *I* caused, I bet you can too."

"What turned it around for you?" Somehow Merry couldn't imagine this bubbly little elf carving the sort of swath of destruction she herself seemed to specialize in.

Serafina rubbed her rounded belly as if consulting a crystal ball. "I had to ask for help."

Help, thought Merry. *From whom?*

Sera seemed to read Merry's mind. "Simple, right? But it wasn't easy. Still, when I finally broke down and admitted I needed it, my friends, my family . . . heck, people I barely even knew, they all supported me."

Merry's lips twisted. "You don't know my family."

"They couldn't be any weirder than mine," said Sera. "Trust me."

At that moment, a woman wearing what Merry could only assume was a full-scale Frida Kahlo costume threw back the tent flap and pounced from within it, her posture shouting "Ta-da!" without so many words. The woman, sporting a tower of salt-and-pepper braids and about four hundred frothy skirts, skipped to a stop as she saw Merry. Her eyes traveled up and down all six feet, three inches of her.

"Hey, gorgeous! How'd you like to be the subject of my new seminar, 'Tall women in sex'? I need a model so I can demonstrate techniques for my new reverse-action sex swing."

Before Merry could respond to this invitation, the apparition was followed by a shorter, plumper, and altogether more mainstream one, sporting a tasteful array of hand-knit accoutrements upon her comfortable frame. "Pauline Wilde! What have I told you about accosting strangers with your sex swing shenanigans!"

The Frida Kahlo impersonator looked anything but abashed. "Horsey, if you want me to stop issuing invitations to strangers, there's a very simple solution."

"I told you no, fool. My back was out for three weeks after that last time."

Asher emerged from the tent and put his arms around both women's shoulders and kissed their foreheads, effectively shutting them up as they beamed up at him with adoration.

"See what I mean, Merry?" Serafina said. "Family. There's nothing like it."

CHAPTER THIRTY-FOUR

I knew you'd come to your senses, darling."

Fresh as a lily and smug as could be now that her daughter had finally returned her increasingly insistent summonses to talk, Merry's mother leaned into the Skype screen.

Merry leaned away from it. "I haven't come to my senses, I'm afraid. But I have come to ask your advice."

She shifted on the booth's vinyl banquette to ease the discomfort in her leg. She was back in Aguas Milagros, at Bob's, and exhausted after a weekend that had taxed both her emotions and her muscles. Dolly had won her hard-fought blue ribbon, and Fred Astaire had earned a treat of feed and fifteen minutes of "fun time" with the lady alpaca of his choice. (Merry had been surprised at his selection of Ginger Rogers over Cyd Charisse, but there was no accounting for taste.) They'd sold out of amigurumi, and most of Dolly's hand-spun yarns were spoken for as well. Yet for all that, it had been a more solemn occasion than it should have been, with the pall of Dolly's ex hanging over them both.

Merry adjusted the screen of her laptop to see her mother's face better, and her own as little as possible. She sipped her latest latte, which Bob had decorated with an elaborate curlicued question mark, and broke the bad news to Gwendolyn. "I'm not ready to accept Grandmother's bequest yet, Mother." *I'll never be ready,* she thought, but this wasn't the moment to tell her mother that. She needed Gwendolyn's expertise. And she still wasn't sure that when this was all said and done, she *wouldn't* take the money. Her bills weren't shrinking, and she still hadn't got a home to go to when this crisis was over. "What I *am* ready for, if you're willing, is to pick your brain a bit."

Gwendolyn patted her hair, as if to guard what lay beneath. "I'm sure I don't know what you're talking about, Meredith." She tried to laugh, but she just looked uneasy—an emotion that didn't set well with her customary poise.

"I'm talking about your life's work. Fund-raising. Getting people to get behind a cause that's dear to your heart."

"And why would you suddenly care about that?" her mother asked. Gwendolyn seemed genuinely surprised. "I thought what I did bored you to tears."

For the first time, Merry realized disdain might be a two-way street in the Manning family. *Her feelings are hurt*, she marveled. *All this time I was feeling shitty because I could never do right in her eyes . . . could she have been feeling the same way about me?*

Confident, self-righteous, mother-knows-best Gwendolyn Manning?

Nah . . .

"It's not what I'm passionate about," Merry admitted. "But that doesn't mean I don't think it has worth. I do. It just isn't right for *me*. But maybe . . . maybe you could use your skills to actually save the day for us here."

"You're asking me to come to your rescue?" Her mother looked more intrigued than offended. It was a start. Asking her mother for anything put Merry on uncertain footing. She felt like she was staring down the barrel of a steep chute, knowing she had to ski the run of her life. Only this time, lives other than her own depended on it. *What if she says no? What if she tells me the things I care about aren't worth pursuing?* Merry's coffee went sour on her tongue. *Then again, what have I got to lose?*

"Yeah, I guess I am." Merry smoothed her eyebrows nervously. "Truth is, you were right, Mother. My column isn't always a good thing. In fact, it's really fucked things up for someone I care a lot about."

"Language, darling."

Despite the fussing, Merry noticed Gwendolyn had declined to gloat. *Well, that's new*, she thought. *Huh.*

"Sorry, Mother. *Messed* things up." Merry outlined what had happened with Dolly and her ex-husband. "Anyhow, I need to find a way to come up with two hundred grand in the next couple weeks, to prevent Mr. Dixon from selling the Last Chance to that ugly corporation."

Gwendolyn made a tiny moue with her lips. She was no fan of big corporations—they had an unfortunate "homogenizing in-fluence," in her opinion. "Darling, I cannot recommend investing in some little farm in the middle of nowhere, but if you were to accept your grandmother's bequest—"

I.e., join the dark side...

"—you would of course be free to make such purchases at will. If you'd only stop being so stubborn..." Gwendolyn studied her manicure, letting the silence speak for itself.

Merry sighed. "Even if I weren't a pain your butt, Mother, agreeing to your terms wouldn't help with this anyhow. Dolly won't accept my money."

Gwendolyn's brow rose. "Really? I'm impressed."

Merry shrugged. "You'd actually like Dolly, Mother. It might surprise you to hear this, but in a lot of ways the two of you are alike. I mean, not to look at, of course. You're far more glamorous. And well preserved. I mean in the way that counts. Your standards. Your dedication to your causes."

"As a matter of fact, it doesn't surprise me at all, Meredith. I read your column, you know."

She does?

Gwendolyn ignored Merry's surprised expression. "It's clear to me Mrs. Cassidy is a woman of character. More so if she won't accept charity. But if she won't, then what exactly *is* your plan to help her?"

Merry slugged more coffee. She'd thought about this, and she was convinced it was the only way. "Crowd-funding. It's when you—"

"I know what crowd-funding is, Meredith," Gwendolyn said tartly. "My donors may be of a different caliber, but I *am* familiar with the concept."

"Right. Sorry, Mother. I got the idea after people started up a Kickstarter campaign for Sam's Survivors—the teens he mentors." She saw her mother nod impatiently and gesture for her to continue. *Guess she read that post too. Wonder what she thinks of Sam? Or the fiction of him I've been creating, anyway.* "All told, thousands of dollars were raised for the kids, when we didn't even ask for anything." The jury was still out—on walkabout, with Sam Cassidy—on whether that had been a good thing. "Anyhow, I figured if people would open up their wallets on a whim like that, maybe we could get them interested in doing some real good for Dolly. I read last year some guy raised fifty thousand dollars for a *potato salad* party, and I thought, if he can do that for picnic food, surely I could get Dolly the money to buy out her husband's interest in the ranch."

Gwendolyn considered this. "Won't that be harder now that *Pulse* is no longer publishing your work? Not that they weren't beneath you, darling, but they did drive a lot of traffic to your column."

It took Merry a minute to digest the fact that Gwendolyn seemed completely up to speed with all her doings, including getting fired by *Pulse*. *I thought she'd lost interest in what I do after the accident. Except to criticize, of course.*

"In some ways, it actually frees me up to write what I like, instead of just being sensationalistic," Merry said. "Right now, I need to remind folks why Aguas Milagros and its inhabitants are important, why it's crucial they don't get bulldozed by the forces of big-box stores and crass commercialism. Single them out, like that Humans of New York guy does with his photographs. If I feature the townsfolk on my site, make people care about their fates, I thought maybe I could get my readers to open their wallets on Dolly's behalf."

Gwendolyn was nodding as she listened. "Yes, I think it could work." Then she frowned as a thought occurred to her. "But why would she be willing to accept a bailout from a thousand strangers who owe her nothing, and not from one person she knows well, and who *does* owes her?"

Merry squirmed. She wasn't about to confess, *Because she doesn't want me under your thumb for the rest of my life, Mother.* "She just is, I guess. Better to be beholden to many than to one, or something. And anyway, she's promised to name all her new crias after the biggest donors, and make amigurumi for the others."

Gwendolyn looked skeptical, as best her Botox would allow. "Well, whatever the case, I find with fund-raising, there's always one key to success."

"And that is...?" Merry asked, when her mother seemed content to stretch out the suspense.

"Sincerity."

Merry choked on a laugh, then pretended to have swallowed coffee down the wrong pipe. Gwendolyn Manning was many things. Poised. Graceful. Beautiful. But she swam in a realm of artifice and glitter as easily as koi in an ornamental pond. Hers was a world not known for welcoming candor. Or Merry, for that matter.

"I know you won't think it of me," said her mother, who had clearly not failed to note Merry's reaction. "You've never given me credit for so much as a soupçon of humanity. But it's quite simple, really." She leaned forward into the webcam, fixing her daughter with a gaze that was more direct than Merry could ever remember. Despite the distance between them, the technology making their connection possible, Merry felt *seen*. "You speak from your heart, Merry. Tell people plainly why your cause is so important, and they'll make it their own."

∽

What makes Aguas Milagros so special—its charm—is also what is endangering it now.

No. You know what? That's not true. I am what's endangering it.

I came here, snark in tow, to make hay of the very people who have so graciously welcomed me into their world. The very name of my column has been an insult to my hosts.

"Don't Do What I Did."

Well, that's true. Don't blunder into a person's home and imperil their livelihood. Don't assume you're more sophisticated, more worldly than the folks you meet, even if the entire population of the town they live in could fit into your apartment building back home. And don't assume your presence won't have a lasting effect—or that theirs won't have one on you.

What I'm saying here is, I've come to love Aguas Milagros and the people who call it home. They've made me feel welcome, and valuable, and accepted in a way I can't ever remember feeling anywhere else. And in return?

I thought I was doing some good. I hoped that by sharing with you some of the wonderful personalities and talents around here, you'd see the value I've come to appreciate—not just in their handicrafts, which are world-class—but in their way of life.

Instead, because of me, the forces of commercialism have come calling, and the Last Chance Llama Ranch is in danger of being sold off to feed the faceless maw of corporate banality. Unless Dolly can come up with the scratch to prevent a "hostile takeover" in the next couple of weeks, she'll lose everything, and so will the llamas (and alpacas, goats, chickens, dogs, bunny, and cat).

I'm not going to try to be cute here. I'm just going to say it plainly. Dolly needs your help. I'm starting a crowd-funding campaign to help her keep the Last Chance from being sold out from under her, and I'll be featuring more profiles and stories from Aguas Milagros each day while the campaign goes on. Donate if you can, and please pass the word along to your friends.

❧

TravelBiatch: Done.

Moby'sDick: Done

Grammahnazi: Done. Period. End quote.

GrlyGrl: Done. But I want an alpaca named after me.

SnoreKelli: I just want an alpaca, period. End quote.

Grammahnazi: Are you mocking me?

SnoreKelli: Yes. Shut up and fund.

$\mathcal{S}$am's been gone nearly two weeks," Merry remarked, trying very hard to sound as if it made not the slightest difference to her.

"Eh, he just gets like that," Dolly said to Merry. They were sitting at her kitchen table, savoring a plate of biscuits and green-chile-smothered scrambled eggs before making their morning rounds around the ranch. "When he does, best to let him walk it off."

"But, er, he will come back, won't he?" Merry asked. Sam had been "walking it off" for rather a while now. And though *she* might not mind the surly llama wrangler's absence, her readers were beginning to notice. Though a gratifying number of them had followed her when she'd decamped from under the *Pulse* umbrella, and they'd loved her pieces about Jane, and the Happy Hookers, and the other inhabitants of Aguas Milagros these past days since she'd "gone rogue," her site stats showed a distinct bump whenever Sam's name was mentioned. If she wanted to keep up their interest in Aguas Milagros and crowd-funding Dolly's ranch buyout, she needed the star of the show to make an appearance—or at least, her sanitized version of him.

And, hell, if she were being honest, she *did* mind his absence. *If nothing else, I'd like to apologize*, Merry thought. On reflection, she could see why Sam had taken it amiss when his kids got swept up in the Internet's fickle concern. A man as private as Sam

Cassidy, as prickly and proud, must hate to find himself and those he cared for under scrutiny by an uncaring and capricious outside world. *I certainly never meant to drive him away from his own home*, Merry thought. She ached to tell him so. But when Sam went on walkabout, apparently he went on *epic* walkabout. He hadn't left so much as a bare-toed footprint round the ranch since he'd taken off at dawn after their confrontation at Café Con Kvetch. He'd simply packed up a llama, left Dolly a note slipped under her door, and taken to the mountains.

Strange how much she missed seeing his grumpy face around the ranch.

"I miss that fool boy," said Dolly, sipping her coffee and causing Merry to wonder if she'd read her mind. "But this late in the season, we're hardly taking tourists up into the national forest anymore, so his sulk's not hurting business—least not more than business already hurts. Sam's got a stubborn streak, and he's been touchy as all get-out ever since he and Jessica split, but he's never left me hanging when it counted."

"Jessica?" Merry blurted out the question before she could call it back. *I don't need to know about his past relationships*, she told herself. *In fact, the less I know about that man, the better for my sanity.* She already found herself thinking of him, wondering what made him tick, far more often than she should. Better to stick with the romance novel fantasy she was creating for her readers than fall for the much more complicated reality.

"His ex-wife," Dolly said, making a face. "Back east. Did a real number on his head, that gal. He hasn't been the same since, though in a lotta ways *I* think he's better. He's got her to thank for the turn his life took, all those years back."

Merry leaned forward on her elbows. Her heart, she realized with surprise, was beating faster than even Dolly's highly caffeinated coffee could explain. Maybe, just maybe, Dolly's explanation would allow Merry to understand why Sam seemed to hate her so much. "Could you say more?"

Dolly snorted, shaking her finger at Merry. "No. I couldn't. Not when it's just between you, me, and a million readers on the Internet. Now c'mon, we got fluffies to feed."

CHAPTER THIRTY-SIX

*M*erry woke, and wished she hadn't. So long as she'd been sleeping, she could pretend she was warm, and cozy, and not—mere days before the crowd-funding campaign was to end—still nowhere near saving the Last Chance. John Dixon hadn't returned, but he'd had that lawyer send over a raft of legal documents, and it was getting harder and harder to see how Dolly was going to avoid having to sell off the ranch. It was a chilling thought.

Or maybe there was a more practical reason for her shivers. Once her eyes opened, Merry could see her breath, as well as the reason why.

Her nocturnal caller had been by again. The cabin door was open a crack, and Merry's boots had been dragged to the doorstep, as if inviting her outside—or warning her she'd need them. More curious than creeped out by now—her recurring intruder didn't seem intent on any real harm—Merry wrapped herself in Dolly's afghan and penguin-walked to the doorway, toes curling against the cold floorboards. She shivered and blinked in the sudden light.

Whiteness. As far as the eye could see, a soft layer of snow had descended overnight, blanketing the pastures and blunting the outlines of the hacienda and outbuildings. The mountains were shrouded in capes of low-hanging clouds, and more fat flakes fluttered down from the steel-gray skies by the minute. The yellow-blooming autumn chamisa were no more than frosty humps in the crystal-white landscape, and Merry could see Dolly's disparate herds clustering beneath their corrugated steel shelters both to munch on the hay in the mangers and keep their woolly hides from piling up with snow. Merry doubted they'd have to worry much about staying warm, however, what with the eight inches of wool insulation most of them were sporting.

Unlike me.

Thank God for the Cosby sweater, Merry thought, shivering again and heading back inside the cabin to dress for the day. Randi had donated the eye-poppingly bright item to Merry's wardrobe upon learning Merry—who hadn't planned to stay more than a couple of weeks—had nothing suitable for the late-fall weather, not even a jacket warmer than her windbreaker. The sweater was an impressive tribute to the eighties in a rainbow array of stripes, swirls, and even, if she wasn't mistaken, a sequin or two. And it wasn't the only new addition to Merry's wardrobe. In the past couple of weeks she'd been deluged with homemade leg warmers, hats, scarves, and post-punk mittens from the Happy Hookers, and she'd been grateful to accept, even if sporting all their largesse made her look like a schizophrenic Christmas tree.

It's not like I'm out to win any beauty contests out here. But lord, if Mother could see me now...

Hell, Merry thought, *maybe she'd even be proud of me.*

Stranger things had happened—such as Gwendolyn's tacit support of Merry's efforts to save the ranch.

And speaking of strange... Something seemed out of place in the pen nearest the barn. It took Merry a moment to realize what it was—three fluffy lumps, where there should have been four. Quickly, Merry layered on socks and leg warmers over her stupid (and increasingly threadbare) skinny jeans, then sweatered up, wrapping a scarf around her neck and plopping a hat with about six too many pom-poms over her messy hair. She stuffed her feet into her boots and headed out the door to investigate.

Snow! sang a little, gleeful part of Merry that would never get over the delight of a field of untouched powder. *Snow-snitty-snow-snow-snow!* Even with the usual morning stiffness in her left leg, Merry found herself skipping a little as she headed out into the pristine white pasture.

One alpaca, two alpacas, three alpacas...Nope, just three alpacas.

Jane had sequestered the expectant mothers who required a richer mix of feed in their diets into a pen of their own. Travis McGee, Mike Hammer, and Jack Reacher (all girls) were where they should be, eyeing the brightly colored apparition in their midst with mild interest, but one was missing.

"Dashiell!" Merry gasped. The delicate young mother had been a source of worry for Jane and Dolly, as well as Sam, since she'd lost her cria in childbirth last year. Now her *absence* was a source of worry for Merry. *Alpacas don't just vanish.* And Dashie's coat was a rich, coffee brown. She wasn't likely to blend into the snow, which wasn't deep enough yet to bury her even if she'd been lying down, in distress. Which Merry sincerely hoped she wasn't.

I have to find her!

The snow had swirled up in a dense drift along one edge of the pen where hay had been stacked, Merry saw, creating a natural ramp a determined camelid could have climbed. The two-toed footprints and, more alarmingly, tiny dots of blood in the snow told Merry one *had*. The tracks, already disappearing in the worsening snowfall, headed up and into the mountains beyond Dolly's property.

Oh no . . .

Merry ran for the hacienda, calling Dolly's name. But when she got there, flinging herself through the mudroom and into the kitchen without even stopping to wipe her boots on the mat, she found a note waiting for her on the table.

Needed some kerosene and some treats from town. Looks like it's fixing to be a real doozy of a snowstorm, and we can't be expected to weather it without our cocoa, now can we? See you in a couple hours. —D

Shit.

Merry grabbed Dolly's phone, an old rotary dial that felt like ten pounds of lead in her hand. She found Jane's number taped to the fridge and dialed as fast as her shaking fingers would allow.

"This is Jane Kraslowski, your friendly neighborhood on-call vet. I'm not here to take your call, but if you leave a message, I'll be sure to have your horsies and chickens and assorted fluffsters feeling up to snuff in no time."

Double shit.

There wasn't time to wait for Dolly to get back, or to go in search of Jane, even if she'd had access to a car. The MINI Cooper would never make it past the driveway in this weather, let alone all the way into town. Within minutes, if Merry was any judge of snow—and she was—the alpaca's tracks would have been completely covered, impossible to follow. She grabbed a pen and scrawled a note to Dolly, telling her what had happened and that she'd gone out after the wayward critter.

On her way out the door, Merry said a quiet prayer.

Then she ran full tilt into the storm.

I am a woman with vast experience of snow. Over the years I've carved it, crunched it, and cursed it by turns. I probably know more names for the stuff than your average Inuit.

Today I just called it dangerous.

I followed Dashie's trail for at least a couple of miles up into the mountains abutting Dolly's property. For a gal about eleven and a half months into an eleven-month pregnancy, she could really hoof it (I know, I know, alpacas have feet, not hooves). Up and up into the trees her two-toed tracks went, rapidly filling in with the ever-strengthening snow. Up and up into the trees I went after her, like a sweater-clad abominable snow woman. The wind was rising, and there was less light than I'd have liked, especially with the dense ponderosas towering over my head.

In the past couple of weeks, Jane had taken me traipsing about the trails with which Aguas Milagros abounds (visitors, by the way, rhapsodize over their unspoiled beauty, so if you get a chance, and there isn't a monster storm, I recommend hiking them), so I'd come to know my way around a little. But now everything looked unfamiliar. I'm not ashamed to say, I was a little afraid, both for the alpaca and myself. Yet there was nothing for it. Dashie had made a dash for it, and I must dash after.

It was more luck than skill that sent me stumbling into her, in the lee of some tumbled-over trees that had formed a sort of shelter. She was down on her side, legs out, and rolling around in a way that scared me silly. I could see—and pardon me, I know this is a PG column—her vulva doing something one could only associate with imminent birth, and I thought, Oh, crap. I'm about to be an auntie.

I ran to Dashie, who seemed reasonably glad to see me despite having absconded into the woods to avoid exactly that, and checked her breathing. Having zero veterinary training, I couldn't say whether it was okay or not, but I was relieved to see her rise to her feet and shake the snow off her fleece. She paced around, looking at me with those limpid black eyes, and I knew...

I could not let her down.

∾

The darn creature had made a beeline for the forest as if trying as hard as she could to ditch any possible rescuers. *Probably true,* Merry thought as she caught up to the laboring alpaca about two miles into the trees. Didn't cats and other prey animals tend to hide out when they were in distress, so as not to make themselves a target for predators?

If so, Dashiell was a sterling example of her species. She was shivering in the lee of a clump of trees, breathing hard, trickles of amniotic fluid staining her back legs as she attempted to birth her cria. Merry could see a nose and two tiny forelegs sticking out already.

"Hey there, Dashie," Merry cooed, trying not to startle the alpaca. The cold air was scraping her laboring lungs, and her voice came out as a rasp. "Hang on, sweetie. This is no place to 'drop cri,' as Jane would say. Let's find you a proper spot to have this sucker." Merry scanned the woods. Wind and swirling snow were making it hard to see, and she was, quite frankly, cold as fuck. The layers of woolens were great, but no match for temperatures that had suddenly dipped down into the thirties, with a sharp wind dragging the chill down even further.

Bad as it is for me, it's worse for this poor mama. Better get her somewhere warm and out of the wind. But where? A darker area in the trees began to look familiar. *I'm on the trail Jane showed me the other day*, she realized. *The one with that historic mine shaft...*

Mine shaft!

❧

Ah, the miracle of birth.

No, seriously, it's a miracle anyone manages to ever get birthed. Great googly moogly, what a process. If ever I'd wondered (and I hadn't) why they call it labor, I wondered no more. Dashie stood patiently, stamping occasionally and straining, while from forth her nether regions poked a wee nose, and then spindly little legs I was glad to see had little feltlike caps over the tiny toenails. Not having much experience with motherhood or the impending thereof, I tried to think what might be comforting, and settled upon some old campfire songs.

It was halfway through the third rendition of "Kumbaya" that the young'un was born. A perfect little boy with darling brown curls and a neck like the stalk of a flower seeking the sun, he came sliding into the world in a slop of what I assume was normal mama-made goo, and Dashie began cleaning him almost immediately.

Me? I began cleaning house. Er, cave.

❧

There wasn't much Merry could do about making the mine shaft more hospitable, but she was damn well going to try her best. After the awesome job Dashiell had just done bringing her baby into the world, there was no way she'd do less than full duty as doula. Fire was out of the question at the moment—any wood she might have been able to scrounge up would be wetter than her limited fire-making skills could overcome—but that didn't mean their asses had to hang out in the breeze.

Merry used a scoop made of tree bark to dig away the snow that had accumulated on the cave floor until she'd exposed enough bare earth for them to rest on. She used the snow piles she'd made to build a windbreak by the entrance, leaving room to let in light and air, but sheltering them from the worst of the weather.

Then she set about slicing her sweater to ribbons.

"I don't know much about crias," she told Dashiell as she ripped the sleeves of the Cosby sweater from their seams, "but I do know babies oughtn't ever be cold." The alpaca, seeming much more at ease now that she'd expelled her offspring, hummed at Merry, watching her with gentle eyes as she nuzzled her little one. The cria was struggling to rise now, wobbling adorably on twig-like legs, and Merry took the opportunity to rub its damp wool dry with one of the sleeves she'd hacked off. Then she worked the rest of the giant, rainbow-striped sweater over the new baby's body. The cria squirmed a bit at the unaccustomed touch, but it was so woozy from its recent experience that it didn't know up from down, let alone fashion faux pas. In moments it was engulfed in an ode to the eighties.

"Good," Merry pronounced, seeing the shivers start to subside. For good measure she took the remaining sleeve and slid it over the baby's long neck like a sock. The effect was...awesome. Despite the circumstances and the biting cold, Merry smiled with delight.

"I shall call you Bill," she announced to the cave at large.

Before it even occurred to her how ridiculous it was in this situation, she had her phone out and had snapped several pictures. Dashiell seemed to approve, crowding closer to both Merry and the babe as if wanting to star in her first proud-mama photo. Belatedly, Merry thought to check her reception. No bars, of course, and the battery was winding down fast. She'd find no help from that quarter. *Nope, I think we're stuck here 'til the weather lets up. No way Baby Bill there is gonna be able to trot down the mountain in a storm, two hours after making his first appearance on the planet.*

Merry wrapped her arms around her torso, feeling the cold keenly now that the sweater had been donated to its worthy cause. She tightened her scarf around her neck and chest, and seated her pom-pom hat more firmly on her head. "Now we just have to wait for the snow to stop," Merry informed the beasts in a tone far heartier than she was feeling. "Or the cavalry to arrive."

CHAPTER THIRTY-EIGHT

*T*he beast attacked at dusk.

Merry had huddled as close to the alpacas as mama would allow, but the cold still had her in its grip, and the wet snow had dampened everything from her boots to her mittens. Her lips, she was sure, were probably blue, though the darkness would have made it impossible to tell even if she'd cared to find out for sure. Her eyes were drifting closed in any case. She'd dragged in some evergreen branches that hadn't been *too* wet, and scrabbled together some pine needles and other leaves from the floor of the mine shaft, but there was barely enough greenery to insulate her from the heat-stealing ground, let alone burrow under, unless she wanted to go out foraging in the woods for more.

Her shivers weren't as bad as they'd been earlier, and somewhere in the back of her mind Merry knew she ought to be worried about that, but right now she was too busy reenacting *The Empire Strikes Back.*

She was Luke Skywalker, investigating a suspicious probe that had crashed into the ice planet Hoth. The snow was endless, and the fate of the galaxy rested on her shoulders, but she was so tired . . . slipping in and out of consciousness in the snow. . . .

And then the ice monster reared up before her.

The windbreak blew apart in a flurry of exploding snow, and a huge, hairy creature lumbered into the mine shaft.

Merry screamed, or tried to scream, but her throat was so cold she could only squawk. Her torpor vanished in a puff of terrified adrenaline, and she leapt to her feet, fumbling a branch into her freezing-cold hands, trying with all her worth to whack the snow-covered Sasquatch.

"Quit it!" yelled the yeti. "Merry. *Merry!* Calm down, it's me, Sam."

Merry flailed about for another minute, the fading light and the wild hair in her eyes not helping matters. She squinted, pushing her hat back from her forehead. "*Sam?*" she croaked.

"Yeah, it's me, Wookiee." He stripped off his gloves with his teeth, and a second later, warm hands were cupping her face, turning it so he could see her in the waning light. She gasped at the contrast of his hot palms against her cold cheeks. "Jesus, you're whiter than milk."

And my eyes won't seem to focus, Merry thought. *Maybe they're frozen too.* Because, right now, Sam Cassidy looked every bit the dashing romantic hero. Dressed in a long shearling coat and a wide-brimmed leather hat, bandana shrouding half his wind-chapped face, he was the ultimate mountain man. Merry wobbled on her feet.

"Hey! You're wearing shoes," she observed. A dopey smile crept across her face.

"Of course I'm wearing shoes," said Sam, as if this was in no way remarkable. "There's two feet of snow out there."

"Bah," she said. "*That?* That's barely a dusting. You should see the gnar pow in Portillo this time of year." She tried to snap her fingers, but they wouldn't cooperate.

Sam took her hands into his own, and started to chafe the blood back into them. "Christ, you're frozen half to death. What were you thinking, running out into a snowstorm without a coat?"

"I *had* a coat. Well, a sweater anyway," she amended.

"Then why the hell aren't you wearing it?"

"Because *he* is."

Sam followed her gaze, squinting further into the mine shaft. His eyes widened at the sight of the tiny cria cuddled into its customized outerwear. He left her for a moment, just long enough to ascertain that mama and baby were okay. "Well, if that doesn't beat all," he murmured, shaking his head. A grudging grin tugged at his rough-hewn features. He returned to her side, shrugging off his coat and draping it around Merry's shoulders. Even tall as she was, the garment hung generously about her narrower frame.

Thank the gods, it was *warm*. "Thank you, thank you, thank you," she chattered. Her knees seemed unable to take the added weight of the sheepskin, and they buckled, sending her into a sprawl on the cold ground.

Sam followed her down, kneeling at her side. "Don't thank me yet," he told her, running his hands up and down her legs to chafe some life into them. "When I saw the note you left Dolly, I ran out here like some greenhorn without grabbing anything useful. Goddamn it! Of all the rookie mistakes, this has to take the biscuit."

⚘

Sam's the guy you want to be holed up in a cave with in the dead of winter...

Suddenly, Jane's casual words in the yarn shop seemed prophetic.

She'd gathered a pile of dry leaves for tinder as Sam had instructed—growled, more like—and was back to huddling inside his coat now, trying to stop her entire body from convulsing with shivers. She'd warmed up just enough to understand how close she'd been to being cold *permanently*. Her dreamy state had vanished, and she was back to seeing Sam for what he was...one grumpy-ass, unpredictable troll.

Who, as she recalled, had no great love for *her*. And now here they were, trapped together for God knew how long.

"How did you find us?" she asked between chatters. "I'd have thought the snow would have covered our footprints a long time ago."

Sam was checking on the alpacas again, making sure mother and babe had a cozy spot in which to kush, out of the wind and wet snow. Seeming content with the nest he'd arranged for them, he looked over at Merry. "It did. If you hadn't stacked up those rock cairns along the way as you went up, I doubt I'd have found you until morning," he admitted. "The giant X shape you built with those boughs outside the cave didn't hurt either." In the dim glow of her phone's flashlight, Merry saw a reluctant smile crease his features. "Guess you did listen to some of the survival lessons I taught the kids."

Merry forbore to mention that she'd learned this not from him, but from her first ski instructor, after he'd determined Merry could not be convinced to stay on the tame runs most other kids were content with. Rescue 101, he'd called it.

She could use rescue *102* right now. But Sam was disappearing on her...toward the back of the mine shaft. She'd given it only a cursory exam earlier, and hadn't found anything that seemed useful. "Where are you going?" she asked, a bit more shrilly than she liked.

Sam was rummaging in the rafters. "To save our asses, unless you'd rather freeze all night. I may not have brought anything useful with me today, but fortunately I'm not always this big of an idiot." He dragged down a bundle that had been stashed up there. "Fatwood," he said, holding up a cord of resin-impregnated kindling. "And firewood." He started tossing down some logs that had been tucked up in the support beams as well. Soon he had a pile sufficient to keep a fire going several hours. "Always keep it high and dry, out of the wet."

It would have been nice to know about that three hours ago, Merry thought. "Isn't that cheating?" she chattered. "I mean, aren't you supposed to, like, start the fire with the power of your studliness?"

Sam snorted. "I save my studliness for special occasions. Times like these, I prefer my trusty Zippo." He fished around in the back pocket of his jeans, coming up with a worn silver lighter. In moments he'd dug a fire pit, fashioned a bundle out of the tinder she'd gathered, and arranged the fatwood and logs atop it in some arcane arrangement clearly designed for maximum ignition potential. Another moment, and he had a decent fire going. It wasn't doing much to heat the place— and wouldn't until they got a nice base of coals going—but the light was enough to allow Merry to turn off her phone's flash-light.

"Lucky thing you left all that stuff up there," she said, pock-eting the phone. She shuddered to think what might have hap-pened if he had not. Then again, right now shuddering was about *all* she could do.

"I always leave caches of supplies around natural shelters in case of emergency. I've got about six others stashed around these trails."

"Ah." Of course he did. "I don't suppose snacks are included?" Merry hadn't eaten since the night before, and she was hungry enough that she'd begun to wonder if Dashie had a little milk to spare.

"Wouldn't be much of a cache without them," Sam said. He rummaged some more, then held up a rectangle that crinkled with a distinctive candy-wrapper sound. "PowerBars," he said, and tossed one at Merry, who caught it gratefully.

"Now eat up, and let's get naked."

CHAPTER THIRTY-NINE

I suppose you'll want me to be the back spoon," Merry said through clenched teeth. Despite his high-handed command, they weren't clenched in annoyance, but to keep them from clacking violently together. Even in his coat, even with the fire crackling in the pit he'd dug for it, she couldn't seem to generate enough heat to bring up her core temperature. She knew this was unavoidable—she'd had enough avalanche and snow rescue training to understand that much—but she didn't have to like it.

I'd like it a whole lot better if the man I'm about to suck body heat from didn't despise me, she thought.

Sam sighed, arranging the pine boughs he'd gathered into an impromptu pallet for them to share, with a second pile ready to do duty as a cover. "Just get down on the ground and strip."

Under other circumstances—with a different man—the command would have been kinda hot. But Merry was too cold—and too nervous—for cheap thrills. "Fine. But just so you know, this is totally going to be way sexier on my blog."

"I thought you were calling it a column?" Sam's tone was dry.

"Whatever." She started to unbutton the coat and unwind the scarf Sage had made her.

"Did I say strip, *then* lie down?" Sam said sharply.

"What's the difference?" she half chattered, half hissed.

"About three degrees of lost body heat. You're halfway into

an epic case of hypothermia already. You want it to get worse? Stand around bare-assed in the breeze arguing. You want to get warm, you get on top of those boughs with me and *then* we'll worry about stripping off."

"Yes, *sir*." She aimed an ironic salute at him. But Merry was secretly relieved she wouldn't have to face Sam's gaze on her mangled body. His *body* on her mangled body was going to be bad enough. As best she could, she crawled atop the layer of prickly branches Sam had arranged. At least they smelled good, which was more than she could say for herself, after today's adventures. Or Sam, most likely. Not that she planned on sniffing him.

"Now take off the coat and lay it like a blanket over you."

Merry complied.

"Sorry it's not a Beautyrest," he said as he climbed under the coat with her. Even with their clothes still in place, the effect was immediate. The man was a *furnace*. She felt him wriggle and rustle as he loaded their bier with the second bunch of branches atop the coat. Then the air between them got even hotter as he shed his shirt. His pants, thankfully, seemed to be staying in place. "I couldn't find any pillow-top mattress trees in this neck of the woods."

His tone sounded almost . . . *humorous?* But Merry wasn't feeling much like laughing right now. The feel of his very solid body behind hers was making her . . . uneasy. "I'll manage," she gritted. Merry shut her eyes and forced herself to start stripping off her shirt. But she'd barely gotten it unbuttoned when Sam sighed and stilled her with a firm hand.

"Stop. You're knocking all the boughs off. Let me." Suddenly, Sam's hands were all over her torso, sliding the shirt off her shoulders, briefly pinning her arms at her sides before the sleeves came free. There was a puff of frigid air, and then his chest made contact with her bare back. Merry jumped.

Hot.

Hard.

Furry.

He wrestled around a bit and made their discarded shirts into a blanket atop the boughs—to sandwich the warmth in, Merry supposed. But it also kept Sam's *scent* in, and it wasn't stanky after all. No, this was honest, and musky...and weirdly, undeniably *delicious*. It wasn't something you could put your finger on. You just knew you wanted to keep inhaling it, like fresh-baked bread or new snow atop a pristine mountain. Or your beloved after sex...

Sam wrapped an arm around her body and drew her in.

"Before you ask—yes, it's necessary."

Merry bit back the several things she wanted to say. She knew damn well the fastest way to raise one's core temperature was for skin to feed off skin. She could feel the theory bearing fruit already as the convulsions loosed their grip on her aching body, and a warm lassitude replaced them. A knot of tension uncurled inside her belly, only to be replaced by another sort of tension altogether.

"Shoes too."

Merry did as he bid, kicking off her damp boots. She drew her feet as far as she could up into their nest, cursing her height, but Sam didn't give her a hard time—in fact, he wrapped his legs around hers, tangling them together and making sure her cold soles were sandwiched by his calves, which felt warm even through his jeans.

Jesus. I've had sex less intimate than this, Merry thought. She was quiet a minute, listening to the sounds outside their little shelter, the suckling of tiny Bill at his mother's teat. She breathed shallowly so as not to encourage more contact between their bodies—or inhale too deeply of Sam's scent.

Okay. This wasn't so bad.

Then she felt something stiff poking into her lower back. It hadn't been there a moment before. She lurched forward, but Sam's arm held her in place. "Is that your...?!" she hissed.

"It's a branch, Wookiee," said Sam, sounding half-asleep. Yet...was it her imagination, or did his voice hold a certain tension?

"Do branches *throb*?"

There was a pause, which Merry couldn't interpret.

"This one does. Just ignore it. A little wood is all part of nature."

How the hell was Merry supposed to ignore that rhythmic pulse against her back...or the one that was beginning to match it, low in her own abdomen? The woodsy smell of him was overwhelming in the tight space. Outside, the wind howled and the snow piled up. They weren't going their separate ways anytime soon. Just thinking about it made her shudder.

Sam pulled her closer, rubbing her upper arms with his rough hands. "Okay?" he asked, sounding for once like a nice, normal person. "Or still cold?"

Merry was not cold. Not remotely. But that was no reason to believe Sam had the hots for her. As he'd said, "wood" was natural, even when you didn't care for the person whose proximity caused it. *He probably just doesn't want his reputation as a survival teacher to be ruined. Otherwise my ass would be out in the snow.* "I've endured worse," she said shortly.

He grunted, but he moved his pelvis a few inches back.

Merry told herself she was glad.

The silence grew awkward. Finally, Merry couldn't stand it anymore. "Look, I'm sorry, Sam. I appreciate you rescuing me, and doing this." She gestured to indicate their bower. "I know it can't be fun when you hate the person you're spooning up with."

"I don't hate you, Merry." Sam sounded almost...*surprised?*

"Baloney. You've loathed me from day one. And you seemed pretty damn angry a minute ago, bossing me around."

"I'm not angry," he said. "Well, I *am*, but not at you. I'm angry at myself, for not looking after you. It's my responsibility to watch over everyone and everything on the Last Chance ranch."

"I can look after myself," Merry said stiffly.

"I can see that. And you did really well, Merry," Sam surprised her by saying. His breath was warm against her neck, his voice a rumble she could feel as well as hear. "Getting Dashiell to shelter...keeping her cria warm...that was impressive. I know Dolly will be grateful. And...so am I."

"A compliment?" Merry rolled her eyes. "I must have whacked you harder with that branch than I realized. Or did you forget I'm the entitled rich girl, exploiting you folks for my own gain?" Merry's tone was more bitter than she'd intended. But she had to defend herself against this new, confusing Sam somehow. She didn't trust this niceness...not after the look in his eyes the last time she'd seen him. That had *hurt*.

Sam gently swept aside a strand of her hair that had tangled in his stubble, tucking it against her neck. His arm settled back around her waist like it belonged there. "I might have been a bit harsh on you," he admitted. He paused a beat. "Hell. I *know* I was, and I know I owe you an apology."

Merry tried to pull away, but there was nowhere to go, except out into the storm. "Don't bullshit me, Cassidy."

"I'm not. Look, I had a lot of time to think, while I was out in the woods. I realized I never gave you a fair shake, from the day you first arrived at the ranch."

"And now, suddenly, you've changed your mind?" She wanted to roll over and look at him, to read the expression in those electric blue eyes, but that would have brought her bra-clad breasts into contact with his chest. And her heart perilously close to his.

He sighed, propping himself up on his elbow. She could feel him looking down at her profile, as if willing her to look back at him, but she just stared into the fire stubbornly. "Not *changed* it, so much as realized it wasn't you I've been fighting with, all along."

Merry waited. Her heart was beating fast.

"When you arrived at the ranch, Merry, it wasn't you I saw; it was my ex-wife. Jessica." He blew out his breath. "Christ. I can't believe I'm about to tell you this. I don't talk about her—with *anyone*."

"So why tell me?" Merry asked. It was weird, talking to Sam in the dark, skin to skin, intimate, and yet unable to see the expression in his eyes. She stared instead at the tableau of mother and baby alpaca, drowsing together across the fire. So sweet, so peaceful. She wished she and Sam could be at peace with one another too. What would it be like, to feel trusting and safe with Sam? From the moment she'd met this enigmatic, often hostile man, she'd wanted to know what made him tick. Yet suddenly she wasn't sure she was ready to hear his story, to feel something real with him. He'd turned on her too many times. "Why now?"

"I guess I owe it to you, after the way I treated you."

"You don't owe me anything. Not..." She hesitated. *Give the dude a break. It's obviously killing him to be this nice.* "Not unless it's something you really need to say."

"You know? I don't know why, but I think I *do* need to tell you." He sounded mystified. "Just promise me this stays between us. No posting it online."

"Of course not. Jesus, Sam. What kind of person do you think I am?"

"I don't know," he said seriously. She could feel his gaze searching her face, and her cheeks heated up. "But I do know you're not Jessica. It's just, when I saw you that first day, all dolled up in that fancy coat and freaking out about a little llama spit, I couldn't help comparing you two.

"She was glamorous, worldly," he went on. "Accustomed to the best. And she..." He paused, and Merry could hear the working of his jaw as he ground his teeth. "She had certain expectations. Of me, of what I should provide. How I should look, behave, what I should value." Merry could feel him shaking his head. "It was a bad match from the start. But I was young, and she was...so beautiful. So confident. When she took an interest in me, I couldn't believe it. I was just this nobody kid from Jersey City. I wasn't handsome. I wasn't suave. But somehow she picked me."

He sighed. "I was fresh out of school. We met at some fancy-ass benefit. I was only there because my friend had won tickets off a raffle, and Bruce Springsteen was playing. *Not* Bon Jovi, by the way."

Merry smiled at the reminder of their conversation up on Wheeler Peak.

"She thought I belonged," Sam continued, "and I wanted her to keep thinking that. I was crazy about her. I wanted to be everything she expected from the man on her arm. So I took the job she wanted for me, pursued the career path she funneled me down. I schmoozed with the friends she thought were suitable. Hell, I even dressed in the monkey suits she bought me. And still I couldn't make her happy. Over time, it got really bad. I could see the disappointment in her eyes when I couldn't fit in with her crowd, when the money I brought in wasn't enough. We started fighting all the time, and we both said some pretty terrible things. It was killing me not to be the man she needed, and I knew I was standing in the way of the life she really wanted. So finally, I left."

Merry couldn't imagine this younger Cassidy. Sam had always seemed so self-assured, so comfortable in his own skin and confident of his skills. She'd never pictured him as someone with vulnerabilities, insecurities.

"It took me a long time, and a lot of roughing it, but I found my way in the end. Where I belonged wasn't in some stock exchange, parsing derivatives, and it wasn't drinking appletinis on some douchebag's tax-write-off yacht. I lost myself in the woods—but I *found* myself there too. I was finally the man *I* needed to be, not the man she'd demanded I be. I was content— or getting there, anyhow. And then you came along."

"And when you saw me, I reminded you of her?" *Confident? Glamorous?* Was he kidding?

Sam lay back down. "Yeah."

"Oh, Sam." Her shoulders started to shake. Little choking sounds escaped her chest.

"Shit." Sam sounded alarmed. "I'm sorry, Merry. I didn't mean to make you cry."

A wild cackle escaped Merry's lips. She was laughing so hard she could barely speak. "Samuel Cassidy, you have to be the biggest idiot I've ever met in my life."

"I do?" He reared back, but the cold outside their bower prohibited much distance.

"If you think I give a shit about being 'glamorous,' or moving in high society, you've obviously had your head up a llama's butt. I've spent my entire life running *from* exactly that sort of shit. You think *you* were a social misfit? Try being six foot three with shoulders like a linebacker when you're the daughter of a diplomat and a fucking *peer of the realm*. The only place *I* ever felt like I fit in was on a podium with the national anthem playing. And then that ended." Merry's voice grew tight. "But when I got to the Last Chance...it just seemed like a place I could go and not have to worry about all that."

Sam was silent for a while. "And I made you feel unwelcome. Hell, I'm sorry, Merry. I think I can see that now. You're not like my wife was. I mean, not that you're not poised, or confident, but that you're...I don't know...genuine. Unpretentious. You weren't trying to use us, or the ranch. I should've seen that when I read your stories. But all I could think was that you were making fun of me."

"*Fun of you?* After the way I made you out to be such a romance novel hero?"

"*Because* of that. I know I'm no prize to look at."

"You're not so bad," Merry said grudgingly. "If one likes the Pa Ingalls look."

Sam chuckled.

God, it would be so nice to revel in this moment. To feel this kindness, this acceptance from Sam. But he didn't know everything. And when he did...his earlier anger would be nothing to what he would feel. "Before you get too warm and fuzzy, you need to know, you weren't wrong. I *was* oblivious. And self-absorbed. I didn't think enough about the effect my column would have on the kids, or the rest of Aguas Milagros. And it's worse than a little camping gear." Merry started to tell him about John Dixon's arrival, his ultimatum.

Sam put his hand on her shoulder. "I already know, Merry. I ran into my aunt in town, and she told me all about it on our way back to the ranch."

So why isn't he tossing my ass out into the snow?

"She *also* told me how hard you've been working to make things right. How you offered to buy the ranch with your own money, even though it would mean making yourself miserable."

"It was the least I could do," Merry said. "I had to take responsibility."

Sam let silence settle over them for a while. "You couldn't have predicted what my uncle would do. He's been a thorn in Dolly's butt for the better part of two decades, one way or another."

"Still..."

"Hush, Merry."

Merry hushed. She liked that he wasn't calling her Wookiee anymore.

Sam's hand was in her hair again, she noticed, gently smoothing it away from her neck. "You know, while you're going begging for blame, there *is* something else you're responsible for." He pressed closer, making it clear what he was talking about. The "branch" felt more like a tree trunk now, rubbing up against her ass.

"I am *not* responsible for that!" Merry protested. But somehow, she wasn't pulling away like some outraged virgin. In fact... her ass seemed to be doing some rubbing of its own.

Sam sucked in a breath, then let it out slowly. "Oh, it's definitely on you, Merry," he said.

On me? How about in *me?* The thought set her pulse thrumming. Merry bit her lip. "Purely a physiological thing, I'm sure. Just a natural biological response to the circumstance?"

"Of course." There was a smile in Sam's voice. "I'm a guy who's close to nature, and this is my 'natural biological response' when I'm lying beside a beautiful woman."

Ice doused Merry's desire.

Suddenly she was colder than she'd been before Sam had come to rescue her from the storm. *Just when I thought we were friends... and maybe* more *than friends...* How could he be such a snake? Merry flipped over to face him. "*Fuck* you, Sam Cassidy," she said fiercely. "I knew you could be a dick sometimes, but that was just plain cruel."

Even in the dim light of the little campfire she could make out his bewildered expression. "*Cruel?* The hell did I say?"

She glared at him. "Look, you didn't like it when I made you out to be all gorgeous for the magazine? Fine. No problem. No more Studly Sam in the column. But I'd appreciate it if you'd do me the same courtesy and not blow smoke up my ass. I know I'm not beautiful. Not now... not before the accident. Not *ever*. If you're trying to get back at me by mocking me—"

"I'm not mocking you, Merry," he said.

And then he kissed her.

This time, it was no accident.

CHAPTER FORTY

Sorry to disappoint you, ladies and germs, but Sam was a perfect gentle-man. While the storm raged outside, and my hormones raged inside, our mountain man kept Mama, cria, and Merry warm and toasty inside the old mine shaft where we'd sheltered from the storm. Beneath a blanket of boughs and outerwear, we passed the night in pleasant conversation while Dashiell nursed her sweater-draped offspring and hummed counterpoint to the swirling snow blowing past the mouth of the cave.

I have to say that I've rarely felt safer, or, frankly, as comfortable as I did that night in the abandoned mine. Without the comforts of electricity, running water, or even a mattress, we yet managed to pass a productive and informative evening, chatting about everything from survival strate-gies to favorite childhood TV shows (mine was Twin Peaks, *while Sam preferred* The X-Files). *I learned that our Mr. Cassidy is passionate about a great many things, when you take the time to get to know him, and he's generous with his time, his expertise, and, of course, his body heat.*

❧

Merry had to smile. Sam had been generous alright...with his lips, his tongue, the caress of his callused hands. From the mo-ment he'd captured her mouth with his passionate kiss, Sam had taken full control, and she'd never for a moment felt her superior height. In his arms, she'd been all woman, and he'd been all man—a hot, muscular presence thrumming with desire, hands tangling in her hair to hold her still for his kisses, body sliding over hers to enfold her in his embrace.

Making out with Sam was hot as hell, Merry had discovered. It was also *fun*. His kisses had been mischievous and mind-blowing by turns, his lips capturing and cajoling hers into an ever-deepening response, his teeth nipping gently at her bottom lip, then soothing the sting with his tongue and smiling lips. His hands had cupped her face, his elbows braced on either side of her head so that he became her whole world, her focus entirely on the superheated maleness of him. And yet there was something about the encounter that had been about more than passion—it was an invitation to play, to explore, and simply enjoy each other in the moment.

Because that was the essence of Sam, Merry realized. When he wasn't keeping tight wraps on his past, or protecting the little corner of the world he'd come to call home, Sam was a man with a great love of everything life had to offer; someone who was fully in his body and deeply engaged with his surroundings. And his passion last night had made Merry yearn for a taste of that courage, just as she'd yearned for the taste of him. Since the accident, she'd lost sight of her own passionate, spirited side—the side that had been fearless on the slopes.

Now Merry wanted to be fearless with Sam.

But Sam had wanted to be a gentleman.

"Go slow, honey," he'd said, though she could feel his heart racing where it was pressed up against her chest. "Slow...slow..." he'd murmured over and over as he kissed her deep, kissed her slow like he promised, kissed her *everywhere*.

She wasn't quite sure why they'd stopped when they had—

the lack of protection had certainly factored in, but Merry had also sensed a hesitation in Sam that was more about wanting to do things right than wanting to avoid unintended consequences. At first she'd been stung when he'd pulled his lips away, his body held tense above hers, but the undeniable evidence of his desire for her and his labored breathing against her neck had told her it was no easier for him to stop than it had been for her to find her desires thwarted.

It had been a long night.

Even remembering it made Merry squirm . . . in the best possible way. She sipped her latte, which Bob had decorated with a simple but rather cheeky heart, a Cupid's arrow piercing it.

"How do you always know?" she asked Bob, who had a huge platter of nachos in one hand and a beatific smile on his face.

"I'm good like that," he said. He slid the piping hot plate down in front of Merry, narrowly avoiding her laptop. The smell made Merry's mouth water. She'd already been feted with Dolly's best breakfast efforts upon returning from their adventure this morning—Dolly had been overjoyed to see them safe—but she found she was a bottomless pit today. She and Sam had worked up quite an appetite . . .

"Share these with me?" Merry invited.

"Sure."

They crunched chips and savored spicy jalapeños in companionable silence for a while. "So how's it going, Lady Hobbit?" Bob asked at last. "Any news?"

Merry's face turned pink.

"About the Kickstarter campaign, I mean."

"Right! Of course." Merry pecked at her keyboard for a minute or so, squinting at her site stats and following the link to the crowd-funding site. "We're doing respectably, but we're nowhere close enough," she reported glumly. "If only we had more time...I really think we could have made it. As it is...I don't see a way."

"I'm sure your story about last night's adventures will help," said Bob. "The pictures you posted of little Bill were out of sight. Sounds like quite the tale."

A tale I have no intention of sharing in full, Merry thought. What had happened was for her to savor. And Sam too, she hoped. They'd fallen at last into an exhausted sleep—at least Merry had, though she suspected Sam had lain awake after she'd passed out, watching over them. At dawn he'd gotten them all up, checked to see that mother and baby were still thriving, then wrapped Merry in his coat again, along with every other item of clothing he could spare. The sun had come out, and the snow had been sparkling like a field of diamonds, already starting to melt as the temperature climbed. Merry had been almost sorry to say good-bye to their little haven, but she knew Dolly must be frantic. She herself was rather desperate for a hot shower...and some time to think.

Sam had been quiet too, hard to read in the light of day, and Merry hadn't pressed. He'd picked up baby Bill in his arms, and led them all back to the ranch, breaking trail without even breaking a sweat. At Dolly's door he'd refused her offer of his coat back, ignoring her protests. "You'll need it," he'd said, "if you're gonna stick around awhile." Then he'd traced one hand down her jaw, tucking a strand of her hair back under her ridiculous hat. "You *are* going to stick around awhile, aren't you?"

"If I'm wanted," she said simply.

"Oh, you're wanted." His blue eyes had burned into her. "I'll see you later, Merry Manning."

Standing there in Dolly's doorway, clad in mismatched knitwear and a coat she could have wrapped around herself twice, dirty and disheveled in a way that would have given her mother fits, Merry had known she must look a fright. Yet in his eyes...she had felt anything but. "Later," he'd said, and somehow Merry knew it was a promise. A promise she was looking forward to him keeping.

✀

"Banana Hammock! Banana Hammock!"

Bob eyed Merry's phone in mild alarm. "Your device appears to be having an identity crisis," he remarked. It was jumping and jolting all over his Formica-topped table.

"That's my brother," Merry said. "Or his text message tone, anyhow." She picked up the phone and checked the screen, glad of the distraction from her heated thoughts about Sam.

How's tricks in llama town, Sis? Gotta say, I'm a bit disappointed in our boy Sam there. Doesn't he know what a sweet piece of ass you are? I'll be sure to tell him how overrated gentlemanly behavior is when I see him.

Ha. *That* day would never come. The thought of Marcus descending on Aguas Milagros was so incongruous it made Merry snicker. But that reminded her...she hadn't heard from her parents in a suspiciously long time. She knew she'd have to deal with them soon enough, but she was more than happy to let that one slide while she faced the far more immediate—and important—crisis facing Dolly's ranch. If G&P were letting her off the Thanksgiving Day hook, Merry wasn't about to quibble.

Don't you dare, she typed. I've got enough going on around here without "Manning Meddling" to add to it. Thanks for keeping the 'rents off my back, by the way. I assume that was your doing.

Ass. U. Me, typed her brother. There was a pause. Oops, speaking of asses, my spectacular buns are due on set in a sec. Got a shoot for Armani Privé and my privies are anything but private in it. Just wanted to tell ya I love ya while I had a minute, Squatchy. I'm proud of you too. So are Mom and Dad, if you can believe it.

I *can't* believe it, Merry typed back, but her brother had already moved on.

Which is what we're all going to have to do, she thought with a pang. *Unless I can save the Last Chance.*

"What will happen to Aguas Milagros if I can't save the ranch?" Merry said to Bob, who was crunching meditatively on the last of the nacho chips.

"Why don't you ask the mayor?"

Merry followed Bob's gaze to the gentleman entering the café.

CHAPTER FORTY-ONE

So what do you do in Aguas Milagros?" Merry asked, wriggling her tush more comfortably into the worn vinyl of the booth's bench seat. She poked at her phone until it coughed up the voice-recording app, turning the device on the table so that the speaker faced Federico Rios y Valles. She wanted to get everything on record properly, so she could do him justice in her column. His demeanor demanded it.

The gentleman straightened his bolo tie, as if the phone could see him. "I'm the town barber, but that didn't keep me busy enough, so they made me the mayor." He took a sip of the cappuccino Bob had left at his elbow. It had a pair of scissors painted onto the foam, but they were fading under the predations of his tidy mustache. He looked, Merry thought, rather like John Waters, with a dash of Salvador Dalí thrown in. "I think they believed they were doing me a favor." He sniffed.

Merry raised her pirate brow. "Isn't being the mayor kind of an honor?"

Federico pursed his lips. "Have you seen this town?"

Merry's own lip twitched. "Things do move pretty slow around here, I guess."

"An understatement," he said with a tiny sigh. "No one cuts their hair in Aguas Milagros. The men barely see fit to shave themselves more often than their sheep. Dolly's buzz clippers saw more action at shearing time than mine did all year." He clicked his tongue. "I daren't speak about the women."

"That must be a drag," Merry said.

"You cannot imagine," he said. "I have certificates of excellence from every major academy of cosmetology. I have decades of experience styling celebrities, public figures, and Fortune 500 executives. My shave is so smooth it makes Julio Iglesias look rude. Back in the day, it took months to score an appointment at my salon. Now? I'm lucky if I get asked for the odd updo for a girl's quinceañera." His gaze was dejected as he stared out the diner's window, obviously seeing more-glamorous horizons. "You have very nice hair, by the way," he said, returning his gaze to eye Merry's long, coppery waves.

Merry blushed, glad she'd taken the time to scrub up after her adventures overnight. She hoped Sam would appreciate it too. He'd seemed to enjoy running his hands through her hair plenty last night... "Thank you," she said, fiddling with a strand self-consciously. "So what, if you don't mind my asking, brought you to Aguas Milagros?"

Federico's eyes darted about the diner, as if someone might be watching. "I had a bit of trouble, back in the city of my birth."

Merry raised her eyebrow again.

"Let us say that I was moved here... for my own protection."

"Like, *witness protection?*"

"I did not say that. But...a man of my accomplishments... well, you may extrapolate as you wish."

Merry examined the immaculately groomed gentleman before her. He seemed completely serious, and not obviously delusional. *We all have a past, I guess*, she thought. *Some of us are just more eager than others to leave theirs behind.* "So you'd leave if you could?" she asked.

"I did not say that," Federico said again. He examined his manicured fingernails. "Country life does have a certain piquance. And the privacy has its benefits too."

Merry raised the brow further.

"Oh, alright." He leaned forward conspiratorially. "I will tell you, since you are so insistent. I . . . grow a little something on the side. For extra cash. You might want to ask Steve Spirit Wind and his woman about that." He nodded over at the two, who had just entered the café in a cloud of patchouli and pleasant vibes. They grinned and waved energetically back.

"See you tonight, Mer-Ber?" called Steve.

Right. She'd promised to interview the hippies tonight, at their home, and feature *their* side business while she was at it. Which meant she wouldn't be spending "quality time" with Sam again as soon as she'd hoped, but . . . duty called. Her readers were loving the profiles of the townsfolk, and each article she posted on her site spurred a fresh wave of contributions to the cause. They were still far from their goal, but Merry was holding out for a last-minute miracle. After all, the holidays were coming up. People would be in a giving mood, she hoped. Meanwhile, she'd share Steve and Mazel's gifts with the world, as best she could. "Sure thing, guys," she called back.

"Groovy." They grabbed a booth and started chatting with Bob.

"You won't discuss that on your blog, I hope," Federico said. He was eyeing her phone and its recording app with belated alarm. "And you won't feature my photo? Not that I'm averse to pictures in the normal run of things, but there are certain people who, shall we say, ought to remain unaware of my current where-abouts." He twisted his mustache ends anxiously.

"Oh, no," Merry assured him. "I wouldn't dream of it, though of course you *are* tremendously photogenic, Mr. Rios y Valles. Actually, what I wanted to talk to you about today is Dolly's ranch, and the impact the potential sale to Massive Euphemistics would have on the town. My readers will want to hear the opinion of the town's foremost elected official." *Now that I know there* is *an elected official*.

The mayor puffed up with pride. "Well, as you may know, Aguas Milagros is a town of some historical significance. The great Navajo Chief Manuelito made a stand here, back in the 1860s. In fact I believe Mrs. Cassidy's hacienda is built around the site, but you'd want to consult Rebecca, our archivist, about that."

"I'll do that," Merry promised, though it wasn't uppermost on her list. She wasn't sure how keen her readers would be to read about bloody battles and the ignominious history of the US Army's pogroms against the indigenous peoples of the Southwest. *Maybe after I do the bit about the hippies*, she told herself. "Are you a fan of local history, Mr. Rios y Valles?"

"Not really," he said, deflating with another sigh, as if maintaining even a minute's worth of enthusiasm were beyond him. He picked a nonexistent fleck of lint off his crisp sport jacket sleeve. "But again, there's not much here to occupy a man of my talents. One must read *something* on cold winter nights." He stared out at the single street, watching the fast-melting snow drip glistening into the gutters in the slanting afternoon light.

He wasn't giving her much she could publish for her readers. She tried again. "I know the hot springs are a big deal with the locals. Do you think having a corporate retreat center nearby will help to spread the word? Boost tourism?" *Say no*, Merry mentally coached. *Corporations = bad, little folk = good. That's the message we're going for here.*

"It will probably end up like Truth or Consequences, in Southern New Mexico." Federico made a face. "'Miracle waters, now available through your bathroom tap!' They'll be building water slides, next thing you know. So tacky. No one here wants that."

Steve and Mazel might get a kick out of it, Merry thought. She looked over at their booth, where they were tickling one another with their long braids, and smothered a laugh at the image of the two of them whizzing buck-naked down a water slide into the springs.

"The town is sure to go to hell if the ranch gets bought out by those people," Federico continued. "Because it's never just one incursion, is it? No," he said bitterly. "First they want 'protection money.' Next they're demanding you launder their ill-gotten gains. And before you know it, they've destroyed your business, and you're forced to testify against them..."

Somehow Merry got the feeling they weren't talking about Aguas Milagros anymore. "Um...right!" she said. "We don't want any of that here, do we?"

"Oh, I don't know," he said wistfully. "Might provide some excitement, at least."

Federico looked so full of ennui Merry couldn't help herself.

"You wanna do my hair?"

The smile on the dapper man's face made the resulting foot-high bouffant worth it.

The beehive is a noble hairstyle, with decades of history and tradition to, er, prop it up. It is the very pinnacle of coiffage, and only the finest stylists can achieve such heights, be they literal or follicularly figurative.

One such cosmetological genius abides in Aguas Milagros, where he also happens to do double duty as the town's esteemed mayor. Today he had a go at my hair. The attached is a picture of the magnificent results.

P.S.: If you dare laugh I will so pop out of this computer and smack you upside your head.

⌘

"Don't say a word," Merry warned, glaring at Sam. She was in Dolly's front yard, eyeing the MINI Cooper's clearance with despair. Between her natural height and the extra foot of shellacked helmet-hair, it was looking like she might have to walk to Steve and Mazel's tonight. And while yesterday's surprise snow had melted away, she didn't think she wanted to walk home in the evening chill, despite Sam's donated coat. "I promised Mr. Rios y Valles I'd leave it up for the night, so as not to waste his talents."

"You'd need the SWAT team from Los Alamos to dismantle that thing," Sam said, swallowing snickers. He was leaning against the low adobe wall that enclosed his aunt's front yard, barefoot again now, wearing a heavy Clint Eastwood–style poncho over his jeans. Merry wondered which of his llamas had donated the wool to make the rough-spun garment, but she thought it was actually rather fetching. Unlike her hair.

"I *said* not a word, buster," Merry warned, but she was grinning. His presence was making her the *teensiest* bit giddy. "I'll have you know this hairdo wins friends and influences people." She tried to pat it in a ladylike way, and ended up sending it sideways into a tower to rival Pisa. "Buddha thought I'd brought him cotton candy when I came to give him his evening treats," she informed him. "Didn't even spit at me today. And Dolly thanked me for cleaning the rafters. Cleared away years of stubborn cobwebs in one fell swoop, she told me."

"Can I touch it?" Sam asked, eyeing the coppery cloud. "Will it purr?"

"It won't, but *I* might," Merry said before she could stop herself. She bit her lip.

She wasn't sure they were quite "there" yet in their relationship...or if there actually *was* a relationship between them. *A few kisses—okay, a lot of kisses—do not a love match make*, she reminded herself.

But Sam was already taking hold of her lapels, pulling her close. "I'd like to make you purr," he said. He began nuzzling her neck in a way that sent her blood pressure soaring.

Oh, goodie.

"And I'd like to let you," Merry told him. She ran a lingering finger along his jaw, tucking a strand of his blond hair back behind his ear. It didn't seem so much like straw to her anymore. "But I promised the Wind-Tovs I'd interview them tonight for the column, and I don't want to disappoint them—or my readers. We haven't got much time left before Mr. Dixon comes back with his papers and his ultimatum. We probably won't make the funding goal, but maybe if we're close enough, Dolly will be able to get a bank loan or something to make up the rest." Merry's throat went tight. "It might take a miracle, but I have to try, Sam, and this is the only thing I can think of."

"This isn't all on your shoulders," Sam told her. "We'll work something out. Us Cassidys have faced tough times before, and we'll survive whatever happens this time as well. And, Merry— you may not have been here long, but I can tell you're a survivor too. We'll work this through together. You're not alone." He smiled up at her, blue eyes twinkling. "Besides, if anyone messes with you, you can always head-butt them with your beehive."

Merry smiled wryly, pulling away to open the MINI's driver-side door. "Speaking of butting heads, if you wouldn't mind giving me a shove, maybe I can even wedge myself into this blasted Matchbox car."

Friends, do not pass up the hospitality of hippies. At least not in Aguas Milagros.

The home of SSW and his ladylove may be small, it may be creaky, but at least it makes a great getaway vehicle if you ever find yourself in a Partridge Family *escape caper. They live, you see, in an ancient school bus painted every color in the rainbow, and then some. Generations of local kids have been invited to hone their exterior decorating skills by adding some element of whimsy to the rusting metal sides, which are a wonderland of mythical beasties, Cubist portraiture, and frankly rude suggestions.*

Inside, it's even trippier.

"Shawl-chic" is how I'd describe Mazel's overriding ethos when it comes to home decor. Tie-dyed pareos, Spanish mantillas, African batik, Indonesian ikat . . . you name it, it's hanging from the walls, draping the seats, or carpeting the floors of the lovebirds' abode. I entered with some hesitation, seeing that they'd removed the seats from the back half of the bus, replacing them with a makeshift kitchen, and a futon bed plumped high with what I at first assumed was the family sheepdog, but only belatedly realized was a hand-woven blankie of some sort. (Mazel is a sometime member of Dolly's hookers, though she practices something called "arm knitting" that involves using—you guessed it—your arms in place of knitting needles. Imagine wrestling with an octopus and you'll have a fair idea.)

SSW and MT were seated on the sheepdog, but they rose to greet me with eager hugs.

"No, no," I demurred, "please don't get up." Please, I was thinking, do not, for the love of God, get up.

But alas, I got a heaping helping of hippie hospitality. Naked, balls-out hospitality. For you see, the Wind-Tovs do not believe clothing has any place in the home. Most folks leave their shoes by the door. My new friends leave everything.

"Care for a cocktail, hon?" Mazel inquired.

I did.

Soon we were sitting around the sheepdog, Rob Roys in hand, my gaze hopping overtime to evade exposure to the bits of my hosts I'd already had seared into my memory at the springs. They were eager to share the good word about their little side business, and I was eager to think about anything other than nudity.

"So what are you selling?" I asked brightly.

"Good karma," they told me. "Good vibes."

⁂

Merry wobbled out of the bus, a grin on her face so huge it threatened to go sliding off into the night. She squinted, her eyes reddened from the smudge-stick fumes, and tried to locate her car. She found it at last under a cottonwood tree by the little acequia that ran along Only Street. It seemed to swell and shrink, breathing like a puffer fish as she approached. "Hey, Minnie!" Merry said to the rental. "Thanks for being such a great l'il car. You really are my best friend, you know?" She fumbled in the pocket of Sam's sheepskin coat, looking for her keys. The pocket seemed as deep as a mine shaft, her arm lengthening endlessly into its depths. She stumbled and bumped her hip against the car door, giggling helplessly.

Something roared behind her, and Merry wobbled around to see what was what.

The floof-mobile was idling in the middle of the road, headlights and fog lights ablaze. Sam stuck his head out of the window. "You doing okay over there?" he called.

"Heeeeeyyyyyyyyy, Sam!" Merry cried, the smile floating around her like fireflies. "How's it hanging, man?"

Sam's eyebrows shot up, and then his head disappeared back into the truck. A second later she heard the parking brake engage, and the rusty squeal as the driver's door creaked open, then slammed shut. Hobbit feet hit the dirt and padded around the front of the vehicle. Merry squinted against the light at Sam's silhouetted figure.

"Are you *drunk*?"

"I only had one Rubbery. I mean, Roy Rogers. Dang it—Rob Roy!" Merry dissolved in another fit of giggles.

Sam looked back in the direction from whence she'd come, seeing the Wind-Tovs' bus lit up from within and leaking smoke from every open window. His nostrils flared as he inhaled deeply.

"Jesus, Merry. You didn't let them smudge you, did you?" He sounded alarmed.

Merry's head was suddenly very, very heavy. The beehive weighed a hundred tons. She leaned it against the door of the car—or tried to, but missed. She slid down the side of the MINI, her butt thumping into the dirt. "Smudge, fudge, drudge, pudge," she sang, looking up at him with a wondering expression. "Man, that sage is some powerful juju."

Sam scrubbed a hand down his face. "That wasn't sage, Merry."

Merry blinked owlishly at him. "They *said* it was sage." She paused, considered. "Or maybe they said sense...sensi...

sinsemilla?" She shook her head, then shrugged. "Something like that. Oh, look, here are my keys!" She thrust her fist up at him triumphantly, fingers clutched around her pocket hairbrush.

He rolled his eyes. "C'mon, sweetheart. You're clearly in no shape to drive. I'll give you a ride home, and you can get your car tomorrow when you've come down." He extended one callused paw.

"But Minnie might get lonely," Merry protested, patting the tire nearest her.

"Okay, time to go!" Sam padded up to her, giving Merry a close-up view of his bare feet. *They're really not that bad*, she thought. *Not even all that furry.* She reached out to pet one, but before she knew it, he'd gotten an arm around her and lifted her as if she weren't a full three inches taller than he was.

"Whee!" she shouted, directly in his ear. Her nose landed in the crook of his neck, and she snuffled. "Hey, you smell good, you know? Like man-juice." She laughed hysterically.

Sam peeled her nose away from his neck, but he was smiling. "Maybe I'd better take you to my place instead," he said. "I don't think I can trust you alone in the cabin tonight. You might go chasing centipedes with an axe."

"Oooooooh, Sam. You naughty boy." Merry threw both arms around him. "I'd *love* to come back to your hobbit hole. Let's Bag End it, baby!"

Sam bit his lip, but a smile leaked out anyway. "Okay, honey. Let's get you in the truck." He suited words to actions, hauling her around to the passenger door despite her efforts to play peek-aboo with his poncho.

"This is like pushing Jell-O through a sieve—with chop-sticks," Sam muttered.

Merry found this uproariously funny. She did not, however,

find the starch to keep her legs from folding up underneath her, and Sam was forced to keep her upright. Finally, he got her settled inside the vehicle, leaning her head against the door. She was still snickering softly, her hair bent like Marge Simpson's against the roof of the vehicle.

"Haven't you ever smoked pot before?" Sam asked, giving her the side-eye.

Merry shook her head. "Random drug testing," she said, turtling her head deeper into his jacket, then nibbling experimentally on the collar. "Couldn't take the risk."

Sam gave her a look.

"Ski team, not prison." Merry gnawed on the jacket some more, looking pensive. "Same diff, some of the time."

∝

My dear ones, when a man takes you back to his lair, it's just good form not to go ravaging through his kitchen, scaring his bunny rabbit while you go scaring up something to eat. Unfortunately, your fearless heroine displayed very poor form indeed, a veritable Tasmanian Devil devouring PB&Js, cold pizza (Sam makes the pizza himself, in a kiva brick oven of his own devising), and guzzling fresh goat milk from a pitcher in the fridge (only because I did not know it was goat milk, I assure you).

Sam was patient throughout the scourge, allowing me to ravish his larder to my heart's content. As for other sorts of ravishments, well, that's between a girl and her llama wrangler...

CHAPTER FORTY-FOUR

𝓜erry lay in Sam's loft, tummy full of stolen treats, admiring the view. She wasn't looking at the skylight he'd installed in the roof above his surprisingly cushy bed, through which she could see a thousand pinpoints of light. She wasn't looking at the beautiful woodwork of the loft, which was essentially a tree house, nor the rustic-yet-handsome furnishings that decorated the space in Lothlórien chic.

She was watching the mountain man who hovered above her, tucking her tenderly between his sheets.

She liked this view indeed.

Merry sat up against the carved headboard of his bed, then took a deep breath of Sam-scented air, wondering if his pheromones were making her dizzy. Or maybe it was still the smudging the Wind-Tovs had given her. Because suddenly, she felt the urge to confess her innermost secrets. *Here goes nothing*, she thought. "You may as well know, my name's not Meredith." She bit her lip as she watched his face. "It's Meriadoc."

"Oh, honey," said Sam.

His eyes watered. His lips curled upward. His chest lurched and hitched as he tried manfully to stifle it. But the laughter leaked out, in snorts and chortles and snuffles, until finally it burst forth full blown. Even as she stiffened with affront, his arms wrapped round her, hot against her sinsemilla-sensitized skin.

"Oh, *honey*." His hands came up to frame her face, and his mirth-filled eyes were lively. He laid a smiling, yet tender kiss upon her lips. "If you got any cuter, I don't think I could stand it."

"I'm not cute," she sniffed, even as her own lips curled in a smile. "I'm *statuesque*."

"You're adorable, is what you are." He set her back gently against the pillows again, being careful of the battered bouffant. "And I may as well admit, my name is..." He paused dramatically. "...*not* Samwise. It's Samuel. Samuel Adams Cassidy." He shrugged. "What can I say. My dad liked patriots. And beer."

"I like beer," Merry told him. "And I like you." She made a grab for his arm. "C'mere."

"Merry, you're in no condition," Sam protested.

"I'm totally fine!" she said...or tried to say. An enormous yawn threatened to crack her face in two. She tried to cover it with her hand and ended up slapping herself in the face.

"Not fine," Sam said firmly. "But adorable." He kissed her forehead, stroked her cheek lightly. "Get some rest." He made to get up.

Merry had captured one of his fingers and was nibbling it, though the munchies were gone now. Somehow, in the course of one day, she'd grown very fond of sleeping next to Sam Cassidy. She suspected the experience would be much nicer without the bed of branches and the freezing-cold cave. "*Can't* rest," she said, "unless you stay."

"And I can't rest if I do, honey. You're too tempting by half."

"Tough shit," Merry said, yanking him down beside her. She wrapped his arm around her like an extra coverlet, and within seconds, her breathing had grown slow and regular.

"Wookiee," said Sam around a mouthful of beehive, "you are *so* going to pay for that."

"Mm, hm." Merry smiled into the darkness. "G'night Sam."
Two seconds later she was fast asleep.

∾

She awoke the next morning deeply refreshed...and deeply in need.

"Hey, Sam...?" Merry poked his shoulder. Dawn light was flooding the loft, giving Sam's messy hair a golden glow, and burnishing his deeply tanned skin. *How did I ever think this man wasn't sexy?* she wondered. *Was I blind?* She saw him clearly now—and she loved what she saw. The man sleeping at her side was so much better than the "Studly Sam" of her column. This was a real, flesh-and-blood hero. A man who cared deeply for his family, his home, and all those in his charge—even, she hoped, herself. He was warm, and kind, and soulful, even if at times he did jump to conclusions or stomp around like a grumpy bear. He was funny, and passionate, and *exactly* the guy you'd want to find yourself with in a hairy situation. Someone who made you feel safe.

Also, horny.

At some point in the night Sam had removed his shirt and seemed to be sporting only a faded pair of jeans—and a faint, boyish smile. He looked peaceful, Merry thought. *Not for long, boyo*, she vowed.

"Saaa-aaaam..." She poked him some more, until those blue eyes blinked open.

His blunt features lit up at the sight of her, as if she were a prize he'd just won. It made Merry flush with pleasure.

"What, honey?"

"You know how you said I was in no condition last night?"

His eyes crinkled. "Mm, hm."

"Well...I'm pretty sure I'm in condition now..."

"Is that right?" He smiled some more.

"Mm, hm."

Sam proceeded to show her exactly what condition *he* was in. It was quite an impressive condition.

He slid atop her like he was born to be there, and his lips captured hers in a kiss that spoke volumes about his desire for her, his pleasure in her company, the playful tenderness he wanted to share. His hands came up to cup her face, and for a moment Merry went still, remembering the tiny surgical screws beneath her skin, aware of all the subtle flaws he must surely see, with his face so close to hers in the full light of day. In the cave, in the kindness of firelight, she'd been brave, but now, suddenly, her bravado evaporated.

She was raw. Vulnerable. And about to be naked.

With Sam as her lover.

She looked up at him, seeking some truth in his eyes. He stopped, aware of her regard. "What is it, Merry?" His thumbs traced her cheekbones, featherlight. There was nothing in his gaze but desire.

"You really see me, don't you?" Her tone was wondering. *And you're not repulsed.* Just the opposite, if the hardness growing against her belly was any indication.

He didn't laugh, or make a joke. He didn't try to pretend he didn't know what she was talking about. "I see you," he said. And he kissed her like he was seeing her very soul.

Merry kissed him back like he was saving it.

Tongues twined, breath exchanged in little sighs and gasps while their hands roamed, stroked, told each other without words of their delight in this moment, the strength of the desire that washed over them in Sam's sunlit loft. His scent engulfed her, his body pressed against hers with an urgency she shared. Merry's skin seemed to *know* his, somehow, to recognize it as something she had been missing far too long, and she couldn't seem to get close enough. Sam matched her every step of the way. His hands tangled in the mass of her mangled hairdo, and instead of being mortified to realize how she must look in the forgotten bouffant, Merry just laughed and yanked out the pins, shaking her head to let her coppery hair cascade around her shoulders.

"Better," Sam growled. His arms came around her and he flipped them both with an effortless twist so Merry was on top, her hair blanketing them both in messy waves. He held her tight to him, clamping one big hand around her nape to kiss her deeply, ravishing her mouth.

Merry had never enjoyed being on top, never liked the reminder of her size. Now, she was aware of nothing but Sam, his heat, his passion, the pleasure she took in the strength of his body and the kindness in his soul. "You're beautiful," he told her, and in that moment she believed him. She *felt* beautiful.

"You're better than beautiful," she said. "You're mine." Then belatedly, hesitance took hold. She bit her lip, staring shyly down at him. "That is . . . if you want to be."

"I want to be."

And for the next two hours, he showed her how much.

∽

"Dolly's probably wondering what became of me," Merry said. Her body felt like six kinds of awesome, and climbing out of Sam's bed was the last thing she wanted to contemplate. But duty called. Thanksgiving was tomorrow, and Merry was sure Dolly could use help with kitchen prep, even though she'd claimed to have everything well in hand. It was just going to be Dolly, Sam, Jane (whose family was far away, and none too keen on holistic medicine practitioners), and Merry. It probably wouldn't be an occasion for much thankfulness, however, with the specter of John's return on the horizon. He could be back any day now, waving papers and demanding they pay up or sign away the ranch. *Least I can do is help make the holiday as nice for Dolly as I can*, she thought. *Even if I cook about as well as I dodge llama spit. And hell, I can celebrate having evaded my own family, anyway.* She'd been ducking them like mad these past couple of weeks, not wanting to face their ultimatums or expectations while she was so busy facing the immediate crisis at the ranch. They must have gotten the message, because she hadn't heard anything further about having to spend Thanksgiving with them, and it was too late now to meet them anywhere even if she'd wanted to.

Yay, she thought. *So much yay.*

"I'd better get dressed," she sighed. *Boo. So much boo.* "I don't want Dolly to send the search llamas after us."

"She knows where we are," Sam said on a yawn, tugging Merry back down when she made to rise. "I went by and dropped her a note after you fell asleep, so she wouldn't worry."

"Oh my God," she groaned. "*So* embarrassing." She buried her face against Sam's chest. "It's like some corny old joke where the traveling salesman seduces the farmer's daughter."

Sam chuckled. "I'm happy to be the butt of that joke. Especially if it brings me into contact with *this* butt." His palm glided over her hip to grasp the area in question, and Merry purred with pleasure.

She stopped purring, however, as Sam ran his finger down the line of her hip to her thigh...the mangled thigh. His fingertip traced gently around the edges of the longest of the scars. "I hate that you went through so much pain," he said when she twitched.

Merry rolled away, drawing the comforter around her. Her body was suddenly tense.

"Why do you do that?" he asked.

"Do what?" Merry burrowed deeper under the covers, refusing to meet his eyes.

"Hide your body like that."

It must seem stupid to him, after the intimacy they'd just shared. But that had been under covers, in the moment. Now...Merry was suddenly shy all over again. She didn't want him to see her as damaged goods. The scars belied that. "You wouldn't understand."

"About your scars? Merry, I've seen them, a few times now. They don't change anything—except to make me admire you more."

"Admire me? For what, being a loser?"

"A *loser*?" Sam looked shocked.

"I lost, didn't I?"

"Maybe one race, Merry. Not your worth as a human being."

Merry looked away. She wanted to believe him. And these past weeks, here at the Last Chance...maybe she *was* coming to believe that—slowly. Yet the years of being drilled to come home with gold or not at all...it was hard to truly see herself the way the Sam, Dolly, and the others here in Aguas Milagros seemed to. As *enough*. She recalled the despairing look on her mother's face at her sweet sixteen. Remembered how her parents had erased all traces of her skiing career after the accident, as if she were a dirty secret. She shrugged uncomfortably. "I know I'm nobody's idea of the ideal woman."

"Why on earth would you say that?" Sam asked, seeming genuinely bewildered.

"C'mon, Sam. Look at me. I'm *huge*." A trace of bitterness entered her voice. "And since the accident, I trip over my own feet half the time. You have no idea what it's like..." Merry stopped, fists clenching in the sheets.

"Then tell me," Sam said softly. He propped himself up on one elbow, looking down at her. "Merry, I care about you. I want to know."

Merry hesitated. To tell him what was in her heart, what she feared, felt like the ultimate exposure. But she was already naked before him in every way that counted. She could let Sam in... or she could go on fighting her battles alone.

She let him in.

"When I was growing up," she said, "I was a sore thumb everywhere my family wanted me to fit in. Not only was I about a foot taller than the other girls from the time I was seven, I just couldn't seem to get the hang of 'girl things' like everyone else. How to dress, what music was cool, which boy to have a crush on. I didn't care about any of that stuff, honestly. I didn't *want* to go to fancy parties, or vacation in the most exclusive resorts. But that's what a Manning was expected to do. I was an embarrassment to my parents, and a joke to my peers." Again, Merry remembered her sweet sixteen, the disappointment in her mother's eyes. "The one thing I always had—the *one* thing—was my physical prowess. I might look like some hulking Valkyrie, but I could kick ass like one too. When I skied, all my awkwardness slipped away. I was graceful on the slopes. No. I was better than that, Sam. I *owned* them. And then, the day of the accident, they owned *me*. And I owned nothing but this fucked-up, ruined body."

She blew out a breath, knuckled away the moisture that had gathered in her eyes. "I'm afraid I'm not...*whole* anymore, Sam. That I'll never be whole again."

Sam looked at her levelly. Then he rolled to his feet, naked as the day he was born, and planted his hands on his hips. "Get up, Meriadoc Manning. We're going skiing."

CHAPTER FORTY-FIVE

The Taos ski area doesn't announce itself with any great fanfare. Though it's got runs that can compare to some of the hairiest in the world, and those in the know treat the mountain with caution and respect, you'd hardly guess it was there from the casual—okay, haphazard—signage along the road. Which was fine with me, as I'd rather slink in under the radar, if I had to go at all.

Sam seemed to think I did.

"I'm tired of your shit," quoth he. "You're no more broken than I am, and I'm going to prove it to you."

How he intended to prove I wasn't crippled by asking me to perform the action that had crippled me, I wasn't sure, and I told him so in rather vociferous terms. (There may have been a few imprecations, aspersions, and—to be frank—pillows cast at his head during this exchange.) But Sam would not be dissuaded. It was opening day at the Taos Ski Valley, and we would, damn the torpedoes, be amongst the first to carve the pow.

We took the drive in a sort of charged silence, determined on Sam's part, fearful on mine. All I could think of was the last time I'd skied. How I'd stood at the top of that run, so sure of myself, so ready to take on the world—and how I'd been taken off the mountain, unconscious, hardly expected to live.

I don't talk about this much, my friends. Those of you who read this column regularly know I'm not about airing my dirty laundry (whatever my mother says), nor maudlin maunderings about the past. But the fact *is, skiing was my life for many years. And when I lost it, I kind of lost my way.*

Sam was determined to help me find it again—whether I liked it or not.

With his permission, I'm going to tell it like it was. So here's the truth:

Sam sucked.

I sucked.

And sucking was a beautiful thing.

⌘

Merry leaned on her rented poles, staring down the slope. "You, Sam Cassidy, are an asshole."

"And you, Merry Manning, are chickenshit." Sam adjusted his hand-crocheted hat atop his head and gave her a look that dared her to tuck tail and run.

Talking smack was not exactly unfamiliar territory to a professional athlete. But Merry was in no mood just now. She glided her feet back and forth on the unfamiliar skis, digging grooves into the fresh powder. Using rented gear felt weird, but no weirder than being up here in the first place. Taos didn't have many beginners' runs—it was a notoriously steep and wild valley, great for the experienced but offering less for the novice than the more commercial areas nearby, like Sipapu or Telluride. Still, of all the slopes here, this was the bunniest of the bunny.

And Merry was scared shitless of it.

Two kids, who couldn't have been above seven, whizzed by, hollering "Yeeeeeeeeeeaaaaaaaaaaaaaaaahhhhhhh!" as they dive-bombed the slope without benefit of poles.

Merry watched them go.

A man in his seventies gingerly duckwalked to the edge of the hill, and then glided over it, shushing and swooshing with no visible effort.

Merry watched him go.

She watched the next dozen skiers too, hearing their whoops and hollers and giddy laughter as they took advantage of the glorious early-winter day. Sunlight glanced off the fresh dusting of crystalline snow. Evergreens scented the thin mountain air with a crisp, sharp flavor that prickled in the nostrils, exactly as Merry remembered. What she did *not* remember was the abject terror that suffused her now. She'd strapped on her first set of skis at the age of three, and she'd been conquering runs ever since. Today, her fingers shook as she clutched her poles, staring down at the mildest slope in the valley.

"You can do this, Merry," Sam said.

"Can *you* do this?" she snapped. On skis, wrapped in donated knitwear from the Happy Hookers to replace the coat he'd given her, burly Sam looked about as comfortable as a potato balancing on toothpicks.

"Probably not," he said...and launched himself over the edge.

...Only to tumble, ass over teakettle, helplessly down the hill.

To Merry's horrified eyes, Sam was a blur of arms and legs and scruffy blond hair, the hat Dolly had crocheted for him flying off into the snow, his skis unlatching and skidding every which way. He pinwheeled down the slope, past openmouthed moms and dads and kids and ski patrol alike.

"Sam!" Unthinking, Merry launched herself after him.

She skied like she'd never skied before.

Muscle memory took over. She didn't think, she just acted,

carving and turning, leaning into the slope to give her speed, flashing past the startled parents with their kids, the ski patrol dudes who were just beginning to turn toward the commotion.

When she caught up to him, Sam was sputtering and spitting snow, his blue eyes watering and his cheeks flushed red. He was making little hitching noises, as if the wind had been knocked out of him.

"Sam, are you okay? Can you hear me?" She'd tossed her poles and was kneeling at his side, feeling his limbs for breaks. "Say something!"

Sam scraped hair out of his eyes, shook his head as if to clear out cobwebs. His breath was coming in little sobs that sounded scary to Merry. Then she realized what the sounds were.

He was laughing his ass off.

"Knew you could do it," he said once he'd stopped sucking air.

Merry's jaw dropped open. "You fell *deliberately*?"

Sam struggled to sit upright. "I wish I could say that," he said ruefully, "but no, that stunning display of grace and athleticism was all natural."

"Have you never skied before?" she asked, incredulous.

He shook his head. "First time."

"Not even a lesson? Sam, you could have seriously injured yourself."

"I knew you'd come rescue me." He gave her a smug smile.

Merry's eyes narrowed. "You think this is funny? You scared the *shit* out of me, Sam Cassidy!"

"Got you to the bottom, didn't it?" The grin he gave Merry was utterly unrepentant.

She smashed a handful of snow in his face.

❧

We chased each other down the slopes all morning, snowballs flying, skis sliding out from under us, until the ski patrol had to sit our asses down and give us a stern talking-to. (We were setting a poor example for the kids, they said.)

Fact is, I'll never compete again. That much hasn't changed. My leg isn't up for the kind of strain the pros routinely subject themselves to, and it never will be. But what I can still have is fun. Long before skiing was a career—and quite frankly, an obsession—once upon a time it was just something that made a little girl named Merry happy.

It made me happy again today.

And so did Sam Cassidy.

❧

"I don't know how to thank you, Sam." They were back in his truck, sweaty, disheveled, and flushed from the morning's exertions. Merry's legs were shaky and sore, but hardly worse than anyone who was unused to a day of strenuous exercise—and fantastic sex—could expect to feel. Her weeks at the Last Chance had improved her body's physical condition much more than she'd have guessed was still possible. But it was what they'd done for her soul that had made all the difference. Merry's eyes grew misty as she looked at the man who had become her lover. "You've no idea what a gift you've given me today. I feel . . . I don't know . . . *healed*. Complete." She smiled at him through trembling lips.

Sam ran his thumb over them, stilling the trembling with his touch. "That smile is reward enough."

"Then let me give you that too," Merry said, and pressed it to his lips.

She was, she thought, happier than she could remember being in a very long time.

And then Sam's phone rang.

CHAPTER FORTY-SIX

*W*e had some unexpected guests at the Last Chance for Thanksgiving. Visiting dignitaries, you might say.

Yup. Uh-huh. My parents.

❧

A vision in Arctic fox alighted from the chartered Learjet, Manolo Blahnik boots barely seeming to touch the ground. Ice-blond hair didn't dare flutter in the breeze off the hangar, and ice-blue eyes scanned it as if surveying some new fiefdom. The woman's glamour made the Taos Regional Airport seem even more provincial than it actually was—and that was saying something. Behind her followed a tall, somber gentleman with dark hair graying at the temples and a greatcoat that could have graced a prime minister or James Bond equally well. And behind *them*, bounding down the stairs two at a time...the most gorgeous man in the world.

Fuck.

All the joy of this incredible day drained from Merry. *It can't be*, she thought. The sight of the Manning clan in the wilds of New Mexico was so incongruous as to be hallucinatory. But of course, it only made sense. *If the mountain won't come to Mohammed...* the Mannings would come to Merry.

But had they had to come *today*, of all days? *It's like Mother has this radar that goes off anytime I dare to love myself just a little bit. And then she sends in the bombers to blow my self-esteem out of the sky.*

"You *had* to answer your phone," she muttered through teeth clenched in a simulacrum of a smile. "Since when do mountain men even *have* cell phones?"

Sam rolled his eyes. "I'm a survival expert, remember? Which means being prepared. I keep the phone for emergencies, in case my aunt needs me. Looks like it was a good thing I did. Can't believe Dolly forgot to tell me we were having tourists for the holiday. A few minutes later and we would have missed the call to pick them up. Would've been a shame for them to have to drive themselves all the way out to the ranch."

"Yes. A shame," Merry said woodenly.

Sam caught her tone. "I think it's sweet, a family wanting to spend Thanksgiving together at the Last Chance."

"Sweet has nothing to do with it, Sam." Merry sighed.

Understanding dawned in his eyes. "Wait—you know these people?"

"Hardly. They're my family."

Whatever Sam might have said next was cut off by Gwendolyn's trill.

"Meredith! Darling, is that you? Pierce, are you quite sure we've landed in the right airport? Surely that cannot be our Meredith. Why, she's covered in filth!"

Merry looked down at her outfit. *She has a point*, she thought. The clothes she'd been sporting since she'd arrived at the ranch had not exactly benefited from constant contact with barnyard animals, and today's snow-tastic outing had left her both bedraggled and water stained. Her hair, which still hadn't recovered from yesterday's beehive, had to be a complete disaster.

"Your *mother* calls you Meredith?" Sam murmured. "Didn't you just tell me...?"

Merry didn't have time to explain her mother's idiosyncrasies. Smoothing her eyebrows nervously, she started forward.

And was tackled to the ground.

"Squatchy!!!!" Marcus snatched her off her feet and spun her in a circle—or tried to. Merry had a good couple of inches on him, and his model's diet, while great for ropy-looking muscles that showed well in underwear ads, left him less effective at hefting hefty sisters. They ended up crashing to the concrete together in a tumble of limbs and hair and outerwear.

"Oof!"

Marcus took flight again a second later as Sam yanked him off her. Merry blinked up at the two men. *Oh, my.* Sam had hold of her brother's collar in one massive fist, and he looked about ready to use the other one. "You wanna explain why you're assaulting my girlfriend, buddy?" he demanded. Though his tone was level, Sam's latent Jersey boy had most definitely risen to the surface.

Merry rose hurriedly, brushing herself off. *Girlfriend? That's interesting...* "Sam, wait..."

Marcus's eyes widened as he took in the mountain man from head to toe. "Don't tell me *you're* Studly Sam," he drawled. He turned his gaze to his sister. "Merry, your column did *not* do him justice." The fist in his coat collar tightened, and Marcus gulped theatrically, rolling faux-terrified eyes at Merry. "Um, a little help here?"

Merry snorted. "Sam, you can let him go. That's just my idiot brother's way of saying hello."

Sam's fingers slackened as he looked back and forth between Merry and the supermodel. A grin broke out across his blunt features, and he let go and stuck his hand out for Marcus to shake. "Sam Cassidy. Pleased to meet you."

"Marcus Manning." Marcus straightened his collar and smiled his blinding white-toothed smile. "That's my baby sister, if you hadn't guessed."

"I see the resemblance."

Merry rolled her eyes. *Yeah, right.*

"I didn't know Merry had a brother," Sam said. "Actually, she hasn't told us much about her family at all, come to think of it…" His gaze took in Merry's parents, who were approaching at a more stately pace than their son, then slid over Marcus again. Light dawned.

He gets it now, she thought. She knew what he was seeing. *The swans… and the ugly duckling.* She avoided his eyes, focusing on her parents instead. "Mother. Dad. I wasn't expecting you." *The understatement of the year.* She bent to give her mother a kiss on one cool cheek, then accepted one from her father. They were distracted by the sight of Sam, however. Gwendolyn was eyeing him, clearly none too pleased about the roughhousing between her precious baby boy and this rough-hewn stranger. Pierce put a bracing arm around his wife, and she leaned into it as if she needed its strength. "Meredith, do introduce us to your… friend," she said.

Merry's manners kicked in. "Mother, Dad, this is Samuel Cassidy. His aunt Dolly owns the Last Chance. Sam, these are my parents, Pierce and Gwendolyn Manning."

"Pleasure to meet you, young man," said Pierce, putting out a hand. Sam shook it gamely.

"Glad to meet you too, Mr. and Mrs. Manning. Let me get you settled in the truck and then I'll tend to your bags." He ushered them toward the floof-mobile. "I hope your trip wasn't too tiring. Seems Dolly neglected to mention we'd be having guests for the holiday, so I'm afraid we've only got the utility truck with us today." He eyed Gwendolyn's fur coat and impractical boots. "It's not much for looks, but it rides pretty smooth."

One could say that about Sam, too, Merry thought, distracted for a moment into smiling.

Gwendolyn's lips pursed, but she gave him her hand when he made to help her up into the truck's cab. "I'm sure it will do nicely, Mr. Cassidy."

"I'll ride in the back," Merry offered. "So will Marcus."

"I will?"

"Yes, Banana Hammock," she hissed, "you will." She started dragging Marcus toward the rear of the vehicle, which was thankfully poop free today.

"You got some 'splainin' to do," she growled as she shoved him up the ramp and locked the fold-down seats into place for them to sit on.

Marcus gave her his best ingénue face—the one that had allowed him to continue modeling for American Apparel well into his thirties. "Such as?"

"Such as, what the hell you three are doing in New Mexico!"

"Mrs. Cassidy invited us, of course. Didn't she tell you? Seems kinda odd that she wouldn't."

Very odd indeed, Merry thought. Dolly had some 'splainin' to do too.

CHAPTER FORTY-SEVEN

I ain't apologizing, so don't start with me," Dolly said. She met Merry's betrayed look with a pugnacious one of her own.

"But why would you—" Merry looked furtively around the living room, but her parents and brother were out of earshot, availing themselves of the facilities to freshen up. "How *could* you invite my family here without telling me?"

Dolly gave an exasperated huff as she pulled blankets and pillows from the chest that did double duty as her coffee table. "It's plain as day you needed to make your peace with them. Besides, it just didn't seem right, you spending Thanksgiving without your loved ones." She shoved the stack of linens at Merry. "Here. Take these out to the cabin for that scamp you're calling a brother. I already made up the spare bedroom for your folks, if they ain't too fussy for homely things." She gave Merry a measured look. "I figure you and Sammy won't find it too much of a hardship to bunk together at his place."

Merry blushed—*hard*—but she refused to drop the subject. "Dolly, you don't understand about my parents..."

"What's to understand? You love them, don't you?"

Merry made a face.

Dolly whapped Merry with one of the pillows—gently, but hard enough to make her point.

"Yeah. I guess." Merry sighed.

"And they love you, don't they?" Dolly persisted.

"I assume so," Merry allowed, "though sometimes it's hard to tell."

Dolly didn't smile. "You ought to know better than that, child. They just flew halfway around the world to see you, didn't they?"

To scold *me*, Merry thought. *To bend me to their will.* "It's complicated," she said.

Dolly rolled her eyes. "When *isn't* family complicated?"

Right. Dolly had a troublesome family member of her own breathing down her neck in the person of one John Dixon. *I need to get my head out of my ass and remember I'm not the only person in the world with problems. And mine are the kind plenty of people would be glad to have.*

"Seems to me you've got yourself a golden opportunity to straighten things out, child," Dolly said, interrupting her thoughts. "Whatever's between you and them, if you don't work it out now, I guess you never will."

I could have lived with that, Merry thought. But there was no help for it now. "I hear you, Dolly, and I appreciate what you're trying to do. I just don't want them to ruin your holiday, is all."

"Way I see it, the only one fixing to ruin the holiday is *you*, child, if you don't adjust that attitude. So slap on a smile and help me make your folks feel welcome."

Merry plastered a hideous grin across her face. "Don't say I didn't warn you."

❦

My mother ruined Thanksgiving.

A woman of unparalleled grace, charm, and breeding, she is also the last person you want in your kitchen. (Sorry, Mom, but it's true.)

Or your mudroom, in the chill confines of which Dolly had left the turkey to brine. Apparently the vinegary scent of the mixture—Dolly's patented secret recipe—proved too much for my mother's nostrils in the night, and she left the exterior door open to ventilate the hacienda.

Someone—or—something—took this as an invitation to abscond, Grinch-style, with the gobbler.

There was only one thing for it. Café Con Kvetch.

❦

"I'm dreadfully sorry, Mrs. Cassidy," Gwendolyn said. "I'm afraid I've spoiled your festivities."

They were gathered in the hacienda's kitchen, staring out into the mudroom at the remains of the brining bag that were scattered, reeking of apple cider vinegar, across its floor. Of the turkey itself, there was no trace.

In addition to their mortified expressions, Pierce and Gwendolyn had on matching dressing gowns in maroon quilted silk. It was scarcely dawn, the light just peeking over the snow-capped mountains, the air cold enough to make Merry, clad only in Sam's hastily donned red union suit, shiver uncontrollably. Sam, in just jeans and the Carhartt jacket he'd snatched up at the sound of Gwendolyn's screams, chafed Merry's arms to warm them. He started to give her the jacket, but Merry shook her head sharply, giving him a warning look. She had no desire to scandalize her parents with the sight of Sam's brawny naked chest. Pierce and Gwendolyn hadn't questioned the sleeping arrangements last night, and Merry wasn't eager to announce she was shacking up with her host's nephew—if the union suit hadn't already given it away. *We've got enough to deal with around here*, she thought. *Hardly need Dad grilling my boyfriend about his prospects and intentions.*

The fact that Sam was—or wanted to be—her boyfriend, was still far too new. But pretty awesome, Merry had to admit. Unable to help herself, she leaned subtly into him. Sam leaned back, just as subtly, but she had a feeling she wasn't fooling her sharp-eyed mother. After the night they'd shared, Merry was lucky the hobbit hole was halfway across the ranch, or her parents would have gotten an earful. Instead, they'd woken to an earful of Gwendolyn's even more impressive screeches, along with the howling of wild animals fighting over Dolly's heritage turkey.

"Thought I heard the call of the wild Hollingsworth Manning," said Marcus, wandering through the front door sporting a wifebeater and low-slung pj bottoms. "What's cooking?" He yawned, looking over their shoulders to survey the crime scene.

"Not us, apparently," Merry muttered. She yanked Marcus's pj's up before he could moon them all, and he returned the favor with a wedgie that made her yelp and dance away. "Quit it," she whispered, smacking his arm. "This is serious business."

"If you wanted to be taken seriously, you should've worn something a little less *Honey Boo Boo*," he said. "So what's going on? Heard a noise outta Mom I didn't think was humanly possible."

"It was the most ungodly cackling sound," Gwendolyn said, one hand held to her throat. "Just like those jackals—remember, Pierce, when you were stationed in Egypt and we spent the night bivouacked in the Valley of the Kings? On our honeymoon?"

"How could I forget?" Pierce said, his expression saying he remembered the occasion fondly. "It did sound like jackals."

"Coyotes," Sam corrected. "They're all over the place round here."

Gwendolyn tied the sash of her dressing gown tighter around her waist. "I'd no idea," she murmured. "Of course, I should have realized, we're so far from civilization..."

Merry winced at her mother's snobbery, but neither Dolly nor Sam blinked an eye.

"You weren't to know about the coyotes," Dolly said to Gwendolyn. Already dressed for the day in a flowered cotton shirt and corduroy pants, she was also wearing what Merry had come to know as her "brave face."

"When I went out to investigate," Pierce explained, "I saw a pack of animals running away, carrying the turkey with them. It was too late to intervene, I'm afraid, and I don't suppose they'd have listened to reason even if I'd had my wits about me to sit them down at the negotiating table." He smiled at his own joke.

"We had the occasional fox at Father's hunting lodge," Gwendolyn added apologetically, "but they'd never be so cheeky as to run off with one's supper."

"We'll just run down to the market and buy another turkey," Pierce offered, patting his wife's shoulder. "There'll still be time, won't there, if us boys head off now for the store?"

Dolly sighed. "Nearest grocery's a forty-minute drive, and it's closed for the holiday anyhow. I got my bird from a fella who raises 'em on his spread across the valley, but he'll have sold 'em all by now, even if we had time to slaughter and pluck a new one."

Gwendolyn looked a bit green.

"What if we ate at that café we passed on the way in yesterday?" Marcus asked. "I think I saw a sign that said they'd be open for the holiday."

Now Dolly looked green.

"I think it's a great idea!" Merry said. "I'm sure Bob would be happy to have us. And Thanksgiving *is* all about mending fences, after all...right, Dolly?"

Dolly was all too aware of Merry's meaning. "Touché, child," she murmured. "Sam, why don't you call over there once the sun's more up, and tell Bob to expect six more for supper." She headed for the sink. "Meanwhile, who's for coffee?"

Four hands shot up, and four sets of eyes stared at Dolly like dogs begging for a treat. "Alrighty then. Tea for you, Gwen?" Dolly asked.

"If you have it," Gwendolyn said, not correcting Dolly's use of the diminutive, though it looked like it cost her. *Points for class, Mother*, Merry thought. But then, class had never been Gwendolyn's issue. Warmth, on the other hand...

"While it's brewing, you might like to put on some clothes," Dolly said, eyeing Merry's union suit and Sam's bare chest. Merry blushed.

"Excellent idea for all of us," Pierce said heartily. "Come, darling, let's make ourselves scarce." They decamped. Marcus seemed in no hurry to take off, however. He was too busy trying to sneak pics of Merry's onesie with his phone, which he'd had tucked in his pajama pocket.

"That goes for you too, Crest Commercial," Dolly said tartly. "Quit cluttering up my kitchen and go get decent. I got Jane coming over in a bit to check on the new cria, and I don't want you upsetting her with all that handsomeness." She ignored his baffled expression and shooed him out the door. "Go on now."

It was a less disheveled Manning clan that reconvened around the kitchen table an hour later. Dolly was doling out flapjacks adorned with fresh fruit, maple syrup, and homemade whipped cream, and an enormous rasher of bacon sat in the middle of the table.

Sam dove in, and Merry couldn't blame him. It had been a *very* active twenty-four hours, after all. Pierce, too, helped himself to a healthy portion, eyes alight with pleasure at the homely fare.

"Your cholesterol, dear," murmured Gwendolyn, placing a hand on his wrist.

"My cholesterol is on vacation, *dear*," he said, stuffing a bite of pancake in his mouth.

She tsked, but she left him to it.

"None for you, Gwennie?" Dolly asked.

"Oh, no thank you. I don't eat..." She waved at the stack of crisp, golden goodness.

"Mother doesn't eat anything that tastes good," Merry explained.

"Meredith, please..." Gwendolyn sighed.

"Well, you can't go all morning on an empty stomach," Dolly exclaimed.

Merry was fairly certain Gwendolyn had gone the better part of the nineties on an empty stomach.

"Come now. What can I make you, Gwen honey?"

"Perhaps just some egg whites if you have them, Mrs. Cassidy."

"Sure, I can do that," she said, "if you'll call me Dolly like I asked. But what about you?" she asked Marcus, whose plate was also empty. "You on hunger strike as well?"

"My trainer says carbs are off-limits until after the 2(x)ist shoot next month." Merry could swear tears were gathering in Marcus's eyes.

"I don't see any trainers at this table, young man," Dolly said, waving a thick, perfectly fried slice of bacon under his nose.

"Hm, that's true." He perked up. "Fuck it!" A second later his plate was packed full.

"Language, darling."

"Shorry, Muffer," Marcus said around a mouthful that threatened to choke him. "Oh mah gah, thish ish so fugging goo."

There was silence for the next few minutes while the Mannings masticated. Merry, having little appetite, fiddled with her fork, then caught her mother's reproving expression and set it back down. For good measure she removed her elbows from the table. "So," she said brightly, "when are you all headed home?"

Sam choked on his pancake.

"We have family business to discuss before anyone goes anywhere, Merry," Pierce said. "We've been patient while you've sorted yourself out, but now it's time to make decisions. It can't be put off any longer."

"Pierce, darling, I hardly think it's proper to discuss this in front of the Cassidys," Gwendolyn murmured.

"No," Merry said. Her gut was churning. "I've got no secrets from Sam and Dolly—or if I do, I don't want to anymore." She took a deep breath. "Truth is, Sam, I'm worth twelve million dollars."

Sam swallowed his bite, took a sip of coffee. "That a fact?"

"Well, that's what I'm worth if I play Mother's game. If I leave the Last Chance and never come back." Merry's voice was rising, but she couldn't seem to control it. "If I spend the rest of my life raising money to renovate drafty old castles in Cornwall and sipping martinis with her bridge partners or betting on polo matches with Dad's diplomat cronies."

"Meredith! Is that what you think of us?"

"She did kinda hit the nail on the head, Mom," Marcus said, chomping more bacon.

Merry shot him a look. "*Not* helping, Banana Hammock."

"Just sayin'."

"Marcus, this is between your sister and us. You've already made your decision about *your* bequest."

"Cool," he said, rising from the table with lazy grace. "I'll be off then. Got about ten thousand crunches to do if I'm going to work off all those pancakes. Great grub, Dolls," he said, flashing Dolly his signature smile as he made to leave.

"Marcus, stay," Pierce said in his nonnegotiable voice. "Merry, we'll discuss this with the gravity it deserves—and in private—*after* the holiday."

"There's nothing to discuss, Dad," Merry said. Her hands were shaking, her breath coming fast and tight. She felt as if she were standing at the top of some insanely steep chute she'd never skied before, preparing to hurl herself into the unknown. *Come and get me, debt collectors*, she thought. *Here goes nothing!* "I've made my decision," she told them. "I'm not taking the money. And I'm not coming home."

"Don't be ridiculous, Meredith. You need this!" Gwendolyn snapped. Then she shut her mouth, mortified at having been caught arguing over something so gauche as money in front of outsiders. "Pierce, talk some sense into your daughter."

"We'll have plenty of time to talk everything over at the appropriate time and place," he said soothingly. "Right now, how about we focus on accepting the gracious hospitality of our hosts while we're at the Last Chance?"

"We're happy to extend it, for as long as you care to stay." Sam slugged back the last of his coffee and rose from the table, freeing them all from the awkward tableau. "Delicious breakfast, Aunt Dolly. How about I help clear?"

"No, you go on and look in on the critters." Dolly paused. "Actually, now that I think on it, since we've got the morning unexpectedly free, why don't we all show Merry's folks around the ranch? Jane'll be here in a moment to check on little Bill."

Merry winced. After the scene she'd just made, she'd rather hide in a pile of llama beans than hang around with her parents in Dolly's barnyard. "Oh, I'm sure they wouldn't care to...I mean, Mother hasn't got the shoes for it, and I'm sure Dad wouldn't want to slog around..."

"We'd be delighted, Mrs. Cassidy," Pierce answered for all of them.

This will not end well, Merry thought.

"Alright then, go get suited up for the outdoors, folks. Looks to be a beautiful day for it."

"Beautiful day for what?" asked a voice from the doorway.

"Jane—right on time." Dolly smiled at her friend. "Everybody, this-here's Jane Kraslowski, our resident vet, and the reason my fluffies stay that way. Jane, these are Merry's parents, Pierce and Gwennie—"

"Gwendolyn," Gwendolyn gritted.

"I didn't know you had parents, Merry." Jane grinned.

"Seems I do," Merry said, cheered by the sight of her friend. "A brother too. That spaz over there is Marcus."

"Right, I think you mentioned him once." Jane's gaze barely glanced off the supermodel. "C'mon, let's go see about that cria."

And out they trooped, into the barnyard.

CHAPTER FORTY-EIGHT

*T*hanksgiving might have started with an unfortunate incident, but there soon proved something to be grateful for. A mystery was solved this morning. And it was my darling brother Marcus who proved the catalyst.

"Merry, can I ask you something?" he whispered to me. We were touring the ranch with our parents, Dolly, Jane, and Sam leading the way, but Marcus held me back with a hand on my arm as the others kept going. "You're going to think I'm crazy, but . . . is that cabin haunted?"

My mouth dropped open. "Why, what did you see?"

"It wasn't seeing, so much, as, um . . . I don't know . . . smelling. Hearing things." My sibling shook his head. "It was dark, so I couldn't tell what was going on, but, ah, something was definitely with me overnight. I could hear some sort of . . . snuffling. And something stank. And when I woke up, all . . ." He stopped.

"All what?" (I couldn't wait to hear.)

He squirmed. "All my, er, underwear was gone."

I stifled a laugh. "The 2(x)ist samples they sent you?" (Marcus was to be the face—and more importantly body—of their newest campaign.)

Marcus blushed. "Um, yeah. I mean, they weren't my favorite or anything—even I think there should be limits on how teeny a guy's bikini should be—but it's kinda freaky, don't you think?"

"Yes, I'd say that qualifies as freaky," I replied. "But not as freaky as that." I pointed to the goat pen we were approaching.

And to the baby goats who were, with evident delight, munching on his multicolored banana hammocks.

In the midst of her offspring, proud as a mama could be, stood Betty White.

Wearing a pair of Marcus's panties on her head.

*It all made sense now. It wasn't a poltergeist who'd been haunting the cabin. It was a polter*goat.

~∞~

"You doing alright, honey?" Sam asked, pulling her aside as they continued their rounds. The sun was beaming down on a scene of such bucolic splendor one could almost hear Edvard Grieg's *Peer Gynt* playing. The alpacas were frolicking, the goats were pronking, and the llamas looked on languidly as they chewed their cud. The air was fresh and crisp as only New Mexico could scrub it, and snow frosted the distant mountains, sharp against the cloudless blue sky.

Ah, go fuck yourself, Merry told the day.

"Not even a little bit," she told Sam. She dug her hands into her hair, ready to tear out chunks. "Jesus, Sam, why did they have to come here? I was *just* starting to feel good about myself. It's like they've got a sixth sense that tells them when I'm about to have some self-esteem, so they can swoop in and obliterate it." She kicked a clump of cholla, then regretted it when the spines stuck in her boot.

"It can't be that bad, can it?"

"Remind me to tell you about the time my mother offered to buy me a boob job for Christmas," Merry said.

Sam shuddered. "Thank God she didn't succeed. I'm rather partial to your boobs the way they are." He slid his arm around her and copped a gentle feel.

Merry smiled wryly. "Apparently they weren't 'proportional' to my great height, or so my mother claimed."

"Oh, honey." Sam tightened his arm around her as they walked.

"Anyhow, thanks for not freaking out about the money."

"About you having it, or you not accepting it?"

Merry sighed. "Either, I guess."

"Why would either one freak me out?"

"In my experience, people tend to have a lot of opinions about what one should do with money—my mother being a prime example. But Sam, I need you to know something..."

"What's that, honey?"

"I wanted to use mine to help you and Dolly. I offered it to her when John first threatened the ranch. And I'd still do it in a heartbeat, if Dolly would let me."

"I can see why she wouldn't," Sam said. "Don't get me wrong—a bailout would make life around here much easier, for the animals as well as ourselves. But we didn't come here for an *easy* life; we came here for a life we could live with—and we want no less for you, Merry." He stroked her cheek with one rough thumb. "Whatever path you walk, it's got to be one that suits your soul, not someone else's idea of who you should be. I learned that one the hard way."

Merry looked down at Sam's bare feet, thinking of how he walked his path with such commitment, such honesty. She wanted that for herself. "It's just so hard to remember who I am when they're around," she confessed. "I revert back to some stammering sixteen-year-old lummox the minute they arrive. Which is why I tend to avoid them whenever possible."

"Do you think maybe they came here to make amends? Start over?"

Merry thought about how her mother had given her such honest advice about fund-raising a few weeks back, how she'd seemed completely up to date on her doings—almost as if she truly cared. It would be so nice to think they could have a grown-up relationship, without threats, bribes, or coercion. "Maybe," she said dubiously.

"Well, how about you give them the benefit of the doubt while they're here? Worst comes to worst," he joked, "we'll sic the llamas on 'em."

"It may come to that."

It did.

∽

"Meredith," her mother said. "I'd like a word."

I get pulled into any more sidebar conferences, Merry thought, *and I'm going to have to change my career again—this time to attorney.*

The hand Gwendolyn placed on her daughter's arm was light enough scarcely to be felt through Merry's borrowed coat, yet enough to stop her in her tracks. Again, she watched the others outpace her, Pierce with hands in his greatcoat, studying the livestock soberly, Marcus tucking stray panties in his pockets as Sam and Dolly expounded on the animals' admirable qualities and Jane checked them over to be sure all were operating at full fluff.

She'd have given a great deal to be with the others right now. But she knew that look. Gwendolyn would have her say. "What is it, Mother?"

Gwendolyn paced a few steps forward, her fur collar turned up to her chin, stiletto heels somehow not catching in the grass the way a lesser mortal's might. She paused delicately. "Darling, what I'm about to say is for your benefit, so I do hope you will hear me out without your customary hysterics." She looked up at Merry as if daring her to engage in said hysterics. "It's all well and good, your helping these people out. Clearly they need it, and I raised you to know your duty. But if I were you, I wouldn't get too...close...to anyone here."

"You mean, to Sam." Merry's face grew stony, though her cheeks had gone red. The borrowed union suit had not gone unnoticed then.

Gwendolyn didn't try to deny it. "Yes, Meredith, that is what I mean. A man like him...well, I'll grant he's a strapping specimen, and we all have needs...but, darling, let's be realistic. He's got no real prospects. You've as much as said he'll be out of a job if the ranch folds. And maybe *he* can pitch a tent in the woods and live off the land—I will admit his survival skills seem impressive if your column is to be believed—but he'd never be able to take care of you properly. You'd always be scraping by, never afforded the privileges you were raised to enjoy. Surely that can't be what you want for yourself. A woman of your breeding, your background...well, you were never meant to make a life with someone like that, in a place like this." She placed her hand back on Merry's arm. "Please, Meredith, reconsider your rashness, and accept my mother's bequest."

There's the mother I know.

The politeness she'd displayed at breakfast might mask her true feelings in front of the others, but Merry knew better. People like Dolly, Jane, and Sam were no more than peons to Gwendolyn—peons who ought to be grateful she deigned to grace them with her presence.

Anger flared. "What if I *did* make a life here, Mother? What if this is *exactly* the place I'm meant to be, and Sam Cassidy is the man I'm meant to be with?" In truth, Merry's thoughts hadn't gone that far yet—she and Sam were just beginning to enjoy each other—but once she entertained it, the notion felt *right*.

To me, maybe. But not to Mother. Gwendolyn was pursing her lips, looking past her daughter at the sturdy rancher. Sam was leaning against a fence post, laughingly letting Fauntleroy lip his hair as he extolled the llama's virtues to her father and brother. Merry saw him as her mother must—as she herself had done when first she arrived. Scruffy. Unrefined...

Then she saw him with her own two eyes. As the man she'd fallen for.

Yup. She was crazy about every last scruffy, unrefined inch of Sam Cassidy. He was perfect for her—a man who saw her worth, not her size or outward accomplishments. And maybe that was exactly what her subconscious had been trying to tell her all along, the reason she'd found it impossible to say a bad word about him in her column. Now, she didn't want to *hear* a bad word about him—from her mother or anyone else.

"You know what, Mother?" Merry rounded on Gwendolyn. "You are an inveterate snob. These people have been nothing but kind to you, and all you can do is look down your patrician little nose at them and say they're not good enough for a daughter bearing your pedigree."

"I am *not* a snob, Meredith..."

"It's *Merry*!"

"I'm not a snob, *Merry*. And I have nothing against the Cassidys. They seem like quite decent people. But you're still finding your feet after the accident, darling. You can't possibly know what you want, what's best for you. As your mother, it's my responsibility to ensure you don't make a terrible mistake."

"A *mistake*? Rejecting Granny's money isn't a mistake—in fact, it's probably the most rational thing I've ever done! You know what my *real* mistake has been? Trying to please *you*." Merry raked a hand through her hair, determined not to let tears fall. "Because obviously it'll never happen. And certainly not since I stopped being the precious little Olympian you could trot out at parties decked in gold medals!"

"Darling, keep your voice down," Gwendolyn shushed, eyes darting about to see who might have heard her daughter's over-loud rant. But Merry didn't care. She was done worrying about Gwendolyn Manning's delicate sensibilities.

"You want to know the first thing I felt when I woke up from that coma two years ago, Mother?" she demanded. "It was *relief*. Relief! Because I knew I would never have to please you again. I'd never be *able* to please you again. And then maybe you'd leave me alone."

Gwendolyn's face went ashen. "Never *please* me? Good God, is that what you think I care about? Your pleasing me? Merry, I didn't care about your medals because of how they reflected on *me*. I cared because they meant you'd found something you were passionate about—a place to fit in, to excel. I only pushed you toward skiing in the first place because I thought it would give you a sense of pride, of accomplishment..."

"It *did*, but..."

"Let me finish, if you please."

Merry instinctively obeyed her mother's tone, though her blood was boiling to pursue this long-overdue fight.

"From the time you were little, I knew you weren't well suited for the life I had to offer, but I simply didn't know how to help you. It was never about your height, or your appearance; it was about how *you* felt about them. How you seemed to set your-self apart from the rest of us. Please try to understand where I was coming from, Merry. I only knew my own way, the way the women in my family have done things for generations. It was my duty to provide that upbringing for you, but over the years you've made it abundantly clear you have nothing but contempt for the life we live."

"*I* have contempt? You're the one who was disappointed with me all the time."

"I wasn't *disappointed*, Merry . . . or if I was, it wasn't with you." She passed a hand across her cheek, swiping away a tear, and suddenly, to Merry, Gwendolyn looked her age. "It was with *myself*. Frankly, I didn't know what to do with a daughter like you. Marcus? Well, he was easy. He's always moved in our circles seamlessly. I didn't have to worry about him. But you were so unhappy, and I knew it was because I was failing you. It broke my heart to see you miserable every day. I thought if I pushed you harder, provided more opportunities, you'd find a way to fit in. But that day of your sweet sixteen, when you told me you'd tried to harm yourself just to get out of a little party . . . I saw that I was going about things all wrong."

"A *little* party? Half the UN was there!"

"It was what was expected for a girl of your station. But I never expected you'd hate it so much you'd . . . do what you did." Gwendolyn's voice broke. "After that, I suppose I became obsessed with your skiing career, because the only time I ever saw a smile on your face was when you'd cross the finish line. You were so talented, so dedicated. You had a gift that put the rest of us to shame—my own small talent as a skater was never anything to compare to your greatness. And then, when you lost it . . ." She stopped, and tears trembled again on her lashes—real tears, ugly tears this time. "When you almost died . . . Oh, Merry, I was afraid you'd never find another place where you'd be happy. Ever since, you've seemed so adrift. The only thing I could think was to bring you home, so that I could provide a safe place for you, and a purpose."

Merry felt as if Betty the poltergoat had butted her square in the solar plexus. She'd never heard so much raw honesty from her mother. Could she trust it? Or was this just another trick to get her to conform? "But what if where I'm happy is *here*? What then, Mother?"

Gwendolyn sighed. "Merry, it hasn't been that long since the accident. There's still a whole world out there for you—and I'm not talking about hamam horror stories or pub crawls in Copenhagen. Here, all you have is..." She prodded a clod on the ground with the toe of her twelve-hundred-dollar boot. "*Manure.*" She put her hand on Merry's arm again. "I'm not asking you to stop caring about these people. Of course it's natural for you to care, especially when you've been struggling so hard to find your way. I'm simply trying to make you see what you'll be giving up if you limit yourself to this little village. If you turn your back on all the Hollingsworth and Manning names can offer."

Merry blew out a breath of frustration. "You've no idea what *Aguas Milagros* has to offer, Mother. How about you give it a chance before you decide they're all rubes? Get to know them, instead of just assuming they're 'too limited' for your daughter. Maybe I'm not the one who's missing something. Maybe it's *you* who can't see. You're in the middle of a ranch, for Christ's sake, and you haven't even looked at the animals! I mean, what kind of woman thinks an alpaca isn't adorable? Who couldn't love a llama?"

"I have nothing against these people *or* their livestock, Merry."

"Prove it!"

And she did.

᪐

"*Mother, wait!*" *I cried, but Mother was already striding up to the paddock fence. Buddha's neck drew back with alarm, his ears flapping agitatedly.*

I knew what came next.

Apparently, so did my mother. As the stream of spit arced through the air, my mother ducked.

Ducked, I tell you. And she did it so gracefully it was no effort at all—like a character in The Matrix *dodging bullets in slow motion. I could almost hear sound effects, I swear.*

My mouth dropped open. Unfortunately for my brother, who was standing behind Mother, so did his.

Thwack. *Buddha scored a hole in one.*

"Auugggggggggghhhhh!" Marcus gargled. His face was covered with slobber and contorted with horror. "Call the CDC!"

So that's what I looked like, that first day at the ranch, I thought. I looked over at Sam, who was biting his lip manfully. Jane didn't do such a great job hiding her mirth. "Hold still, crybaby," she snickered. "I've got you." She tugged a hankie free of her back pocket and flapped it open. While the elder Mannings watched in appalled fascination, she wiped their pride and joy clean. "There, good as new," she pronounced. "Or, as good as you're gonna get, anyway."

I must tell you, our dear vet did not look impressed.

Marcus, however, looked intrigued. "Thanks, babe," he said, slinging an arm around her shoulder. "You're a real lifesaver."

Jane shrugged out from under it. "Save it," she said. "You're not my type."

᪐

"Gay, huh?" Marcus side-mouthed to Merry as they continued their tour.

"Who, Jane? I don't think so." Merry was still so rattled by her fight with their mother that she could scarcely pay attention to Marcus.

"C'mon. She's got to be."

Merry looked over at Jane, who was measuring little Bill from stem to stern, jotting down notes on a pad. She tugged the cria's ear playfully as it nosed in her pockets for treats. Jane's joy was contagious, but Merry couldn't share it. She was too busy trying to wrap her mind around everything her mother had revealed. So much that she'd believed about Gwendolyn had just been called into question. But one thing Merry knew: Her mother *was* a snob. And Gwendolyn wasn't the only Manning with a penchant for pretention. "Hate to break it to you, Uglymug, but not falling for your charms doesn't make a woman homosexual."

Marcus didn't look offended. "In my experience it does."

"Well, you're in a different world now, Banana Hammock."

Marcus grew serious. "I can see that, Sis. And I can see how good it's been for you. This ranch seems to have worked a kind of magic on you. I don't think I've seen you this happy since... well, *ever*."

Merry forgave Marcus's arrogance. As always, he saw straight into the heart of her—the only one, before Sam, who could. *If only our parents could do the same...* "You're right. This time at the Last Chance... it's given me a *second* chance. A place to start over, and maybe even belong."

"Are you seriously thinking of staying on? Even if it really does mean telling Mom and her money to bugger off?"

"I am," Merry said, and saying it aloud made her feel suddenly light—and not merely in the wallet. "That is, if there's anything to stay for."

"What about Sam? The guy's clearly willing to go twelve rounds in the ring for you."

Merry blushed. "He's part of it. But I meant the buyout. Dolly's ex will be back any day, and he'll spend the rest of their lives hauling Dolly through the courts if he doesn't get what he wants."

Marcus nodded. "I can understand why you'd be upset if Dolly lost the ranch. I'd help you out, out of my own inheritance, but..." He paused. "That might prove tricky."

Before Merry could ask what he meant, Pierce strode up. "Merry, I've just made acquaintance with the most astounding creature!" He linked arms with her and tugged her to the pen where Jane, with Dolly's help, was finishing up Bill's wellness exam. Dashiell had her head over the rail, batting her lashes at them both, while Bill, all curly chocolate wool and sweet innocent cheeks, nuzzled her for milk. Pierce seemed smitten. "Dorothy's been telling me how you helped save this young fellow's life." He shook his head. "Amazing!"

Merry beamed under her father's praise. "He is pretty cute, isn't he?"

"Gwendolyn, isn't it something? Look what our Merry's done!"

Gwendolyn, following in her husband's wake, tried on a smile. "I'm sure we're all very proud of Merry's...animal husbandry." She pulled the hem of her coat away from the cria's questing mouth.

Guess we're not holding hands and singing songs around the campfire quite yet, Merry thought.

"Neither Dashie nor her cria would have made it through the

night if it weren't for Merry," said Sam, clearly trying to cut the tension.

"And *I* wouldn't have made it through the night if it weren't for Sam." Very deliberately, Merry slipped her arm about his waist.

Sam looked surprised at the way she'd just claimed him in front of her family, but his eyes were warm as he gazed back at her. He looped his arm around her in return, and Merry was buoyed by its solidity. "I think you'd have done alright, honey, but I was glad to help where I could."

"You've helped our daughter quite a lot, it would seem," Gwendolyn said, eyeing their body language with an inscrutable expression.

Pierce cleared his throat, and Marcus smothered a laugh. Jane gave the supermodel a scowl.

"How about we hit the road, folks?" Dolly suggested.

The stampede for Sam's truck left llamas blinking in their wake.

CHAPTER FORTY-NINE

$\mathcal{S}$am held the door open for Merry's family, then snuck a kiss on her neck as she passed him as well. "Hang in there, honey," he said with a twinkle in his eye.

"I'm trying." Merry looked around the diner. At least there'd be plenty of warmhearted folks to dilute her parents' chilling influence. Every booth was taken, and several tables had been pushed together to make a communal seating area running the length of the restaurant. The Happy Hookers were represented by Randi, Rebecca, Pam, and Sage, all sitting together at one end of the community table, wearing their finest fiber arts. Steve and Mazel were at the other, and Federico had joined them, talking earnestly with them about something Merry suspected had to do with a certain "side business." Mikey and Bernardo were sitting with their parents at one of the booths, and Joey was with a woman who looked tired but determined, and kept stroking his hair as if he might disappear at any moment. Those who weren't sitting were clumped around the café in little clusters, chatting.

Café Con Kvetch was bursting at the seams.

Its owner was unraveling.

For the first time since Merry had known him, Needlepoint Bob looked less than sanguine. He had an apron slung haphazardly about his paunch, and a hairnet was doing little to tame his salt-and-pepper mane. His eyes were wild as he hustled up to them.

"Dolly, I need you," he blurted.

Dolly's eyes widened.

"You're the only person who can save Thanksgiving," he declared. "Feliciana had an existential crisis this morning, up and quit with the turkeys half-baked. 'Nesto took off in a show of solidarity, so now I'm in the weeds up to my neck. We've got no one to bus or bartend, and half the town showed up in search of sustenance."

The Mannings exchanged glances. Merry looked around the restaurant. The natives were definitely getting restless.

"Overwhelmed, eh?" Dolly took a moment to relish Bob's discomfiture. "No way to feed your charges? Heavens, I can't imagine how *that* feels."

"Revenge may be a dish best served cold," Bob sighed, "but stuffing's better piping hot." He put a hand on her shoulder and gave her a searching look. "Please, Dorothy."

Dolly gave a put-upon huff, but her eyes were alight with energy. "Show me to the kitchen," she ordered. "And no philosophizing while we cook, or I'll show *you* hot stuffing."

Bob blew out a breath of relief. "Whether in this life or the next, you'll find your karmic reward." Now that help was on the way, some of his customary poise returned, and he seemed to see the rest of their party for the first time. "You must be the Mannings. Sam said you were coming." He pressed his hands together in a quick Buddhist salute. "Welcome, and thank you for the gift of your daughter. She's brought a lot of joy to us here in Aguas Milagros these last few weeks." He turned to Sam. "Sam, can you play bartender?"

"Sure." Sam shrugged out of his coat, hung his hat on a hook by the door.

"I think we could all do with a drink," said Pierce. "Single malt, if you have it?"

Sam nodded. "I'll see what we've got back there. White wine for you, Gwendolyn?"

"Vodka martini, and make it a double, if you please."

"An ultralight beer for me, Sam," said Marcus.

"Hit me up with a shot of tequila when you get a chance," Merry side-mouthed to Sam. "Or maybe just bring the bottle." Out loud she said, "How about I get the tables set, and some snacks going round so folks don't get too hungry while you finish up in the kitchen. You've got some bar snacks stashed away, haven't you, Bob?"

Bob nodded gratefully.

"I'll grab the nibbles," said Jane, shrugging off her jacket.

"I'll help you," offered Marcus.

"*You* can check coats," Jane told him. "Since you're basically a walking clotheshorse anyhow."

To Merry's surprise, Marcus meekly did as bid. And was that a hint of a blush on his high cheekbones?

"What would you like us to do?" Pierce asked Bob, piling his and Gwendolyn's outerwear in the hapless Marcus's arms.

"Oh, you guys don't have to do anything, Dad," Merry answered for him. "Just find a seat and make yourselves comfortable."

"Nonsense, Merry," Gwendolyn said. Her spine was steel. "I'm sure we're not as useless as all that."

"Well in that case...how about you help me with the place settings?"

My father earned his stripes in the diplomatic corps. Over decades of dedicated service, he's brokered peace between feuding tribes, forged bonds between entrenched enemies, fostered understanding amongst the estranged.

His mission today? Find common ground with the folks of Aguas Milagros.

With a little help from his lovely wife.

∞

Gwendolyn glided about the café as if born to waitress, graceful as the figure skater she'd once been. She set tables and arranged glassware—even slipping outside for a moment and returning with her arms full of autumn boughs, which she arranged into centerpieces the guests all oohed and aahed over. Pierce, meanwhile, pored over the jukebox until he found music to set the mood, settling on some Bing Crosby. Sam made sure everyone was liberally supplied with libations, and very quickly the atmosphere grew more convivial. Marcus, Merry noticed, spent most of his time attempting to catch Jane's eye. From the kitchen came the sounds of pots clanking, food sizzling, and two old friends slinging good-natured insults while they saved the day for Aguas Milagros.

I may survive this meal after all, Merry thought as her family rejoined her.

"Hey, Mer-Ber, who're the squares?" Steve Spirit Wind wanted to know.

Or not.

SSW studied the Mannings. "I'm getting a heavy vibe here. I think they could benefit from our product," he confided to his woman.

"You speak truth," Mazel concurred. "My fellow travelers in

the light, in the spirit of this holiday—and ignoring, for the moment, the insult to our Native American brethren—we would like to offer you a gift." She rummaged in her macramé tote and came up with a mini bong and a baggie containing an unmistakable herb. "It's a special blend of our own. Also great for waking the appetite—not that we'll need help in that department with Dolly in the kitchen."

Marcus stepped in front of his openmouthed parents. "Allow me to accept on their behalf," he said.

Mazel gave Marcus a look that said something had woken *her* appetite. Steve offered him a distinctly less friendly appraisal, and changed the subject. "Our Merry's been a real gift to this town," he told the Mannings, using nearly the same verbiage Bob had. "Brought a breath of fresh air into the place—and I ought to know about that!"

"This is Steve Spirit Wind," Merry explained to her nonplussed parents. "And Mazel Tov, his, er..."

"His more enlightened half," Mazel finished for her. "Be welcome, travelers." Before they could fend her off, she'd enveloped the Mannings in a patchouli-scented embrace. Steve came around the other side and sandwiched them in, squeezing until Merry heard her mother squeak.

She started to rescue her parents from the hippies' embrace, but was foiled when she was engulfed in hugs herself. Mikey and Bernardo jumped her, hanging off her like a jungle gym, eager to introduce their parents. Joey trailed them more shyly, while the woman she'd seen earlier stood uncertainly behind him.

"Check it out, Ms. Manning, look what I got!" Mikey stuck a foot out, clad in top-of-the-line winter boots. The rest of his clothing was new too, and scrupulously clean.

"You should see the space-age sleeping bag I scored," Bernie

chimed in. "Don't tell Sammy, but it *totally* beats a bag of leaves."
He cast a sheepish glance at Sam, who was slinging brewskis behind the bar.

"Our folks want to meet you," Mikey said, waving the adults
over. Merry stuck her hand out...and was pulled into more back-
slapping hugs.

A man with hair as wild and woolly as Bernie's gave her a
breathtaking squeeze, then introduced himself and his wife. "Lou
and Lydia Ruis," he said. "Our son can't stop bragging about how
he's famous on the Internet! Now he and Mikey want to take
computer classes so they can have their own blog."

"*Column*, Dad," Bernie said.

"We've never seen the kids so enthusiastic about anything,"
said Lydia. "We spoke with the mayor and he's going to see about
getting better Internet around here, and one of the schoolteachers
from Angel Fire is going to come teach classes once a week."

"That's amazing," Merry said, seeing the excitement on the
kids' faces.

The other parents nodded shyly. "Thank you for what you've
done for our boy," said Mikey's mother, a chubby brunette who
introduced herself as Melissa. "We've seen such a change in him
these past weeks. He's trying harder in school. More outgoing.
Confident."

"*Mom*," groaned Mikey. "Embarrassing much?" But he didn't
look embarrassed. He looked proud.

His dad ruffled his hair. "Anyhow, we're glad you came,
and we hope you'll stay awhile longer in Aguas Milagros." He
beamed at Merry's parents. "You must be so proud of your daughter."

"Oh...ah, yes, of course," said Pierce. He patted Merry's
back. "Very proud."

Ha, Merry thought. If Gwendolyn had her way, she'd probably be airlifted out of Aguas Milagros by commandos before dessert was served. "I hope I *can* stay," she said. She extended her hand to the nervous-looking woman, who was still hanging back behind Joey. "And you are?"

"Joey's mother," said the woman, coming forward shyly. "Christa Ramirez. I wanted to thank you for what you did for me too."

"What I did for you?" Merry was confused.

"You woke me up, Ms. Manning. Made me realize how much my Joey needs me." She stroked the boy's hair again, her eyes damp with tears. "I haven't always been the best mother, but I want to be there for him now." And before Merry could react, the smaller woman threw her arms around her too.

If hug collecting were a job, I'd be out of debt in no time, she thought, patting the wraithlike Christa on the back.

And speaking of backs, Merry could feel laser-like eyes on *hers*. She turned to see her mother watching her with a peculiar expression on her face. *I don't even want to know what that look means*, she thought. She turned back to the kids.

"Where are Zelda and Thaddeus?" she asked Bernie.

"Zel dragged Thad to her parents' place for Thanksgiving," he said. "Poor sap."

Mikey snickered. "T and Z, sitting in a tree...Better him than you or me!"

Merry smiled, but a thunderous voice brought her up short.

"Woman, why aren't you wearing that sweater I gave you?!"

Merry glanced around, and saw Randi bearing down on her. *Oh, no*, she thought. "Randi, I'm so sorry...I had to cut it up..."

"You *what?!*" Randi feigned fury for a moment, then burst out laughing. "I'm just messing with you, woman. L'il Bill wears it well! Hey, these your folks?" She slapped Merry on the back. "You did great with this one, y'all. Can we keep her?"

"Really, Randi. Try not to look like a lunatic in front of Merry's parents," suggested Rebecca, who had come up behind her fellow hooker. Today her braids had been adorned with autumn leaves, giving her a fairy-queen-ish feel. She held her hand out. "I'm Rebecca Donovan. We've been delighted to have Merry here in our town. You must be so proud of your daughter."

"Of course," Gwendolyn said stiffly, accepting the handshake. "And what do you do here, Ms. Donovan?"

"I'm the town historian," she said. "I keep the archives for Aguas Milagros."

Gwendolyn looked intrigued. "I'm something of an amateur historian myself," she said. "I run an institute dedicated to historical preservation. You may have heard of it—the Hollingsworth Heritage Foundation?"

"I can't say I have, but I'd be happy to hear about it now." Rebecca put an arm around Gwendolyn. "How about you join me at the visitor center down the street while we wait for dinner? It's where we keep all the old records, for want of a better location. I'd love to pick your brain." She turned to Merry. "You won't mind if I steal your mother for a bit, will you?"

Merry stifled the several things she wanted to say. "Feel free."

The two women disappeared out the door. Was it her imagination, or did the temperature inside Bob's café warm up a degree?

Marcus was certainly feeling the heat. The mayor had sidled up to him, placing a hand on Marcus's biceps. "Merry, who is this charming young man?"

Marcus flexed like the showman he was, and Merry stifled a grin. "Federico, this is my brother, Marcus. Uglymug, this is our town mayor, Federico Rios y Valles. He's also a fantastic stylist."

"I do appreciate a cutting-edge haircut," Federico allowed. He examined Marcus's expertly gelled coif. "*And* a man who knows how to show himself to his best advantage. Of course, you don't need help with that, do you, gorgeous?"

Marcus cast a triumphant glance at Jane, as if to say, "Now here's someone who appreciates me!"

Jane merely snorted. She couldn't have looked less impressed examining mange on a dog.

Marcus turned his back on her. "So, Mr. Mayor, what's your favorite product?" he asked, and soon the two men were deep in conversation about pomades versus waxes. Jane wandered off to swap amigurumi advice with Sage.

And Merry found herself alone with her father.

"Seems you've had quite an impact here, young lady," Pierce said.

He'll probably be calling me "young lady" well into my sixties, Merry thought, looking at her father fondly. "I hope so," she replied. "They've had quite an impact on *me*, Dad. Dolly and her friends... they're pretty amazing people."

"Then they're in good company, sweetheart. Because I think you're pretty amazing too."

Merry warmed under her father's words. "Wish Mother thought so," she said, then wished she'd kept the thought behind her teeth.

"Your mother loves you very deeply, Merry," Pierce told her. "I know she regrets how hard it's been for you two to see eye to eye. When Dolly reached out to us with her invitation to share the holiday, your mother jumped at the chance—even knowing there'd be barnyard animals."

Merry couldn't bring herself to laugh at her father's lame attempt at humor. "I wish I could believe that. But it seems like she just wants me to come home, toe the line like a good little daughter."

Pierce shook his head. "She wants you to be *happy*, Merry," he corrected. "It's what we all want."

A lump formed in her throat. "I...I think I *am*, Dad."

Pierce pulled her in for a hug, and for a moment Merry inhaled the scents of childhood—of tweed sport coats and the cigars her father still snuck when he thought Gwendolyn wouldn't notice. He kissed her cheek. "Then your mother and I are happy too, sweetheart. It just may take her a little longer to realize it." Pierce clinked glasses with her, then drained his as he watched his wife reenter the restaurant with Rebecca. "Be patient."

"You've been patient long enough!" shouted Dolly, emerging from the kitchen. She banged on a pot with a huge wooden spoon. "Take your places, people. It's chow time!"

CHAPTER FIFTY

*W*hat Bob and Dolly drew forth from the tiny café kitchen was an astounding culinary feat.

What they drew forth from yours truly was both simpler and more savory.

Gratitude.

Happy T-day, friends and neighbors. I hope your holiday was as full of love and good cheer as was mine.

❧

There was a mad scramble for the tables, now laden with fragrant dishes from marshmallow-topped sweet potatoes and cranberry relish to green bean casserole, chestnut stuffing, and of course, perfectly browned turkeys. Plate after plate of Dolly's prized biscuits rounded out the offerings, with gravy moored alongside in deep boats. The smell alone was enough to make Merry's knees weak. She found herself seated between her brother and Sam, her parents across from her. Dolly took her mother's left, with Bob on *her* left. Jane had landed up beside Marcus, seeming none too pleased about it.

"I'd like to start tonight's festivities with a traditional thanksgiving blessing," Bob said, loudly enough for all to hear. "The author of this one may be lost to the mists of time, but his message still rings true today. Everyone grab hands, and I'll expound." He inhaled a breath and took on his toastmaster tone.

"Count your blessings instead of your crosses;
Count your gains instead of your losses.
Count your joys instead of your woes;
Count your friends instead of your foes.
Count your smiles instead of your tears;
Count your courage instead of your fears.
Count your full years instead of your lean;
Count your kind deeds instead of your mean.
Count your health instead of your wealth;
Love your neighbor as much as yourself."

He settled back, beaming at the assembled guests. "And... go!"

Across the table, hands reached out to snatch whichever dish was nearest.

"Hold on, heathens!" Dolly shouted. She smacked Bob's biscuit-thieving hand with her spoon. "No one eats until he or she says one thing he's grateful for."

Groans rang out around the table. Dolly ignored them in queenly fashion. "I'll pick a victim to get us started," she said. "How about you, Randi?"

"I'm grateful for my fellow hookers!"

Gwendolyn looked alarmed.

"I'm grateful for *The Walking Dead* being back on!" said Sage.

"For another year with my main squeeze," said Steve, kissing Mazel.

"For Aguas Milagros!"

"Hear, hear!"

Around the table, sentiments both sweet and silly were shared, until finally, it was Dolly's turn. The guests grew quiet, apart from the growling of stomachs.

"I expect you've all heard this might be the last year for us Cassidys at the Last Chance," she said. Heads nodded solemnly. "And it's true; we may have to fold our tents if we can't find a way outta this mess pretty quick. But I'm not one to bemoan what's lost, or worry about things I can't change. I'd rather focus on what we've *got*, and right now, that's each other."

"And some damn fine biscuits, Dolly!" Randi shouted from down the table.

"And some damn fine biscuits," she allowed. "Thing is, this year, I can't think of a single thing to be grateful for." Eyes widened as people stared at Dolly. "That's because I'm grateful for so *many* things. My nephew Sammy, of course." She looked over at Sam, who gave her a little salute. "Couldn't imagine running the Last Chance without him these past seven years. And Janey, who keeps me in stitches while we're stitching. And yeah, even Bob here. I'm glad to let bygones be bygones, and be grateful for all those years of friendship we've shared—as well as the ones to come." She cast him a fond glance, and he returned it.

"But there's one unexpected gift that came my way this year, and that's our Merry." She turned her gaze to Merry, and her eyes were moist. "Child, you've been a revelation, and an inspiration too. From day one you've given it your all. I've never known a woman with half the grit you've got, and it's given me the gumption to keep fighting in the face of whatever comes my way, whether its bankruptcy or something unexpected down the road. So here's to Merry!"

And as one, two dozen glasses were raised. "To Merry!"

Merry blushed a deeper crimson than the cranberry sauce.

"I'd like to second that," said Bob when the shouting had died down. He cleared his throat. "Since she's been here, Merry's made us all see ourselves more clearly. She's held, as Hamlet once said, 'the mirror up to nature: to show virtue her feature, scorn her own image, and the very age and body of the time his form and pressure.' Her stories have exposed our foibles, celebrated our uniqueness, *and* improved our business. Plainly said, Lady Hobbit, we're glad you're here."

"I'll third that," said Jane, elbowing across Marcus to muss Merry's hair. "Here's to Merry! Maybe you can't crochet worth a damn, but you sure have wound your way into a lot of hearts around here." She toasted Merry with her wineglass.

Merry was too blinded by tears to toast back.

Before she could begin to gather her emotions, Sam spoke up. "My thanks this year go to Merry as well," he said. He reached out and cupped her cheek, gently wiping the tears away. "The moment Buddha hauled off and hawked a loogie in your face, Merry, I knew things were never going to be the same around here. From summiting Wheeler Peak on a bum leg to birthing an alpaca all by yourself in the middle of a snowstorm, you're the bravest woman I've ever known. And that bravery healed something in me I didn't know was broken. You've opened my heart, Merry Manning." He paused, and Merry saw there were tears in his eyes as well. "And you've claimed a piece of that heart—if you want it."

Merry found her hands were trembling, and she knew only one place they'd find shelter. She tucked her fingers inside his own. "Oh, I want it," she said.

"Gag! Retch! Puke! Jesus, you two, if you were trying to get me back on my diet, you've succeeded. Who could stomach such treacle?" Marcus shuddered.

"Your sister was trying to have a moment there, sport," said Pierce, calmly unfolding his napkin.

"And the rest of us are trying to have dinner. So can we hurry it up?" Marcus winked at Merry, and, snuffling back both tears and laughter, she pulled a face at him.

Gwendolyn refrained from cautioning Merry against the potential ruination of her face. Instead, she cleared her throat. "Pierce and I are also very grateful to be with you all today," she announced. "I honestly can't remember when we've had such a charming country holiday. Isn't that right, dear?"

Pierce nodded. "Beats Turkey Day at the White House, hands down."

"So today I'm grateful for..." Gwendolyn looked pensive. "Well, for having a lot to chew on, I suppose."

Considering the minuscule portion she'd ladled onto her plate, Merry didn't think her mother was talking about food.

"Can we eat now?" Bernie yelled.

They could eat.

They have a post-Thanksgiving tradition here in Aguas Milagros. And while the town is salutary in so many ways, I cannot "get with" this particular one.

Who in their right minds would want to get naked with stomachs as full as ours still were the day after a festival meal as rich, satisfying, and altogether egregious as the one served to us by the inimitable team of Dolly Cassidy and Needlepoint Bob?

Who, moreover, would want to get naked with their parents, their hostess, and their supermodel brother, in the company of their brand-new boyfriend? (Sorry, fans, I'm afraid Studly Sam is officially off the market. He says "hi" though.)

Despite my better judgment, off we went to the hot springs, for Aguas Milagros is a town deeply rooted in tradition, and who was I to change that? (Seriously, I asked, but apparently I hadn't the power to change it.)

Unfortunately, I was proven right in my protestations.

Because the springs were already occupied. By a big, fat snake.

⚬

"We are totally getting out of this," Merry assured Sam. "No *way* Pierce and Gwendolyn are going naked in public."

Sam gulped. She'd never seen him disconcerted before, but

she was sure as hell seeing it now. "It's one thing to meet your girlfriend's parents," he muttered, tidying his ponytail as they approached the hacienda from his hobbit hole in the early-morning light. "It's another to...you know, *meet* them."

"Thought you were all about *au naturel*," Merry teased.

"There's *au naturel* and there's *'au, please gouge out my eyes with a melon baller.'*"

"Never fear," she said, patting his arm as they entered the house. The Mannings were sipping coffee at the kitchen table, looking bright-eyed and rested, while Dolly fussed around them. *Let's see if I can blow their Zen*, she thought. "Guys, there's something they probably didn't tell you about the springs at Aguas Milagros." She paused. "It's *naked-only*."

Puzzled looks met her pronouncement.

"What other way would there be to visit a hot spring, darling?" Gwendolyn said. Merry couldn't tell if it was the Botox or if her mother was truly unfazed.

"Naked, as in *you* have to *get* naked. In front of other people."

"I'm game," said Marcus.

Merry rolled her eyes. Of course he was. Her brother never missed an opportunity to shuck trou. But it was her parents' blasé reactions that stumped her.

"When in Rome," Pierce said with a shrug. "And believe me, they do stranger things in Rome—or at least the diplomatic corps do, when they're off the clock."

"Darling, don't be so provincial," Gwendolyn drawled. "A woman of the world doesn't blush at such things. Why, your father and I visited the baths in Kyoto countless times when we were stationed there."

"But you said...you *totally* gave me hell when I did it in Istanbul, and that wasn't even coed!"

"One *does* it, Merry. One doesn't *tell* people about it." If Merry hadn't known better, she'd have sworn she saw Gwendolyn wink.

Sam chuckled, and she shot him a dirty look. "Mother, it's a mile up the mountain, and you don't have the right shoes. And...and..." Merry ran out of reasons.

"A walk in the woods will be bracing," said Pierce, bouncing on his toes. "Especially after all that food yesterday." He patted his stomach.

"Yes, and Dorothy's been kind enough to lend me a pair of quite sporty walking shoes." Gwendolyn stuck out one small foot, clad in a pair of Keds. "We're all keen to set off, Merry, so do stop dawdling."

"Sam, help!" Merry whispered.

"Look, I'm one hundred percent with you on this one," he said, whispering just as low. "But I know when I'm licked. Let's just get this over with, and pray for a steamy morning at the springs."

∽

Dorothy had been unusually quiet this morning, and Merry knew she was more worried about John resurfacing than she let on. She stuck close to Sam as the party set off, leaning a little on his arm, and Merry let them have their time together. She could use a little time with her closest relative too.

Merry trod the path alongside Marcus, envying him his smooth stride, though she had to admit her own gait was far stronger than it had been just weeks ago. "So, what'll you do with your big sweaty wad o' Granny-cash?" she asked. "You must be slavering to get spending now the bequest's come due."

"I didn't take it, actually."

Merry did a double take. "You're shitting me."

Marcus shrugged. "I started thinking about what you said, about the strings attached. And the more I thought, the more I realized that I wanted to...I don't know...be my own man, I guess. The business I'm in...it doesn't exactly promote responsibility. Fashion is all about the illusion of eternal youth. But we both know I'm near the end of my shelf life. Another year or two, and I'll be lucky to get print campaigns for Eddie Bauer. I wasn't wise with my money because I knew I had Grandmother's fortune to fall back on. Figured I'd spend the rest of my days making Mother happy by sucking up to old biddies for her charitable campaigns. Or I could marry Penny Aberdeen, the way she's been hoping for about the past ten years. But then I thought about all *you've* been doing...and, well, it sort of shamed me. You've always been the better of the two of us—"

Merry's jaw dropped. "Marcus, nobody thinks that—"

"Sure they do. Let's face it, Sis. You've always been the driven one, the talented one. Me? I just had a pretty face. But you...the whole world knew your name. You were America's next great champion. And when your first career was taken away, you got back up on your feet and found a new way to win people's hearts. That's the kind of person you are, Merry. Tough. Resilient. A fighter. You may be my little sister, but I look up to you. And not just because you *are* a big ol' Sasquatch."

Merry stopped right there on the trail and gave him a hug.

"So what *do* you want to do?" she asked when they resumed walking.

He shrugged again. "I thought I'd try the other side of the camera for a change," he said. "Maybe some nature portraits, or even documentary filmmaking. There are a lot of great causes I could champion, instead of just exploiting my body for cash. It's

scary as shit to think of going it alone, but I've got enough con-
nections to get me started. Hell, maybe I'll go to grad school."
His mouth twisted wryly. "Imagine me, a student at nearly forty.
Maybe I'm being ridiculous."

Merry beamed at her brother. "For the first time in all the
years I've known you, Marcus, I don't think you're the *least* bit
ridiculous."

The sight that met their eyes at the hot springs, however, was.

CHAPTER FIFTY-TWO

Yep, Merry thought. *That's a briefcase.* No amount of eye rubbing or arm pinching would change the fact that an alligator leather attaché was propped between two rocks on the edge of the steaming mineral pool.

It belonged, presumably, to the fellow in the three-piece suit. Who was dabbling his pasty white toes in the pool.

The person *inside* the pool was properly naked. Well, except for his feather-festooned cowboy hat.

Heading up their party, Dolly stopped so short the rest of them piled into one another like Keystone Cops. Pierce and Gwendolyn merely looked confused by the unusual occupants of the springs. Marcus seemed to be treating the scene as just one more Aguas Milagros weirdness. Sam bristled at Merry's side when he saw who it was. But Dolly was steaming hotter than the springs.

"Is there even one damn thing you won't ruin, John Dixon?"

Dolly's ex leaned his head back against the smooth stones that lined the pool, flinging his arms wide. He smiled through his brushy mustache. "Why, Dolly, what a surprise! We were just enjoying a nice morning soak. Weren't we, Twat?"

"*Watts*," sighed the lawyer, swishing his feet in the water. He eyed his wingtips with longing, as if he couldn't believe his current sad state of affairs.

"There's something you should be soaking, alright, and that's

your fat head," Dolly spat. "Don't try and tell me you ain't here
to bedevil me, because even you couldn't be that full of bull."

Marcus guffawed, but Merry elbowed him and he quieted.

"Fine. You got me." John shrugged. "Knew I'd get the business end of your shotgun if I showed up at the ranch," he said,
"even if it *is* still half mine. And I knew you always visit the
springs the day after Thanksgiving. You ain't exactly known for
being quick to change your ways, Dolls. I figured best to meet on
neutral ground. Didn't realize you'd be having a party." He eyed
the Mannings curiously.

Dolly became aware of their audience as well, but she wasn't
about to tuck tail. "These springs aren't neutral ground, they're
sacred ground. And your greed pollutes them like poison."

John scoffed. "Nothing's sacred, woman, not even your precious ranch. You're gonna have to face reality sometime...and I
hate to tell you, but that time is *today*. Twat here drew up the
contracts, and I expect you to sign, or there'll be trouble."

Sam strode to the lip of the pool. "Are you threatening my
aunt?" Merry had never seen him so furious. She grabbed his arm
lest he drown his uncle-in-law.

John smoothed his mustache. "Now simmer down, Sammy.
This ain't your business. It's between Dolly and me."

"I'm *making* it my business," Sam said. Merry bit her lip.
She'd like to make it her business too—with a knuckle sandwich
straight in Dixon's smirking face—but this hardly seemed the
place.

Her mother disagreed.

"Sir, I don't know who you are, but I do know you are *sin-
gularly* rude." Gwendolyn strode to the fore, regal as could be.
"What business brings you here, and why are you harassing Mrs.
Cassidy?"

"I can answer that one for you, Gwen," said Dolly. It broke Merry's heart to see the defeated expression on her weathered face. "This is my not-ex-*enough* ex-husband, John Dixon. And that over there's the lawyer he brought with him to try to force me to sell the ranch."

"Ah." Gwendolyn pursed her lips.

"Ah, nothing," John said, rising up to point a finger at his former wife. "I gave you fair warning, woman, but you wouldn't budge. Now you're gonna. This fella's got the papers that say so." He jerked his thumb at the lawyer. "Says if you won't buy me out for the same's they're willing to offer or better, I have the right to petition the court to a force a sale through, and you'll just have to take what you get in the settlement. So 'less you got the cash today, you're out on your rump."

"I'll give you a *kick* in the rump!" Dolly stomped forward, suddenly fired up again.

"Hang tight, Dolly." This came from Sam, who looked positively murderous. He laid his hand on his aunt's arm. "Let me take care of the pest removal."

"Should we be calling the police?" Pierce murmured to Merry. She shook her head. "Dolly's a tough lady. She can handle it."

But it was another tough lady who took charge.

"Sir, am I correct in the presumption that you are attempting to sell the Last Chance ranch to this..." She waved at Watts. "Person, or to those he represents?"

"You can presume anything you like, lady." John smirked, but Gwendolyn's manner had clearly caught him off guard.

Gwendolyn was not to be deterred. "And further, that the buyer intends to use the ranch for large-scale commercial purposes?" Her ice-blue eyes skewered Watts now, cross-examining him.

The lawyer nodded meekly, looking like he wanted to dive for the bottom of the pool. "That's right, Mrs....?"

"It's *Lady. Lady* Gwendolyn Hollingsworth Manning."

Hoo, boy, Merry thought. *Mother doesn't whip out the honorifics for just anybody.* She put her arm around Sam, who still seemed ready to leap into action. "I think we're in for some fireworks," she murmured to him.

Sam gave her an uncertain look. "It's a good thing," Merry assured him. *At least*, she thought, *it's a good thing when the Wrath of Gwendolyn isn't directed at* me.

Watts gulped. "That's correct, Mrs.... er, Lady...um...your grace." He wiped a bead of sweat off his brow. "Massive Euphemistics, whose interests I represent, plans to run a corporate retreat and conference center out of the Last Chance ranch."

"Well, they'd best make *other* plans, I'm afraid," Gwendolyn said. She examined her manicure. "It so happens the Last Chance is an historical landmark. I ascertained as much with the aid of that delightful Ms. Donovan yesterday," she said, turning to look at Dolly. Merry could swear there was a glint of mischief in her eye. "We spent a very rewarding half hour in the Aguas Milagros archives yesterday, and as it turns out, there was a fascinating record of a certain Indian chief...Manzanito, was it?"

"Chief Manuelito," Dolly said.

"Yes, Manuelito. That was it. Well, apparently he had quite the history in Northern New Mexico in the mid-1800s, and one of his many rebellions took place on the site of your very ranch. Part of the hacienda actually dates back to those days, and may have been where he made his stand against US government forces."

Dolly's eyes lit. "That's right! We've got a plaque and everything, on the wall by the yard. I never thought much about it, honestly."

"Well, whoever sold you the ranch should have told you, because it's listed in the National Register of Historic Places, and that has repercussions." Gwendolyn turned to the two men in the pool. "You see, gentlemen, the ranch is a site of national historic significance. As such, it cannot be renovated, repurposed, or materially altered in any way that would mar the historical value of the site."

"All because of some stupid plaque?!" John was sputtering through his facial hair.

Gwendolyn's expression was serene. "That's right. Whoever owns the ranch must continue to preserve it *as is*. Of course, Mr. Dixon, you could still take Mrs. Cassidy to court over the property, but without a buyer such as—what were they called, Massive Mistakes?—you'll hardly find it worth your time. And if you'll take a little friendly advice, I'll tell you this for free: You don't want to tangle with historical preservationists. Believe me, that's a battle even Admiral Nelson couldn't win." She allowed herself a tiny smile. "Better to allow Mrs. Cassidy to buy you out for the fair market value of the ranch in its current state." She turned to her hostess. "How much is that, Dolly dear?"

Dolly looked dazed. "About a quarter of what the Massive Pains in the Ass are offering."

"I'm correct in assuming that Merry's crowd-funding campaign can cover that much, am I not?" Gwendolyn looked to her daughter for confirmation.

Merry felt like cheering. "Totally, Mom!"

"Well then. That, as they say, would appear to be that." Hands on hips, she stared Dixon down. "Now, I'm sure we'd all thank you if you and your toady would see fit to stop hounding this dear woman and *bloody well shove off!*"

Bloody well shove off! echoed through the forest, bouncing off the steaming surface of the water. Birds stopped chirping. Bees stopped buzzing. Gwendolyn looked a bit taken aback at the volume she'd achieved, but that was alright. Everyone else was looking pretty poleaxed too.

Not least, John Dixon. He sputtered. He blustered. But there was, in the end, nothing much he could say.

"You can be sure we'll check your story," he vowed, hauling his towel off a branch and wrapping himself in it. "C'mon, Twat."

"Did you know about the plaque?" Watts asked, hustling his pruny feet back into his socks and shoes. "Because if you knew and you entered into negotiations with our organization anyway, you could be open to a nuisance suit." His expression said *that* would be a legal battle he'd relish.

John just shot the man a look. Then he turned his gaze on Dolly again, sizing her up and down, and all at once he seemed more rueful than wrathful. He shook his head. "Well played, woman. You always did have a knack for finding defenders wherever you went. Prob'ly why that fool Bob Henderson's been in love with you since the day we hit this jerkwater town."

"Humph," said Dolly, turning pink. "Well, feel free to *leave* this 'jerkwater town,'" she suggested tartly. "But this time don't forget to file the divorce papers on your way out. We'll work out a settlement about the ranch later—a *fair* settlement."

As the group watched, Dixon settled his hat more firmly on his head, turned tail, and skedaddled, lawyer at his heels.

"Now, who's for a soak?" Gwendolyn asked when the two men had disappeared down the trail. "I, for one, could jolly well do with a bath after all this kerfuffle!"

CHAPTER FIFTY-THREE

*T*hey weren't out of hot water yet.

"Your mother and I have been talking," said Pierce.

He sloshed about, settling his arm around his wife. Gwendolyn's creamy skin flushed in the steam...or was it something else? Merry didn't want to think about where her father's other hand might rest. She was distracted enough by the very pleasurable sensation of Sam by her side—and the total weirdness of being naked with her entire family, plus Dolly, in a pool the size of one of Gwendolyn's smaller limousines. Merry sank deeper under the water until it lapped at her lower lip. "Have you?" she murmured.

"Yes," said Pierce. Somehow, soaking in a mud puddle in the middle of nowhere did nothing to diminish his dignity. "We've done a lot of thinking in the course of the last twenty-four hours, and we have something to tell *both* you children."

Oh, goodie, thought Merry. She exchanged a look with her brother. Marcus, lolling in the shallow end where his body just *happened* to be most exposed, only shrugged. He clearly had no idea what was coming either.

"You folks want some privacy for this?" Sam asked—rather too eagerly. He made to rise.

"As a matter of fact, Sam—I may call you Sam, mayn't I?"

Sam nodded. "Of course, Gwendolyn." He subsided back into the spring, giving Merry an "Oh, help" look.

"Well, it's partly because of yourself and your aunt that we need to say this, so, if you don't mind, we'd like you to stay."

This was getting weirder by the minute. Merry looked about the pool, but there seemed no easy escape—for her *or* for Sam. *Sorry*, she mouthed to him. But she didn't feel sorry, she realized. She felt *happy*. At peace, in a way that was unshakable, no matter what her parents might say next. She'd seen a side of her mother she'd never seen before today—the side that stuck up for her offspring and their friends—and it was something she'd cherish forever. All the money in the world meant nothing next to the support they'd just shown her.

Feeling a spurt of mischief, she ran her hand up Sam's thigh under the water. He went red and shot her a look that promised vengeance. Merry just grinned.

"Sure thing, Gwen," Dolly answered for them both when Sam couldn't find the breath. "Please, Pierce, have your say."

Pierce looked at Merry and Marcus in turn. "The first thing we want to say is that your mother and I are both extremely proud of the people you two have grown into. Marcus, you may play the reprobate, but lately we've seen there's far more to you, and we want you to know it hasn't gone unnoticed. We think you'll do well in your new career, make your mark the way a Manning should. And Merry—sweetheart—watching you yesterday with the people of this town...well, it's clear you've made one hell of an impression."

"When I saw how deeply loved you are here," Gwendolyn put in, "I was truly moved. And it's clear to me you love these people too. You're comfortable in Aguas Milagros in a way I've never seen you before, and—even though I'll admit it's somewhat foreign to me—I can see this is where you're happy. That's all we've ever wanted for you, darling."

Pierce patted his wife's shoulder proudly. "The second thing we wanted to say is that you've helped *us* become better people."

Gwendolyn cleared her throat. "The fact is, you've *shamed* us into doing so. We've realized—well, *I've* realized—we never should have tried to control you by means of money—"

"—and the fact that you've both refused it just lets us know you're mature enough to *handle* it—" Pierce added.

"—so your father and I have decided that, effective immediately, you will both have your inheritance from your grandmother, to do with as you wish."

Merry's jaw dropped so hard she got a mouthful of mineral water. Sam put a finger under her chin and gently closed it for her.

Marcus's reaction was less subtle. "*Wheeeeeeeeeeeeeee-hooooooooooooooooo!*" he shouted, so loud he could have been heard all the way into town. He did a backflip in the water that drenched them all. "*Yeeeeeeeeeaaaaaaaahhhhhhhhhhhh!*"

"Way to show you're mature, Banana Hammock," Merry snorted. Her mind was reeling. To be out of debt...to be able to breathe...but more than that, to do whatever felt *right*, without worrying about pleasing her mother or anyone else...Could it be true?

"So, if I wanted to buy a million buckets of green paint with the money, and dye myself like the Jolly Green Giant, you wouldn't have a problem with that?"

"It would be none of our business, I should think." Gwendolyn patted her perfect hair. "But do think twice. Green's never been your color, darling."

Merry grinned. Her heart was soaring. "I have a better idea, anyway." She turned to Dolly. "Didn't you once tell me there's a lot of lonely llamas out there, looking for love?"

CHAPTER
FIFTY-FOUR

*W*ell, *it's official. Cleese says we're staying, and I make it a policy not to argue with the wisdom of turtles. (Besides, he's formed a fast friendship with Sam's bunny, Arwen, and I couldn't bear to break them up.) From this day forth, my bedazzled reptile and I shall make our home in the town of Aguas Milagros, where we will find ourselves in good company with the thirty...excuse me, now thirty-ONE alpacas, sixteen llamas, assorted goats, chickens, dogs, cat...and the single best people we've ever known.*

Stay tuned for more news from the Land of Enchantment. Until then, I'll be...

On My Merry Way.

Oh, and Don't Do What I Did. (Seriously, the hot springs can only hold so many at a time.)

Epilogue

Aguas Milagros

Six months later

*A*lright, alright. I know you've been clamoring for updates, and I've finally found the time to fill you in. So here's the skinny on what's been happening in Aguas Milagros since last I checked in.

Dolly got her wish, dear ones. With the money we invested turning the ranch into a full-scale rescue outfit, her llamas (and several more from neighboring areas) are comfortable in their retirement, with the occasional tourist run to keep them in fine fettle. The alpacas continue to slay one with sweetness while producing the silkiest yarn anywhere in New Mexico. Luke (the ranch hand I had the good fortune to fill in for) finally made it back from his much-extended honeymoon, bringing his blushing bride with him. With the increased herd around here, they've both got their hands full. Sam still teaches survival classes (he's even got my fire-building skills up to snuff!), and with Jane's help, our amigurumi sell out faster than ever in the shop. Marcus stops in from time to time to take nature photographs (he's making quite the name for himself in the art world), but I'm afraid Jane scarcely gives him the time of day. (Keep at it, Banana Hammock, I think she's warming to you.)

If you come to visit (and we hope you do!), be warned: You may not see much of Dolly. After years of tireless toil, she's finally found the time to travel the world, and Bob accompanies her as often as his duties at the café permit. We get plenty of postcards to track their movements, however, each with a certain theme:

Alpacas of the Andes

Llamas of Tibet
Candid Camels of Arabia
(You get the idea.)
    And I? Well, I'm hard at work on my novel, and I've been loogie free
for 107 days now. Yet my heart has been thoroughly captured: by this
land, by these people, and by the second chances so freely offered at the
Last Chance Llama Ranch.

Acknowledgments

And now the part where I tell on myself:

Aguas Milagros, I'm afraid, does not exist. I pulled inspiration from real towns around New Mexico like Mora and Questa, but Aguas Milagros itself is a product of my imagination, hot springs, hippies, and all.

Llamas and alpacas *are* known to spit upon occasion, but not nearly as much as I make them out to, and they mostly only do it to each other. Really. Don't be scared.

Generally speaking, if the powder base is good, ski season in the Taos Valley opens the weekend after Thanksgiving. I moved it up a few days for my own nefarious purposes.

For similarly nefarious reasons, I moved the Wool Festival at Taos back about a month. It's usually held the first weekend in October.

Chief Manuelito, a fierce Navajo warrior and leader, obviously never spent time in a fictitious town, but he did move around northern New Mexico a lot in the 1860s, and he was well-known for his battles with the US military. I just created a little rest stop for him on his travels, for which I hope I may be forgiven.

And now the part where I slobber with gratitude:

To Susan Barnes at Redhook, for patience, guidance, and a truly humbling degree of faith in me. (And for obligingly squeeing every time I sent her *another* llama or alpaca picture.) It's a privilege to work with you.

To Holly Henderson Root, agent extraordinaire, for being as ever the voice of complete calm, competence, and professionalism. Never were there sweeter words than "Let me take care of this for you."

To my friends Rebecca Parish, Pam Watts, and Randi Ya'el Chaikind, the Santa Fe NaNoWriMos who made this last year a time of copious caffeine, laughs, and kick-ass fiction. I think we must've slurped coffee (and hogged outlets) in every café in Santa Fe.

To Jim Garland and Diane Thomas of our little Eldorado writers' group, for invaluable suggestions and generosity with their time. I hope to be able to return the favor someday.

And lastly, to those who rescued me from rivers of tears this past year: my brother, Jason Fields, Amanda Morris, Leslie Kazanjian, Diane Schwartz, Caz McKinnon, Arna Elezovic, Bernard Balizet, Shana Hack, Lucinda Marker, Pierre Barrera, Susanna Kirk, and of course, the women of the sanity-restoring Eldorado Thursday night women's meeting.

Thank you, thank you, thank you.

And now the part where I acknowledge my inspirations:

I doubt I'd have dreamed up this novel without my serendipitous meeting with real-life mountain man Stuart Wilde of Wild

Earth Llama Adventures up in Questa, New Mexico. The idea for "Lunch with the Llamas" began with a lunchtime trek with his majestic llamas, and he was gracious enough to share freely of his wisdom and expertise on several occasions while I plied him with llama questions. I recommend you check out Wild Earth at www.llamaadventures.com or on Facebook at www.facebook.com/llamatrek for a wonderful wilderness experience!

The folks at Victory Ranch in Mora, New Mexico, were an invaluable resource. (Plus, they let me pet their alpacas to my heart's content.) With two hundred of the cutest camelids you ever did see, set in a gorgeous, mountain-ringed valley, this is probably the squee-fulest ranch you can visit. Darcy Weisner and her family graciously fielded my many questions, *and* let me fondle all the yarn in their shop. They run visiting hours where you can meet and feed the animals year-round, and once a year, you can even watch the 'packies get shorn. (It's not traumatic at all, I swear.) Visit them at www.victoryranch.com or on Facebook at www.facebook.com/victoryranch. (Oh, and I have to fess up: I stole the idea of "theme naming" cria from them.)

Anne Stallcup at Que Sera Alpacas gave me a more thorough tutoring on the topic of microns, staple length, and "well-organized fleece" than I could possibly do justice. I'm just grateful she let me get to know her herd and take lots of adorable pictures. Check her out just outside Santa Fe proper at www.queseraalpacas.com or on Facebook at www.facebook.com/queseraalpacas.

And of course, I have to acknowledge the inimitable Cody Lundin. I was lucky enough to attend Cody's "Nothing" Course through his Aboriginal Living Skills School in Prescott, Arizona, last summer, where I learned all about being "the outside penguin," garbage bag blankies, and roasting de*lic*ious ash cakes over an open fire. (Blech!) Cody, thanks for your wit, your wisdom, and for not razzing me *too* much about jonesing for Diet Coke. I hope you don't mind my borrowing your bare feet for my character Sam! Information on the Aboriginal Living Skills School can be found on Cody's website at www.codylundin.com.

meet the author

Photo Credit: Jenn Adams

A scion of Manhattan's Upper East Side, HILARY FIELDS wrote her first romance novel at sixteen, and continued to write women's fiction even as she studied classics and philosophy at St. John's College, a tiny liberal arts college in Santa Fe, New Mexico. In the spirit of cognitive dissonance, she continues to divide her time between Manhattan and the Land of Enchantment, and enjoys cooking, crocheting, and her obligatory feline companions.

introducing

IF YOU ENJOYED
LAST CHANCE LLAMA RANCH,
LOOK OUT FOR

BLISS

by Hilary Fields

Nothing says "oops" like your naked ass skidding in the salmon mousse...

    A year ago, pastry chef Serafina Wilde's seemingly perfect life fell to pieces. So now, when her eccentric aunt Pauline calls from Santa Fe needing her help, Sera jumps at the chance to start over. Pauline even offers to let her take over the family business, "Pauline's House of Passion," and turn it into a bakery...provided she agrees not to ditch the "back room." Cupcakes and sex toys don't exactly mix, but Sera is willing to try, and what she finds in the beautiful City Different is the best life has to offer—if she has the courage to go for it.

Chapter 1

Neither here nor there
Albuquerque airport, present day

$\mathcal{P}$auline Wilde didn't look like a woman in mourning. Unless by widow's weeds one envisioned a lemon yellow and sky blue broomstick skirt studded with what had to be at least half a quarry's worth of turquoise and intricately worked Native American silver disks, topped with a ratty, oversized T-shirt proclaiming, in half-faded but still defiant lettering, "Orgasms Aren't Just for the Young!" Add to that a fiercely pink headscarf barely binding a wild-and-woolly extravaganza of hip-length salt-and-pepper hair and a pair of ancient gardening clogs with roses and kittens hand-stenciled on them in flaking acrylic paint, and you had the very picture of a woman *not* suffering the loss of her beloved life partner. But then, Serafina thought, that was Pauline—she didn't believe in catering to societal expectations. Never had, never would.

"Bliss! Helloooooo, Bliss! Over here, kiddo!"

Her aunt's voice was exactly as it had always been—warm, slightly fruity, like a cross between Julia Child and Jane Goodall, blended with a dash of throaty Kathleen Turner for good measure. Sera smothered a grin at the sight of her impatiently elbowing past the rest of the folks waiting for friends and loved ones at the terminal. Only Pauline ever called her by her ridiculous middle name—a name Pauline herself had gifted her, and which was now echoing through the boarding area to the amusement of the other passengers disembarking from Sera's flight.

The Albuquerque airport was surprisingly posh, Sera saw as she took her first gander around at the fabled Southwest. *Not at all what I imagined from the place where Bugs Bunny made his wrong turn.* Airy, clean, and decorated in pinkish earth tones and expensive native pottery, it was a far cry from the chaos she'd left behind at JFK just a few hours earlier. But she didn't have much time to absorb her surroundings—her aunt was treating the place like a linebacker in a championship game, barreling past all obstacles to get to her objective.

Nothing had ever stood in Pauline Wilde's way. Not for long, anyhow. Ever since Sera could remember, Pauline had been pushing boundaries, defying convention, sticking her middle finger in the face of anyone who told her she couldn't do something she wanted to do. She was a woman utterly estranged from the concepts of shame, modesty, and deference. In comparison, Sera, raised by stolidly conventional yuppie parents until she was thirteen, had always felt somewhat small and apologetic, though Pauline had done her utmost to yank her niece from beneath her towering feminist shadow and lend her some chutzpah when her own wouldn't take Sera the distance.

It hadn't worked, even when Sera had gone to live with Pauline after her parents' sudden deaths. If anything, the contrast between Sera's shy, repressed thirteen-year-old self and her ballsy aunt had made Sera shrink down even smaller, despite her deep love for the older woman. She knew Pauline would be horrified if she realized her efforts to toughen Sera up had done more to make her squirm than make her strong. She admired Pauline's ideals of striving for self-fulfillment, even as she doubted her own ability to advocate for her deepest needs and wants. She simply didn't feel she had the *right* to happiness the way Pauline so obviously did.

Shaking herself firmly, Sera reminded herself she was nearly thirty, and had been self-supporting since college. She'd faced—and conquered—some extremely tough demons, particularly in the last year. She'd seen a bit of what her inner mettle was really worth, and learned to trust her instincts more and more. Pauline's support had done a lot to set her on that path. Now it was time for Sera to do the supporting.

Her aunt's frantic call had come just yesterday.

Hortencia's gone. I need you, Baby-Bliss.

Sera's heart had sunk. Pauline and Hortencia had been insep-arable for the last few years. Her aunt must be devastated. *I'm coming, Aunt Paulie,* she'd assured her aunt over the phone. *I'm on the next flight.* And she had been.

Before Sera could so much as set down her carry-on, Pauline had wrapped her arms around her niece and was squeezing for all she was worth. Instantly, Sera was swamped with that famil-iar Pauline smell: part musky herbal—mugwort or pot, she'd never been sure—part fairy godmother. Tears sprang into her eyes.

"Fuck, it's good to see you, Aunt Paulie."

"Ditto, kid-bean. Aren't you a sight for sore eyes, too." Pauline took her time eyeballing her niece, flipping the short, chin-length ends of Sera's new bob approvingly, putting her hands on Sera's hips and turning her this way and that. "Lookin' good, kiddo! I see all those sweets you bake aren't hurting your sweet figure any. You've still got a tush on you like a couple of hot cross buns. You didn't get that from me, that's for sure. Tuchas like a freakin' pancake, that's what I've got. A crepe even, these days. Ah, but what am I babbling about? Baby Bliss, let's get your shit and blow this taco stand. I can't wait to finally show you what heaven's all about."

Bemused, Sera trailed after her aunt down the long, wide ramp that led to the baggage claim. Had grief made her loopy? Er...loopier than usual? Because she'd expected sorrow-stricken. Wan. Shaken. All the sad emotions the joyful, fearless Pauline Wilde had never seemed susceptible to, but surely must be feeling after the death of her life partner.

At least, that had been the impression she'd given Sera when she'd called to tell her that Hortencia was suddenly gone. *I'm devastated, Bliss. Utterly wrecked,* she'd said. Could Sera please drop everything and fly to New Mexico to help her deal with her loss?

Given that Pauline was, quite simply, Sera's single favorite person, she hadn't hesitated for a second. *After all the times she's saved my bacon,* Sera thought fondly, *she'd be within her rights to ask for a kidney. Hell,* both *kidneys.* In any case, considering how little anchored her to New York these days, taking time out was no great hardship. And she'd been missing Pauline a lot lately.

"So how's your love life, kid?" Pauline asked—loudly—over her shoulder as they headed for the bag claim. Her skirt jingled in counterpoint to her strides. "You getting any?"

I didn't miss this *part,* Sera thought with a mental wince. She avoided the smirking glance of the college-aged bohunk trotting down the ramp to meet his gloriously tanned, crunchy-granola girlfriend, her arms outstretched as if to announce to all and sundry, "Now you...*you're* getting some."

"Um, I'm doing okay," she said weakly. "Not dating anyone seriously right now. Mostly trying to keep the catering business out of the red, keep myself on the straight and narrow. That kind of thing."

"That wasn't what I asked," Pauline said, huffing a little as they made it to the conveyor and started scanning the bags. "I asked if you were getting *laid*. Don't really need a boyfriend for that, though of course, it never hurts to know where your next O's coming from. One of the benefits of a steady relationship, I s'pose." Her face clouded over momentarily.

"I'm so sorry about Hortencia, Aunt Paulie," Sera jumped in, eager to change the subject, and also to comfort the woman who'd once been *her* sole solace after her parents' deaths. "It must have been quite a shock, her passing so suddenly. I had the impression she was healthy as a horse, with all that hiking and mountain climbing you two were always doing. I'm just sorry I never got to meet her. From everything you've told me, she must have been a really special lady." Sera patted Pauline on the shoulder. "How are you holding up?"

Was it her imagination, or did her aunt flush, just slightly?

Pauline made an impatient, fly-shooing gesture. "Don't get me started with the wailing and weeping just yet, kiddo. I need these eyes to see. It's a long drive to Santa Fe, and we have a lot of catching up to do. So," she finished, briskly clearing her throat and pointing at the luggage rattling around the conveyor, "I'm gonna guess yours is the one that looks like a giant pink cupcake with rainbow sprinkles on the front?"

Sera had to admit it was.

"Great, let's get that cupcake to go."

As she stepped out into the sunlight, Sera took her deep first breath of New Mexico's thin, dry air. Goose bumps rose along her arms, but somehow she didn't think the cool September breeze was to blame. She sensed a weightlessness, a sense of potential—

as if destiny had taken a vacation and left her with a wide-open fate. She couldn't say how she knew, but she had a feeling her life—her very being—was about to change.

And considering the woman she'd been until recently, that might be a very good thing.

Because *that* chick had been a real fuckup.